Praise For *Th...*

"Mystery lovers make way f... ...1 female detectives of *The Women of Wy...* ...e stops at every floor and leaves you breathless and wanting more."

–DiAnn Mills, bestselling author of *Lethal Standoff*

"Step back into the 1950's with this picture-perfect mystery! Donna Mumma has recreated the era with her delectable descriptions of fashion, as well as the social nuances of the time period in *The Women of Wynton's*. I couldn't turn the pages fast enough to learn how these four different women would save the department store where they work—and become friends in the process. Really hoping this is the first book in a new cozy mystery series, as I can't wait to spend more time with these women—and their wonderful clothes."

–Sarah Hamaker, award-winning and bestselling author of *Justice Delayed* and The Cold War Legacy Series

"An eclectic cast of quirky women in a small town in the 1950's. Throw in a mystery, and what's not to love? Donna Mumma has penned a page-turner in *The Women of Wynton's*."

–Ane Mulligan, award-winning author of *By the Sweet Gum*

"Donna Mumma is a master of characterization and attention to detail in her setting. I felt transported to a different time, full of glam but also marred by prejudice and social injustice. This 1950's mystery picked up speed with each chapter and had me turning pages until justice was served."

–Kristen Hogrefe Parnell, author of the Crossroads Suspense romantic suspense series

"Stylish. Spunky. Intelligent. Ahead of their time. Blissfully in love. Unlucky in love. Sleuthful. Hard-working. Creative. *The Women of Wynton's* embellish all the adjectives and more! They'll have you cheering on the main characters, flipping the pages to see 'who done it,' and wishing for another installment by the time you reach the last page. It's a fashion show you don't want to end, punctuated with a bit of gossip and rumors, a couple of murders, and a bonding of unlikely women to save their jobs and the department store they adore."

–Julie Lavender, author of *Children's Bible Stories for Bedtime* and *Strength for All Seasons: A Mom's Devotional of Powerful Verses and Prayers*

The Women of Wynton's

A Classy
1950's Mystery

DONNA MUMMA

BARBOUR
PUBLISHING

©2024 by Donna Mumma

ISBN 978-1-63609-885-2
Adobe Digital Edition (.epub) 978-1-63609-886-9

This book is a work of fiction. Names, characters, places, and incidents are either products of the author's imagination or used fictitiously. Any similarity to actual people, organizations, and/or events is purely coincidental.

Cover illustrated by: Alessandra Fusi

Published by Barbour Publishing, Inc., 1810 Barbour Drive, Uhrichsville, Ohio 44683, www.barbourbooks.com

Our mission is to inspire the world with the life-changing message of the Bible.

ecpa Member of the
Evangelical Christian
Publishers Association

Printed in the United States of America.

Dedication

To JP and D
And an interrupted story

Chapter 1

AUDREY

RESERVED FOR AUDREY PENAULT
WYNTON'S DEPARTMENT STORE
VIOLATORS WILL BE TOWED

Oh, how this sign set the bees a-buzzing in the wives' and mothers' bonnets in Levy City—that and her shiny new 1955 Thunderbird convertible parked beneath it. Why should she have what their husbands, sons, or brothers deserved after fighting in the war?

Audrey checked her hair in the rearview mirror and finger-combed the windblown tendrils. Florida's heat was the ruination of hairdos and makeup. At least driving with the top down dried perspiration and shrank the pores. A few mussed curls were worth the ride.

Part of her couldn't blame folks for not liking her. Sixteen-year-old girls in this town didn't run off to New York City alone, then return fourteen years later, sprinkling everyday conversations with French phrases locals wouldn't understand. And Audrey had money—far more than what people suspected Daddy left her when he died.

But she wasn't the typical Levy City girl.

A business degree hung on her wall at home, not wedding or baby photos. Her love for the inner workings at Wynton's Department Store irritated Levy City's female population like sand grit in the eyes.

C'est la vie.

Mr. Wynton considered her a vital part of the store and believed she deserved her own space. His opinion reigned above all others.

She opened the car door. With knees pressed together, just as Miss

Evelyn's Charm School had taught her, Audrey stood in one swift motion.

Mother always said long-legged, long-necked girls like her must be mindful to move gracefully and swanlike to avoid looking like a drunken spider.

One of the few pieces of Mother's advice worth remembering.

After fastening her car's convertible top into place on the windshield, she patted the door's candy apple–red finish.

Audrey gathered her hat, handbag, and work satchel from the seat. A quick push with her hip closed the door.

"Good thing you put that top up," a deep voice called. Nelson, the store's overnight security guard, limped toward her. "Going to rain today." He stopped at the front of her Thunderbird.

She settled her purse into the crook of her arm. "Your knee giving you fits?"

"It's never wrong."

Audrey peered at the driver's side window, a perfect mirror to help position her Breton hat. Its beige-and-white-striped brim and black grosgrain ribbon matched her beige suit trimmed in black.

Nelson reached out his wrinkled brown hand and patted the hood of the Thunderbird. "You still got the best car in the garage."

No one but Nelson and Smokey, her mechanic, was allowed to touch her car.

"Wish I was there when you whipped out your checkbook and told that car salesman you'd pay cash on the spot."

The color had been the first thing she'd noticed when she spied the two-seater through the windows of the dealership. The showroom's overhead lights had glinted off the car's finish like moonlight on a lake. The white leather interior trimmed in red screamed, *I'm sophisticated and free as the wind. Come have fun with me.*

She needed fun.

"He practically choked on his tongue." Audrey readjusted her hat so the most flattering number of curls framed her face. "He and his manager kept saying I needed to talk to my husband before making such an important purchase. Their eyes bulged like gigged frogs when I told them I could buy *whatever* I wanted *whenever* I wished."

Their next question grated even more. "How's it no man's snatched up a beauty like you?"

She'd flashed them what someone once called her 24-karat smile. "I'm too slippery to catch," she'd replied.

Her return to Wynton's an hour late—in a flashy new car—kept the gossip mill humming for a month.

She met Nelson's gaze. "It's 1955. Things shouldn't be that archaic."

"Lotta things not the way they should be right now."

They shared a long, quiet look before she did the only thing she could. She nodded.

Nelson had fought for his country in the war and come home with a bum knee. That same country now prevented him from using restrooms or drinking fountains designated WHITE'S ONLY. He couldn't even shop in the very department store he worked for.

Yes. Lotta things needed changing.

Audrey unzipped her satchel's top and removed a white paper bag plus a red-and-green plaid thermos. She held them out to Nelson. "Two just-baked cinnamon twists from Tiner's Bakery and one thermos of freshly brewed Maxwell House coffee."

He took both and set the thermos nearby on his "resting chair."

Nelson opened the bag and inhaled the twists' fresh-baked fragrance, then slid one out and took a bite. His eyes closed, and the crinkles on his dark face deepened as he chewed.

Audrey tilted her head toward the red Corvette convertible parked in the space next to hers. The car belonged to Mr. Wynton's son, John T., who worked as head of store finances and, thank goodness, wasn't hers to manage.

"Junior's here early." She stifled an irreverent grin at the use of the Wynton's employees' secret name for the man.

Nelson swallowed. "Got here an hour ago. Brought his missus with him."

Strange.

She kept Mr. Wynton's calendar, scheduled every minute of his day down to his lunch breaks, doctor visits, and pick-up times for his dry cleaning. He ran the smallest of details by her before asking to have them penned in his book. There'd been no mention of this meeting.

Nelson slid the second twist from the bag. "Junior zoomed in so fast he almost slammed his car into the wall."

This secret meeting didn't bode well for the day. Audrey zipped her satchel, then withdrew a pair of black gloves from her black purse. "You off in an hour like usual?"

Nelson winked as he munched.

"Leave the thermos in the usual place. Go home and sleep well, Nelson."

"You keep 'em dancing in the store today, Miss Audrey." He spoke around the bite bulging in his cheek.

"You want a jig or a jive?"

His expression curled into a smile. Nelson moved the thermos of coffee and sat in his chair. "The Charleston."

Sounds of another car's wheels thumped across the parking floor above them. A car door slammed.

Nelson swallowed his bite. "You'd best get going into the store."

The heels of her black pumps clicked across the pavement as she passed the top-floor executives' spaces on her way to the exit. Scents of fresh bread wafted through the garage, mixing with the smell of oil and gas. The Negro cooks in the cafeteria and the Grove, Wynton's premier restaurant, arrived at six in the morning to start their baking.

But Junior never arrived before ten. What was going on today?

Once outside the garage, Audrey gazed up at the store's white-bricked walls gleaming as the sun glowed in the windowpanes of the upper floors and large display windows at street level. The two acres of shopping glory were emblazoned with Mr. Wynton's name on both street-facing sides.

The smaller seventh floor sat on top like a pillbox hat. Windowed on three sides, it held business offices and the conference room. An auditorium and ballroom rounded the last of the square footage along the windowless back, the home of special events like Levy High School's homecoming dance and prom. Grand gatherings she'd helped organize.

Unlike today's meeting between father and son. Was Mr. Wynton trying to put to right something Junior had fouled up in his quest to launch Wynton's into the future?

Launching *him* into the future with no means to return might better serve the store.

God love him, but Junior came up with the worst ideas. He was forever devising new ways to manage billing, changing the merchandise displays, or rearranging the shopping floors to optimize the current customer buying patterns.

None of his improvements worked. Ever.

She resumed her hurried stride as the massive clock above the store's entrance ticked away the time.

When she entered the main level, the gray-and-white granite floor sparkled. Clerks set out today's specials, arranged merchandise on shelves, and polished the glass display cases. A familiar three-note melody chimed through the store's intercom, and employees stopped to listen to the morning announcements.

Even the air smelled sweet, thanks to Cosmetics spraying today's featured scent around the perfume counter in hopes that lady shoppers would catch a sniff and wonder, *Wouldn't that smell wonderful on me?*

Alvid Ashley, a first-floor manager, maneuvered around one of the white, fluted columns flanking the main floor's center walkway. No matter how he moved, he always looked like a crane wearing a cheap suit.

And a loud tie. Today a lemon-yellow necktie festooned with a bright parrot screamed against his charcoal-gray jacket. Alvid never resisted the lure of the loud.

Or a juicy bite of gossip, especially if the tidbit sullied Audrey.

He blocked her progress. "Matching purse, gloves, and hat. Perfectly put together as always, aren't we?"

She pointed to his tie. "Burdines' or Maas Brothers' new line?"

He smoothed his hand over the fabric. "Junior didn't seem to mind it. Shot me a compliment when he breezed through earlier."

"We'll discuss publicly supporting the competitors later."

"Is that part of your job description now? I had no idea you'd been promoted." Alvid widened his stance, as if trying to wall her in somehow.

She had no time for his nonsense. Audrey whooshed around him and past the escalators in the middle of the atrium, hurrying to the elevators located in the back corner.

As soon as the operator pushed the gate back on the sixth floor, she bolted from the car and rushed to the executive suite.

Audrey opened the outer door to hear angry voices filling the air.

"We can't operate the same way you did thirty years ago, Dad." Junior's voice blasted through the cherry-paneled walls of his father's closed office.

"We just completed a multimillion-dollar renovation of the store, including updated air-conditioning. That's enough for now," Mr. Wynton countered.

Audrey put her gloves and hat in the coat closet situated behind her desk. She eased the door closed, then locked her purse in the desk's bottom drawer.

As the volume between Mr. Wynton and Junior rose, she removed the folder holding papers she'd gone over the night before from her satchel.

Junior roared foul words hot enough to curl the carpet from the floor, causing her to jump and send the papers flying. Mr. Wynton would hate that. He was a man's man in every sense but also ascribed to the thought that a gentleman never uttered such language in the hearing of a lady.

He needn't worry. She'd had worse directed at her.

Audrey gathered the scattered papers. The sooner they were locked in the filing cabinet, the better.

As she pulled the handle to confirm the cabinet's drawer was secured, Junior burst from his father's office. He slammed the door so hard it sounded like a gunshot, then stomped past her desk.

"He's ruining everything." His words crackled around the room.

Junior grabbed one of the dark green plastic chairs from the waiting area and catapulted it toward his father's office door. It missed the intended target and crashed against the wall.

He kicked the upended chair. "He won't block me forever."

Audrey moved to the outer office door and held it open, plastering her best *you may leave now* expression on her face as she stared Junior right in the eyes. He spewed more oaths at full volume as he exited.

When she was certain he and his opinions weren't returning, she shut the door, put the chair away, then knocked on Mr. Wynton's door.

His face still shone crimson when he answered. "I could use some fresh coffee. Please."

"Yes, sir."

He closed the door.

She crossed the room to the alcove where the coffee cart was kept and set the coffeepot to brew. But there were no cups. A trip to the storage closet in the hall offered the perfect excuse to give Mr. Wynton a few moments to cool off.

While she was pulling a package of cups from a top shelf, one of the store's bookkeepers joined her. "Is Mr. Wynton busy at the moment?"

Audrey tucked the package under her arm. "Very."

The woman chewed on her bottom lip.

"Is there a problem?" Audrey led her from the closet into the hall.

"The back-to-school sales numbers aren't reconciling with the invoices. Bookkeeping wanted Mr. Wynton to look over the paperwork."

Audrey motioned to the manila envelope in the bookkeeper's hands. "Are those the invoices?"

The bookkeeper nodded and handed them over.

"I'll make certain he sees these right away."

Audrey went to the office and laid the invoices on her desk.

As she prepared the coffee, she added less sugar and cream than usual, per the doctor's orders. Her boss's stomach might love rich foods, but his heart needed a break from them.

She rapped on his door.

No response.

Peering inside, she found the space empty. Had he gone to the washroom? No, the light was off.

Where was he?

A groan sounded from behind his desk. She rushed into the room.

Mr. Wynton lay on the floor, looking like wadded-up paper with his arms and legs tucked against him. Sweat drenched his shirt collar and spread in dark patches on the back of his suit coat.

"Mr. Wynton!"

Perspiration soaked his snow-white hair. His eyelids were swollen shut, and his tanned skin paled as he struggled to speak. "Help me." He slurred each word.

Audrey dropped the steaming cup, sending scalding coffee across her new black pumps and puddling on the carpet.

She grabbed the phone receiver. Finger shaking, she almost couldn't press the red emergency button.

A voice on the other end answered. "Store security."

"Call an ambulance for Mr. Wynton. Now!"

Chapter 2

MARY JO

Mary Jo pressed her hankie against her nose. She wasn't the store-clerk type. Ten minutes into the new employees orientation, the proof of that had slapped her in the face. If she could just get to the ladies' lounge, have a quick cry, then sneak out and go home.

But she had to make this work. No. Other. Choice.

What if she couldn't?

Tears coursing down her cheeks, she pushed open the heavy ladies' room door and plowed into one of the lounge's wingback chairs. She fell forward over the arm and lost her shoe.

"I hate this place." A sob escaped her as she wiggled her foot back into her pump. "Even their restrooms are better furnished than my house."

She rounded the corner to wash her face but drew back. Another woman stood at the sinks, bent at the waist, holding her stomach and sucking in short breaths. She seemed to be having a spell of her own.

Mary Jo's cheeks burned. "I'm sorry, I didn't mean to intrude."

"You're not." The woman straightened and squared her shoulders. Surprise brewed in her wide brown eyes when she looked at Mary Jo. "I'm Audrey."

Mary Jo caught a glimpse of herself in the mirrors. "Oh. My. Word."

Her lashes clumped together like wet cat fur, and mascara ran down her face in black stripes to her cheek hollows. The entire left side of her lipstick was smudged.

Meanwhile, Audrey looked like she'd stepped out of a high fashion ad, right down to the powdery-floral scent of her perfume. Her beige outfit highlighted her long legs, tiny waist, and the double strand of pearls encircling her neck. She was the picture of grace and composure, except for the pale pallor to her peaches-and-cream complexion.

Mary Jo cupped her hands around her face. "I look like something a cat spit up." More tears. "I'm not going back to orientation looking like this."

Audrey pulled a paper towel from the nearby dispenser and dampened it. "Wipe off as much makeup as you can."

"What?"

Her high heels clicked on the white tile while she glided toward the door. "Keep wiping."

In less than a minute, Audrey came back with a small silver case. She pulled one of the wingback chairs from the lounge and motioned. "Sit."

Mary Jo complied, settling against the soft pink upholstery.

Audrey set the case on the sink counter. "Welcome to Wynton's." Her sweet words soothed Mary Jo's ruffled spirit.

"I'm Mary Jo, and you must be the hundredth person I've met today. I'll never remember all these names. Except for Mr. Wynton." She blew her nose on the wet paper towel. "I couldn't believe the owner of the store met with a nobody like *me*. He was such a gentleman during my interview."

Audrey unsnapped the fasteners on the case, careful to protect her manicured nails, which matched the color of her lipstick. "You aren't a nobody, so never say that again. Mr. Wynton views all the employees as his extended family. He wants to know you the moment you set foot in the store." She removed a jar of cold cream and unscrewed the lid. "Let's fix your face."

Mary Jo looked at her watch. "I've only got fifteen minutes left on the break."

"Perfect." Audrey spread a pearl-sized dollop of cream across Mary Jo's cheeks, then smoothed it over her face. She removed compacts, rouge, eye shadow, mascara, and lipstick from the case. "I'll have you freshened up in ten minutes or less."

She dotted foundation about Mary Jo's face, then patted cheeks, chin, and forehead with a powder puff from a gold compact. "Some ladies prefer pancake makeup, but here in Florida, it's best to set your makeup with powder. Keeps us from sweating everything off." She patted a few more times.

Next came the rouge. "With your beautiful chestnut hair and baby blues, this peachy pink works best." Audrey swished a brush over the highest point of Mary Jo's cheek. "Let's show off that great bone structure of yours."

"That's the nicest thing anyone has ever said to me."

Audrey scowled. "No one's ever told you that before?"

Mary Jo shook her head. "My mama and daddy weren't much for makeup or passing out compliments. I grew up with six older brothers, and they were too busy telling me I looked like a snapping turtle. My husband gushes over me, but he's biased."

"I mean every word." Audrey put the rouge back in the case.

Mary Jo's stomach butterflies settled. If Audrey was any indication of how the employees of Wynton's treated one another, maybe she could fit in here.

Audrey checked the time. "Five minutes left." She took out a gold tube of lipstick. "Revlon's Fire and Ice. I'm sure you've seen the ads. The latest must-have and it's going to look fabulous on you." She handed the tube to Mary Jo.

Rushing footsteps pounded down the hall outside. A man barked orders, but the restroom's thick walls blocked the words.

"What's going on out there?"

Audrey paled again. "There was an incident in the executive suite. The store detectives and the store's doctor are handling it."

"My goodness. Is that why the man came into our orientation and told us to clear the room?"

Audrey nodded, then pointed to her lips, reminding Mary Jo to keep applying. When she finished, Audrey handed her a paper towel to blot the excess.

The commotion outside stilled. "I hope everything is all right."

"Me too." Audrey stepped back, like a painter surveying her work.

She rotated the chair so Mary Jo now faced the mirror.

She nearly gasped at her reflection. "I can't believe that's *me*."

Audrey placed the cosmetics back in the case and closed the lid. "Applying cosmetics is akin to a coloring book. You use lines, shading, and color selection to enhance your features. I can teach you if you'd like, especially since you'll be working in Cosmetics." She snapped the fasteners closed.

"How did you know I'm in Cosmetics?"

"You're Mary Jo Johnson, right? I saw your name on this morning's new-hires list." Audrey lifted the case from the counter. "Mr. Wynton sends those to the employees so we can be on the lookout for the new folks and offer our help."

"I was ready to tuck tail and run."

"And now?"

"I feel a little better."

Audrey cocked a brow. "Is your orientation instructor Vermelle Harris?"

"Yes."

"And Vermelle started off with the 'you must have at least ten separate work outfits so repeat customers won't think you're pathetic' speech?"

"That's why I cried." Mary Jo looked at the floor. "I shouldn't be saying this, but. . .my husband, Kenny, has been out of work for three months. We're broke."

"I'm so sorry." Audrey paused. "That must be difficult."

Mary Jo dabbed at her nose with her lipstick blotter. "He worked in construction. There was an accident." She released a long, shuddering breath. "He lost his right arm."

"Oh my."

"If we want to pay our mortgage or buy groceries, I have to work. Our girls are outgrowing every stitch of their clothing faster than I can sew new outfits. Even the hand-me-downs from my friends. And then there's Kenny's medical bills." She met Audrey's eyes. "All I ever wanted was to be a mama and a housewife." She sighed. "But now I'm here."

Audrey squeezed her arm. "You've got great fashion sense. Your hair lays so smooth, and the way it turns under at the ends is gorgeous, like Grace Kelly's. You've paired this wonderful blue sweater with your tartan skirt. Pure class." She removed her pearls and fastened them around Mary Jo's neck. "Now you look *très chic*, and our customers will love you."

Mary Jo tried to protest, but Audrey held up her hand. "We all mix and match regularly. Even Vermelle." She gestured to the pearls. "Borrow them for today, and don't worry so much."

It would be nice not to worry anymore. Too many nights all her problems stampeded in her head while Kenny tossed and turned, trying to find a pain-free sleep position.

Audrey thrust the makeup kit toward Mary Jo. "Take this. It's filled with the brands we carry. You can become more familiar with them on your own time."

"But I'm just a perfume spritzer—"

Audrey held up her hand. "We have tons of these sample kits. You'll make the cosmetics counter soon. No doubt." She held out the case until Mary Jo took hold. "And when you do, you'll know all about Max Factor, Maybelline, and Elizabeth Arden and can help our customers learn too."

"I was hoping to someday be promoted to Ladies' Accessories. I just adore cute purses, gloves, and hats. Spending all day showing evening bags and dressy gloves to ladies and hearing where they will wear them seems fun to me." She patted the case. "Thank you, Audrey."

"Of course. I hope you have a wonderful rest of your first day."

"You've made it so much better." In fact, it hardly seemed real. Meeting Audrey was like something from a movie, she was so amazing.

"Good. Vermelle can be a bit much, but she means well. And you're going to be great."

"Audrey, would you like to meet for lunch?"

That sounded so sophisticated, like something from a movie. Ladies working in department stores met for lunch too, didn't they?

"Can't do lunch, but I will come to Cosmetics later and say hey."

Mary Jo smiled through her disappointment, like Mama taught her. "I'd like that."

"My pleasure." Audrey hurried to the door. "I've got to run. You'd better get going too." The door slammed closed behind her.

Mary Jo looked at her watch. "Good golly."

One minute to spare. Mary Jo scurried down the hallway, meeting Vermelle at the door just as she pulled it closed.

"You've returned, Mrs. Johnson?" She peered down her nose at Mary Jo.

The drumming in her heart and stomach resumed. But Audrey said she'd be great at this job.

No. Other. Choice.

"Yes, ma'am. I'm here to stay."

For Kenny and the girls.

Chapter 3

VIVIEN

Making brides happy brightened the spirit or grayed the hair, depending on the girl and her wedding dreams.

"You're certain you put the box with the veil caps on this bottom shelf." Vivien Sheffield perused the storage room of her bridal salon once more.

"Yes," Mirette called back. "While you were consulting with the Peterson girl yesterday."

Strange. In the twenty-seven years Mirette had been her assistant and seamstress, she'd never misplaced items before.

"I've looked three times, and the box isn't there. Where else could the caps be?"

"Perhaps I spirited them home to wear for myself. You know how I'm always doing that."

"No need to get snippy this early in the day." Vivien walked from the storeroom to the alterations and fitting area. "Miranda Paulson is coming in this afternoon, and she has changed her mind for the fifth time on what style of veil she wants."

Mirette sat in a nearby chair, her silvery head bowed as she sewed pearl accents onto a satin wedding gown bodice. "I thought she'd decided to wear her grandmother's veil. She made such a big to-do over carrying on the family tradition."

Vivien sighed. "That was two days ago. She called as soon as I got to the shop, gushing about how Elizabeth Taylor looked in *Father of the Bride*, and asked if we could somehow adapt her grandmother's veil to look just as *darling.*" Vivien drawled out her last word, sing-songing both syllables.

Mirette stopped midstitch. "Her grandmother's going to have a conniption fit if we start taking that veil apart. It's nearly a sacred artifact."

"Of course she will. I told Miranda we would make the change if and only if Mother and Grandmother gave their approval. In person."

"And she agreed?"

"I gave her no choice. They'll be here at three."

"Thanks for the warning. I'm taking my lunch break then."

Vivien put her hands on her hips. "You most assuredly are not. We are *both* going to convince that girl to stick with the heirloom veil. I'm not about to tangle with her mama or grandmother."

Mirette cut her thread. "Then I'll quit and go home."

"You do that"—she looked Mirette directly in the eyes—"after we've finished with Miranda."

As Mirette groused softly, Vivien retrieved her appointment book from her desk drawer, then ran her hand along the desktop's smooth surface.

"Can't believe you keep that monstrosity around." Mirette positioned the satin bodice over a dress form.

The black lacquered desk, with its thick gold vines adorning the wide, curved legs, clashed with the white French provincial furniture she used for displays in the showroom. The chair's red velvet cushions were better suited for a rowdy bar. The drawers stuck, and the splintering old wood snagged her stockings so often she had to keep extra pairs in the storeroom.

But she loved the gaudy thing with all her heart. Carter spent hours scraping away dust and grime so she would have a place to consult with the brides they hoped would patronize her first shop.

"It goes when you go." Vivien opened her appointment book.

Mirette grinned as she pinned a satin sleeve on the bodice.

"We've a busy day ahead. A girl is coming in at ten and another at eleven thirty. Both want to shop for a gown and bridesmaids dresses, and choose china and silver patterns."

Brides had flocked to "Miss Vivien's" salon for twenty years since Mr. Wynton wooed her to move downtown from her first shop on Laurel Street. She and Mirette had built their salon at Wynton's from scratch and now took up most of the fifth floor.

"Best make sure I look my part before the girls arrive. I do have my reputation to uphold."

"Someone's on their high horse today." Mirette pretended to fluff her hair.

They laughed as Vivien took her purse from a desk drawer, pulled out her compact, and checked to make certain hair and makeup were in order. The sand in her hour-glass figure had shifted, and the gray hairs appearing in her hairbrush reminded her that Father Time held her in his crosshairs. At fifty it was no surprise, but she'd toyed with finding a boxed color to bring back her blond highlights.

Vivien stashed her purse. With a sigh, she popped open the small locket hidden among the charms on her bracelet.

Her heart pinched at the image of a handsome, youthful man pictured inside.

Carter Sheffield, I still miss you every day.

She'd never intended to age alone. Age was etching a road map across her face, and life sent her a road full of potholes. But she'd gleaned wisdom from every single bump—and still held her head high.

"Time to head to the sales floor."

Mirette set aside her sewing to join her.

"Have you heard any more about what happened to Mr. Wynton earlier?" Vivien opened a drawer and retrieved the glass cleaner and rag to begin polishing a display case filled with snowy-white gloves.

"Josiah said he heard Mr. Wynton had some sort of episode. He stopped breathing right before the ambulance got here, but the store doctor got him going again."

"What on earth happened?"

"Folks think Audrey poisoned his morning coffee. Junior met with him just fifteen minutes before. His father was fine when he left."

Vivien clicked her tongue. "Y'all need to quit spreading rumors about Audrey. It's downright ugly."

"She's snooty, bossy, and thinks she runs this entire store."

Vivien crossed her arms. "And you've witnessed this yourself?"

Mirette poked out her chin. "No, but only because you keep me prisoner in this shop all day."

"You need to stop riding the employee elevators and use the stairs. Those tongue waggers gossip far too much."

"I don't see you cozying up to Audrey." Mirette tossed her head.

"And you know why. A woman can't do half the evil things y'all claim she's done."

Vivien flipped a wall switch, and the opening strains of a Mozart symphony floated from the ceiling's speakers, a separate system from the rest of the store. The last thing her brides needed was Frank Sinatra crooning about a broken heart as they selected their wedding dresses or trousseau items.

"That Muzak puts me to sleep," Mirette grumbled.

"It helps your brain recover from all the gossip."

Voices hummed outside, and people filed from the elevators across from the shop, led by a woman in a pleated, navy silk dress, carrying a clipboard.

"Must be Vermelle's day to lead the new-hires tour."

Vivien walked to the salon's front door. Mirette joined her.

Vermelle brought the group inside. "Let me introduce a Wynton's legend, Miss Vivien Sheffield. Her renowned bridal salon attracts brides from every corner of Florida. She has dressed the daughters of two governors, a university president, and a Hollywood producer. Brides have driven from Georgia, Alabama, and as far away as New York City just to have a Miss Vivien original. Brides may also have their nuptials planned by Miss Vivien herself."

Vermelle signaled to a young woman standing in the back of the crowd. "Mrs. Johnson, I'm sure you purchased your wedding gown here, and maybe china and good silver when you married. Yes?"

Mrs. Johnson's face went beet red. "No, ma'am. I made my gown, and my husband brought my china back from Korea."

"Oh." Vermelle addressed Vivien and Mirette. "Thank you, ladies." She raised her hand high. "Now we'll make our way to Formals and Fine Dresses on the other end of the floor. Come along."

The group followed like ducklings.

"I feel sorry for Mrs. Johnson," Vivien said. "Having to live through your husband going off—" Her voice caught, and she swallowed back the emotions brewing within.

Carter went off to serve as a doctor in a military hospital in Algeria during the war. The man who came home sat in silence and stared out the window for hours, barked orders for the amputation of limbs in his nightmares, and gathered their children in hugs so tightly that they'd cry out.

Six months after his homecoming, he died.

Mirette gave Vivien a soft hug around the waist. "She seems a bit mousy for this store."

Vivien dabbed her eyes. "If she's married, I wonder why she's working."

"Better keep her away from Audrey. She might try to poison her just for sport."

Vivien elbowed Mirette's side. "You need to hush. I want to give her a little boost."

She cantered to the back of the tour group and tapped Mrs. Johnson on the shoulder. When the young woman twirled around, Vivien held out her hand. "I'm Miss Vivien."

"I'm Mary Jo. Nice to meet you."

Vivien sandwiched Mary Jo's hand between her own. "Honey, I think you're going to do just fine here." She tilted her head toward the group, which was now trailing down the hallway. "You belong here too."

Mary Jo smiled then hurried off to join the others.

The door to the stairs opened as Vivien joined Mirette.

Mirette's eyes widened as she whispered in her friend's ear. "My stars. Speak of the—"

Vivien shushed her. "She'll hear you."

Mirette glared. "What in the world does she want? She *never* graces us with her presence."

Vivien shielded her lips with her hand. "She's sure in an all-fire hurry."

Audrey approached, clutching a manila envelope tight against her chest. "Good morning, Miss Vivien." She swept her gaze left. "Miss Mirette."

A nervous, jumpy air surrounded Audrey.

"What brings you down to the salon?" Vivien asked.

"I was hoping I might put something in your safe."

No one in the store was supposed to know about the safe Vivien used to house the dainty diamond tiaras, cultured pearl chokers, and fine bracelets her high-end clients chose.

"How did you know—"

"Mr. Wynton." Audrey held out the envelope. "May I?"

Mirette pinched Vivien's arm. When she had her employer's gaze, she shook her head hard. *Don't*, she mouthed.

Audrey kept her gaze on Vivien, seeming to make a point of ignoring Mirette's rudeness, which she must have seen.

Her insistence made no sense. "Why not in the store's safe? I'm sure it's far more secure than ours."

Audrey checked the room around them as if looking for spying eyes or ears. She held out the envelope. "Please. Mr. Wynton insisted."

Chapter 4

GIGI

S he needed a job without hairnets. Every night, she washed her hair, set it with curlers, slept on the rotten things, only to have her curls flattened at work. Why couldn't she get the jobs where she started and ended the day with powdered cheeks and fresh lipstick, rather than smelling like the daily special with a side of onions?

"Miss Woodard, if you please."

Her boss's reprimand snapped Gigi back to the overcrowded cafeteria housed in the back of Wynton's first floor. Had the entire town come out for the meatloaf special?

A tap on her right shoulder brought relief. "Hey, Blondie, lunch break."

Gigi grinned at the young woman now standing beside her. "About time, Lenore." She handed the long-handled serving fork to her replacement.

Lenore squeezed into her place on the serving line. "Not having fun?"

Gigi removed her stained apron, then smoothed wrinkles from her light blue uniform. "A girl can only take the smell of meatloaf and simmering green beans for only so long."

Lenore forked a large slice of meatloaf onto a plate. "Go eat."

Gigi headed into the kitchen, inhaling the aroma of fresh baked goods coming from the huge commercial ovens.

She waved to Lilla as she removed a tray of biscuits. "Getting your facial?"

Lilla set the tray on the counter. "Days like this should give me the nicest skin in Levy City." She chugged half a glass of ice water in one gulp.

"I think I've made enough biscuits to feed the whole county. Haven't seen this many people here in a long time." She brushed flour from her light gray uniform.

"Busy days like this kill my feet."

"Mine too." Lilla downed the remaining water, then removed another tray of biscuits. "I'm glad I'm in the kitchen. Can't take all that noise, even if they would let me eat out there." She gestured toward the cafeteria.

Some things were just wrong. Customers ate Lilla's cooking without complaint, but they would fuss up a storm if she joined them in the cafeteria.

Things needed changing. But it wouldn't matter if Gigi hollered that from Wynton's rooftop. Folks in this town wouldn't listen to her for all the meatloaf and sweet tea in the world.

"Forget them, Lilla. Less foolishness to deal with back here."

Lilla squared her jaw. "Avoiding foolishness doesn't make it stop."

"No, it doesn't."

Lilla removed a tray full of Wynton's famous peanut butter cookie bars from the oven. Gigi reached for one, but Lilla slapped her hand. "You're as bad as my kids. You'll burn the skin right off your fingers. Let them cool a minute, and I'll give you one."

Gigi grabbed a sweet tea from the serving line. When she came back, Lilla held out a napkin-wrapped bundle. "Gave you two. You're looking a little scrawny today."

"I am many things, but scrawny ain't one." Not with Daddy's big bones stuffed into Mama's medium frame. No, she was built like a silk oak. Straight and solid, lacking a waistline, with a few well-placed knots so folks knew she was a girl. Even her hazel eyes resembled the color of leaves.

And she'd inherited Daddy's penchant for being hungry all the time, making the warm bundle in her hand all the better. "Thanks."

Lilla smiled and returned to her baking.

Gigi went to the employee's locker room to get her bag lunch. Same old bologna with cheese on Wonder Bread and an apple. At least the cookie bars would add a little glamour to her meal.

A girl needed a little glamour sometimes.

Back in the cafeteria, all the high stools at the lunch counter were occupied. Those red leather seats trimmed with chrome were the best ones in the house. Marlon Brando could walk into Wynton's, sit down on one of those stools, and look cool.

Or James Dean. Wouldn't that be a hoot? James Dean and Marlon Brando at Wynton's lunch counter, drinking Cokes, having a confab while munching on cheeseburgers and fries.

But this was Levy City. Where nothing exciting ever happened.

All the booths were full as well. Nothing left but the square tables arranged in the middle.

The noise there could make a body deaf. The added nuisance of smelling the concoction of grease, cologne, and perfume was enough to spoil even her healthy appetite.

She spotted Alvid and a woman she didn't know sitting near the back with two open chairs. He beckoned her over.

Alvid slid out the chair next to him when she reached the table. "It's a mob in here."

Gigi sat. "Been like this all day. What's going on?"

"New employee orientation is the only thing I know about." He motioned toward the young woman sitting across from him.

"This is Mary Jo. . ."

"Johnson," Mary Jo finished.

Alvid pointed at her with both index fingers. "Right. She's our new perfume spritzer."

Just what Wynton's needed. Another young, fine-boned girl with a sugar-sweet drawl and big blue eyes. She looked like she'd stepped out of a TV commercial. The average American housewife gushing over a new refrigerator. Right down to the pearls around her neck.

Gigi moved so she could avoid tagging Alvid with her elbow. "Nice to meet you."

Mary Jo's eyes fell to Gigi's name tag. "You're Georgia?"

Gigi shook her head. "I go by Gigi. My manager doesn't care for nicknames." She stuck out her tongue.

"Oh," Mary Jo answered.

Gigi unwrapped her sandwich and motioned for Mary Jo to pass the salt and pepper.

"You like perfume?" She seasoned her bologna.

"I do, but I hope to move to another position soon."

"We'll see." Alvid spooned up a bite of potatoes.

Mary Jo's eyes dropped to her empty tray.

Alvid deserved a kick in the shin. Couldn't he see this poor girl had dreams? Nobody should stomp on those.

"So, Mary Jo, other than putting up with this squirrel of a man"— she motioned to Alvid—"how's your first day going?"

"A little nerve-racking." She looked around the room. "I'm used to being at home with my two little girls."

Well, she'd pegged little Miss Wifey into the right hole.

Alvid squinted at Mary Jo. "You didn't tell me you're a mama."

"Two little girls, aged six and seven." She smiled for the first time, and the scared, rabbity look in her eyes dimmed.

She probably read bedtime stories and worried when her little darlings ate too much candy. Maybe married the star quarterback from high school. Alvid weeded little prom queens like her out fast.

"Alvid, did you hear what happened this morning?" Gigi finished off her sandwich.

"About Mr. Wynton passing out in his office?" He swatted at the air as if shooing away a fly. "That's old news."

"Was it his heart?" Gigi crunched into her apple.

A wide *I know a juicy secret* grin spread across his face. "Nope. Wasps."

Gigi stopped chewing. "What?" She covered her mouth to prevent apple bits from tumbling out. "How on the good green earth did wasps get up to Mr. Wynton's office on the seventh floor?"

Alvid shrugged. "I don't know. But Ruth—you know, the curly-headed brunette from Children's—"

"Don't know her."

Alvid continued. "Well anyway, Ruth said they found the bite marks."

She pushed away the thought. "How would a wasp sting send Mr. Wynton to the hospital?"

Alvid held out his hands in surprise. "He's allergic to them."

"If my cousin gets stung by a bee, her face swells up like a watermelon. She has to go to the doctor and get some kind of shot to get better," Mary Jo said.

Alvid swept his hands toward Mary Jo. "See, perfectly reasonable explanation." He tapped Gigi on the arm. "You know what your problem is? Paranoia. You think the whole world is out to get you."

Like he knew so much. The world snatched people up and stomped on them every day.

"I still think the store detective needs to keep his eyes on you-know-who." Gigi took another bite of her apple.

Alvid raised his brows in mock surprise. "You really think the Hatchet had something to do with this?"

"Why not?" Gigi wrapped her core in her used napkin. "Once he's gone, she could take over completely."

Alvid threw his head back and laughed. "How? Once the old man is dead, Junior and Cissy get everything."

"How do you know?"

Alvid shook his head as if in complete disbelief. "Everybody knows Junior is heir apparent."

"I have no idea what *hair apparent* means." Gigi broke off a small piece of cookie bar. "Anyway, the Hatchet would fix things where she gets everything. She's got some kind of spell over Mr. Wynton."

Alvid's silverware clinked as he crisscrossed his fork and spoon on his plate. "Mr. Wynton is a big boy and knows exactly what he's doing." He winked to finish off his thought.

"Your mind lives in the gutter sometimes."

"Who's the Hatchet?" Mary Jo asked.

Alvid motioned for Mary Jo to huddle in close. "Audrey Penault. She's the old man's secretary, his eyes and ears. When an employee makes a mistake"—he axe-chopped the tabletop with the edge of his right hand—"gone."

Gigi eyed Mary Jo. "You'd know her if you'd met her. Really tall, fancy-pants kind of woman. Dark hair, wears expensive clothes and thinks she's better than everybody."

Mary Jo's eyes widened. "She gets people fired for making a mistake?"

"All. The. Time." Gigi swallowed her cookie bite fast. "My boyfriend,

Bobby Bridges, used to work here in the loading bay. Audrey didn't like the way they unloaded the trucks and put up the stock. Bobby told her to mind her business and go back to the sixth floor where she belonged. A week later, he got a pink slip. She's flat-out somebody you want to avoid."

Mary Jo fingered her pearls. "I think I'd better take care of something."

Alvid looked at his watch. "Lunch break is over in five minutes." He wagged his finger. "Don't come back late on your first day, or I might have to tattle to you-know-who." He guffawed.

Mary Jo sprang from her chair, fumbling to get her purse on her arm while still holding the tray with one hand. "Where do I leave this?" Her face paled more by the minute.

Nope, this girl was never going to last. Gigi held out her hand. "I'll take care of it."

"Thank you." Mary Jo slid the tray across the table. "It was lovely meeting you."

She weaved through the tables as she rushed away.

"Alvid, you've scared her to death."

He held up his hands. "Don't blame me. I just met her. And you didn't help with that talk about the Hatchet."

Gigi stacked the trays. "Do they think Mr. Wynton will be okay?"

"Joe up in Furniture heard the boss's personal doctor wants him to stay in bed for a week after he gets out of the hospital. Which leaves Junior in charge. That should send Audrey through the roof. You know how well she and Junior get along."

Gigi finished the last of her tea, refolded the wax paper sandwich wrapper, and put it in her bag along with the second cookie bar. Both could be used for tomorrow's lunch.

"Let me know if you hear any more about Mr. Wynton."

"Okey dokey. Hopefully Mary Jo What's-Her-Name found her way back to Cosmetics. I hate having to track one of my new little rabbits down." He rose. "My wife won't be happy about my working with another young one. She complains that I'm around too many women."

Gigi put her glass on Mary Jo's tray. "She won't be here long."

"Nope." Alvid stacked his tray with Mary Jo's and motioned to take both. "Have fun slinging hash." He walked to the dirty dish conveyor belt.

Gigi headed back to the kitchen.

Mr. Wynton couldn't die. She hadn't been to church in years, but to-night she'd send up a prayer for his recovery and hope God was listening.

After answering want ads all over town, he'd been her last hope. She was thirty-five, twice divorced, and rejected by every other place with a job opening in town. Mr. Wynton, however, met with her himself, called her "Miss Woodard," like she came from quality. Even though he was a member of all the fancy-pants organizations whose shields hung on the welcome sign at the city limits. Mr. Wynton offered her a job within five minutes. And when she got up to leave, he held the door open, even thanked her for the interest in working at his store.

Then he'd said something that rocked her to the core. "Miss Wood-ard, you're going to be a valuable asset to this store, and I look forward to seeing how high you rise." He'd taken her by the hand. "I hope you're ready, because you're poised to go places."

If something happened to him, where would she go then?

Chapter 5

AUDREY

Audrey glanced at the clock. Junior arrived in fifteen minutes. She opened her top drawer, opened an aspirin bottle, shook two pills from within, and popped them in her mouth.

As she downed the tablets with a cup of water, Mary Jo peeked around the door. "I need to talk to you."

She dropped a bundle of tissue paper on Audrey's desk, then knitted her fingers together. "Here are your pearls. I rushed home to fix supper and forgot to give them back yesterday."

"You needn't have worried. I trust you." Audrey retrieved her purse and stored the pearls inside.

Mary Jo squeezed her hands together, and they streaked red as a candy cane.

"Is there something else?"

"Yes." Mary Jo inhaled as if extracting courage from the air around her. "Please don't get me fired. I know I was a mess yesterday, and I don't have any idea what I'm doing."

A tear slid down her cheek. "But I'll learn."

Audrey pulled a hankie from her desk and handed it to Mary Jo. "Why would you think I—"

She stopped. In a single day, the store's gossip vines had twined their way to Mary Jo.

"Your job is safe."

Mary Jo sniffed. "Promise?"

Audrey held up three fingers. "Scout's honor."

"Thank you." Mary Jo blotted more tears. "I'm a complete mess. Again."

Audrey sat on the edge of the desk, crossing her legs at the ankle, as Miss Evelyn had taught her. "Sometimes a girl just needs to cry. Then she wipes her face, throws back her shoulders, and gets to work."

Mary Jo wiped her nose. "Mama used to tell me the same thing."

"Most mamas know best. I—"

"Is this an all-girls meeting?"

The voice jolted Audrey and she shot up from her perch on the desk as a woman entered.

She beelined on red stilettos to Mary Jo and held out her hand. "We've not met. I'm Clarissa Wynton, Mr. Wynton's daughter-in-law. You can call me Cissy. Everyone does." She stretched her lips into a smile so wide Audrey swore she could see bits of her bright red lipstick flecking off.

Cissy grabbed Mary Jo's hand and shook it as if she were priming a pump. "Who are you, honey?"

Mary Jo stood wide-eyed, taking in Cissy's form-fitting red silk dress with oversized white bow drooping from the neckline.

A dress costing more than her weekly bills no doubt.

Her stunned silence wasn't surprising. Audrey and Cissy had grown up together, and she always entered a room with the subtlety of an avalanche.

"Doesn't she talk?" Cissy's high-pitched giggle overpowered Audrey's fast-acting aspirin.

Mary Jo blinked from her stunned trance. "I'm Mary Jo Johnson. I'm new. In Cosmetics."

"Pretty as you are, you'll have all the ladies rushing to Wynton's to buy up every stitch of makeup we've got." Cissy swung to Audrey. "Don't you agree?"

"Mary Jo is going to be a valuable asset to this store."

"Of course she is." The clump of gold charms on Cissy's bracelet jingled as she draped her arm about Mary Jo's shoulders. "The ladies are going to adore you."

She shifted her eyes to Audrey. "John T. said to be ready when he arrives. Lots to go over."

"Perfect." And, like Junior, completely unnecessary. Mr. Wynton gave her instructions during their meeting at his home earlier. And she'd witnessed him commanding Junior over the phone to make no changes in operations.

Mary Jo wriggled from Cissy's grasp. "I'd best be going. Mr. Ashley will have my head if I'm late." She looked at Audrey. "Please remember what you said."

If only she were the gushy type who'd reassure Mary Jo and take away her concerns. Or gather her in like a lost chick, as Cissy did. Instead, she drew a cross over her heart.

When Mary Jo moved to leave, Cissy caught her by the hand. "Let's have lunch today. What time does Alvid let you go?"

"One o'clock."

Cissy squealed as if this were the most wonderful news she'd heard in years. "Wonderful. Save me a seat in the cafeteria."

"I'd love to Mrs. Wynton."

Cissy wagged a finger at her. "No, no. I'm just plain, simple Cissy."

Audrey blinked to hide her eye roll.

A knock caught their collective attention. "Am I interrupting a hen party?"

Junior strolled in, his slick-backed hair glistening underneath the lights. He wore one of his father's red silk ties.

Cissy glided to him as if they were partners in a dance competition. She play-slapped him on the chest. "You're so bad."

She swept her arm toward Mary Jo. "Hon, this is—"

"Mary Jo Johnson." Audrey finished for her.

Cissy sent a side-eyed look. "Yes, thank you." Her eyes flashed with enough anger to shoot a bowling ball through a drinking straw.

Audrey swallowed back a giggle.

"She's new." The sugar-sweet tone laced Cissy's voice again as she ushered Junior toward Mary Jo.

He offered his hand. "Nice to meet you."

Though he had about as much sense as a fence post, Junior had inherited his father's strong chin and bright green eyes. Add in the same voice resonating with the mellow tones of a cello, and many would say he was quite a package.

Mary Jo blushed as she shook his hand. "Nice to meet you too."

"She and I are having lunch today. I'm so excited," Cissy cooed.

Junior stepped aside. "I won't hold y'all up." He slid on his well-practiced flirty grin and winked at Mary Jo. "Bye now."

She understood her dismissal and scurried to leave. Cissy caught up with her in the hall, and their voices faded as they headed for the elevators.

Junior strolled to the open doorway of his father's office. "I love how Cissy takes all the new hires under her wing. She just has a knack with people."

His lips curled into a smirk. "Unlike some folks. You know the type well, don't you, Audrey?"

Oh, he thought he'd fired a good shot with that one, all that smug satisfaction shining in his eyes.

Audrey walked around her desk and sat in her chair. She pulled a fresh sheet of paper from the tray and loaded it into her typewriter. "I know all kinds of folks. What did your father say was first order of business for today?"

She forced back a grin as a red hue crept up his neck. Always nice to remind Junior which Wynton she answered to. He might dress up in Daddy's clothes, but he could never fill his father's shoes.

He glared, and she half expected him to blow a raspberry at her. "Get me some fresh coffee. And your steno pad. Meet me in my office."

No little man. That will never be your office. Ever.

"Pep it up, Audrey. I don't have all day."

When she brought his coffee, he snatched the cup from her, causing a drop to spray onto his hand. He spat utterances worthy of a soapy mouth-washing as he shook away the scalding liquid.

She thrust a napkin at him. "Don't ruin the desktop."

"The desk and I are fine." He mopped both. "Sit."

Audrey settled in the chair across from him and opened her pad to a clean page. She crossed her ankles and held her pencil poised to write. "Whenever you're ready."

Junior swiveled the chair to face the window, forcing her to take notes while looking at the back of his greasy head.

He propped his feet on the credenza as he rattled off a list of letters to be sent to vendors, items to be included in the agenda for the monthly meeting with the board of directors, and the budget for Wynton's annual Christmas parade and fashion show.

Every five minutes he'd stop. "Are you getting all this? I won't waste time going over details again."

She'd been the fastest stenographer in her class. Mr. Wynton teased she wrote like liquid lightning. She transcribed at the same speed Junior spoke.

But she copied nothing he said. She'd taken down all she needed to know this morning when she talked with his father. Since Junior couldn't read shorthand to save his life, Audrey filled the page with comments about him she was too ladylike to say to his face.

She tuned in when Junior failed to mention the invoices the book-keeper discovered. Mr. Wynton put reconciling those figures at the top of the list and mentioned the same to Junior during their earlier phone call.

"Are you certain that's everything?"

Junior swung around. "Don't question me." He waved toward the office door. "Go. You have enough to keep busy for a while."

Audrey uncrossed her ankles and dug her heels into the carpet. "Mr. Wynton always checks the invoices—"

Junior sprung from the chair, sending it crashing into the credenza. "I'm in charge." His unspoken *not you* hung in the air. "Take your Chanel suit and get out."

She flipped her steno pad closed, slid her pencil into the spiral at the top, and stood.

Any store owner worth his grits would have recognized she wore Dior today. Junior wouldn't recognize quality if it came and bit him on his. . .chair cushion.

She shut the door behind her when she exited. A moment later, she heard him speaking in hushed, nervous tones on the phone.

He was up to something. Something big.

Audrey went to her filing cabinet and pulled out the envelope with the invoices that she'd retrieved from Miss Vivien's safe that morning and slid it into her satchel.

Chapter 6

VIVIEN

How had she forgotten to pack lunch last night? She wasn't that old. Yet. Vivien searched the cafeteria for empty seats. Wynton's employees filled them all. The noise of all those voices buzzed in her ears as she paid the cashier for her sweet tea, chicken salad sandwich, and soup.

She heard her name above the din. Seeing Mary Jo Johnson and Cissy beckoning her to their table was a shock. Mirette was never going to believe Cissy lowered herself to eat with the employees.

She seemed an unlikely friend for Mary Jo, but as Vivien sat down, they melted into titters like a couple of schoolgirls.

A woman in a waitress uniform sat with them. "I'm Gigi Woodard."

"I'm V—"

Gigi held up her hand. "You're Miss Vivien."

A dash of sass flavored her words. Vivien stirred her sweet tea. "Is that good or bad?"

Gigi gnawed a large bite from her sandwich, taking time to chew and swallow. "Good for you. I'm sure your bills get paid."

"Now Gigi, don't fuss at Miss Vivien." Cissy patted Vivien's hand. "Don't mind her." She lowered her voice. "You know how Mary Margaret gets ever since she became the cafeteria manager. Well, she's in a real mood today, and all her employees are suffering."

"I see." Vivien shifted her gaze to Gigi.

She stared back, and the corners of her mouth curved down as if she were a boxer aiming to land a punch. And right then, Vivien believed she could.

"Best not to stir the pot then."

Gigi half shrugged. "Who's stirring? I'm working my shift and going home."

"Smart girl." Vivien raised her tea glass in salute, then took a sip.

Surprise mingled with suspicion in Gigi's eyes. "Thanks."

Vivien spooned a bite of soup.

"How is life in the salon, Miss Vivien?" Cissy laid her knife across the uneaten slab of roast beef and butter beans on her plate.

"Seems a box of veil caps sprouted legs. Disappeared two days ago, but when we opened the salon this morning, the box came back."

"What an odd thing," Mary Jo piped in.

"Too many strange things are happening around here. First Daddy's little spell." Cissy swept her gaze to Mary Jo, then Gigi. "I've called him Daddy ever since John T. and I got engaged." She switched her attention to Vivien. "And now someone's been messing in your shop. I don't know what to think."

"I know who I'd be watching." Gigi laid her elbows on the table and leaned in. "The Hatchet."

Cissy pushed her tray away. "Who on earth is the Hatchet?"

Mary Jo cupped her hand around her mouth. "That's what they call Audrey behind her back."

"Who came up with such a name?" Vivien set her spoon in her empty bowl.

"Sounds like Alvid. He's not fond of Audrey," Cissy said.

"It fits." Gigi shoved the wrappers from her lunch into her crumpled lunch bag.

"She's been nothing but nice to me." That came from Mary Jo.

"Give her time, Mary Jo, and you'll see."

"And what is she going to see, Gigi?" Vivien swirled the last drops of her tea around the bottom of her glass.

Gigi puffed up like a rooster ready to spur a chicken snake in the henhouse. "Us lowly workers have to watch her like a hawk, or we lose our jobs."

This echoed Mirette's daily rants. "Audrey has no say over—"

"She got my boyfriend, Bobby, fired." Anger blazed in Gigi's eyes. "He's broke, and I've been stuck at home for the past three weekends. A girl can only watch so much TV on a nine-inch screen before she goes bonkers from boredom."

She shot Vivien a defiant look. "We all know about her and Mr. Wynton." Gigi peered at Cissy. "I don't blame Mr. Wynton. He's a good man. But a good man can be tricked by a bad woman."

Mary Jo gasped. "Gigi, you shouldn't say such things."

This was the exact reason Vivien avoided gathering with Wynton's employees. The tales of the tongue waggers permeated every conversation.

Years ago those strangling vines almost caused her to turn Carter out for no good reason. Then the truth slapped her sensible before she ruined both their lives.

Cissy gazed around the table. "May I share something?"

Vivien braced for what was coming because Cissy loved drama, and best when it encircled her.

She laid her hands over her heart. "I've always been shattered by how Audrey's twisted Daddy around her little finger. She's caused so many fights because he favors her over John T." Cissy fanned her face. "If I'm not careful, I'll start bawling and flood this whole table."

Mary Jo threw her arms about Cissy's shoulders as Gigi blew a loud breath through pursed lips. "I'm not surprised."

She'd had enough, so Vivien rose from the table. "I need to get back to the shop. Mirette's going to think I got lost."

"Look out." Gigi tilted her head at the cafeteria's main entrance. "The Hatchet's headed our way."

"What's she doing down here? She only eats what she packs or the Florida Salad from the Grove," Cissy said.

Vivien gathered her dishes and was ready to take them to the conveyor, when Audrey came by.

"Mrs. Wynton, your husband needs to speak with you."

Cissy erupted in a whirl of fluster. "I'd better run. Miss Vivien, take my tray up for me?" She vaulted from her chair and landed on her high-heeled pumps. "Lunch was a dream, ladies." She scurried through the parting crowd.

Vivien took the discarded tray and stacked her own dish on top.

"Miss Vivien, may I speak with you?" Audrey took the dishes from her.

Behind her, Gigi muttered, "Uh-oh," to Mary Jo.

Vivien vowed never to eat in the cafeteria again. Maybe she'd install a refrigerator in the back room and stock it with food. Mirette would love the idea.

"Shall we?" Audrey motioned toward the door.

After dropping off the dishes, Audrey remained quiet until they reached the stairwell. She opened the entrance door, then looked around as Vivien walked inside.

Their heels clicked in unison as they climbed. Audrey finally spoke when they reached the second-floor landing. "I went to get Mr. Wynton's papers from your safe, but there was a problem."

"What?"

Concern filled Audrey's eyes. "I originally put them on the bottom shelf, under the jewelry boxes. Today I found them on the middle shelf. Did either you or Mirette move them?"

"No."

Color drained from Audrey's cheeks. "Has anything in the shop gone missing?"

Vivien hesitated. "A box of veil caps disappeared two days ago. We store it on the shelf to hide the safe's door. This morning it returned rather mysteriously. Is there something wrong, Audrey?"

Audrey jerked at the sound of a door banging on an upper floor. The tapping of clipped footsteps sounded as someone descended the stairs.

"May I leave those papers in your safe for now?"

"You can leave them as long as you like."

"Thank you, Miss Vivien. Please let me know if you see anyone acting strangely around the salon."

She scurried up the steps, silently passing the other employee.

Vivien continued to the salon. At the moment, the only person acting up was Audrey herself.

Chapter 7

AUDREY

The figures on the page blurred, but she had to keep digging. Somewhere in the invoices, statements, write-offs, and store accounts, Junior's unsavory activities lurked.

The coffee had run out three hours ago, and she still needed to wash the pot and cups in preparation for Junior's constant demands of "a hot cup of joe."

But the sooner she found out what Junior was up to, the sooner she'd be rid of him and his cup of joe. She resumed thumbing through her notes.

Someone cleared their throat behind her. Audrey shot around to see Nelson standing in the doorway of the office.

"You nearly scared the life out of me." Her heart galloped like a pack of wild horses. "What are you doing up here on the seventh floor, Nelson?"

"When your T-Bird is still here after midnight, I come checking."

"You're sweet." She swept her hand toward the piles of papers, account books, and used coffee cups. "I'm digging for buried treasure."

Nelson limped to a chair in the waiting area and sat down.

She padded across the room in her stocking feet and sat beside him.

Nelson frowned. "You'd better sit at your desk." He rubbed his bad knee. "I won't stay long. Soon as this thing quits throbbing, I'm back to the garage."

"There's no one here but the cleaning ladies, and they finished this floor hours ago. Dessie's polishing the marble tiles on the main floor, and Mae is cleaning the display windows facing the street."

Audrey rubbed the small of her back, urging the kinks to unwind. "They'll keep going until those floors and windows are sparkling like diamonds. I'm fine here."

A wide yawn escaped her. "I used to be able to stay up all night."

"You used to be a lot younger too." Nelson chuckled.

"Well, I surely don't need you to remind me of that."

"Age creeps up, then all of sudden grabs and won't let go." He groaned as he straightened his knee.

Audrey yawned. "I lived in Paris before the war. Sometimes I'd stay up all night, then sleep until late afternoon for days in a row."

She continued. "I once went to bed and slept for two days straight. Only got up if I had to, then went right back to sleep."

"I was in Japan during the war. Okinawa. Kept them same kind of hours." Nelson shook his head. "But not for fun."

A silence settled between them. "Were you treated badly during the war, Nelson?"

He clammed up, and she worried she'd insulted him.

She was about to apologize when Nelson answered. "No different than here." He massaged his knee. "Did what they called me to do. Came home. Don't think about it anymore. Got enough to do here."

A finality seasoned his words. He'd say nothing else.

Living in Paris had opened Audrey's eyes to relations between Blacks and Whites she'd never seen in Levy City. In France, no one was treated less because of their skin color. They were simply people who lived, loved, created art and music she fell in love with, and mingled together as friends.

Which made her return home two years ago difficult. She'd accepted Mr. Wynton's job offer without thinking about how much she'd grown beyond the old ways and rules. There were lines here she couldn't or wouldn't cross. The price to pay was too great for her and for others involved.

But those Blacks who, like Nelson, served in Europe, France, Japan, and later Korea now wanted the freedoms already extended to Whites and the foreigners they'd fought for.

She'd heard stories from Lilla and Eunice about cousins who'd fought against unfair treatment. Blacks up north and as far west as Kansas protested the department store practices that excluded them or made shopping more difficult. Gains in their favor came slowly.

But they came. And Wynton's needed to follow.

Nelson's voice brought her back. "Junior the reason you're working late?"

"He's a child running around in a grown man's silk shirt." Another yawn overtook her. "But he's up to something. And I'm going to expose him."

She walked to her desk and swept her hand across the piles. "Somewhere in all this is a trail of breadcrumbs. Once I find them, I sink Junior and save Mr. Wynton a lot of trouble."

"How?"

"Nelson, did I ever tell you I went to business school?"

He raised his brows. "Do tell."

She nodded. "In New York City. I had to attend class at night. The administration believed female students would be too much of a distraction if we attended class with the men. Imagine that."

Nelson grinned. "I can."

"I paid my own way and earned a degree. I know how businesses are supposed to be run."

She patted one of the piles. "Junior's an oily snake who's lying and stealing from his father. I'm bound and determined to stop him dead in his tracks."

Nelson unfolded from his sitting position and rose. "I've been gone too long."

He made his way to the door, then looked back. "Be careful, Audrey. Even black snakes have a nasty bite. Especially if they work in pairs."

"Is Junior working with someone here at the store?"

Nelson steadied himself on his bum knee. "When folks ignore you, they forget you still see and hear."

Audrey rushed to him. "Nelson, what do you know?"

He held up his hand. "Three weeks ago, before he had his spell, Mr.

Wynton came to the garage and showed me a news clipping with a picture of three gentlemen. He said if I ever saw any one of them in the store, I was to come and tell him, but no one else, including you. The day after Mr. Wynton went to the hospital, I saw Junior driving past the store with two of those men riding in the back of Mr. Wynton's Cadillac."

Chapter 8

MARY JO

Mary Jo tugged her blouse into place over her lacy slip. The brown, full-skirted corduroy jumper waiting on the hanger would be the fourth outfit she'd tried on this morning, and her final choice.

She wasn't Audrey, who must have dozens of closets stuffed to the rafters with beautiful clothes.

After hearing Cissy's worries at lunch last week, she'd have nothing to do with Audrey ever again. She could excuse being snobby. Even demanding perfection. Why, her own family expected perfection from themselves and everyone else. But Audrey was a two-faced home wrecker. Using her feminine wiles and beauty to influence a man as kind and gentle as Mr. Wynton, coming between a father and his only son— that boiled the blood. Pretty was as pretty did, and pretty should never try to tear a family apart. It wasn't decent.

A high-pitched wolf whistle sounded behind her. Kenny sat up in bed and rubbed his hand over the soft bristles of his crew cut.

Mary Jo unbuttoned the top three buttons of her jumper and stepped into it.

"You want some help with all those buttons? There must be twenty of them down the front of that thing. I'd probably have you finished by lunchtime." Kenny laughed, but the hollow sound echoed through their bedroom.

"I'm done." She smoothed the fabric about her slender waist.

Ever since she had started working, he'd begun picking on himself, and she hated this new habit with a passion. He was her hero, the first person in her life to tell her she was pretty. He bragged to all their friends about her cooking, her mothering, even her housekeeping. At night before they turned off the lamp to go to sleep, he'd tell her he was the luckiest man in the world.

Who cared that he only had one arm? The doctor said that as soon as all the healing finished, Kenny could find a job. He gave them pamphlets about programs that offered training for war veterans with injuries. When he'd complain about his new struggles and all the things he couldn't do, she'd remind him how strong and smart he was.

But Kenny laughed her compliments down, saying he was going to run away and join the circus.

"I'll become the world's first one-armed lion tamer," he'd declare, and he'd chase the girls around the room, roaring and snarling until they all fell in a giggling heap on the sofa.

But in their alone times, he'd stew over her being the breadwinner. He wasn't a man, he'd say, and then slip into his dark mood and sit for days, staring at nothing and refusing to eat, sleep, or talk to her and the girls.

He came up behind her and gave her a one-armed hug around her middle. The scent of Ivory soap wafted around him as he kissed her cheek. "I think you're the cutest perfume spritzer in the entire state of Florida." He gazed at her reflection.

Mary Jo surveyed herself from head to toe. "This outfit needs something."

Like that necklace she saw yesterday at the jewelry counter. Nestled on the black velvet form, those gold links glowed like a sunbeam when she walked past on her way to lunch. She'd turned around for a second look.

"Isn't this stunning?" The clerk had noticed Mary Jo staring. "This is the latest from Trifari." She ran her fingers over each loop of the chain. "So chic and goes with everything. Would you like to try it on?" She lifted the necklace from the velvet.

But Mary Jo backed away, and the clerk looked at her as if she'd grown another head.

"No, thank you. I'm just browsing."

The clerk smiled. "Trying on is free." Her smile widened.

Falling in love with the necklace, which she'd done, wasn't good. She'd glanced at the tag and walked away.

Ten dollars.

She couldn't because there was always another expense. Grocery money. Payments on the doctor bills. New shoes for the girls because their feet grew a size every two weeks these days.

And they still weren't keeping up.

She went to her jewelry box and chose Grammy Lyla's brooch with the mother-of-pearl center surrounded by silver filigree.

No girl needed a flashy gold necklace when she had free pieces filled with family love.

She'd hoped for a new dress or skirt for Christmas to add to her work wardrobe. Like one of the new ladies' suits Wynton's carried. For $25.50, she could get a lined jacket, a reversible vest in solid red on one side and red plaid on the other, a red skirt, a solid blue skirt, a plaid skirt, and a white blouse. Six new pieces she could mix and match. She wouldn't be on the same level as Audrey and her designer clothes, but she'd have more than four choices to try to wear over her workweek. And no more trying to hide the worn spots.

If her parents gave her a little bit of money for Christmas, as they did last year, she could buy some fabric to match the new suit and make another skirt and vest herself, expanding her wardrobe more for next year.

She shuddered. Thinking about clothes for next year meant working at Wynton's far longer than she'd hoped.

Kenny came out of the bathroom in his blue robe. "Hey, you look like the gals in those fashion magazines you love so much."

"I know I don't, but thank you."

He pulled her close and bent his head to hers. "Those girls have nothing on you." The scent of his minty toothpaste tickled her nose as he moved in for a kiss.

Mary Jo wriggled free and retrieved her kitten-heeled black pumps and slid them on her feet. "If I don't hurry, Mr. Ashley will fuss over my being late again."

She grabbed her purse from the dresser top. "I've got to tell the girls goodbye. Love you." She pecked him on the lips, then scurried past in a flurry of last-minute hair fluffing and checking in the mirror to make sure her stocking-seams were straight.

Both girls whined as she gathered them in hugs and showered kisses on their silky cheeks while they sat at the kitchen table eating breakfast.

Her mama always made sure she and her brothers had hot breakfasts before school. But she didn't have the time to whip up pancakes or biscuits and gravy or scrambled eggs no matter how much she wanted to.

"Don't go to work, Mama. Stay home and play," her oldest, Carrie Rose, cried as she held a dripping spoonful of cereal above her bowl.

"Wouldn't that be nice?" Mary Jo choked back tears as she tapped the tip of her daughter's nose. "But you have to go to school today."

She hugged her youngest, Penny. "And so do you."

Mary Jo rushed to the door, and the girls followed. "Daddy needs to walk y'all to school, and if you don't hurry up, you'll be going in your nightgowns."

She threw them a final wave as they stood at the front door watching her back the car down the driveway.

Driving was another thing Mama never did. But God had handed her a different road than Mama got.

As she pulled into a space on the top floor of Wynton's garage, a small group of female employees walked past. Most were dressed far more stylish than she.

For single girls, Wynton's was the place to work. Many of the older ladies kept their jobs after the war, saying they could never go back to being "just a housewife" and were glad they didn't get pushed out when the men came back from the wars.

Mama would faint dead away if she ever said a thing like that. And Mary Jo wouldn't. She'd happily trade all this sophisticated freedom for another quiet day at home to make beds, bake cookies, and do the laundry. She even missed scrubbing the floors and the bathrooms.

Footsteps clacked from behind as Mary Jo punched in her time card. She swirled around to face Alvid.

"Skating in at the last minute again, Mrs. Johnson?"

She slid her card into a slot on the board. "Yes, sir."

Mary Jo rushed from the employee locker room to the main floor. As soon as she reached Cosmetics, she stopped to catch her breath.

"What's the special scent today, Edie?" Mary Jo leaned against the corner of the case and patted her chest to calm her racing heart.

"Isn't it Youth Dew?" Edie set out a new receipt pad.

"No, that was yesterday."

"Oh, that's right. Today is White Shoulders." She removed the tester bottle from the case and passed it to Mary Jo. "My mama loves this."

Mary Jo spritzed the air. "Mine never wore perfume. She wasn't a fan of cosmetics." She sniffed the air. "Mmm, that's nice. Like a combination of gardenias and jasmine. This should sell well today."

"Hey, there's my new friend." Cissy headed her way, walking and waving so fast she looked like a two-legged pinwheel.

Edie leaned over the counter. "You know Mrs. Wynton?"

"We had lunch earlier this week."

Edie pursed her lips as if to say, *My aren't we grand?* as Cissy grabbed Mary Jo in a strangling hug.

"How are you?" As she squeezed tighter, Mary Jo feared her cornflakes would come back up, which would be mortifying as Cissy was dressed in a green-and-pink floral dress.

Mary Jo sucked in a quick breath as Cissy released her. "What brings you by this morning?"

"I forgot to put on my perfume, and I feel absolutely naked without it." She motioned to the decanter in Mary Jo's hands. "What's that?"

"White Shoulders." Mary Jo held out the bottle. "Would you like a spritz?"

"Gracious no. My spinster aunt wears that." Cissy went to the back of the perfume counter. "I never wear anything except Chanel No. 5."

She pulled out a new box, tore away the wrappings, and dropped them on the countertop. "Put this on my store credit."

She pulled out the beveled stopper and dotted the scent behind each ear, on the inside of each wrist, and finished with a few drops rubbed in both palms. "I love having my perfume on my hands so that everything I touch throughout the day smells nice and shows I've been there." She giggled. "One of my funny little quirks."

Cissy kept the decanter, blew a kiss at them both, and walked through the center of the floor, greeting all the employees as she made her way to the elevators.

After throwing the discarded box in the trash, Edie rolled her eyes.

"What was that about?" Mary Jo asked as she spritzed the air again.

"Mrs. Wynton."

"I think she's nice."

Edie huffed. "She has her own way." She looked past Mary Jo. "You'd better get into your proper place. Here comes Mr. Ashley."

Chapter 9

GIGI

Not even the needle scratching at the end of the record would make her let him go.

Gigi snuggled her cheek against Bobby's shoulder as they swayed around the floor in her apartment. She'd pushed the table and two chairs that came with the place against the wall and stacked the ottoman on the sofa to create more space for them to dance.

He pulled her closer, and she breathed in the scent of English Leather.

"Forgive me yet?" He kissed her ear.

"I don't want to smack you silly anymore."

Bobby nuzzled her neck. "A guy can't be in trouble for working hard so he can take his best girl out to a nice place someday."

"I'd rather go to the drive-in and have you all to myself."

He swung her around in a circle and kissed her.

"Darlin', very soon I'll take you anywhere in town any night you please." He dipped her, then gave her a lingering kiss.

Her head went all fluttery, like she'd been on the merry-go-round she loved to spin on in grade school.

She pulled away before she lost all control. "I've got to turn off the record player before that scratching drives me to distraction."

He ran his finger down the length of her arm. "Didn't even notice."

Goosebumps chased the shivers wriggling from her head to her toes. Gigi moved to the player, set the needle in the cradle, and clicked off the machine.

Bobby set the tattered ottoman on the floor, then plopped on the sofa and spread one arm along the top of the cushions. It was then she noticed the large silver watch hanging on his wrist.

"Did you get a new watch?"

He glanced at the face, then twisted his wrist to offer her a better view. "Yeah, I did."

Gigi leaned in. "Wow, that's dreamy."

He could afford an expensive new watch but couldn't take her rollerskating or buy her a cheap hamburger at the drive-in?

"How'd you pay for that?"

He flashed a wide grin. "I didn't. My old one got broken at work, so my new boss bought me this one."

"You've got some nice boss. I saw one like that at Wynton's costing a few pretty pennies."

"Yeah, but I've got an even nicer girl." He patted the empty spot beside him and flashed a smile like the gangsters in the old movies he loved to watch at the Tropic Theater downtown.

She'd gained two ex-husbands' worth of experience to know this moment needed a cooldown.

"I need some sweet tea. You want some?" She headed to the small kitchenette in the corner of her one-room apartment.

"I'm not in the mood for tea." Bobby wiggled his brows upward.

Gigi pulled the door to the refrigerator open. "Tea is all you're getting, Romeo."

Bobby yanked his arm from the cushion. "Pour me a glass." He propped his ankle on the opposite knee and bounced his leg.

He could sit there and stew all he wanted, because she wasn't doing anything to cost her job at Wynton's. Working there gave her the hope of moving out of the cafeteria to something better.

"What's the newest at the store?" He took the glass of tea.

Gigi settled in the chair across from him. "My boss asked me to set the schedules again and fill out the weekly orders."

She wiped a bead of perspiration from her forehead. Her little above-garage apartment held in the heat worse than an oven. Gigi cranked open the windows to allow some of the cooler night air to creep in.

Bobby took a swig of tea. "You up for a promotion?"

"No."

"Then why take on extra work?"

"People who help get noticed."

He snorted. "Tell her to give you more money if you're doing her job too." He uncrossed his legs. "That's your trouble. You don't stand up for yourself at that place."

He beat his chest with one thumb. "I didn't take their guff, especially from Audrey." Bobby swiped the air with his hand, causing the face of his new watch to catch the light. "Getting fired from there was the best thing that ever happened to me."

He puffed his chest like Daddy's old banty rooster used to. She loved Bobby to death but was not in the mood to hear him go on about how he bested Audrey.

"I met Cissy Wynton at lunch the other day."

His eyes widened. "No kidding?"

"She ate lunch with me and the new girl, Mary Jo."

Bobby leaned forward with his elbows on his knees. "In the cafeteria?" He shook his head. "I'm sorry, darlin', but I don't believe you. Cissy Wynton's got too much class to eat with regular folk in that grease pit."

"Bobby Bridges, are you calling me a liar?"

He choked back laughter. "No, honey. I just think you're mixed up. Cissy Wynton is one of the richest ladies in town. Why would she sit with the employees at her own store?"

"She doesn't own the store. Mr. Wynton does. And since when did you take a liking to Cissy Wynton? You said if she had her nose stuck any higher in the air, she'd drown in a downpour."

Bobby held his hands as if shielding himself from her anger. "I got nothing against her. I hear she's not half-bad. And everybody knows she and Junior inherit the store when the old man dies."

The ice cubes clinked as he downed the last of his tea. "By the way, how is Mr. Wynton?"

"His heart is still giving him fits. Junior's running the store, and Cissy said she's jumping in to help." She leaned in closer. "But you know the worst of it? She said Audrey has pushed her way in between Junior and his daddy. Stirred up all kinds of trouble between them." She sat back. "Isn't that awful?"

He rubbed his hand along the stubble darkening his jawline. "That woman is something I won't repeat in front of mixed company because my mama taught me better. The old man needs to step down and let Cissy and Junior run things. And get rid of Audrey."

Her heart lurched at the thought of these changes. "Mr. Wynton is perfectly capable of running the store, Bobby. Everybody knows Junior isn't nearly as smart."

"I've heard Cissy's pretty smart herself. She could step in. She's already the top fashion buyer and practically runs the personnel department."

"Where did you hear all that?" She shifted in her seat so her elbow didn't press against the underside of the foldout bed she tucked against the wall during the day.

"Everybody knows how hard she works. Junior too."

"I didn't." So how did Bobby know? In search of a new topic that didn't make her stomach knot, she changed the subject.

"Did you hear what happened to James Dean?"

Bobby scowled. "Wasn't he in that movie you love so much? The one where he's a wet blanket?"

"He wasn't a wet blanket in *East of Eden*. He was tragic. Anyway, he was killed in a car wreck out in California today. So sad."

"He didn't even know you existed. You're just a faceless fifty-cent admission at the Tropic Theater. You need to get interested in something other than movies."

She motioned to her record player. "Just bought a new record from Wynton's. Got to use my employee discount."

"Oh yeah? Which one?"

" 'Rock around the Clock' by Bill Haley and His Comets."

Bobby laughed again. "That's real high-brow, honey." He made a motion as if he were drinking tea with his pinkie stuck up straight. "You aren't a teenybopper. Need to think about more grown-up things."

"Such as?"

He gave her a look as if she were six and asked for the moon. "Cooking, cleaning, keeping house. Reading books."

"I have a job, you lunkhead. And when was the last time you read a book?"

She drew in a breath to calm her boiling nerves. "You love rock 'n' roll too. At least you did before tonight. And you're older than me."

"I've learned to love other things a whole lot more now." Bobby rose from the sofa. "I gotta go."

Gigi sprang to her feet. "Go? You've hardly been here an hour."

"This new job keeps me hopping. I gotta get some rest."

"What is this mysterious new job?"

"It's hard to explain."

She planted her hands on her hips. "Try me."

He hesitated. "I do small jobs for my new boss. Like deliveries or fixing things. Some days I'm just a gofer." He headed to the door.

Bobby beckoned her with his hand. "No more third degree. Come kiss me good night."

Heat shot up her neck and settled on her cheeks. "If I'm not good enough for you to spend time with and so dumb I couldn't even understand what you do at this fancy new job, I'm not good enough to kiss you."

He pushed the screen door open. "Your loss."

Gigi flashed him the cold shoulder. "Don't flatter yourself."

His footsteps thudded down the wooden stairs that led from her apartment. She hoped the loose railing didn't give way, causing him to fall to the cement driveway below. No way did she feel like dealing with him if he conked his head.

Knowing full well she'd roast tonight, she slammed the main door shut and set the lock.

The circles of light from the headlights of Bobby's car shone on her front window as he backed from the driveway.

Gigi shut the blinds.

After washing their tea glasses, she settled on the sofa, where the smell of Bobby's aftershave and perspiration still lingered.

He'd certainly gotten full of himself. With this new job, he acted as if he were doing her a favor by dating her. Had he forgotten she met him when he was still a stock boy at Wynton's?

Now he behaved as if he'd moved up the social ladder high enough to sit next to Mr. Wynton.

New watch. New attitude.

What in the world was going on with Bobby Bridges?

Chapter 10

Audrey

S he was checking the last of the questionable invoices when the phone rang.

Audrey never answered until the third bell. Miss Evelyn said a lady makes sure to appear relaxed and unrushed in all activities. The advice worked wonders in business.

She lifted the receiver. "Mr. Wynton's office. May I ask who's calling?"

"This is George Crawford. I need to speak with Mr. Wynton."

She retrieved her message pad and pencil. "Mr. Wynton is unavailable at the moment." He'd told her not to tell any of his business associates he was still on bed rest. "May I take a message?"

"He told me to call his office today at this time."

Audrey looked at the closed door of the inner office. Junior hadn't decided to grace the store with his illustrious presence yet. "Are you wishing to speak to John T. Wynton, Mr. Crawford?"

George Crawford chuckled into the phone. "I love your sweet southern drawl. Like listening to silk. Yes, I wish to speak to John T."

She wrote *Mr. G. Crawford* and the time on the notepad.

"He's out as well." Junior had resumed the habit of not arriving before ten. "May I ask what this is in regard to, please?"

"You're so polite," George cooed into the phone.

Audrey tapped the eraser end of her pencil on the notepad. Good manners were the backbone of her upbringing. And they often came in handy when one wanted to know something without seeming nosy. She flipped her pencil over with the lead poised over the paper.

"I'm calling to let John T. know that my investors are ready to talk numbers. They'd like to meet at the beginning of October, then set the deadline for the sale in December, preferably before Christmas."

Audrey snapped her pencil in two. *The sale?*

She pressed the phone tighter to her ear. "And what sale are you referring to?"

"We're buying Wynton's Department Store."

She covered her mouth to keep from shrieking like a batty banshee.

"Hello? You still there?" George called from the other end.

The phone receiver slipped from her hand and fell to the floor.

"Hello? Hello! What's going on down there?"

Audrey yanked the cord, reeling in the receiver like a fish on a line. She exhaled, then answered Mr. Crawford's long-distance bellows. "Forgive me, Mr. Crawford." Her hand shook as she gripped the receiver. What kind of son did such a thing when his father was ill?

"Let me read back your message to ensure I've taken down all that Mr. Wynton needs to know." And she meant father, not son. "You wish to inform him that your investors are interested in the sale of Wynton's Department Store and are ready to discuss numbers with him. You wish to meet with him at the beginning of next month, and you want negotiations finalized by December first. Is there anything else you'd like to add?"

"Not a word. What's your name, dear? I'd like John T. to know how well you took care of me today." George practically purred the words to her.

And if she could have reached through the phone, she'd have strung him up faster than a body could say "Jack Robinson." "How kind of you."

"I'd love to meet you when we—"

"I'll pass your message on to Mr. Wynton. Thank you for calling." She hung up before George could respond.

Audrey threw the broken halves of the pencil at the inner office door.

"Junior, you dirty, rotten skunk." She retrieved her satchel from under her desk and thumbed through the notes she'd worked on at home.

She'd discovered the questionable figures first. Then invoices written for goods never received by the store and payments sent to a strange vendor the store never used. There were instances of altered accounts receivable, numbers that didn't add up, and refunds given to customers without any record of an original sale.

She found dormant accounts, now suddenly full of activity, along with new revenues not matching the number of daily sales.

She was a whisper away from burying him. If she could put all the pieces together, soon enough he'd be dragged from the store by his shirt collar, his well-manicured hands secured in handcuffs.

Before Christmas preferably.

The handle on the outer office door clicked, and she slid the papers back in her satchel.

Junior entered, encircled by a cloud of cologne. She bit her lip to keep from vomiting out the volcano of hot words boiling in her throat.

"Did I get any calls this morning?"

"Mr. George Crawford."

Junior stopped his trek and froze like a deer in rifle sights.

"Bring me a cup of fresh coffee." He strolled to the office door as if nothing were amiss, but he paled beneath his tan.

He kept his eyes on the paperwork on his desk when she arrived with the coffee. Audrey carried the memo of the call in her free hand.

She set down the coffee, then lowered herself in the chair directly opposite Junior.

He wagged his fingers at her. "Give me the message."

Audrey crumpled the paper and tossed the ball on the desk by the steaming coffee cup.

"How dare you sell your father out, you oily snake."

"What are you babbling about?" Anger flared in Junior's eyes.

"You're trying to sell the store."

Junior lifted the coffee and took a swig, then choked and tried to spit the steaming liquid back into the cup. He cleared his throat and set the coffee off to the side of his papers.

"Groups like George Crawford's call all the time. They're always trying to acquire a midsize store like ours. Having five successful locations across the state makes us more desirable." He acted as if she'd said Santa Claus had called and wanted to order a new sleigh.

She leaned against the edge of the desk. "For your information, I screen calls from prospective buyers regularly. I know how they operate. Mr. Crawford believes you have a deal in place. With deadlines."

"A sales tactic. Just business."

"Then why are you sweating?" She pointed to a drop of perspiration pooling above his brows.

Junior's face went red as he wiped his forehead. "You'd better be able to back up those accusations. The store's in my care now."

She wouldn't trust him with the care of a dead frog. And his veiled threat scraped her nerves worse than the sneering smile he'd flashed after he spoke.

George Crawford must have been one of the men from the news clipping Nelson had mentioned.

"Does being in charge include courting buyers your father banned from the store?"

Junior's sneer fell as his eyes bulged. "How did. . . ?" He forced a smile. "You've been listening to the store's gossip chain."

She rested her elbows on the armrests of the chair. "I've found much more than gossip."

He steepled his fingers together. "I've got news for you, lady, and I use the term loosely when applied to you. I've appointed Cissy as the new head of store personnel to protect Wynton's employees from you. She and I will have you out of here and out of my father's life by December."

Junior pointed his finger like a gun at her and dropped his thumb as if it were the hammer. "Guaranteed." He winked.

Audrey rose. "I've dug up some pretty interesting things that have your fingerprints all over them. Like fraud, theft, skimming from the store's coffers, and cooking the books."

She wiggled her fingers in Junior's line of sight. "All these little threads are coming together"—she laced her fingers for emphasis—"and weave quite a tapestry of unsavory activities."

Junior erupted with an overly loud belly laugh as she walked to the open doorway. "You're one delusional—"

She slammed the door behind her before he could finish his thought.

A bearlike bellow erupted from the office, finished off with Junior's yelling at her over the intercom for a towel to sop up spilled coffee.

She pressed the button to respond. "Towels are in the washroom. Help yourself."

Audrey drew in a deep breath as she switched off the speaker. A wasp sting started all this. Now she'd stuck her hand into the hornet's nest of Junior's sordid activities. All while poking the baby bear to let him know his days of dipping into his father's honeycomb were numbered.

And it wasn't even lunch yet.

Chapter 11

AUDREY

Her car lights illuminated the long, fingerlike branches rimming Mr. Wynton's driveway. They seemed to reach out as if to stop her from her quest as she pulled into the usual spot and cut the ignition.

Junior warned her days ago to stay away from his father. He forbade the nightly visits to talk store business. Her phone calls were disconnected as soon as he or Cissy heard her voice.

Not knowing the truth about Mr. Wynton's health ate at her, kept her from sleeping, and now compelled her to jump in her car well after midnight.

The damp mid-October night air stroked her cheeks as she grabbed her satchel and purse. She locked her car out of habit. Mr. Wynton lived so far off the road, no one would bother taking the long trek through the black woods to stir up mischief.

The shadowy outline of the house towered above the yellow domes shining from the outside lights. They spotlighted her path, and she made sure not to wander too far beyond the boundary where they sliced away the darkness. She'd encountered too many raccoons in these woods not to remain cautious.

Audrey fought to keep from running to her car and leaving the property. But she had to tell him what Junior was doing because December loomed, and she was running out of time to protect the dream.

When she went to knock, the door suddenly swung open. A figure cloaked in the interior's late-night gloom called out. "Audrey?"

His voice sounded weaker than usual, but she released her pent-up breath as Mr. Wynton switched on a light.

"Yes, sir."

He grabbed her wrist. "Hurry and get in here before the night nurse calls John T. and Cissy."

Mr. Wynton shut the door and quietly set the locks. "She's upstairs watching TV in her room. We'll go in my study."

Watching him shuffle across the pine floor as she followed behind him shredded her heart. A few weeks ago she had struggled to keep up with him as he made his daily rounds visiting employees and greeting customers.

He slid the amber-colored pine doors closed as soon as she entered the study. "Have a seat."

She looked away as he winced and lowered himself into his favorite chair. The brown leather groaned as he settled his full weight in the seat and leaned against the overstuffed back. "What brings you here?"

He took his glasses from the end table and slowly unfolded each bow before sliding them onto his face.

Audrey drew her notes from her satchel, and he held out his hand. "Let me see."

She kept them close, not ready to blanket him with the truth.

He met her eyes. "I know he's been stealing from the store. And he secretly owns some of the clothing vendors we've been buying from. He's charging us double what the clothes are worth, using old accounts to move funds around to hide assets from other side deals. I found invoices for goods never delivered, ordered from dummy companies. Sound familiar?"

"Yes, sir. But there's something else."

"Worse?"

She tightened her grip on her notes, wishing she could squeeze the paper hard enough to erase their truth. "He's made plans to sell the store out from under you."

Her boss tapped two fingers against his lip as he absorbed her news.

She had to drop the balls all at once and get the ordeal over with. "The deadline is December first."

"How did you find out?"

"Last month I took a call from a man named George Crawford. He's one of the buyers."

Mr. Wynton grunted. "George Crawford runs United Merchant's Federation. They're a conglomerate bent on owning successful midsize department stores like us. We're one of the last still being run by the family whose name is on the store's front."

"What are you going to do?"

He sighed, deepening the new creases lining his cheeks and jaw since the last time she'd seen him. "The same thing every old, male animal does when a younger one comes along and threatens his territory. Fight."

The grandfather clock in the corner of the study ticked a steady rhythm like a distant battle drum. On her previous visit to this room, weeks before his health declined, the sweet, grassy aroma of his favorite cigars seasoned the air. He'd paced the floor as they talked, plopped in his chair a moment only to resume his pacing, talking at speeds she struggled to match as she took notes.

Tonight he stared with red-rimmed eyes resembling an old bloodhound's. Droopy, glassy, and longing for rest. A myriad of pill bottles and elixirs covered the top of the side table.

He had become an old man.

"How can you fight this? There's so little time."

The hollows in his cheeks burrowed deeper as he set his jaw. "This battle's mine. You're not to get involved."

She started to protest, but he silenced her with a look. "On my desk is an envelope. I want you to keep it at your house. Don't open it unless. . ."

Mr. Wynton stared directly into her eyes. "Understand?"

He'd never locked her out of the store's business before. But he wasn't going to budge. "Yes, sir."

He inclined his head toward the desk. "Go."

Her shoes sank into the deep pile of the crimson, Persian-patterned rug as she crossed the room. The folder lay on top of his black leather blotter pad.

As she lifted her secret assignment from the desk, the blank white boxes on his huge calendar glared at her. Never, in all her time spent in this room, had she seen those boxes empty.

He had nothing to fill them with. His days bore no purpose.

She bit her lip to stave off the tears. She'd cry on the way home where he wouldn't see.

Audrey slid the envelope into her satchel with the rest of her notes, then looked up to find him dozing.

He'd be so embarrassed if he thought she'd noticed. She walked back to the desk. "Mr. Wynton," she called in as loud a voice as she dared to avoid catching the attention of the nurse.

She dropped her gaze to the desktop as he stirred, rubbed his eyes behind his glasses, then fixed his attention on her.

"Yes?"

"Is there anything else?"

He massaged the back of his neck as he yawned. "You're taking on far more than I should be asking of you."

Audrey painted on the fake smile she'd perfected long ago. If he'd allow it, she'd snatch every bit of trouble from him and tie it to her own shoulders. "You never ask too much."

He shifted so he could see her better from his chair. "Let me do something for you. As thanks."

She shook her head, but he pounded the armrest with his fist. "I insist. Whatever you ask."

"Well, there is one thing you might do."

Chapter 12

VIVIEN

Vivien showed Mirette the sketch of her newest bridal creation. She rather liked this gown, especially the rounded shape of the skirt and the oh-so-current shin-length hemline.

"This silk tulle skirt will float as the girl walks down the aisle." She tapped the drawing. "And see here on the bodice—I wove strips of the chiffon together to give a little texture and interest and catch the eye."

She flipped the page. "I continued lacing down the back, ending with this bow. The ribbons will trail down the skirt. What do you think?"

Mirette cocked her head to the side. "Looks like a cupcake with blobs of icing crisscrossed over the top."

Vivien elbowed her in the ribs. "Stop it. We saw plenty of gowns with this shape at the bridal expo in New York last spring. This style is fresh and new right now, and plenty of our girls will appreciate not having to sweat through their wedding day in the middle of summer, lugging around a long, heavy gown."

She tapped her pencil along the top of the bodice. "The only change I could see is maybe making this a bateau neckline."

Mirette drew back and stared at her. "A what neckline?"

"Bateau."

"What on earth is that?"

"The fabric is cut straight across at the collarbone in the front and back of the bodice, leaving an inch-sized gap at the shoulders." Vivien drew her hand across her chest, miming her description.

"And what is that called again?"

"A *ba-toe*. It's French."

"My, aren't we getting fancy." Mirette bounced her head in rhythm with each word.

"Keeping up with the latest styles. Girls these days want what they see in the movies or *Modern Bride*."

"There's also that TV show about weddings." Mirette snapped her fingers as she tried to wring the irretrievable answer from her brain.

"Are you talking about *Bride and Groom*?"

"That's the one!" Mirette screeched so loud she gave Vivien a jolt. "Such a phony-baloney mess."

"Be that as it may, we do a difficult dance here in the South. Our girls want to carry on family traditions for generations and be modern at the same time. We must keep up, my friend." Vivien closed her sketchbook and filed it away in the cabinet where she kept her designs.

Keeping up.

Every year the fear of being left behind hovered closer and closer. Women her age, widowed with married children, found themselves chasing the calendar instead of purpose.

But she had her salon, a hard-earned reputation, and her name. And thank God, the creative gifts He'd given her didn't diminish with her age. She could still design with the best of them. And find the dress for any bride who crossed the shop's threshold, even though she'd passed through the dreaded "change of life."

"We had a delivery last night," Mirette called from the storeroom. "A big box. It's either Miranda's bridesmaid dress or the gown you ordered from Boston for Tricia Gant."

"I'll meet you there." Vivien grabbed her scissors from her desk drawer, making certain she'd grabbed the sharp pair. Not the ones Mirette dulled when she scraped away some splinters on Vivien's desk.

She'd just cut the tape from the top of the box when a voice called to them from the sales floor. "Who would be here this early?"

Mirette took the scissors from her. "I'll unpack."

Vivien pulled up on a nearby bench as her legs offered little help in rising these days. She smoothed the full skirt of her black taffeta dress about her knees and adjusted the thin belt around her waist.

She found Cissy rifling through a rack of bridesmaid dresses, pulling certain gowns out and draping them over her arm.

"May I help you, Cissy?"

She swung around so fast the dress fabric flapped back and forth like laundry dancing in a breeze. "Miss Vivien. Good morning." She held up the bundle in her arms. "I'm sure you're wondering what I'm doing here, aren't you?"

All the dresses she'd taken bore Vivien's personal label. "The thought did cross my mind."

Cissy made quite the picture as she moved toward Vivien. Her gray pencil skirt constricted her legs, and she could take only short, toddling steps in her heels.

Thank the good Lord, Mirette opted to stay in the storeroom, because there would have been no controlling her mouth around Cissy today.

"Cissy, why have you gathered my dresses off the rack?"

She paused, as if she were thinking how best to answer. "I noticed these are older styles and wondered if you have to send them to our discount store on Latham Street to keep your inventory current."

"I don't send any dresses to Latham."

Her brows rose at the response. "None of them? What do you do with those that don't sell?"

Vivien crossed her arms about her waist, cradling one elbow in the opposite hand. "All my designs sell."

"But these are older. Why would you keep them on the sales floor?"

Her innocent stare failed to cover her implication that good taste seemed to be running far ahead of Vivien.

She drew in a deep breath. "Cissy, just what exactly are you saying?"

Cissy shifted the load to her other arm. "These don't fit the modern bride's tastes."

Flaming heat ran up the back of Vivien's neck, passed over her hairline, and crept across her scalp until the part in her hair radiated with warmth.

She held out her hand. "I'll hang these back up now."

"The dresses weren't my reason for coming in this morning." Cissy said as Vivien smoothed a ribbon on one dress back into place. The unmistakable scent of Chanel No. 5 hung on the fabric. She'd have to air these out later.

"No? What then?"

"The annual holiday fashion show is coming up, and since Daddy's illness, John T. and I have taken on more responsibilities here at the store. I won't be able to run the show this year."

"Uh-oh. I see where this is going," Mirette chimed in as she came to stand by Vivien's side.

Cissy curled her lip and shot a look at Mirette as if she smelled bad. "Miss Vivien, no one else in this store knows fashion or fashion shows better than you. You're the perfect choice."

The nerve. First she insulted her business practices, called her out-of-date, and then possessed the gall to ask her to take on the enormous task of the fashion show.

"What about Audrey?"

Cissy's face flushed crimson. "I wouldn't ask Audrey to put on a dog show, much less one of Wynton's most important events."

"Then you'll just have to ask her anyway, because we don't have time to take this on. We're booked solid with appointments through the holidays, and we have drop-ins coming in every day," Mirette said.

"I've solved that problem for you, Miss Mirette."

Vivien passed a silent *can't wait to hear this* look to Mirette. "How?"

Cissy slapped her hands together and laced her fingers into a ball. "I've hired two new junior assistants to help you through the holidays."

"What?" Vivien and Mirette choked out in unison.

"Is this not the best idea? Now you two can concentrate on the show and not worry about the salon. My new girls will take over for you until after New Year's."

"Do these girls of yours know how to sew? Are they familiar with bridal fashions or experienced in dealing with the bride's family?" Mirette's questions tumbled out like an upturned bag of marbles.

"They're young, so they can relate to your girls. They'll help them find the fashions they want and have better advice on the latest trends."

Vivien let the new slight against her fade before she answered. "Cissy, do they have any sales experience?"

"They both served on our teen advisory boards and worked with me as teen consultants when I was the buyer for Wynton's Young Miss and Collegians Department a few years back." Cissy bounced up and down as if she were about to burst. "They're perfect to take over while you two plan the show."

There were no words, at least not civil ones. Vivien turned to Mirette for help.

For the first time in the thirty years since she'd known her, her old friend went mute. Mirette stood there with her jaw hanging so low she could catch flies.

Cissy rushed forward and grasped Vivien's hands. "Please, Miss Vivien. I want this year's show to be the best we've ever had. This may be the last one Daddy ever. . ." Her words faltered as she broke into tears and propped herself against a mannequin clad in a gown the color of pink champagne. The mascara dripping from her false eyelashes left a black dot on the ruffled neckline of the gown.

As Mirette moved her away from the merchandise, Vivien ran to grab one of the boxes of tissues they kept on hand for weepy brides.

Good thing she'd perfected wearing multiple hats at one time. Another skill that came to good use in the business world thanks to her age. Maybe someday society would see that as clearly as she did.

Miss Vivien pulled tissues free and handed them to Cissy. "Dry your eyes, honey."

She complied, finishing with a soggy nose blowing. "I'm sorry for being so weepy." Another sob escaped, and Cissy held her hand out for additional clean tissues.

After more whimpers, she drew herself up with a deep breath. "I'm not asking just for me, Miss Vivien." She pushed a soggy false eyelash back into place.

Vivien patted her on the back. "I'll take over the fashion show."

At Cissy's brightened expression, Vivien held up one finger. "On one condition."

Cissy clutched Vivien's hands. "Anything."

"I have complete control to choose the clothes, models, music, and theme."

Cissy bobbed her head. "Of course."

"I have one other request."

Cissy stared, waiting.

"I want you to be the commentator."

Cissy responded with a smile so wide Vivien feared her face might split. "I'd love to." She lunged at Vivien and wrapped her in a choking hug.

Vivien unwrapped Cissy from her and stepped back. "I'll work out the script and send everything to you in a few weeks."

Cissy thrust her mass of used tissues into Mirette's hand, twirled on her heels, and floated to the exit of the salon. "Miss Vivien, Miss Mirette, thank you both so much." She laid her hands across her heart. "You're both just loves." She whooshed out the door without another word.

Mirette wrinkled her nose at the dirty tissues. She threw them away, then looked at Vivien.

"I think I may spit up."

Vivien met her gaze. "I think I may join you."

Chapter 13

MARY JO

Mary Jo yawned as she sprayed a cloud of Wynton's perfume-of-the-day around the aisle. Hopefully no customer would ask her the name, because it was French and she had no idea how to pronounce it. At least the floral scent masked the smell of the Vicks VapoRub she'd forgotten to wash off her hands before she ran out the door this morning.

Both girls had fevers and sore throats and kept her awake all night.

And the helpless look on Kenny's face when she left instructions on how to care for them didn't help matters. He was nursing a sore ankle from tripping over the patio chairs when a coral snake crawled by him. He'd hoped to sit with his foot propped up while she and the girls were gone for the day.

At least he'd get a break when she arrived home. Unlike her, because as soon as she came in the door, the girls would start fussing for her to console them.

"Mrs. Johnson, a word," Alvid yelled from across the department.

The entire department gawked and stared. Edie from Cosmetics sidled over as Mary Jo set the perfume decanter down.

"Have you heard the latest?"

Mary Jo waved her hands to stir the air. Today's scent was not only unpronounceable but strong enough to choke a horse. "What's going on?"

Edie cut her eyes toward Alvid, who now came toward them, weaving through racks of shirts and pants.

She leaned in close. "The store's been losing money like water through a sieve ever since Junior took over. Word is layoffs are coming."

Mary Jo's stomach dropped to her shoes. "In what departments?"

"All of them. I heard half of Bookkeeping is ready to walk out because they've had to work until midnight for weeks trying to untangle the mess he's made."

Edie snapped back as Alvid arrived. "We'll talk later."

"Good morning, ladies." Alvid pressed his hands together and bowed his head to Edie. "Miss Mason, allow us a moment, please?"

"Good luck." Edie went back to her counter.

Alvid fixed his face into a sympathetic expression. "Mrs. Johnson, I received word today that Wynton's is letting you go."

Her gut erupted with sharp pains, like when she was eight years old and Georgie Spears kicked her in the stomach.

"Why?" she screeched through the fingers of shock squeezing her throat.

Alvid smoothed his neon-orange-and-red tie against his shirt. "All I know is that Audrey delivered your dismissal to personnel this morning."

Mary Jo dug her nails into her palms. "She promised she wouldn't."

Alvid handed her a pink slip. "Never believe a rattlesnake's friendly overtures. They'll always bite you in the end. It's their nature." He looked at his watch. "I'll give you fifteen minutes to clear your locker out."

"Yes, sir."

"I'm so sorry," Edie said as Mary Jo gathered her things.

Mary Jo couldn't speak. She'd failed Kenny and the girls. Audrey had betrayed her. Her fears whirled like a swarm of mosquitoes attacking from all sides.

How was she going to keep her girls fed and clothed? And pay for Kenny's medical bills?

She trudged her way through the main aisle, keeping her eyes down so she wouldn't see the pity on coworkers' faces as she walked this path of shame.

But then she heard her name. She looked up to see Cissy scurrying so fast her full-skirted brown dress swished in rhythm with each step. "Good morning, friend." She almost sang the words.

Cissy pulled her into an embrace so tight the rhinestone buttons adorning the front of her dress poked Mary Jo. "You look so tired and sad."

She'd done well so far to keep from crying and would save what little bit of face she had left by keeping herself together until the drive home.

"I've lost my job." Mary Jo coughed back the sobs demanding release.

Cissy's eyes widened. "What?"

Mary Jo drew a deep breath. "Mr. Ashley just informed me I've lost my job."

"Come with me." Cissy looped her arm in Mary Jo's and whisked her back to the cosmetics counter, where she promptly called Alvid over.

When he stood before them, Cissy tightened her grip on Mary Jo's arm. "Did you tell Mary Jo that she's been dismissed?"

Alvid fiddled with the back of his collar. At that same moment, Mary Jo spied Audrey coming up behind them in a dark red suit. She still wore a small straw hat and matching gloves, as if she'd just come in the door.

And now she had the gall to stand and watch her dirty work unfold.

"Yes. I got the word from Audrey this morning," he continued.

"Alvid, you've scared this poor soul to death." Cissy released Mary Jo. "She isn't being dismissed. She's being transferred to Ladies' Accessories."

Mary Jo's knees melted, and she swayed on her feet. "Really?"

"Yes." Cissy dipped her chin.

Alvid shook his head as if to knock his brain back into gear. "And who decreed this?"

Cissy gestured to herself. "Me. Right now."

Out of the corner of her eye, Mary Jo saw Audrey scowl. Probably mad Cissy overruled her and took away her power.

Alvid's brows shot up. "But what about the list Audrey—"

Cissy flicked her hand like she was tossing out a piece of trash. "Daddy's returning to the store next week. Until then, Audrey's lists don't exist."

"My mistake, Mrs. Johnson." He bowed. "If you ladies will excuse me, I'd better get to my post so I don't get fired myself." He walked past Audrey without a word.

"Thank you for saving my job, Cissy. You don't know what this means."

"That's what I'm here for." Cissy left without another word. Her heels clacked across the marble tiles as she made her way to the elevators.

Audrey hovered in the background until Cissy was gone. When they were alone, she came closer.

"Congratulations. You're going to love working in Accessories." Audrey appeared to be brimming with excitement, which seemed as real as a three-legged duck, considering how she'd tried to have Mary Jo dumped.

It took every grain of ladylike behavior Mama had drilled into her to keep Mary Jo from saying what she truly thought of the whole affair. "I am. Thanks to Cissy."

Audrey took a step back, as if she'd been slapped by the tone Mary Jo worked hard to weave into her words.

"May I show you to your new assignment?" Even in sweeping her hand in the intended direction, Audrey moved like a ballerina.

Mary Jo shook her head. "I know where to go."

"I hope your new assignment goes splendidly." Audrey seemed to hesitate as if there was more she wished to say, but she walked away.

Mary Jo met the looks from those she'd earlier avoided with her head held high as she walked to her new position.

Her new manager met her with open arms. And Mary Jo laughed out loud when compliments on how nice she smelled came.

And there wasn't a French anything in sight.

As she straightened a hat hanging astray on its perch, she noticed Gigi modeling a purple-and-green scarf in the small circular mirror in the display.

Her friend's jaw popped open when she looked up and saw Mary Jo. "What are you doing here?"

"This is my new job."

"You got a promotion already?"

"I did. And according to my new manager, I also get a ten-cent raise. If I do well, I'll get another by New Year's." She almost burst saying the last part, as she couldn't believe her good fortune in landing this new job.

All thanks to Cissy.

But Gigi didn't beam or wish her well. Her shoulders drooped and her mouth drifted into a sour expression. "How?"

"That's the best part. When I got here this morning, Mr. Ashley told me I'd been dismissed. By Audrey. Then Cissy came and said she'd overruled the decision and put me here. Isn't that wonderful?"

Still no offer of congratulations came from Gigi. "How do you like that?" She dropped the scarf and headed in the direction of the cafeteria.

"Want to meet for lunch today?" Mary Jo called after her.

"Can't." Gigi continued walking.

"Tomorrow then?" Mary Jo asked, but Gigi never responded as she hurried away.

Chapter 14

AUDREY

The gray clouds gathering like giant balls of dirty gray cotton weren't going to ruin Audrey's day. Mr. Wynton was back in the store.

Once she'd parked, she gathered her things. Damp air, chilled by the promise of coming rain, sprinted through the garage, dragging a wave of somersaulting leaves along the concrete.

She waved to Nelson as he came around the corner. "Your breakfast is still warm and dry." Audrey held the bag aloft.

As he limped closer, he pulled his jacket collar up around his ears. "Glad something is, because it sure ain't me." He chuckled as he took the bag and thermos from her.

"At least you can go home soon."

He made his way back to his chair. "And get warmed up." Nelson unscrewed the thermos cap and took a quick sip of coffee.

A gust of wind engulfed them, and Audrey pressed her hand over the crown of her hat to prevent its blowing away. "You ought to go home and get yourself wrapped up in a nice dry blanket."

Nelson opened the bag. "I'm going to sleep, and I might not wake up until next week. Y'all will have to do without me for a few days." He took a bite from one of the cinnamon twists.

"Now, Nelson, you know this store won't run without you."

"Phooey," he grunted while enjoying another bite of his breakfast.

He switched the bite to his cheek. "Mr. Wynton's back. Don't need anybody else."

The weight of her satchel and purse pressed into her arm, so Audrey transferred them to her hands. She held both against the front of her full skirt to keep the silk fabric from billowing in the wind and exposing far more than was decent.

"Especially now that Junior and Cissy decided they needed to get away. I suppose almost driving the store six feet under is taxing. I hope they forget their way home."

Nelson laughed, then choked on his food. He took a long swig of the coffee and worked to clear his throat before he answered. "Soon as his money runs out, he'll come running."

"With Cissy right on his heels." Audrey looked around the garage, and upon seeing no other employees, she reached forward and squeezed Nelson's shoulder. "I've got to go. See you tonight when you're back on."

He nodded as he downed the last of his coffee. "You think you'll still be here that late?"

Audrey rolled her eyes and sighed. "It's going to take weeks of late nights to unravel the mess Junior made."

At the sound of another car entering the garage, Audrey said a fast goodbye and hurried to the employee's entrance.

The smell of fresh-baked sweet potato bread welcomed her when she entered, announcing the arrival of November and soon Thanksgiving. Eunice, the best baker in the county, was in the store's pastry shop, baking up a storm to be ready for the holiday rush. Folks put in their orders weeks in advance for Thanksgiving and Christmas. Once Audrey had devised a way for Wynton's to ship the bread as easily as fruitcakes, Eunice's sweet potato bread became a holiday staple on tables all over Florida and South Georgia. She had designed Wynton's Christmas logo that decorated the boxes in which the bread arrived.

As she looked around the main floor, straw cornucopias filled with fake fruit and vegetables adorned counter spaces, while paper turkeys and smiling Pilgrims hung on the tall white pillars flanking the main aisles.

She passed by a potted palm where light classical music drifted from the speakers hidden within. The styles would change throughout the day. Peppy to raise the energy and spirits of the employees midmorning, and dance tunes and jazz in the afternoon to wake up clerks and customers alike. Soon Christmas carols would be played around the clock, bringing holiday cheer to the hearts of Wynton's customers.

But all these things paled in comparison to the one truth she couldn't stop smiling about. Junior and Cissy hundreds of miles away in Miami Beach. For two weeks. She would have done her best celebratory pirouette right there in the middle of the atrium if Alvid and a few other clerks weren't watching her. As Miss Evelyn taught her, no need to make a spectacle of oneself.

When she reached the executive office, she heard the deep bass notes of Mr. Wynton's voice filling the room. He had mentioned a scheduled call. Audrey put away her things, sharpened a handful of pencils, started the coffee, and waited for Mr. Wynton. She had a steaming cup ready, sans sugar and cream, when he summoned her. With coffee secured in one hand, she grabbed her steno pad and pencil with the other and headed to his office.

The store's latest financials lay open on his desktop. "We took a dip the last two months, didn't we?"

"I'm afraid so." Audrey delivered the coffee and settled into the chair on the opposite side of the desk.

Mr. Wynton turned a page and ran his finger down the columns. "Nothing a strong holiday can't fix." Without looking up from his work, he reached for his coffee.

He set down his cup after one sip. "I missed being here."

"We missed you too, sir."

"I smelled Eunice's bread baking when I came in this morning. Best thing to greet me after being gone so long."

Audrey shifted in her chair. "I wanted to ask you about that."

"You did?"

"Yes, sir. I wanted to talk about her holiday bonus."

Mr. Wynton flipped to another page of the financials. "If you're worried we can't afford to pay her for the extra hours, there's no need. We didn't lose that much in my absence."

"I think we should pay her more this year."

Mr. Wynton cocked his head at her. "More? I'm paying her the highest wage of any Colored employee in Levy City."

Audrey laid her pencil and pad on the edge of the desk. "Mr. Wynton, we both know folks drive from hours away each year to get fresh loaves of her bread. I guarantee they're already lined up in Florida Delights, and we both know they aren't there for the coconut patties, fruitcakes, or saltwater taffy."

She paused, looking for his telltale signs of aggravation—reddening cheeks, balling his fingers, or the highest level, rubbing his hand along his jaw.

He peered over the edge of his glasses. "I know you think I need to pay the Negro employees better, allow them to shop here rather than restricting them to our discount store on Latham, and let them train to be clerks."

Mr. Wynton removed his glasses and sat back in his chair. "I know what you experienced in France." He shook his head as deep sadness filled his eyes. "These are the right things to do. But this is Levy City, and I'm too old, too tired, and too set in my ways to start pushing against those fences."

"But you could start with something small, like raising pay. Others would see you're doing something different and maybe follow." She drew in a breath to bolster her courage. "You're a community leader, president of the Lion's Club, the Rotary Club, and the Jaycees. A deacon in the Baptist church. People respect you. They'll listen."

He rubbed his jaw. "Florida's different than the rest of the South, with all these Yankees moving here in droves, not understanding how we do things, pushing us to be more like where they came from. But we're part of the South. And there are hard-and-fast rules concerning Coloreds and Whites."

"But—"

He held up his hand to stop her.

Mr. Wynton closed the financials and moved them to the corner of his desk, then motioned to her steno pad and pencils. "Let's get on with the rest of today's business."

"Yes, sir." Audrey flipped her pad open and waited to take dictation. For now the subject of Eunice and the other Black employees was closed.

Mr. Wynton continued. "Let's start with the Christmas fashion show. Cissy tells me Vivien and Mirette agreed to take that over this year."

"How did Cissy talk them into that?"

"She says they jumped at the chance, but my suspicion is she cried them into submission."

That sounded like something Cissy would do. "Why did she ask them in the first place?"

He grunted. "Because she's Cissy."

Audrey stifled a laugh. "Oh."

"If Vivien asks for help, I'm hoping you'll step in. You're the most qualified."

"I doubt Vivien would ask, but if she does, I'll be there," she answered softly.

"I knew you would." He tapped the stack of financials. "I need you to set up a meeting today with Accounting. I want to go over what happened while I was gone and how we fix things as fast as possible."

Audrey added his directive to her notes.

He continued. "How were Halloween costume sales this year?"

"We did a 15 percent increase. Not having a hurricane come through has helped with overall sales since August."

Mr. Wynton soaked it all in. "Nice to have some good news today."

Audrey looked up from her pad. "Yes, sir, it is."

He snapped his fingers. "The Florida Delights department needs help for the holidays. Citrus sales and shipping are bustling, and they're shorthanded. With all the northerners sending oranges and grapefruit to their relatives for Thanksgiving and Christmas, we need to move some folks around to meet the demand."

She jotted down the new message. "Yes, sir."

He paused. "About those things you discovered?"

Her heart drummed a few extra beats. "Yes, sir, what about them?"

"My phone call earlier this morning. . .stopped that train in its tracks."

Her relief escaped in a noisy breath. "I'm glad, sir. And I'm so sorry."

The corners of his mouth sagged, and he suddenly looked worn and tired. "Fathers and sons—it's a complicated dance."

He slapped his hands on his thighs. "But that isn't your worry."

"Yes, sir." Audrey rose, closing the door behind her when she exited.

As she was feeding paper into her typewriter, her phone rang. "Wynton's Department Store, Mr. Wynton's office. How may I help you?"

"Audrey, get me Daddy now," Cissy screamed from the other end of the line.

Her next words were so loud and garbled Audrey held the phone away from her ear a moment.

Audrey cut in. "Cissy, I can't understand you. What in the world is going on?"

"I need to talk to Daddy. Not you. You caused this." Another round of ear-splitting wails burst from the phone. Audrey pressed the transfer button.

"Yes?"

"Cissy, line one." She listened for the click indicating Mr. Wynton picked up the line.

She laid the receiver in the cradle and resumed her typing. A moment later, Mr. Wynton opened his office door.

His face had paled to a deathly white. His arms hung limply at his sides.

She jumped from her chair and ran to him. He swayed, and she caught him by the arms to steady him.

He trembled beneath her grip.

"Mr. Wynton, what's the matter?"

He looked at her, but his glassy eyes stared past her, unseeing.

"My boy. Is dead."

Chapter 15

AUDREY

Audrey stood at the back of the mourner's crowd. Alone.

Brother Carol from First Baptist, Levy City, spoke over John T.'s flower-draped casket. His voice hovered over them like somber notes from a jazz trombone. "We offer our last goodbyes to our beloved neighbor, devoted son, and loyal husband."

She shifted her attention to Mr. Wynton. The full-of-life sparkle in his eyes was snuffed.

He'd said nothing to her since the call.

Not. One. Word.

Brother Carol continued. "John Thomas Wynton loved life." He scanned the crowd. "And everyone who crossed his path."

The rays of the late-morning sun warmed her black felt bumper hat. The netting of her bird-cage veil bore holes large enough to allow a cool breeze through. But Florida's fickle weather decided to ignore it being November and bless them all with summerlike heat and no breath of cooler air.

A bead of sweat clung to a tendril of hair by her ear. She dabbed the moisture away with the fingertip of her glove. Miss Evelyn said ladies were to remove perspiration as delicately as possible to avoid drawing attention.

They all stood there like potatoes wrapped in black foil, baking in oven-like temperatures. Several of the ladies in the crowd waved the free paper fans Sayer-Mills Funeral Home provided, but the supply ran out before Audrey joined the graveside service. The entire town seemed to have turned out.

For Mr. Wynton.

He stood erect, shoulders ramrod straight.

Junior was a rascal. But also the four-year-old boy who'd cried in Daddy's arms when his mama never came home from the hospital. The Little Leaguer Mr. Wynton taught how to bat and pitch the perfect, unhittable fastball.

And the man who asked his father to be the best man on his wedding day.

Brother Carol spread his arms wide before the mourners. "We all cry together today. Remember the good times, and pray for his family, who must now go on without him."

Audrey picked out Wynton's employees in the crowd. With the store being closed for the remainder of the week, they'd come to pay their respects.

Near the front, Mary Jo and her husband stood together. No surprise she'd cried through the entire service. He took his place behind her, tall and muscular, exuding a strong male presence despite the empty sleeve dangling from his navy suit jacket. But he glanced at those around them often, readjusting his body to keep his injured side tucked against Mary Jo and out of sight as best he could.

What was his name? Cissy probably knew.

Behind them, Gigi held tight to the arm of Bobby Bridges, who kept wiping the sweat dripping from his swept-back pompadour. He'd spewed plenty of nasty words about the store around town. At least he had the good sense to pay his respects and keep his big trap shut for the moment.

Miss Vivien and Mirette stood in the second row. Mirette shifted from one foot to the other while trying to fan away the heat. Miss Vivien stood still, her head bowed, her eyes hidden from view by the brim of her wide black hat. The unused white handkerchief she clutched stuck out against her black-gloved hands.

Brother Carol's voice called her back. "John T. held us all in highest respect, worked hard to care for his community."

Audrey slid her gaze to the far end of the cemetery.

Nelson, Eunice, Lilla, and a few of the other Black employees stood in their own group separated from the White mourners by a distance far enough to count as respectable. She would have joined them and shown local society they were all human beings with loved ones they'd never see again this side of heaven. But this was Levy City, and that just wasn't done if you wanted to avoid planting trouble seeds for all involved.

Brother Carol raised his hand. "Let us pray."

As soon as the prayer ended, Audrey's attention rested on Cissy, who clung to Mr. Wynton.

She was under the town's microscope and handling her spotlight as only Cissy could. Knowing her neighbors well, she'd chosen a bell-shaped black dress with three-quarter sleeves, accessorized with a simple onyx brooch and matching bracelet from the store's collection. No high heels, gaudy baubles, or skintight fabric certain to set tongues to wagging.

The only part of her outfit true to form was the mink ring hat with a net veil wrapped about her face and tucked under her chin. Only Cissy Wynton would wear such a hat on a hot day like this. If Brother Carol went on much longer, that mink was going to be sitting up and begging for water.

She'd gone to great lengths to hide the accident-caused bruises on her cheek with makeup. Another blackish-purple blotch peeked from under the hem of her left sleeve.

"Father, we thank You for Your mercy, Your grace, and Your love. Give John T. a big hug from us and tell him to save us all a seat. Amen." Brother Carol finished, and the others repeated *amen*s of their own.

Cissy covered her face and doubled over with body-shaking sobs.

How hard it must be to lose the person who'd become your other half. No matter how much the two of them irked Audrey, they were a well-matched team, knitted together by those mysterious cords that bound a man and woman in love. Cissy might drive her to distraction, but she deserved condolences.

"On behalf of the family, I want to say thank you for coming. Keep them in your prayers these coming days, weeks, and months." Brother Carol looked to Cissy and Mr. Wynton once more before turning back to the group. "God bless y'all."

As the preacher stepped away to speak with the funeral home employees, Audrey moved into the sea of mourners, zigzagging her way to Mr. Wynton and Cissy. Before she could break free from the crowd, Ben Evans directed them to their waiting limousine.

Ben opened the door and motioned them to enter. Mr. Wynton held Cissy's elbow as she bent down to get into the vehicle. Audrey increased her pace, causing the limestone in the cemetery's road to crackle under her shoes.

Mr. Wynton must have heard her. The lines on his face softened when he saw her.

She moved closer. "I wanted to offer my—"

"Get away from us," Cissy screeched as she wriggled out of the back seat. As soon as she cleared the door, she shot to Mr. Wynton and clung to his arm. "I don't see how you have the gall to come here when we all know you hated John T. You're probably thrilled he's dead." Her voice sliced through the quiet among the gravestones. The crowd stopped the migration to their parked cars and stared. Some came back to the scene, forming a semicircle around the parked limousine, looking like they were standing at the ready if needed.

Those words hit harder than a freight train, and Audrey reeled backward. She fought to regain her footing while Mr. Wynton tried to maneuver his daughter-in-law back into the car.

Cissy glanced at the assembling crowd. She grasped her throat as shaky sobs escaped her. A second later, she dropped her hands, choked back another sob, then drew a deep breath. "I know you wanted him dead. Then you'd have nothing stopping you from taking over Daddy."

Mr. Wynton grabbed her arm. "Cissy, get in the car."

She cast her attention on him. "No. They need to know what she did to him. To us." Her voice caught.

Audrey moved forward. "You're wrong."

Tears streamed from Cissy's eyes, smearing her mascara in dark blotches beneath her eyes. "Liar. I have proof, and I'm going to make certain you pay for what you did."

Mr. Wynton pushed Cissy into the car.

Audrey caught his sleeve as he went to enter himself. "Mr. Wynton, I never—"

He yanked free and joined his daughter-in-law, slamming the door in Audrey's face.

She stared at her boss through the window as the car pulled away. Her vision swam with tears.

Did Mr. Wynton believe Cissy's accusations?

Mirette's voice floated to Audrey's ear. "Guess she won't be dropping off a casserole after the service."

A loud shushing followed and was most likely Miss Vivien trying yet again to corral her assistant.

Audrey's mind switched to another time when a long black limo drove away from her. She'd learned her first lesson from Miss Evelyn that day. True ladies remained calm in crises. Kept pleasant expressions on their faces and kind words spilling from their mouths. And no public tears. With lifted chin, she swallowed back the emotions now swelling to a stabbing pain in her chest. She swiveled on her heels to face the crowd.

Her gaze fixed on a tree at the far edge of the cemetery, so the staring faces blurred and became clouds of black rimming the perimeter of her runway. Her mind went to the quiet place within, where she could turn off her ears and blank out their whisperings and murmurings. This came easily now, as she'd done it so many times before.

Audrey slid her purse from the crook of her elbow and let it dangle from her fingers as she hung her arms at her side. She took one step, then another, pressing the soles of her shoes firmly on the ground to prevent her knees from buckling. The crowd parted like stage curtains as she moved past.

A lone tear clung to the corner of her eye when she reached her Thunderbird. Once she'd settled into her car, Audrey blinked and let it fall. The crowd couldn't see her now. Miss Evelyn would approve.

Chapter 16

AUDREY

Nelson met Audrey at her parking space. He skipped his usual pleasant greeting as she handed him his breakfast. Warning filled his eyes.

She tipped her head toward the Corvette parked next to hers. "Gives me shivers to see his car here."

"Mrs. Wynton drove the boss to work today." He set his breakfast down on his sitting chair. "She's shook up like a hive of hornets."

Audrey gathered her things together and locked her car door.

Nelson shoved both hands in his pockets so hard the loose coins jingled like tiny bells. She'd not seen him this agitated since he'd spied Junior driving the men banned from the store around town. "What's got you so worried, Nelson?"

"They got out of the car, and she fussed over it being too early to return to the store after the funeral and how he needed to take better care of himself. He took all her fluster for a minute or two, then yelled at her to leave him alone. After that, she started in on how you got to be fired to honor Junior. Today."

"What did Mr. Wynton say?"

"Nothing. Kept on walking to the store, silent as the grave, with her chasing after him."

They shared a long look until Nelson spoke again. "You be careful, Audrey."

Every nerve in her body clicked to attention when he didn't put "Miss" before her name. Whatever he'd seen had stirred up a pot of worry. And he wasn't the worrying type. "I will."

Audrey arrived and found Cissy sitting at her desk, watching the door like a sentry at a fort. She popped from the chair when Audrey entered.

A choking cloud of Chanel No. 5 filled the space. She'd probably be smelling the scent for days before it wore off her chair.

Dressed in a black jacket as tight as a corset and a full black rayon skirt, Cissy carried the air of an awaiting undertaker. She lowered her brows until the skin between them puckered. She pressed the button on the intercom. "Audrey's here, Daddy."

Mr. Wynton's voice boomed through the speaker. "Both of you in my office. Now."

Cissy rose and opened Mr. Wynton's door, then made a wide sweep with her hand. "After you."

Audrey walked to her desk. Cissy remained in the doorway, tapping her black pointy-toed shoe on the carpet as Audrey folded her gloves and placed them in her hat, then locked her purse away in the drawer.

She glided through the door and took a seat across from Mr. Wynton. He made no eye contact with her but motioned to his daughter-in-law. "Shut the door."

He remained silent until Cissy was seated, then switched his focus to Audrey.

She searched his face for any clues to his thoughts. Before Junior's death, he'd been an open tome to her.

But the page before her remained blank.

"Miss Penault, I called you here to ask you some questions."

He rarely addressed her in such a formal manner. Audrey sat straighter in her chair. "Yes, sir?"

"When my son and Cissy were on vacation down in Miami, did you call their hotel?"

"No, sir."

Cissy sprung from her chair. "Liar." She pulled a piece of paper from a pocket in her skirt. "This came from the hotel's front desk."

She shoved the paper in Audrey's face. "Read this out loud."

Audrey took the message written on stationery from the Fontainebleau Hotel. "Your father is gravely ill. Return home at once. Audrey Penault."

She met Mr. Wynton's gaze. "I never left this message."

Cissy tore the note from Audrey's fingers. "She killed my husband."

"Sit down." Mr. Wynton motioned.

Cissy plopped in the chair as commanded but jammed her finger within inches of Audrey's nose. "She was counting on his driving home exhausted because she knew full well John T. would come running as soon as he heard."

"And do tell how I'd know he would be exhausted when he got this message."

Cissy slammed her hand on the desktop. "How you can sit there and tell such a lie is beyond me." She pulled a black handkerchief from her sleeve and buried her face in the cloth.

Audrey gripped the armrests of her chair. "Mr. Wynton, I—"

"We have *this*." Cissy dropped her hankie in her lap and shoved the message before Audrey's face. "The clerk wrote the time when the message was taken."

Mr. Wynton took the now crumpled remains of the note. "Eleven thirty." He looked at Cissy. "When did you get this?"

She drew in a deep breath, as if pulling up the strength to answer took everything from her. "A little after midnight."

Mr. Wynton stared at her for a moment. "They waited thirty minutes before notifying you of this message?"

"Yes. We went out dancing. When we got back, the clerk flagged us down in the lobby. That's when he gave us the message from *her*."

"When did you leave the hotel?" Mr. Wynton's chair squeaked as he leaned back.

"Two."

His brows arced above his eyes. "If John T. was so insistent you return home, why did it take you two hours to leave?"

Cissy ducked her head, then lifted her chin and glared at Audrey. "Because we got into an argument." She turned sad eyes on Mr. Wynton. "You know how John T. loved you. He wasn't staying there one more minute when you needed him."

Mr. Wynton closed his eyes and rubbed his forehead with a single finger. "You still haven't explained why it took two hours to leave the hotel."

"It took the hotel forever to send us a maid to help pack, and then the bellhop was slow as molasses when he came to take our luggage to the car."

Audrey swung on Cissy. "You couldn't pack your own things?"

Cissy's eyes narrowed to slits above her fiery-red cheeks. "We were frantic. And arguing. Because. Of. You."

She switched her tear-rimmed gaze to Mr. Wynton. "We couldn't think straight, and I insisted John T. call you to find out what was going on. His calls wouldn't go through, and that made him mad with fear."

Her father-in-law stared without speaking, and Cissy stared at him with a lost-kitten expression.

Seemed Cissy wanted Audrey hauled off to jail.

Audrey had no alibi. She'd been home listening to a new Frank Sinatra album on her hi-fi. She'd rushed to the music department that same morning and grabbed her copy as soon as the clerk unboxed them.

Never in her worst nightmares would she guess her new favorite song, "In the Wee Small Hours of the Morning," would be describing the timeline of her alleged criminal behavior.

She addressed Cissy. "Where did you go dancing?"

"I fail to see why you must know." If eyes were able to shoot arrows, the look Cissy aimed would have pierced straight through Audrey's skull.

"If you went to a club—"

"Are you insinuating—" Cissy drew up like a rattler ready to strike.

"Ladies." Mr. Wynton's voice sliced through the room.

This was neither the time nor place to tussle with Cissy. Miss Evelyn had taught her better. "Yes, sir. I apologize."

Cissy clicked her tongue against her teeth and huffed. "You should be begging for forgiveness and mercy after what you've done."

Mr. Wynton rose and faced his office window. "Miss Vivien is waiting for you in the salon, Cissy. To discuss plans for the holiday fashion show." Without turning around, he thrust his thumb in the direction of the door. "Go."

Cissy shot from her chair. "I'm not leaving you alone with this—"

"Now." He spoke in a low growl like a hound about to attack.

"Daddy, please."

Mr. Wynton met Cissy's singsong plea with eyes full of icy rage. Audrey looked away. Being a witness to and fearing the emotion now emanating from her boss churned her gut. Pleading her own case could come later.

If at all.

Cissy's shoulders sagged as she slunk to the door and left the office without another word.

Mr. Wynton turned back to the window. His shoulders shook each time he exhaled.

"Mr. Wynton, I'm so sorry."

"Everyone is. At least to my face."

Audrey stood, first thinking of embracing him but then holding back. "Is there anything you need?"

"A ditch around me, filled with sharp spikes. Maybe some tigers at the bottom of it." He moved to the couch along the wall and sat, then scooted down so his head rested on the cushion's top edge. He stretched his legs before him.

"I'm so tired, Audrey." He flashed a lopsided grin, and its saggy corners slashed through her heart.

Audrey sat on the arm at the other end of the couch. "I wish I could change all of this for you, Mr. Wynton."

"This is one mess of his that you and I can't fix."

He pushed up from the couch and went to his desk. "When am I supposed to meet with Sam Loring down in Legal? Ten or eleven?"

Audrey stood. "Ten thirty. And he's coming here."

Mr. Wynton shook his head. "I can't keep anything straight in my head today. Good thing I've got you batting cleanup for me."

She choked back a wad of emotion swelling in her throat. "Always."

He picked up his coffee cup. "Could you bring me a fresh cup? Cissy fixed this when we got in, but this stuff is thick as motor oil and about as tasty."

Audrey rushed to take the cup from him. "Right away."

She hurried from the office, closing the door behind her. As soon as the latch clicked, she leaned her forehead against the cool polished wood.

She heard him clearing his throat, then muffled sounds of nose blowing. If only she could erase his pain. Help him find the way to move beyond, fill the void left behind by Junior's death.

But that was time's and the good Lord's job. She could only support their work, not do the task for them.

Audrey poured the cold coffee in the sink and fixed a fresh pot. She added a half spoonful of sugar and stirred until all was well blended.

After adding a dollop of cream, because the doctor's orders could be ignored at a time like this, she grabbed the copy of the *Levy Times Commercial* newspaper and a small paper bag from her satchel. Mr. Wynton always drank his coffee with the *LTC*. Might do him some good to read the news about the town.

He didn't look up when she entered, but she couldn't miss the moisture glistening in the corners of his eyes. She set his coffee beside him on the desk and then the bag. "I heard Cissy said you haven't been eating much."

"Cissy says a lot of things." He kept his eyes on the papers he was pretending to read.

She tapped the bag. "If you get hungry."

As she walked to the door, she heard the rattling as he opened her surprise. His low chuckle drifted to her ears. "RC Cola and a chocolate Moon Pie. The workingman's lunch."

She twirled around and met his gaze. "Nothing better."

The strain in his face and eyes softened, and he almost smiled. "Thank you, Audrey."

She tipped her head. "You're welcome."

Audrey left the office, pulling the door shut behind her. Work was Mr. Wynton's best escape, and she'd leave him to do what he needed in private.

Chapter 17

VIVIEN

Vivien set out the last of the cream-colored linen napkins she'd stayed up way too late ironing. The purple-and-yellow pansies embroidered along the sides seemed to be casting her the same glance the ladies in the Junior League shot new recruits trying too hard to impress.

"Mind your own business. I know what I'm doing." She rearranged them so the pansy faces stared in the opposite direction.

"Why do I feel like I'm helping the spider trap the flies?" Mirette set two cut-glass plates filled with Vivien's homemade cinnamon rolls and tiny cheese Danish on the table.

"Oh hush." Vivien picked up one of the small dessert forks from her best silver and wiped away a fingerprint with the polishing cloth she'd brought from home.

"Seems like you're puttin' on the dog a bit much. You think you're serving Queen Elizabeth?"

"Go get the box of sugar cubes and fill the dish for me." Vivien gestured to the crystal sugar bowl she'd had since she was a bride.

"Go get this, set that down, fill this up." Mirette headed to the storeroom once more. "I swear I've walked the soles off my brand-new shoes." Her voice faded as she walked to the back of the store.

Vivien touched the side of the teapot to check the temperature as she checked items off on her mental list: food, atmosphere, presentation.

Done.

She hadn't been this nervous about prepping for a show since she and Mirette got the gumption to enter a few of her designs in the Bridal

Week show in New York. And she'd had months to prepare for their debut there.

She had three weeks to put the holiday fashion show together.

Vivien shook away the nerves. She'd hosted the old guard of the League and the Ladies Garden Club. There wasn't a group alive more difficult to please than either of them.

Mirette returned with the sugar box. "I've retrieved the cubes you demanded, Your Majesty." She performed an off-kilter curtsy.

"If you fall, I'll have to leave you on the floor and let the girls walk around you."

"That would be a conversation starter, now wouldn't it?" Mirette laughed and Vivien joined in until they heard the salon's front-door chimes sound.

"I cannot believe you spent good money sending out engraved invitations for this," Mirette said as she and Vivien made their way to the front of the salon.

"I almost didn't get them made. Bill and Sandra were just about booked out. Everybody's been coming into the store's stationery department to get their Christmas cards ordered. Besides, I'm certain Cissy never sent any, and I'm setting a new tone."

Vivien met the group of six young women standing in a pack with a smile. "Good morning." She swept her hand toward the back. "I've set up a table with sweet temptations, coffee, and tea. Go help yourselves."

The girls thanked her in unison as the door's chimes sang out another's presence.

Mary Jo Johnson entered, glancing around as if expecting to be thrown out. Vivien grabbed Mirette by the hand. "Be extra nice to her. She's one of my top choices."

She winked and greeted Mary Jo. "Welcome. We're so glad you came."

Mary Jo flashed a shy smile. "I've never been in a fashion show. I'm so nervous."

Mirette laid her arm about Mary Jo's shoulder. "Don't you worry about a thing, sugar, and come on back with me. You look like you skipped breakfast this morning."

Mary Jo's shoulders relaxed. "I'm starving."

As Mirette led her to the back, she winked at Vivien over her shoulder.

One worry squashed, two more to go before she could truly release a breath and relax.

Vivien walked into the hallway outside the salon. She was missing one more invitee.

The elevator doors opened, and the operator, Berle, moved the metal latticed gate as Gigi disembarked. She scowled as Vivien waved her over.

She held up her invitation. "You sent this?"

"Yes, ma'am. Come on in."

Gigi checked her watch. "I only have twenty minutes."

"Perfect." Vivien increased her speed as she herded Gigi into the salon.

When she had Gigi squared away with a plate in one hand and a cup of coffee in the other, Vivien tapped the side of the crystal fruit bowl with the last of the clean spoons.

"Ladies, thank y'all so much for coming. I know many of you are old hats at the fashion show, but we have a few new folks, so let's make sure we have plenty of time to answer any questions."

Leanna, from Ladies' Sportswear, raised her hand. "Is Cissy coming today, or will she be talking to us later?"

She'd expected such a question and had practiced her response. "Cissy will be dropping by, but she's—"

"Then we'll wait for her. She's in charge, right?" Crystal from Housewares piped in.

"I don't have time to wait." Gigi moved to set down her plate and cup.

Vivien gazed around the group. "I am in charge of the fashion show this year."

The original pack of girls gaped at each other with horrified expressions. One girl cupped a hand around her neighbor's ear and murmured.

Vivien caught Gigi's eye. "You will not be late for work."

The girls quieted, but their lack of confidence came at her in waves. All of Levy City knew Cissy spent the entire year planning for the show. She courted all the best department store designers and the big fashion houses to enter their latest creations as well as Wynton's own labels.

Cissy's shows weren't just a kickoff for Wynton's Christmas season—they had become one of the top social events of the year.

Vivien looked over the girls before her. Most of them had been hand-picked by Cissy and had worked with her in Wynton's past holiday shows. They were a tight-knit little sorority with loyalty to their beloved leader.

Another from the pack raised her hand. "Miss Vivien, are you the buyer this year too?"

"Yes, Betty Anne, I am."

More whispers among the pack. "This is going to be a royal mess" drifted within Vivien's hearing.

It took everything she had to hold her tongue. Her spring bridal extravaganzas drew larger crowds and a higher-paying audience than any of the holiday shows. And she was personal friends with many of the designers and would get whatever she asked for and more.

But bringing that up would be the epitome of gauche and not her style.

At the back of the group, Mirette grimaced and added a resigned shrug of her shoulders.

Vivien tapped the fruit bowl harder. "Ladies." All heads swiveled her way.

She picked up her clipboard filled with her notes. "All is well."

"Good morning. Y'all forgive me for running late," Cissy called as she hurried into the salon.

The pack erupted into high-pitched giggles and greetings as they circled her and smothered her with hugs.

Cissy hurried to hug Mary Jo and Gigi before joining Vivien at the front of the gathering.

"What a great-looking group, Miss Vivien. You sure can pick them." She wiggled her fingers at the pack again, and they responded with more giggles.

"I'm sure Miss Vivien let y'all know I won't be in charge this year." Cissy's declaration was met with a chorus of groans from the pack. She blew a kiss at them. "Y'all are so cute."

Vivien pinched her lips together to stifle a laugh when Mirette held her finger to her mouth and pretended to be nauseated by their saccharine responses.

Cissy continued. "But don't worry. I'm sure she told you I'll still be there as the emcee."

A cacophony of cheers whooped from the pack. "Thank goodness, Cissy will still be part of it. At least now we know there's hope," one girl cooed, then looked to see if Vivien had heard her.

She held the girl's gaze a moment and moved on. "Ladies, we have five minutes left before we all need to return to work. If there aren't any more questions. . ."

Betty Anne's hand shot up once more. "Who's going to wear the showstopper?"

"Oh yes, who, Miss Vivien?" Cissy looked around the group.

High-pitched squeals and mumblings emanated from the pack.

Vivien held out her hands to shush them. "I'll make that decision later. Now I need all of you to grab one of the sheets Mirette has and fill it out."

The pack, plus Mary Jo and Gigi, crowded around Mirette.

The group quieted as they worked until the sound of thudding footsteps across the salon's marble tiles made all heads turn. One of Wynton's store detectives bounded in and slid to a stop before Cissy.

"Mrs. Wynton, there's been an incident in Mr. Wynton's office. I need you to come with me."

Cissy yowled loud enough to scare the dead. "I knew better than to leave him alone with Audrey. What's she done to him now?"

The pack surrounded her, patting and hugging her, and one fanned Cissy with her paperwork as if she might faint dead away at any moment.

The detective stared at the melee, then motioned to the door. "Please. Now."

Cissy latched onto his arm. "I don't have it in me to face much more of this."

He led her away. The pack stared after them, hands clasped in worry or patting their chests.

Vivien stepped before them. "Let's all say a quick prayer for Mr. Wynton."

When they'd finished, she gave new directions. "Hand me your sheets before you go." She ushered them to the front door of the salon. "We'll have another meeting to discuss specifics next week."

The pack made their way to the elevator in silence.

Mary Jo hung back. "Miss Vivien, I don't think I belong here. Those other girls are so tall and glamorous. And I don't even know what a showstopper is."

Vivien shook her head. "I chose them for a reason. I chose you for another."

She paused to let this sink in a bit. "Many women who attend the show are young housewives and mothers. They want to be glamorous but also the epitome of what a wife and mother should be. When they see you up on that runway, they'll know they can be both because *you* are both."

"And who's supposed to be watching me? I'm pretty sure the women of Levy City aren't secretly dreaming of becoming waitresses anytime soon." Gigi stood a few feet behind Mary Jo, looking ready to pick a fight.

Vivien met her eye to eye. "Gigi, have you ever truly looked at the women who come to the cafeteria?"

Gigi lifted one shoulder. "Not really. Why?"

Vivien drew a circle around Gigi's face with her finger. "They're you. They read the same magazines, listen to the same songs. They buy their makeup and perfume from the drugstore, just like you. And"— she paused to make her point clear—"they dream about fancy dinners out. Maybe meeting a movie star. Wearing Audrey Hepburn's perfume. Just. Like. You." She continued, "They want pretty clothes that will look nice when they go out with their special fella. Makeup and perfume that make them feel pretty. You will wear those clothes, the accessories, make-up, and perfume on my runway and show them that Wynton's wants girls like them to live out those dreams."

Vivien scanned their faces. "And an extra little bonus is, everything you model you keep as our thanks for being in the show."

Gigi thrust her paper at Vivien. "I'm in. I guess."

"Mary Jo, I was going to ask if your girls might model dresses from the children's collection. We have a new line of girls coats coming under Wynton's label made by Carinne's that I want to feature. Again, you'd keep everything they wear."

Mary Jo's eyes widened. "I'll have to ask my husband." She handed Vivien her paperwork.

Mirette tapped the face of her watch.

Vivien spread her arms about them like a mother hen. "And the showstopper is a conversation for another day. I'll walk y'all to the elevator."

She hoped one more push would seal their commitment. "Wynton's caters to everyone, not just those who live on Lakeside Drive and the Cottages or look like those other girls. You two belong in my show. More than anyone else." She released her grip on them when the doors opened.

Gigi and Mary Jo went to opposite sides of the elevator.

Vivien found Mirette in her sewing chair. "Well, that was ugly all the way to the bone." Vivien smoothed a stray tendril of hair back from her face. "I'm worried for Mr. Wynton."

Mirette gathered her pincushion and some thread. "Me too, so I'd better get to work or I'm not going to be worth anything today. Can you bring me Cathy Tucker's veil? I left it hanging on the mannequin by the fitting rooms."

"I hope he hasn't had another spell with his heart."

"Sounds like he'd had another spell with Audrey."

Vivien returned with the veil and dropped it in Mirette's lap. "That was uncalled for and plain ugly. Disrespects him. And us."

She walked to her desk and opened her schedule book. "Let's talk about something else."

Mirette worked her needle in and out of the fabric. "How about that new dress in your sketchbook?"

Vivien met her friend's gaze. "Peeking again?"

Mirette finished more stitches before she answered. "You'll never get her to agree to wear the gown."

"I can be pretty convincing when I choose to be."

Mirette rearranged the fabric on her lap and resumed her sewing. "I'd love to be a fly on the ceiling when you ask her."

"I've already asked the one person she won't say no to."

Mirette looked up. "But what if—"

"Don't even think that." Vivien gathered up her book and moved to the salon's main floor to start the day.

Mary Jo looked over the array of cast-off hats covering her counter. "Let me see that darling blue one with the green and purple feathers pinned on the side. Reminds me of a peacock." Mrs. Watson pointed to her next choice.

"This is quite colorful." Or loud enough to awaken someone from a deep sleep, Grandma Dottie would have said. Mary Jo placed the hat on Mrs. Watson's head.

She tipped her head from side to side, eyeing her reflection in the mirror. "This hat really says something, doesn't it?"

"Yes, ma'am, it does."

Mary Jo kept her opinions on exactly what to herself. The customer was always right, even when she liked a hat no other woman in Levy City would be caught dead in.

Mrs. Watson shifted the hat so it dipped daringly near one eye. "Now don't I look jaunty?"

"Yes, ma'am."

"Do you know, my own husband told me on our wedding day that I had terrible taste."

Mary Jo's jaw dropped. What husband would say such a thing to his new bride? "No, he did not."

Mrs. Watson smiled so wide the wrinkles on her cheeks blended into folds like a paper fan. "He sure did. When we got married, my mama and daddy couldn't afford to buy me a new dress, so I wore a black suit, which was all I had. I hated being married in black, so one of my friends took me to buy a new hat for a wedding present."

She erupted into gasping chortles until she regained her composure. "I wanted a dash of color, so I came and picked out the brightest blue straw hat Wynton's had."

She broke into huge guffaws. "When Henry James met me on the steps at the courthouse, his eyes practically bulged from his head." Mrs. Watson looked at her reflection again. "He said, 'Lottie, what in the world are you thinking wearing such a gaudy thing on our wedding day?' And you know what I told him?"

Mary Jo couldn't imagine what a bride might say to that.

"Bless his heart, he was as boring as a fence post and should be thankful marrying me might liven him up." She cackled.

"This is exactly what I want. Our kids are throwing us an anniversary party this weekend, and I'm going to surprise him with this hat and see if he remembers. Won't that be a hoot?"

Mary Jo filled out the receipt. Days like this took away some of the sting of working and not being home with her girls. Didn't she once tell Audrey that's why she dreamed of being in Accessories, so she could help ladies like Mrs. Watson?

As she nestled the peacock hat into the soft folds of pink tissue paper, she heard the tap-tapping of heels on the sales floor's marble tiles. No one but Cissy Wynton walked with such rhythm in stilettos. She rarely came to the sales floors, though.

"Don't you just love our hatboxes?" Mary Jo finished tying the pink ribbon around the box and handed the parcel to Mrs. Watson. "When I was a little girl, I thought those tiny pink roses printed on the sides and the satin lid made them look so fancy."

"Aren't they though?" Mrs. Watson settled the box's corded handle in the crook of her elbow. "This has been the most fun I've had shopping in a long time."

"I loved hearing your story."

Mrs. Watson shot her an unbelieving, side-eyed look as she put her Wynton's charge plate back in her purse. "I'm a boring old lady, but you're sweet to indulge me."

Boring was a word no soul would apply to Mrs. Watson.

"I've got to go to Notions next. Need a new bobbin for my sewing machine. Then I've got to get up to the beauty shop here and get my hair done. Bye now." Mrs. Watson headed away.

Mary Jo spied Cissy standing in the back of Menswear talking with Alvid. Their heads were close, and more than once Cissy sliced the air with wild gestures. Alvid offered her supportive pats, most of which were shrugged off.

Mary Jo put Mrs. Watson's cast-off choices back on their stands or in the case, then wiped the glass on top clean. Clicking heels sounded again, and she looked up to see Cissy coming her way.

She scooted around the counter and pulled Mary Jo into a tight hug. "I want to eat lunch with you and Gigi today."

"I think she's mad at me."

"My best girlfriends mustn't be feuding. I really need to talk with someone." Her bottom lip trembled.

"What's wrong?"

"You know why I left Miss Vivien's so fast on Monday?"

Mary Jo bobbed her head. "I heard Mr. Wynton was sick again."

"They had to take him to the hospital, and they don't know what's wrong. I'm just shattered because I can't be with him around the clock. But I'm the only one left to run the store."

She laid her hand across her heart like she was about to say the Pledge of Allegiance.

"Once he's home, I'm guarding him from you-know-who."

"Do you mean. . .Audrey?"

"Of course I mean Audrey." Cissy huffed like an angry bull.

She drew in a deep breath. "I can't say any more here. We'll talk at lunch." She hurried off.

Chapter 19

GIGI

Gigi clamped her teeth as her boss, Mary Margaret, continued to bless her out. All she'd done was share with Lilla how mad she'd been when Bobby showed up with flowers and candy after being two hours late for their date last night.

"Miss Woodard, were you just not raised right?" Mary Margaret looked down her nose at Gigi.

Heat flamed in Gigi's cheeks. "What's the problem? I like talking with Lilla during my lunch break."

Mary Margaret looked like she might pop a gasket. "People see, people talk. And you should just know better when you're on Wynton's time."

"Is that so?" All the hot words she knew begged to be let loose. "My lunch break is my free time."

"Not that free." Mary Margaret glared at Lilla. "And you, if I ever catch you wasting time in my kitchen, cackling like a turkey, I'll have you out of here faster than you can blink twice. You understand me?"

Lilla kept her eyes down as she rolled a ball of dough flat with a rolling pin. "Yes, ma'am."

"And don't you think for one moment I won't sack you because of your cooking. I could find a dozen Colored women just as good or better, and they would be begging for the opportunity to work here. You hear me?"

"Yes, ma'am." Lilla showed no outward signs of anger, but she'd pressed the dough so hard with the rolling pin it had spread thin as a dime.

Gigi readied to let those words loose like a fire hose.

"I'm afraid you're quite mistaken." A voice cut into the room, and Gigi whirled around to see Audrey standing in the doorway of the kitchen.

She strolled in, and Mary Margaret shrank in her presence. "You have no authority to fire anyone. If Gigi fulfills her responsibilities and doesn't violate store policy, she may spend her lunch break however she pleases."

Standing next to the counter, dressed in a fitted black suit with a leopard-print belt, Audrey looked like a living, breathing *Vogue* magazine cover. But her air of quiet authority shot through the room like lightning, and Gigi now understood why men like Alvid, and even her Bobby, found Audrey hard to take.

Mary Margaret fiddled with the top button on her jacket. "I was only addressing a complaint I'd received from another employee."

"Who complained?" Gigi looked at Lilla, who kept her attention on her work.

"Gigi and Lilla are Wynton's employees and will be respected, no matter who made a complaint," Audrey said.

Gigi persisted. "I want to know who complained about me talking to Lilla."

"Audrey."

All heads turned as Cissy entered the room. "I've been searching for you for fifteen minutes. You need to notify me when you leave your desk. But I do appreciate you coming and taking care of this like I asked."

Audrey's brows arced above her eyes. "Like you asked?"

"Yes, as I asked you." Cissy tipped her head from side to side with each word. "Now, you'd best go. I left instructions on your desk for a few letters you need to type and drop in the mail."

She spoke to Audrey as if she were a little girl, and Gigi couldn't deny enjoying the scene between the two.

Cissy eyed Mary Margaret. "I'll handle the complaint against Gigi." She shooed Mary Margaret away. "Get your food orders ready. They're due soon, am I right?"

"They came in yesterday," Audrey said.

Cissy pressed her hands together and pointed them at Mary Margaret. "You may go now." She moved on to Audrey. "And you too."

Though irritation flashed in her dark eyes, Audrey stayed calm as a clam. She dipped her head and left, giving Lilla a quick smile as she passed by.

Cissy grabbed Gigi. "Get your lunch and come with me."

When she realized Mary Jo was seated at the table, Gigi jolted to a stop.

"What's the matter?" Cissy tried to pull her along.

"You didn't tell me Mary Jo was sitting with us."

"It's time you two made nice." Cissy gave a light shove, but Gigi resisted.

"It isn't like that."

"Then what is it? Mary Jo can't figure out why you're so angry with her. And frankly, from what she's said, I can't either."

Gigi gripped the edge of her lunch bag so tightly her fingernail tore a small hole in the paper. How could Mary Jo and Cissy understand? Like Audrey, they were blessed with the magic ticket to all things good.

Being pretty.

And pretty got what pretty wanted. Like promotions.

The words sounded positively pitiful in her head and would be far worse if spoken out loud. She'd be admitting to the whole world she wasn't good enough.

Gigi clenched her teeth. "All right."

"You're a doll. Let me go grab some tea, and I'll be right there." Cissy worked her way upstream through the crowd as Gigi continued to the table.

Mary Jo jumped from her seat and wiggled around Gigi like a puppy welcoming its owner home. Why did she have to make such a fuss over someone she barely knew at work?

She sat across from Gigi and started with the apologies again. "I'm so sorry for what I said—"

Gigi held up both hands to stop the flow. "Let's just eat." She snatched up her bag and yanked her sandwich free.

The usual hurt look crossed Mary Jo's face. "Sure. Let's." She stirred her fork around in a pile of greens on her plate but never took a bite.

Cissy set down the tea and settled in her chair. "Good friends can't stay mad at one another."

Gigi smiled around the bite in her mouth to humor her.

"Are you excited about being in the fashion show?" Cissy stirred her tea.

Mary Jo set down her fork. "I'm so nervous. Kenny's not sure about me and the girls modeling, even when I told him we'd get free clothes. I haven't told the girls yet."

Cissy swung her attention to Gigi. "What about you?"

Gigi set down her sandwich. "I don't know."

"You don't know?" Cissy stared at her wide-eyed. "Being asked to model for Wynton's is a very special thing. Especially if you're picked to wear the showstopper."

"What is that?" Mary Jo asked.

Cissy held her hands out in disbelief. "Only *the* most important dress of the season."

She looked at Mary Jo and then Gigi. "You two really don't know what I'm talking about, do you?"

Gigi shrugged. "I never paid attention to fashion shows." Only because she couldn't afford the clothes.

"The same goes for me." Mary Jo laid her hands in her lap and leaned in. "Miss Vivien told us she wants this year's show to be for ladies like me and Gigi."

Cissy tossed her head. "I was very particular who I chose to model."

Gigi wasn't sure if Cissy was putting her and Mary Jo down or not. "Miss Vivien knows a lot about fashion."

"*Bridal* fashions. Completely different from high fashion. But I can't worry about the show. I've got to focus on running the entire store."

"Such a huge responsibility on you, Cissy," Mary Jo said. "How is Mr. Wynton doing?"

"Daddy is on complete bed rest. I've hired two full-time nurses to care for him. I moved into the house to be closer to him. And Audrey is there all the time because he insists." She rolled her eyes.

"Daddy says I'm not ready to take over all the store business. I'm sure Audrey put that in his head." Her mouth seemed to curl at the corners. "But I've got her number. I hired a private detective to investigate her."

"You did what?" Gigi and Mary Jo screeched.

Cissy looked like the wolf who'd feasted on the sheep. "When I left Daddy in his office on Monday, he was perfectly fine. Twenty minutes alone with her and he had to be carted out on a stretcher. No one's going to tell me this was another coincidence." She set her tea glass on Mary Jo's tray.

"My plan is to have her gone by New Year's."

"Why not now?" Gigi asked.

"Daddy."

The alert chimes sounded through the store's speakers. Cissy stood. "That's my signal that I'm needed upstairs, so I've got to run. You two girls talk and be friends again. I insist."

Cissy blew them kisses and left.

Gigi avoided making eye contact with Mary Jo.

"It was nice to have lunch together again." Mary Jo looked at Gigi like a dog begging to be let indoors.

"I'm not mad at you. It's just easier for me to eat alone in the kitchen right now."

"Having trouble with your boss again?" Mary Jo rose and picked up her and Cissy's dirty dishes and tray.

Gigi nodded to fend off any more questions.

"I've been hoping you could get a better position."

"You and me both, sister." Gigi shoved her chair under the table and left the cafeteria.

She snuck in through the back door of the kitchen five minutes late.

Lilla looked up from her pot scrubbing. "Good lunch with your friends?"

"I've got heartburn."

Lilla rinsed away soap bubbles under the faucet and dried the pot with a towel. "You need folks to eat with."

Gigi stopped at the swinging door that opened to the serving line. "Why? I've got you."

Lilla shook her head. "That might change. You'd better get to the line because Mary Margaret's coming, and she's fit to be tied."

Gigi shoved the door open and scooted into her place in the line.

Lilla's *That might change* replayed through her mind like a scratched record as she plopped a spoonful of peas onto the passing trays.

Chapter 20

AUDREY

Audrey stood at the railing of the second floor, watching her favorite dance.

Shoppers paraded past the fluted columns, stopping at the counters as they shopped. Two young women stopped in Cosmetics and gazed at the array of fancy compacts. The clerk, Lynette, greeted them and produced one for their inspection.

Nothing topped the well-ordered, delicate waltz of helping a customer find the item of their dreams. Keeping Wynton's in business was a necessity, but providing a place for Levy City's residents as well as the rural folks far outside town was always Mr. Wynton's goal.

And hers.

With the fashion show coming in less than two weeks, then Wynton's Christmas parade the following weekend, the holiday buildup had begun.

Advertising assured her that the parade floats would be ready. The high school band, the local horse club, and Levy City's brand-new fire engine were all scheduled for their march down Central Avenue. Wynton's employees had volunteered to fill in as reindeer and elves to help wherever needed.

A noise from the floor caught her attention. A crowd had formed around a counter in Ladies' Dresses as Alvid Ashley's voice sounded above the din. Other shoppers stopped and craned their necks toward the commotion.

Audrey hurried to the escalator.

Inside the semicircle stood Trina Lee, the longtime maid of Jane Holcomb, one of Wynton's oldest and most loyal customers. She gripped a garment box with Wynton's logo in both hands.

"I don't care what you say; you aren't returning that dress without a note from Mrs. Holcomb," Alvid bellowed.

Audrey moved to the front of the crowd. She slipped between Alvid and Trina Lee. "What's going on?"

"She's trying to return a dress I'm sure was stolen," Alvid sneered.

Gasps and murmurs spread through the crowd. Trina Lee lifted her chin and squared her shoulders. "I'm no thief. Miss Jane bought this dress last week. It's not her size, and she wants to trade for one that is."

Alvid stabbed his finger at the box. "There's no receipt, no note from Mrs. Holcomb. Per store policy, this can't be returned, and I have an obligation to call security on this—"

"May I see the dress?" Audrey resisted saying please. Alvid had primed the crowd into a fit, and she wasn't going to stoke their fires by showing deference to Trina Lee.

She'd campaigned against the rotten store policy declaring that Black customers must present a note signed by their White employers giving them permission to shop at Wynton's in their stead.

Mr. Wynton agreed to think about changing the rule. When she'd mentioned it to Cissy, she was met with laughter. "How would we protect ourselves from the robberies?"

Now she'd have to get around the rule.

Trina Lee held out the box. Audrey looked inside, seeing clearly the garment was never intended for the tiny, frail Miss Jane.

Since her maid wasn't allowed to try on clothes in the store, Miss Jane had purchased the dress for Trina Lee and chosen the wrong size.

"Is Miss Jane not feeling well today?"

Anger blazed in Trina Lee's eyes, but she kept her voice calm. "Yes, ma'am. She woke up feeling peaked and is spending the day resting in bed."

Concern filled Trina Lee's eyes. Miss Jane had cancer, and the whole town knew she was near the end. She'd probably bought the dress as a final gift for her maid after forty years of loyal service.

And friendship. Miss Jane had been an invalid for the past decade, shutting herself up in her big house. She'd moved Trina Lee in and relied on her for everything.

Audrey took the box from Trina Lee. "Mr. Ashley, I'll handle this myself."

Though he bowed with respect, disgust shone in his eyes. He'd had this crowd in his palm, and she ruined his performance.

"Follow me." She heard the soft padding of Trina's thick-soled shoes squishing behind her.

With no more drama to behold, the crowd resumed their shopping.

Audrey led Trina Lee through the employee entrance doors and down the hallway to an empty storage room. She opened the door and motioned for Trina to sit in a chair along the wall.

"I didn't steal that dress. I don't have a note, because Miss Jane's hands was shaking so bad today she couldn't hold the pen. I said y'all wouldn't take the dress without a note, but she told me to come on to the store anyway." She sat back and balled her fists around the straps of her purse, where chips of leather peeled away.

Audrey removed the dress from the box and draped the garment over her arm. "What size do you need?"

Trina Lee met her gaze. "What?"

"The size?"

Trina Lee scowled. "12."

"Stay here. If anyone comes in, you tell them Miss Penault is dealing with you."

"What're you doing?"

"Just stay here."

Audrey hurried out with the dress in hand.

When she returned, she laid a neatly folded dress and a receipt in the box, then closed and tied it shut. "This should fit much better. If it doesn't, have Miss Jane call me. The number is on the receipt."

She held the box out to Trina Lee. "Anytime Miss Jane needs help shopping, she's to call that number, and I'll take care of everything. We'll have her packages delivered to her doorstep."

Trina Lee took the box. "I've been doing Miss Jane's shopping for a long time and did fine on my own."

"I'm trying to make things a little easier now that she needs more help." Audrey held open the door. "Shopping can be one less thing to worry about."

"No, thank you. I'll bring the note next time." Trina Lee left the room.

Audrey directed her down the hallway. "The door at the end leads to the back sidewalk."

Trina Lee tucked the box under her arm and made her way out. Audrey watched to ensure she left the store without trouble.

Someday Wynton's would welcome Trina Lee through the front door. Someday.

Audrey went back to the executive suite and typed the last line of a letter with one hand as she rubbed the clinched muscles in her neck. Every single cramp and throb bore Cissy's name.

The door to the office suite clicked. Expecting Cissy, Audrey faced a tall man with hair the color of coal and eyes as pale blue as the Grecian Sea peeking his head in the door.

"Are you Audrey Penault?"

"I am."

The man entered and extended his hand to her. "I'm Joshua McKinnon."

She took in his old-fashioned navy pin-striped suit and spotted red tie. "Do you have an appointment?"

He dropped his hand to his side. "No, I'm a new hire."

There was no McKinnon on the new-hires list. She'd gone over those names earlier in the morning. "I don't recall seeing your name. Who hired you?"

"Mr. Wynton. He said to come up and introduce myself to you." He extended his hand once again.

Audrey tilted her head to the side. "We both know that's not true."

He grinned like a boy caught sneaking cake before dinner as he pulled his hand back. "Yes, ma'am, you're right. Mrs. Wynton hired me.

I'm the new head detective for the store."

Audrey soaked in the news a moment. "When did this happen?"

"Last week."

How on earth did Cissy know how to hire a detective? "Did you work for another store?"

He nodded. "Yes, ma'am, I've been around a few since I came home from Korea. A mutual friend recommended me to Mrs. Wynton."

"Well then. Welcome to Wynton's." She stood and motioned to the coffee cart. "May I get you some coffee?"

"No thanks. Not much of a coffee drinker."

He stared at the cart. "Do you use ground sugar or cubes?"

She forced herself not to balk at the odd question. "Ground. Mr. Wynton thinks cubes are too feminine."

He chuckled, then walked over and stirred the sugar in the bowl. "How often do you refill this?"

She moved until she stood opposite him. "Whenever the bowl is half-empty."

As she went to take the spoon from him, he flipped the white crystals, and they splayed across the cherrywood surface of the cart.

"Now I've gone and made a mess." He set down the spoon.

Audrey hurried to wet a napkin in the executive washroom and return to clean up the mess.

He motioned for the napkin. "I should clean up the spill."

"I'll take care of it." She held the napkin below the edge of the cart and swept the sugar into it with her hand. After crumpling it into a ball, she tossed it in the garbage can.

Mr. McKinnon reached in and drew the napkin out, then stuffed it in his coat pocket.

Audrey gestured toward his pocket. "If you're looking for a souvenir, we have all kinds of matchbooks, candies, and pens with Wynton's logo on them. I'll get you a pocketful of those before you go." She allowed her smile to spread slowly, appearing friendly, because any man who'd take a soiled napkin for no good reason was just plain crazy.

He was just the type Cissy would hire.

She held her hands toward the door to encourage his exit, but he sat in one of the waiting room chairs. "Mrs. Wynton told me you were clever."

"Did she now?" She highly doubted Cissy said anything positive about her.

He stretched his arm across the back of the chair next to his. "Indeed, she did."

Mr. McKinnon watched her with the same look a mama mockingbird gave right before she swooped down to peck at anything coming near her nest of hatchlings. "You don't want to know what she told me?"

"Not especially."

"You're the first woman I've ever met who didn't care what others said behind her back."

She'd heard. Far too many times, she'd heard.

"*C'est la vie.*" Usually, using French around men enticed them to make a hasty exit, and it would be double glorious if Mr. McKinnon were one of them.

"Yes, ma'am, such is life."

"You speak French?"

He shrugged. "I've picked up all sorts of language through the years." He placed his hand about his mouth as if ready to tell her a most juicy secret. "And most of it is best left unsaid in polite company."

"Well then." Audrey clammed up, hoping he'd catch the hint and go. But he decided to keep talking.

"How close are you to Mr. Wynton?"

"I beg your pardon?" Of course, Cissy would have shared all the best rumors with him.

"Mrs. Wynton says her father-in-law respects your opinion above all others. Including hers and his son's, God rest his soul."

How good telling him off would feel. Instead, she walked to her desk and sat on the edge. "Are you much of a fisherman, Mr. McKinnon?"

"Only when I've found the right lures and bait." He waved his hands as if trying to erase the air around him. "I've taken up way too much of your time."

Without another word, Joshua McKinnon rose and left the suite.

She heard him humming as he walked to the elevator.

When Audrey bent her knees and peeked through the crack between the door hinges to ensure he'd made his exit, the door opened and Miss Vivien pushed it from the other side. "Audrey?"

She straightened. "Miss Vivien." She rubbed her cheek where the doorknob had clocked her.

"My heavens, did I hit you with the door?"

Miss Evelyn always said a true lady was measured by how well she could compose herself when she was in a fix.

Audrey planted her feet a bit farther apart and tugged the hem of her suit jacket into place. A curl fell over her forehead, and she tucked the lock back into her hairdo.

"Do you need to see Cissy?"

"No, I wanted to ask you something."

"Me?" Audrey pressed her heels harder into the floor. She wasn't certain she was up for any more questions today.

Especially from Miss Vivien, who hadn't found a reason to speak to her since she'd cut Audrey and her mother out of her life twenty-five years ago.

Chapter 21

VIVIEN

Vivien was in between clients and stole a moment to look over the latest sketches she'd put down in her sketchbook.

"You never told me how your little confab went yesterday," Mirette called as she smoothed the skirt of a peach-colored dress with the shop's clothes steamer.

"As expected."

Mirette pursed her lips. "Meaning?"

Vivien closed the book. "You remember our first bridal show in New York?"

"We almost passed out the moment our gown hit the runway."

Vivien pulled on the short black jacket that matched her fitted black brocade dress. "Do you remember what I told you right after?"

"That we'd always hold each other up."

"And have we fallen yet?"

"No, but I've got a feeling it's time to glue a pillow to my face."

"Mirette, I've redone my makeup and my hair. Neither of us will be hitting the floor today." She shot her most serious "boss lady" face at her assistant.

Mirette glanced at her watch as the salon's front door chimes rang. "The ducklings only took an hour and forty-five minutes for lunch today."

"I know two little ones who will be getting Timexes for Christmas from Santa's elves." Vivien opened her desk drawer and took out her lunch pail. "I'm off on my mission."

She laid a stern glare on both girls when she met them on the sales floor. "Did y'all have to catch and skin your food today before the cafeteria could cook it?"

"I guess we're a little late. We were talking with some of the girls in the fashion show. They're all wondering who's wearing the showstopper this year." Laurie passed a look with Deanna. "When are you going to tell us?"

"Not today." Vivien motioned to the back of the store. "Mirette has a list for you both."

A duet of sad sighs followed her out of the salon.

Thanks to the ducklings taking their own sweet time to eat and socialize, the noon rush had long left the cafeteria, and several tables sat empty when she arrived.

Vivien scanned the half-filled dining room for two particular faces.

She found Mary Jo first, sitting with a group intent on their own conversation and ignoring her.

Gigi was sitting with Alvid. His mouth was going a mile a minute, surely spilling all the latest from the store's gossip vine.

She'd best work fast.

Vivien joined Mary Jo. "Is this seat taken?"

"Miss Vivien. How nice to see you." Mary Jo pushed the chair out as her tablemates left without a word.

Once settled, Vivien removed the Tupperware with her salad from her pail. "Were those friends of yours?"

"No, ma'am. This was the only empty chair when I arrived."

"Not sitting with Gigi anymore?"

"No, ma'am."

Vivien stirred her homemade mayonnaise dressing into her salad with her fork. "Why?"

Mary Jo stole a quick glance at Gigi. "I don't know."

Vivien forked a tomato into her mouth and planned her response while she chewed.

"Do you think she'd tell me?"

Mary Jo's face went pale. "I don't—"

Vivien held up her fork to stop Mary Jo. "I'm teasing. I know she doesn't like me much either."

"I don't understand her."

Vivien stabbed a lettuce chunk. "I do." She finished her bite.

Mary Jo took her tray to the conveyor belt and came back to the table.

"How much longer do you have?" Vivien asked.

Mary Jo pulled back the edge of her sleeve and looked at her watch. "Ten minutes."

"I'll be back in two."

Vivien moved to Gigi's table. "Do you have a couple of minutes?"

Gigi met her with a suspicious scowl. "What for?"

"I'd like to show you something. For the fashion show."

Gigi traded expressions with Alvid. "Okay."

"Come on then."

Alvid sprang from his chair like a jack-in-the-box. "This sounds fun. I think I'll tag along."

Vivien shook her head. "Really, Alvid, I don't think this is for you."

He tapped his watch's face. "I have thirty minutes."

"Lucky you, but this is girls only."

Vivien herded her troop of two to the employee's elevator entrance and urged them into the car. "Fifth floor, Berle."

The operator pressed the button, and the car jiggled upward.

As soon as the doors opened, Gigi stepped out of the car. "Why are we at the salon again?"

Vivien motioned to them both. "Follow me."

She led them into Ladies' Formals and Fine Dresses, past the racks of flowing gowns, formal wraps, and the door to the exclusive back room where Wynton's housed their own line of furs.

Gigi stared. "Who needs a fur coat in Florida?"

"Those furs aren't about being warm." Vivien recalled the sable stole Cissy wore almost nonstop the year she and Junior married.

She took them past the designer sections to the fitting rooms along the back wall of the department.

Vivien swept her hand across an almost life-size, full-color picture of a tall brunette with her head held high and her long neck stretched like a swan's. The model posed in a red satin gown shining with tones of silver and gold in the light. A red satin cape with a white fur lining fell across her shoulders and cascaded down her side like a waterfall.

Mary Jo moved in for a closer look. "I've never seen anyone look so beautiful."

"She's like Cinderella." Gigi surveyed the picture.

Vivien tapped the frame. "This, my dears, is a showstopper. A gown worn by just the right girl, posed just the right way, looking more like art than a dress. This dress commands every eye in the room."

"Wynton's showstoppers have become the highlight of the holiday fashion show. The gown is a one-of-a-kind creation made by a guest designer. We've had many big names contribute a dress over the years. Debutantes often beg for a copy of this gown, in white of course, made for their coming out in the spring."

"I can't stop looking at the dress, or her." Mary Jo stepped back and continued gawking.

"She looks familiar." Gigi squinted and moved closer.

Vivien grinned. "You've both met her."

They whipped around, both wearing shocked expressions.

Vivien directed their attention to the model's upturned face. "She was one of the most sought-after fashion models in the world. Then she retired and came here to work at Wynton's two years ago. That's Audrey."

"What?" Gigi screeched and swung round for a closer look.

"Will Audrey be in the show?" Mary Jo asked.

"Good grief, no."

They jerked around to find Alvid had followed them to the dressing rooms. "If she showed up, all the other girls would quit, and the audience would leave. No one in this town wants a dress, or anything else, having to do with her. Haven't you heard how she's responsible for Junior's wreck?"

Mary Jo gasped. "No."

Alvid lifted his chin in an exaggerated nod. "Oh yes."

And this was the exact reason she didn't want Alvid to be a part of this in the first place. Vivien stepped in before things got worse. "Alvid,

I've got to talk show details with these ladies."

"Of course, Miss Vivien." He bowed to Mary Jo and Gigi. "Ladies."

Vivien waited until she was certain he was out of earshot before speaking to the other two. "Listen to me closely."

They clicked to attention.

"I don't know what's going on between the two of you. Stop it."

Mary Jo looked at the floor, while Gigi's eyes snapped angrily.

She continued. "Mirette and I have been friends for nearly thirty years, and let me tell you, there have been times when we've wanted to snatch each other bald."

Vivien held up one finger. "But when my life fell apart, Mirette helped me pick up the pieces and glue them back together. Because that is what we southern women do for one another. We pull up our stockings, forgive one another, and hold our friends close no matter what. Understood?"

Gigi and Mary Jo shared a look.

"Yes, ma'am," Mary Jo said.

Gigi stared a moment, her lips pursed as she worked through her thoughts. She brushed Mary Jo's arm. "Want to ride down together?"

Mary Jo nodded so hard her head almost snapped back.

"And one last thing. We don't take anything men like Alvid say seriously if we know what's good for us."

Vivien walked them back to the elevator.

Hours later, she took a last look around the salon's fitting rooms before gathering her things to go home.

Mirette waited, her sweater thrown about her shoulders and her purse already in the crook of her arm. "You showed Mary Jo and Gigi that picture of Audrey, didn't you?"

"I did."

"And?"

Vivien looked in the mirror as she put on her hat. "It's lovely to know we old gals can still pull a fix-it-all from our hats."

"Score one for the old gals." Mirette raised her arms in a cheer as Vivien cut the lights.

They walked out together.

"I'm taking the stairs tonight. You want to join me?"

"Always."

At the fourth-floor landing, Mirette motioned to the window. "It's raining. Did you bring an umbrella?"

Vivien produced a black one from her satchel.

Her friend wrapped her arm about Vivien's waist as they made their way to the main floor.

"Good thing we old gals have weathered enough in life that we know how to be prepared." Mirette pushed through the side door.

"Ain't it, though?" Vivien opened her umbrella, and they huddled together as they splashed through puddles on their way to the parking garage, giggling like two little girls.

Chapter 22

AUDREY

Audrey stood at Mr. Wynton's front door as she pushed her compact, wallet, and handkerchief out of the way until finally locating his house key in her purse. The rising sun shooed away the night as she unlocked his front door.

She knocked on his study's paneled doors.

"Come in."

He was thumbing through a stack of papers at his desk and looked up when she slid the doors closed. "Nurse Nancy won't like us being behind closed doors. And she likes to gossip."

Audrey opened one of the doors. "Better?"

"She'll still gripe because you're here."

Seemed whatever coop she inhabited, she always got on the wrong side of the other hens. Audrey sat down in one of the overstuffed chairs near his desk. "Too many females in your den?"

He propped his chin on his hand. "All day and night it's, 'Don't eat this,' 'Don't drink that,' and 'Put out those foul-smelling cigars before you drop down dead.' Between Nancy, Ethel, and Cissy, I've got all the feminine company I can stand."

Mr. Wynton extended his hand. "Present company excluded, of course."

The grandfather clock gonged, and she stood. "Time for your medication."

He opened a desk drawer and produced two pill tins and a bottle filled with a thick liquid. "Nancy and Ethel won't forgive me for not trusting them with all these blasted pills." He held up the liquid medication bottle. "And I swear this stuff is killing me from the inside out. Only death could taste this awful."

"Doctor's orders." Audrey walked to the small credenza where a crystal water pitcher and matching glasses sat on a silver tray. She poured him a glass.

He shoved the tins toward her. "Count them out for me. I can't remember how many of each I'm supposed to take."

"I wrote down the doses for you." She grouped his morning pills together on the desktop in front of him.

He grunted, scooped up the pills, and popped them in his mouth, chasing them down with a long sip of water.

Mr. Wynton held the glass out. "Fill it up before you pour the pig swill down my throat."

Audrey fixed his refill and measured the liquid in the glass dosage cup. She thrust both at him. "Bottoms up."

"That phrase used to be a lot more fun." He choked down the elixir, then gulped the water from the glass.

He still sputtered when he handed the glass and cup back to her. "See you at six."

Cissy stomped into the room, dressed in a pink satin robe trimmed with flowing ostrich feathers. The hot-pink curlers in her hair flopped with each step. "I don't see why you won't let Ethel or Nancy give you the medicine, Daddy. They know what they're doing."

Mr. Wynton sagged into his chair and focused his attention on his paperwork. He gave no answer.

Cissy glared at Audrey. "You can go now." She crossed her arms and tapped the toe of her pink high-heeled slippers on the rug.

"Do you need anything else, Mr. Wynton?"

"That's all." He opened a small drawer and rifled through the contents.

She held the used glass and medicine cup out to Cissy. "I'll leave these with you since I'm not allowed in the kitchen."

Cissy snatched them away. "For good reason."

"Audrey, bring my black fountain pen when you come back tonight."

Mr. Wynton slid the drawer shut. "I don't have one in my desk, and I need to sign some papers to send in tomorrow's mail."

"You can't do store business tonight, Daddy." The glass and cup clinked together as Cissy slammed them on the table before rushing to his side. "Dr. Bridges told you not to strain your heart—"

"Signing my name is not going to strain my heart," he groused.

"But Daddy, it's bad enough she comes here twice a day to do your medicine when I'm paying two nurses to look after you. But to have her shoving store business on you too. . ." She draped her arms around him in a smothering hug. "I just want to take care of you. You're all I have left."

Mr. Wynton untangled himself from her embrace and patted her on the shoulder. "I'll take a nap this afternoon before Audrey comes back. I promise. If it makes you feel better, I'll take one before lunch too."

Cissy kissed the part combed into his white hair. "Thank you, Daddy."

Mr. Wynton mouthed a goodbye as he continued consoling his daughter-in-law.

Once at the store, Audrey made her way to his office to retrieve the pen. The scent of Cissy's perfume met her when she sat in Mr. Wynton's chair and opened the drawer where he kept his pens. Upon seeing none of his usual favorites, she pulled the drawer out farther to search in the back tray.

She yanked her hand back.

A dead wasp lay among the array of Mr. Wynton's pens.

The very species he was allergic to.

But not old enough or crackly dead enough to be left over from the incident in August.

She slammed into the chairback, her mind reeling. Other than her, only Cissy and Junior knew of Mr. Wynton's allergy to wasps. He'd sworn them all to secrecy because he didn't want folks to know.

Had someone else discovered the truth and used the allergy as a chance to kill Mr. Wynton?

A new thought chilled her blood and sent an all-over shiver through her. No one would suspect Cissy or Junior of planting the lethal insect.

But they'd be jumping over one another to blame her.

The wasp needed to be hidden until she could figure things out.

She ran to the outer office door and locked it.

Audrey went to the cart and poured an opened can of coffee into the trash, then took the container to Mr. Wynton's desk. She slid the corpse onto a page from her memo pad and dumped it into the can. After pressing the lid closed, she ran her finger around the edges to make sure all was closed tight. She pushed the drawer closed with her hip.

Audrey went to the closet and stuffed the coffee can deep inside her satchel.

She almost jumped out of her skin when someone turned the knob and yanked the door so hard it thumped.

"Why is this locked?" Cissy yelled from the other side.

Being seen in such a rattled state would never do.

Audrey set her satchel in her desk chair and pulled the zipper closed around the can.

The knocking sounded again. "Audrey, are you out of your ever-loving mind? Let me in this instant."

From the sound of Cissy's screeching, she was about to throw a hissy fit.

Audrey breathed deeply and grabbed her satchel. She was going to walk past Cissy with that wasp in her bag.

After all, she was the Hatchet, wasn't she? Nerves of steel, heart of stone, blood as cold as ice. No feelings, according to the gossip vine.

With a white-knuckled grip on the leather handle, Audrey exhaled, walked to the door, and released the lock.

Cissy burst in like a cat with its tail on fire. "You'd better have a good reason for locking that door." She cemented herself in front of Audrey.

"I have a good reason for everything I do." Audrey swirled past her and headed for the stairs, striding as fast as she could while remaining ladylike.

After all, ladies were never meant to rush about like a bunch of ants, Miss Evelyn always said.

Cissy yelled something after her, but the walls blurred her calls into echoes as Audrey hurried to the stairs.

When she reached the garage, she surveyed the area to make sure no one was around. Once convinced she was alone, Audrey made her way to Nelson's sitting chair.

After one last look in all directions, she went to the spot behind the garbage can where he'd hide the thermos. She removed the coffee can from her satchel and dumped the wasp's carcass inside Nelson's thermos, then screwed on the lid.

She left the thermos in her T-Bird, locked up tight.

On her way back, she dropped the coffee can into the garbage. Audrey thanked the dear Lord there was enough refuse inside to muffle the sound, because her nerves were pulled as tight as piano strings and about to fray.

As she walked into the office, she heard Cissy on the phone in Mr. Wynton's office.

Audrey sank into her chair. She'd run up the stairs from the garage, no easy feat in her heels. Her cheeks radiated heat, and the edge of her hairline itched with perspiration.

She unlocked her desk drawer to retrieve her compact and freshen up a bit while Cissy finished her phone call.

But when she looked in her purse, her compact was missing.

Chapter 23

AUDREY

Audrey stared at the blank page sitting in her typewriter. No matter how hard she tried to focus, her mind swirled back to the wasp, now residing in an empty cold cream jar in her medicine cabinet.

She'd lain awake well past midnight trying to ascertain who benefited most from the deadly bug's being in Mr. Wynton's desk drawer.

The list stayed short each time she ruminated on the names.

Junior. Cissy.

And her. Only she and Mr. Wynton knew why she must be included.

She swiveled her neck to ease the cricks, flexed her fingers over the keys like a pianist, then dove into the new business proposal Mr. Wynton had assigned her to type.

He'd grumbled through the dispensing of his pills and tonic earlier, but his complaints ceased when she'd delivered the news of Wynton's landing one of the best contracts to be had in the retail world.

And she'd brokered the deal.

Her heart nearly left her when a deep voice sounded behind her.

"Might I interrupt for a second?"

She spun in her chair to see Joshua McKinnon standing in the middle of the room dressed in a gray suit with a red-and-purple tie that Alvid would have loved. "Where in the world did you come from?"

"Birmingham, Alabama."

Miss Evelyn had taught her real ladies allowed gentlemen to have their fun and laughed along with them.

Audrey plastered a grin across her face. "Clever."

He pulled a chair from the waiting area. "May we chat?"

"Sure."

McKinnon settled into the chair.

No sense offering him coffee, which was fortuitous, because she'd been on the phone and hadn't restocked this morning when she arrived. "How may I help you?"

He removed a napkin from his pocket. "Do you know what this is?"

"A Wynton's napkin. I'm guessing the one you took the other day."

He unfolded the sides and shook sugar granules onto the surface of her desk.

"Is there a reason why you've decided my desk needs to look like the top of a sugar cookie?"

"There is." He set the napkin in the middle of his mess. "Who buys the sugar for this office?"

"I do."

"Do you restock the coffee cart?"

"Yes."

Joshua wet the tip of his index finger with his tongue and pressed his digit into the sugar spread on her desk. "You plan on using this to kill rats or mice around the office?"

"What?"

He thrust his finger toward her. "There's cyanide in this sugar. Enough to make a man sick but not kill him."

Icy fingers twined inside her, chilling from the inside out. She resisted rubbing them away. "How?"

He pulled his finger back. "Do you have a washroom?"

"Mr. Wynton's office. Just inside to the left."

He rose and she soon heard the faucet running as he whistled his way through washing his hands.

The high-pitched tune grated on the nerves, especially when trying to piece together where his questions led. Audrey twined her fingers to control their shaking.

He returned to his chair and put the napkin back in his pocket. "Now you see why I wanted to know who buys the sugar."

"Aren't you afraid of the cyanide being in your pocket?" Not to mention how unnerving it was to know the same poison was spread across her desk. She'd have to call maintenance to come and scrub all the furniture in the office once he left.

He screwed his lips into a pucker. "I suppose I should be." McKinnon patted his pocket and stared her straight in the eyes.

She hadn't squirmed under a man's gaze since she was ten and wasn't about to start now. Then a new thought flashed. Audrey reached across the desk and drew a line in the sugar then touched her finger to the tip of her tongue, careful not to smear her lipstick in the process.

McKinnon locked eyes with her. "You know how to call a bluff, Miss Penault."

He'd pronounced her name "Penult," as most folks did.

"When I lived in France, they said my last name as 'Pee-nall.' I fell in love with the musicality of it and have preferred that pronunciation since." She rose from her chair to retrieve a wet towel from the washroom.

"I stand corrected, Miss Pee-nall." He spoke in perfect French.

"Thank you."

Audrey slipped into the washroom and brought a towel to Mr. McKinnon. "You have the honor of cleaning my desk, while also explaining yourself. Mr. McKinnon." She flashed her 24-karat smile at him.

He clicked his tongue as he took the towel. "You certainly live up to your reputation, Audrey. And please, call me Joshua."

Audrey handed her wastebasket to him without bothering to ask what he meant.

Joshua brushed the mess into the trash. "The sugar I snatched the other day did indeed contain cyanide. And I had to ask, since your boss was poisoned."

He shook the towel over the trash can. "Thing is, I can't figure out why you'd want to kill him. Especially since you're so close."

Neither statement deserved a response, so Audrey remained silent.

Joshua went on. "But now we have a new problem."

He held up the towel with a questioning look, and she directed him to return it to the washroom.

"What is this new problem?" The sound of the towel flopping in the sink wafted through the suite.

"Did you go to Mr. Wynton's this morning? Cissy tells me you're the only one he trusts with his medicines, and he won't let the two nurses she's hired near him." He walked back into the outer office.

"I did."

"Was Cissy downstairs when you arrived?"

"No."

"And the nurses?"

"Ethel was in the kitchen. Nancy was upstairs while I met with Mr. Wynton."

McKinnon paused. "Where was Nancy when you left?"

"Still upstairs. She avoids me."

"And Mr. Wynton?"

The chills crept up her arms again. "He was sitting in his armchair, reading the business page of the *LTC*."

"And you gave the medications, as usual?"

"Yes."

"And you dispensed them according to his doctor's orders?"

Audrey sprang to her feet. "He's sick again, isn't he?"

McKinnon rubbed the back of his neck. "Ethel found him passed out cold in his study. She also discovered Nancy dead at the bottom of the stairs. Her killer stabbed her in the neck with a small piece of a mirror."

Audrey's ears pounded in tandem with her runaway heartbeat. "Did Ethel see who did this?"

"No. She said she heard you leave, and when she walked from the kitchen, she found Nancy, then Mr. Wynton. His doctor is with him now."

He walked to the door. "The police are at the Wyntons' house." Joshua lingered in the doorway. "They're heading here to talk with you next. Good luck, Miss Penault." He spoke her name with his perfect French accent and left.

Audrey collapsed into her desk chair.

Her hands shook as if she were in the middle of a blizzard without warm gloves. The police were coming. Because she made the perfect suspect.

Miss Evelyn taught that true ladies solved their own troubles and didn't burden others.

But true ladies never got themselves mixed up in murder either.

She needed help. But who could she call?

Chapter 24

AUDREY

After the police left, Audrey hurried to Accounting. The clicking and whirring of adding machines filled the room as she walked between the rows of desks.

She headed to the fishbowl office of the department manager, Mr. Henderson.

He'd made Accounting one of the best collections of bookkeepers around and was one of the most trusted advisers to the board. But Audrey still watched him with the same caution she would give a black widow spider.

She breezed into his office and laid a folder on his desk. He kept his focus on the stack of work before him. "What are you doing here?"

She tapped the folder with her finger. "Mr. Wynton wants these balance sheets to be redone. You have duplicates here that don't match."

He continued scrawling across his paperwork with his pencil. "I went over those myself. Perhaps Mr. Wynton made the mistake?"

She'd checked each number, each calculation herself. "What are you implying?"

"The boss hasn't been at his best lately. His health is putting a great strain on him. And the store."

"The store?"

Mr. Henderson slowly lifted his eyes. "A ship sinks when the captain can't stand at its helm." He slid the folder toward her. "We are a week away from the holiday shopping season, and for reasons too complicated for me to explain to you, the store is not ready."

"I beg to differ. Wynton's sales have remained stable going into this quarter, our foot traffic has increased, and sales have begun to pick up at a faster rate than last year. All good indicators."

"Did Mr. Wynton tell you this?"

"No. I went over the numbers myself."

"A certificate from secretary school gives you the experience to do this?" He gestured toward his framed diploma sitting on the credenza behind his desk.

"I have a business degree."

"From a correspondence school?"

"No. The same university where you earned yours. Class of '53."

"I have over fifteen years of experience, helped this store weather through WW Two and Korea. You've been here how long?"

"Two years."

He issued her a silent dismissal by returning his attention to the papers on his desk.

But she wasn't finished with him yet.

She put on her sweetest voice. "Mr. Henderson, what about Cissy? I could ask her to go over them."

He pressed his lips into a thin line as he slid the folder she'd brought into his inbox. "I'll go over the papers again and put them on your desk when I have time."

"Thank you." She had another stop to make—Miss Vivien's.

The salon was a hive of female activity. Two young ladies hovered around Mirette as she showed them various bridesmaid dresses, and Miss Vivien talked with a girl and her mother about china and silverware patterns.

Audrey moved to the back where the fitting rooms were, then sat and waited. When Miss Vivien finally arrived, Audrey had mapped out and practiced what to say a dozen times.

Miss Vivien pulled up another chair. "What brings you to the salon?"

"The question you asked me the other day."

"All right." Miss Vivien smoothed a fold in her wide black skirt.

"Would you be free to meet for lunch at the Grove later to talk about it?"

Curiosity showed in Miss Vivien's eyes as she rose from her chair. "I'll see you at noon."

Chapter 25

AUDREY

Audrey stood outside the door of the private dining room of the Grove. Inside, Mary Jo, Gigi, and Miss Vivien waited, all probably wondering why she invited them to lunch.

Fear invited them. Her plain, simple fear.

It rubbed like a rock in her shoe. She'd never begged for help in her life, and here she was staging a sympathy play to save herself and Mr. Wynton.

Miss Vivien and Mary Jo looked up when she entered. The chair next to Mary Jo sat open for Gigi.

"Thank you for coming."

The door flew open, and Gigi rushed in. "I'm sorry I'm late."

"You look pretty," Mary Jo complimented as Gigi scooted up to the table. "I love your blue blouse. Looks gorgeous with the blue-and-black-checked skirt. And that upturned collar is so sophisticated."

Gigi patted her hair as if she'd been windblown. "Thanks."

"Are you off today? Have a big date with Bobby later?"

"No. But I do have news." A wide grin spread across her face. "You're sitting with the newest clerk in Florida Delights. Started today."

Mary Jo squealed while Miss Vivien clapped and offered congratulations. Gigi beamed as they both stood and hugged her around the neck.

"I told you someone would find out you were practically running the cafeteria by yourself." Mary Jo offered another hug.

Audrey watched them. She could balance a column of numbers in a heartbeat and read a financial table with ease. But she couldn't for the life of her understand how to form those long-standing bonds that led to the type of sisterhood Mary Jo and Gigi now shared. Or like Miss Vivien and Mirette enjoyed over the years. There must have been a secret sense for it that she missed at birth.

She cleared her throat as she took the chair next to Miss Vivien. "Shall we order?"

Gigi looked around the room, and her gaze lifted to the crystal chandelier hanging overhead. "I've never eaten in a place that had a chandelier. It looks like an upside-down fountain. Pretty."

She dropped her gaze to the array of silverware spread before her on the light blue linen tablecloth. "What are all these for?" She picked up a silver pickle fork. "This looks like a fancy frog gig."

Mary Jo snickered at the image of a frog-hunting tool on the luncheon table, while Miss Vivien gestured toward the utensil. "That's a pickle fork. You use it so you don't get pickle juice on your fingers."

"Easier to plop the pickle in your mouth." Gigi laid the implement back on the tablecloth.

Audrey opened the menu resting on her plate in hopes the others would follow suit. "They make a fantastic chicken salad here. The shrimp salad is nice too."

"Eunice bakes the chicken potpies here." Gigi tapped her finger on Mary Jo's menu. "The crust is so buttery, it melts in your mouth."

Mary Jo shook her head. "I shouldn't have something that heavy." She tapped another selection. "I want the chicken salad."

Miss Vivien laid her closed menu on her plate. "Me too."

Gigi seemed to deflate and hung her head as she opened her menu again. "Tomatoes stuffed with cottage cheese. And walnuts sprinkled on top. That sounds good. The chicken potpie has too much starch." She closed her menu.

The other women smiled and nodded. Audrey laid her menu aside. Crying shame, a woman always had to feel nervous about eating too much in public.

Once their food arrived, Audrey stirred the cup of tomato aspic she'd ordered, then poked at the blue cheese–sprinkled lettuce wedge on her plate. She couldn't take a single bite.

It was time to move on with her plans. "Ladies, your attention, please."

Three pairs of eyes stared back. She barely knew Mary Jo and Gigi. And Miss Vivien had been mad at her for decades. She'd practiced a million different ways to say her piece.

This wasn't like talking to Mr. Wynton. She had to present this diplomatically, strong enough for them to see the urgency and yet soft enough to avoid coming across as a battle-ax.

Women were complicated. And if they all told her no. . .

Audrey sat straight in her chair. "Each of you owes Mr. Wynton, so I would think you'd want to jump at the chance to help him."

After all the practicing, she still hit them with the finesse of a cannonball fired in the dark.

Miss Vivien cocked her head back in shock. "What is that supposed to mean?"

"Mr. Wynton needs our help."

"For what?" Gigi shared a confused expression with Mary Jo.

"To prevent his being killed."

"Have you lost your ever-loving mind?" Gigi's voice bounced off the walls.

"Really, Audrey, this isn't very nice meal conversation." Mary Jo spoke as if she were upbraiding her own children.

Audrey looked at Miss Vivien. "I suppose you think I'm crazy too?"

"You've thrown quite a lot at us all of a sudden. What brought all this on?"

Maybe the truth could save her. "One of Mr. Wynton's nurses was found dead in his house today."

Mary Jo sucked in a squeaky breath. "Poor Cissy. She must be frightened to death."

"How do you know all this?" Gigi looked to the other women. "None of us have heard a thing."

"Cissy hired a private investigator named Joshua McKinnon. He told me about the nurse this morning." Audrey folded her napkin and laid it next to her untouched plate. "He'll be talking with all the employees, I'm sure."

Mary Jo's face blanched. "Does he think the person who did this works here?"

"Possibly."

"How awful." Mary Jo covered her mouth with her napkin as if she were going to be sick.

"I'm terrified for Mr. Wynton. Whoever is behind this is just getting started and won't stop until he's gone. For good." Audrey searched their faces for signs they understood.

"Why do you think somebody's after Mr. Wynton? A burglar could have broken into his house and killed the nurse because she saw him. Everyone knows he's one of the richest men in town." Gigi stared her down. "And Cissy told us about Joshua days ago."

Audrey's nerves snapped, and her fears rushed to the surface. "Why are you arguing with me? Can't you see? Someone who knew Mr. Wynton had an allergy put those wasps in his office. Junior was working to make a deal to sell the store, but his father would never allow that. The people he was working with won't take no for an answer, and now Junior's dead. The only thing keeping them from taking over the store now is Mr. Wynton."

Miss Vivien tilted her head to the side. "Audrey, you're not making any sense."

She sprang up and tipped over her chair. "I don't have time to make sense. I came to the three of you because I thought you'd help me protect him."

Audrey righted her chair. She should have known better than to approach them. Yet again, she was on her own. "This was a terrible idea. I—"

Mary Jo locked eyes with Audrey. "Cissy would never let anything happen to Mr. Wynton. He's all she has left."

Mary Jo's words drilled into Audrey's brain and heart simultaneously. *All she has left.*

Audrey shoved her chair under the table so hard the dishes rattled and water sloshed from the goblets. "I'll pay the check on my way out."

Chapter 26

VIVIEN

Vivien noticed him outside the salon talking with Cissy, who looked mad as a wet hen. When their conversation ended, Cissy stomped to the elevator so fast the trumpet sleeves on her black dress flapped like a heron's wings.

Mirette peered around the doorway as the man pivoted on his heel and headed down the hallway.

"He's going into the fashion showroom." She turned back to Vivien. "Are they having a private showing in Fine Dresses today?"

Vivien finished writing a note on her clipboard and walked to her desk. "Not that I know of. Maybe he's shopping for his wife."

"He didn't look married to me."

"And just what does a married man look like from afar?" Vivien squeezed the clip open and removed the sheet so it could be filed.

"Miserable." Mirette winked.

"Then maybe that's why he's in the showroom. He needs a special please-forgive-me present."

"He seemed to be having quite the conversation with Cissy out front."

Vivien slammed her desk drawer closed. "There will be no more of that kind of talk. I declare, you get worse every day."

"Want to know what I heard in the employee elevator this morning?" Mirette flashed a Cheshire-cat grin.

"No. I've got enough to think about with Thanksgiving and then the show."

"Have you told Cissy what's happened yet?"

Vivien pointed her pencil at Mirette. "Not. A. Word."

She put up her hands as if surrendering. "I wouldn't dare."

"You'd better not. I've got a few more calls to make. Everything's going to be fine."

Oh, how she'd prayed this would be true. Half of the clothes she'd ordered for the show hadn't arrived yet, one model's new fiancé made her drop out, and Cissy kept making changes to her emcee script that didn't fit with the show's theme. If she didn't get this all pulled together in the next few days, her show—and reputation—were going to burn worse than Atlanta after Sherman went through.

The entrance chimes sounded, and she looked as the dark-haired stranger entered. Men always looked nervous and uncomfortable when they visited the salon.

But this gentleman touched the bow on a dress hanging on a nearby rack, then pulled a yellow lace gown out and looked as if he meant to buy it.

Vivien exchanged a silent *Who is he?* look with Mirette and walked to where he stood. "May I help you?"

The man held the gown next to him. "Not really my color, is it?"

"With the right shoes, earrings, maybe a tiara, we could make it work."

He let out a belly laugh and returned the dress to the rack. He marched toward her with his outstretched hand. "I'm Joshua McKinnon."

The man Audrey had mentioned. She shook his hand firmly. "Vivien Sheffield. Lovely meeting you."

He gazed around the sales floor. "I see you've earned your sterling reputation."

Mirette joined Vivien. They were both old enough to suspect men who talked so butter would melt in their mouths.

"I'm certain you aren't here to buy that yellow gown, Mr. McKinnon, so what can we do for you?"

"Mrs. Wynton hired me to keep an eye on the store. I'm introducing myself to the employees, getting to know the place better."

"You're going to talk to 250 people?" Mirette piped in.

Joshua widened his stance. "Not all at once."

"Let's go back here and have a seat. I've a feeling you've much you'd like to ask us." Vivien motioned to the fitting area.

Joshua sat in the leather bucket-style chair reserved for mamas during their daughters' gown fittings. He looked like an upside-down turtle as he settled into the shell-shaped seat, with arms draped over the sides and legs jutting far beyond the seat cushion's edge.

Mirette pulled her sewing chair next to Vivien.

"Don't let me keep you too late."

Mirette crossed her arms. "We'd be home already if I had any say."

Joshua sat forward and rested elbows on his knees. "I just want to ask a few questions about Audrey Penault."

"I see she's instructed you on how to pronounce her name."

Audrey's insistence on how she wished to be addressed rubbed a few folks raw. Most people thought she was being hoity-toity, but Vivien suspected it came from wanting to be distanced from her mother.

"Yes, ma'am." He tapped his knee. "I hear she's close to Mr. Wynton."

Vivien was sure he had. "I've known Mr. Wynton for a very long time. He's not the type."

She shot a warning side-eye to Mirette to keep quiet.

"I'm thinking she's got quite a head for business." He bounced his foot as he waited for her answer.

"She understands the inner workings of this store well." Far better than Junior ever had.

"You see her wanting to move up in the company?"

"As far as I know, she's happy assisting Mr. Wynton."

Vivien rotated her watchband so she could see the face and check the time.

"I'm told she's also helping in Mr. Wynton's care at home."

"I wouldn't know about that."

"How well did she get along with the younger Mr. Wynton and his wife?"

The entire town knew how Junior saw red over his father's trust in Audrey. And she and Cissy had been rivals almost from the day they were born.

"She ignored them."

Joshua chuckled. "Did you ever get the feeling she was trying to insert herself between Mr. Wynton and his family?"

There was no denying Audrey and the boss were close, but she recalled the scene at Junior's funeral. Mr. Wynton stuffing Cissy into the car, Audrey standing alone, watching the car pull away.

"I've never gotten that impression."

Joshua sprang from his chair. "One more question. Have either of you noticed Miss Penault being friendly with an employee named Francis Tyler?"

"I don't know her. Do you, Mirette?"

"We spoke in the elevator a few times." She hunched her shoulders forward to ease the strain from hours of sewing throughout the day.

Joshua fastened the bottom button on his sport coat. "She works in the children's department. Someone reported seeing Francis and Audrey driving in her car a few weeks ago, and I wondered why." He grinned. "Love the T-Bird. Most beautiful car on the road right now.

"Thank you, ladies. I'll walk myself out."

Vivien got her purse from the storeroom and her sweater from the back of her desk chair.

"You ready, Mirette?" She cut the lights in the storeroom and fitting room area.

"Grabbing my stuff now."

"Don't forget your lunch pail. Or your glasses." Vivien folded her sweater over her arm. "And did you pack the satin for the underskirt of Tammy Colson's flower-girl dress? You said you were going to work on that while you watched *Lucy* tonight."

Mirette held up the items in her arms. "I've got everything. Did you remember your clipboard and the show notes?"

Vivien opened her bag and checked to make certain they were there. "I swear our lists get longer every night. Are we really this forgetful these days?"

"They say after natural hair color, the memory is the next to go."

"At least hair color can be fixed."

"True." Mirette hung the straps of her bag, purse, and lunch pail over her arm. "Let's go before the circulation in my arm cuts off."

As Vivien reached to turn off the sales floor lights, the phone rang. "Honestly." She sighed. "Let me get that in case it's news about the clothes for the show."

She turned the lights back on and grabbed the phone on the fourth ring. "Miss Vivien speaking."

"I'm calling about the clothing orders you placed," the male on the other end said.

She set her going-home items on the floor. "Yes?"

"According to our records, the shipment was canceled last week."

"What?" She pressed the receiver against her ear to make sure she'd heard correctly. "By whom?"

Mirette rushed in, but Vivien shushed her so she could hear better. "Thank you for calling."

She slammed down the receiver.

"What on earth is going on?" Mirette switched her load to the other arm.

"According to Carl in Shipping, my entire order for the show was canceled."

Mirette slapped the top of her head with her hand. "Oh. My. Stars. Above. Who did that?"

"Audrey."

"Why?"

Vivien yanked her belongings from the floor. "Let's go find out."

Chapter 27

AUDREY

Audrey's heart skipped a beat when the knock sounded. Vivien and Mirette stood in the entryway, and from the flashing in both their eyes, this wasn't meant to be a social call.

"We need to talk. Now."

Audrey motioned to the waiting area. "I'll be right with you."

They dropped their belongings on her desk. "Why did you cancel my orders for the show?"

Audrey met their angry stares. "I didn't."

Vivien clenched her teeth. "Carl in Shipping says you did."

"Mr. Wynton approved those weeks ago." She went to the filing cabinet and retrieved the folder.

Audrey thumbed through the contents—twice. "They're gone."

"You lost them?" Mirette looked like a bull with flared nostrils and charging on its mind.

"I don't lose things." Audrey put the file back in the cabinet. "Let me check Mr. Wynton's desk."

When a search of the desk yielded nothing, she checked her satchel. Nothing.

Her heart hammered. How did these orders grow legs and go gallivanting from the office overnight? She distinctly remembered seeing them, mailing them, and filing the notice that the order had shipped.

Audrey retrieved her purse. "I'm driving to the warehouse."

"Not without us." Miss Vivien scooped her belongings into her arms with Mirette right behind her.

Audrey mashed the elevator button and stood ready to jump into the arriving car. As the door opened, Cissy met them.

"My, you ladies are working late tonight."

Dealing with Cissy was the last thing she needed. If the orders for the clothes were indeed lost, this spelled trouble for Wynton's. The show's orders and the holiday stock orders went out at the same time.

The holiday season would be ruined, and the store would lose its most profitable shopping season.

More red marks against Mr. Wynton.

Audrey stepped past and motioned for the operator to press floor 1. Miss Vivien and Mirette rushed past Cissy and entered the car.

"What are—" Cissy's question was lost when the elevator doors closed.

When they reached the parking garage, Miss Vivien caught Audrey by the sleeve. "We'll take my car."

They drove to the warehouse in silence.

Audrey wasn't a favorite of either woman, and she understood both of their reasons. But she wasn't about to allow Miss Vivien's show to fail.

She slid from the back seat when they arrived. "I'll get us in."

Nelson's nephew was the warehouse's night watchman. He recognized her as soon as she stood in the butter-hued beam of the lights. "Miss Audrey, what are you doing out here so late at night?"

"We're looking for an important shipment we think might be here."

Frederick stood to his full height. "There's nothing but the night loaders here. Y'all shouldn't be here."

She walked to the heavy metal door and waited. "Let us in, Frederick."

The flashlight that hung on his belt flapped against his leg as he slid the huge metal door open, grumbling under his breath. "If my boss sees you, you tell him you made me let y'all in."

She agreed.

Once in the building, Audrey led them down an aisle where tall metal shelves towered to the open rafters. Boxes and crates of all sizes filled the space, and she perused the shipping labels. Their heels left trails of dots where they'd walked on the dusty concrete. There was no evidence of Miss Vivien's orders.

"I need to find the manager." Audrey brushed away grit where she'd touched the boxes.

"Hello?" The boxes and crates muffled her voice.

Mirette and Miss Vivien joined in the call until a man dressed in dark blue overalls with Wynton's embroidered above his name tag rounded the corner.

He clomped their way in heavy boots.

"You gals need to get out of here," he huffed when he'd reached them.

"I'm Audrey Penault—"

"Nobody in my warehouse except my workers." He jerked his thumb toward the exit. "Git."

His attitude gave confidence that Wynton's stock was safe in his hands, but he needed to understand they were on a mission for the store. She'd get him to comply one way or another.

"I'm Mr. Wynton's secretary." She swept her hand at Miss Vivien and Mirette. "We're here to find some missing crates that were never delivered to the store."

The manager jabbed his thumb against his chest. "I've been running this warehouse for twenty years, and we ain't never lost an order."

"That's why we're here. Someone canceled a delivery, but I'm certain it's in this warehouse. I'm not leaving without it." She flashed her 24-karat smile.

"And neither are we." Miss Vivien gestured to herself and Mirette.

He ran a beefy hand over his pink, bald head. "What are you looking for?"

"There should be six crates addressed to Vivien Sheffield, care of Miss Vivien's Bridal Salon," Miss Vivien said.

"Come on." He motioned for them to follow. "I'll get the delivery log."

The manager led them to an office tucked into a back corner, so small the three of them had to stand shoulder to shoulder. He sat behind the ancient desk and flipped through a thick stack of papers on a clipboard.

"Here we are. Six crates. Vivien Sheffield." He hung the clipboard back on a nail attached to the wall. "Says they were delivered to the store weeks ago."

"Well, your perfect record is shot. Those crates never made it to the store." Mirette shifted her weight back and forth as if her shoes pinched her feet.

The manager puffed up like a balloon, but before he could pop, Audrey jumped in. "Where would an order like this be stored?"

"Aisle 12-B, at the end."

"May we check to see if they were overlooked somehow?"

The manager grunted. "I'll get Galvin to take you there."

He squeezed by them to a telephone hanging on the wall outside the office. After lifting the receiver, he bellowed for his workman over the PA system.

A young Black man ran up seconds later. His coveralls hung from his lean frame, and his brown, bloodshot eyes looked as though he'd not seen his pillow in a few days. "Yes, sir, Mr. Mitchell."

"Take these ladies over to 12-B. If they find what they're looking for, get a truck and hightail it to the store."

The manager glowered at them. "Don't make visiting a habit."

"Agreed. And thank you. I'll let Mr. Wynton know you've helped us."

"This way." Galvin walked ahead.

As Audrey followed, the manager called behind her, "Just let Mrs. Wynton know. She's been on our backs like a sunburn, and I'd like to get her off it."

She walked back and extended her hand. "If we find the crates, I'll make certain she never bothers you again."

The manager crushed her slim fingers inside his stumpy ones. "Ma'am, if you'd told me that sooner, I would've walked you there myself."

She gave his hand a final firm shake.

"Let's go find your clothes, Miss Vivien." Audrey gestured for Galvin to lead the way.

When they reached 12-B, the three of them, plus Galvin, searched without success. He retrieved a tall ladder to check the highest shelves.

When he'd set it up, Audrey put her hands on the side and went to place her foot on the bottom rung, but Galvin stepped in.

"Ma'am, I can't let you up there. I'll find them crates."

"I'm perfectly capable of climbing a ladder."

"Not dressed like that, you ain't." He noted her suit and heels. "And my grandma would get after me if I let you."

He hopped on the bottom rung and climbed to the top. Galvin scanned each shelf on his way down. "You sure they're here?"

"I'm not sure of anything right now." Miss Vivien looked away from the shelf and stared at a collection of crates piled along the wall, half covered by a tattered tarp.

She craned her neck forward and squinted. "Good gracious."

She grabbed Mirette by the arm and dragged her to the area, then pulled the ragged end of the tarp away from the shipping labels. "These are our crates."

Galvin hurried down the ladder. "You sure? Boss said the store called two hours ago and said they was supposed to go back to the sender. Truck's waiting out back for them."

"What truck?" Audrey pulled the tarp off and fanned the dust away from her nose.

"There's a guy at the loading dock with a paper from the store. Says he's supposed to take these out tonight."

"Show me." Audrey took off in the direction Galvin indicated.

"We're coming too." Miss Vivien and Mirette hurried behind them.

Galvin led them to the loading dock, where an unmarked white delivery truck sat parked next to the loading bay. The driver's door hung open, but the cab of the truck was empty.

Galvin shook his head. "The guy was just here. I was getting the dolly to start loading those crates when the boss called me to come help y'all."

He went down the steps and walked to the truck. "Left the keys behind."

Audrey turned to Miss Vivien and Mirette. "This isn't one of our trucks. They all have the Wynton's logo on the side."

Miss Vivien held out her hands. "Who would want to steal clothes for the show?"

"I don't know. But we're going to get these crates back to the store, and I'm going to help you and Mirette unpack everything tonight. We'll make sure you have what you need for the show. If you don't, I'll be making calls until you do."

She called to Galvin, "Can you move this truck out of the way?"

"Yes, ma'am."

"Good. Pull one of our trucks up to the loading dock. I'll get your manager to give us some more help."

"Yes, ma'am." Galvin climbed in the truck.

Miss Evelyn would have been mortified to hear the tone in her voice, bellowing orders as if she were the man in charge.

She must pause, calm herself. Voices dripping with honey rather than vinegar spurred men on. All southern women learned that from an early age.

When she talked with the manager, she made certain sugar tempered her words. The work was done quickly, with men bowing and doing all she asked, some offering to do more.

Once the truck was loaded, she thanked the manager again. "I'm sending your entire crew loaves of Eunice's sweet potato bread."

"Could you throw in a new coffeepot? The one in our break room broke."

"You'll have the latest model Wynton's sells."

"Lady, you're all right." The manager went back to work.

When they reached the car, Miss Vivien embraced her. "I don't know what we would have done without you tonight." She held Audrey at arm's length. "You've saved our show and my sanity."

Mirette patted Audrey's arm. "I never would have believed *you* would save us."

"Mirette." Miss Vivien shook her head.

"You're welcome." There was so much more Audrey wished to say. But couldn't.

The delivery truck pulled around from the back. Galvin rolled down the driver-side window. "We'll meet you at the store."

The three of them piled into the car. As they followed the truck's red taillights through the quiet streets of Levy City, Audrey settled into the soft leather upholstery of Miss Vivien's back seat.

A deep yawn escaped as she tuned out the conversation in the front seat. As Audrey looked at the inky sky dotted with polka-dot stars, a hard truth hit. David had his sling and rocks, Joshua had his marchers, and Deborah had her faith.

She'd won a small battle on many fronts tonight. But a larger war still brewed.

And she had nothing to aid in the fight.

Chapter 28

MARY JO

Mary Jo patted her middle as Mirette raised the zipper on her dress. She'd put on her firmest girdle to hide all the turkey, corn bread dressing, and pecan pie she'd eaten for Thanksgiving. If the dress didn't fit, she'd just die.

Mirette grinned in the dressing room mirror. "Not worried, were you?"

Mary Jo wiggled into the dress's matching jacket. "A little."

"You look beautiful." Mirette patted her on the shoulder.

She looped a long pearl necklace around Mary Jo's neck. "A perfect look for you to wear to church and work."

Mary Jo noted her reflection. "I can't thank you and Miss Vivien enough for choosing me and the girls for the show. Getting four new outfits, plus coats and shoes. . ." Her eyes misted.

"Audrey will be after you if you get your makeup all runny." Mirette moved on to help another model.

Mary Jo fanned her eyes.

"Mama, you look so pretty." Carrie Rose hugged her around the knees.

She rotated her daughter so they both could see their reflections. "Not as pretty as you."

Mary Jo touched the lace collar on her daughter's midnight-blue velvet dress. "You can wear this to the Christmas service at church."

Carrie Rose held out her feet, clad in shiny patent-leather Mary Janes. "Look at my socks. Lace and flowers that match my dress."

Mary Jo cuddled her. "I love them." She looked around. "Where's your sister?"

"Miss Audrey is helping her." Carrie Rose pointed to where Penny sat in a chair where Audrey kneeled before her and buckled her shoes.

Another woman should not be dressing her child. She'd spent enough time pushing the task onto Kenny. Mary Jo clasped Carrie Rose's hand and hurried over.

"I'll do that."

Audrey stood. "We're done." She grinned at Penny. "She was a big help."

Penny giggled and fluffed the fabric of her red circle skirt. "Look Mama, I'm the color of a Christmas present."

"That's red." Carrie Rose rolled her eyes at her sister.

"It's fancier than just red." Penny stuck out her tongue.

Mary Jo clamped her jaws. If they started fussing and caused a scene, she'd be completely mortified. Kenny was already upset that they were participating, because he thought it made them look like a charity case. Their acting up would only make things worse.

And she wasn't too keen on them being friendly with Audrey. The story of how she saved the show was nice to hear, but Cissy's accounts of Mr. Wynton favoring Audrey still burned her.

But she'd be nice in front of the girls.

Audrey leaned in close. "They'll be fine. And you look wonderful."

"I may faint dead away." Mary Jo held out her quaking hands.

"Here's the secret to runways. As soon as you walk out, find a spot on the opposite wall and focus your eyes there. Head up, shoulders back, point your toes out to the side with each step and stroll to the end. Stop, turn, stroll back."

"Stare, stroll, stop, turn, stroll back," Mary Jo repeated.

"That's it."

"What about me?" Both girls jumped from their seats, waiting for their compliment.

Audrey patted their heads. "You're going to be great too."

Two of the other models rushed up. "We're supposed to be on stage in ten minutes. Is Ruby free to do our hair and makeup?"

"She's got one in the chair and four waiting." Audrey went to her makeup station and pulled a large cape from the chair. "Who's going first?"

"Are you sure Ruby can't?"

Another model dressed in sportswear squeezed by them, and Mary Jo's stomach jumped. The first group was lining up.

"I need all sportswear," Mirette called as she pinballed her way through the gathering throng of models.

She looked at the two waiting for makeup. "Y'all should have been done by now." She gave both girls a stern look. "Get in Audrey's chair."

Mirette looked at her clipboard. "Moms, I need your children here." She waved her hand as other models scooted past.

A crowd of kids and moms circled Mirette. Mary Jo ushered her girls into the mix as Miss Vivien joined the group.

"Everyone looks so nice." Miss Vivien bent down to the children's eye level. "Remember what we practiced. Walk out slowly, stop at the end of the runway, smile, then come right back."

A dozen little heads nodded, and Mary Jo caught herself joining in and stopped, hoping the other mothers hadn't noticed.

"Miss Mirette will tell you when to go on, so I need you to give your mamas a hug, then line up right over there by the black curtains," Miss Vivien said.

The girls squeezed Mary Jo's waist and took their places in line.

"They look so cute."

Mary Jo twirled around to see Gigi all made up and dressed in one of the multipiece suits from Wynton's own label.

"That gray color is fabulous on you. And the cut of the skirt is so flattering."

Gigi opened her coat, showing off a red-and-gray plaid vest. "Look at this." She unfastened the bottom two buttons and folded over the triangular edge of the fabric. "This is reversible. Do you know how many different outfits I'll get with this one suit?"

"Isn't it so sensible? I'm modeling the navy version. My vest is red-and-white checked."

A loud round of applause interrupted their talk, followed by Miss Vivien's opening remarks.

"Too bad Cissy woke up with laryngitis and had to drop out."

Gigi refastened her vest button. "Miss Vivien just marched right out there like she had no cares at all. Do you know who's wearing the showstopper?"

"I know I'm not."

"Three girls in the dressing room were bawling because they weren't chosen. Apparently Miss Vivien made her pick a long time ago and didn't tell anyone. Must be some dress."

A collection of carols mixed with fun Christmas songs began, signaling the beginning of the show. Mirette ushered the first group of models onto the stage, then readied the next one.

Gigi and Mary Jo moved farther backstage to be out of the way.

"You did a great job on your hair and makeup today, Gigi."

"Audrey did it. And you know what she said to me?" She grabbed Mary Jo and pulled her in close as a model rushed by with her hands full of clothes. "She could have let me do my own because I have a knack. Can you believe she said such to me?"

"She helped Penny buckle her shoes and was just a doll to Carrie Rose."

"And how she went to the warehouse and saved Miss Vivien's show. I don't know what to think after our lunch with her. It's like she's a completely different person."

"I hate to say this, but I can't forget all those things Cissy told us. How can someone be so nice and so nasty at the same time?"

They huddled close as the first group of models hurried from the stage to change into their next set of clothes.

"Mirette's calling us over." Mary Jo smiled at her girls as they headed for their first turn on the runway.

"I'm so nervous for them."

"They'll do fine. You've had them practicing up and down your hallway so often this week I'd bet they made ruts in the floor."

Mary Jo pressed her thumbnail against her lips, but Gigi pushed her hand away. "Don't smear your lipstick."

"Separates," Mirette whispered loudly.

The children filed in from the runway, and Mary Jo made sure to give the girls a big wave as they hurried by.

"You're on." Mirette ushered the group to the stage.

Mary Jo's knees melted, and she feared she might fall in front of all of Levy City. Except Kenny, who opted to stay home because he didn't want to be cooped up with a bunch of hens looking at clothes he couldn't afford.

Gigi gave her a gentle push from behind. "Don't look so scared."

She almost tripped on her first step to the stage. Audrey's pep talk rang in her brain.

Stare, stroll, stop, turn, stroll. Head up, shoulders back.

Before she could take it all in, she was backstage again, with Mirette pushing her to change into her next outfit. She'd been in the spotlight for the first time in her life, and she hadn't fallen or fainted.

Audrey motioned her to a dressing area behind a silk screen. She passed the suit ensemble to her on a hanger.

"You've got fifteen minutes."

Mary Jo popped around the screen. "Where are my girls?"

"Dressed and ready for their next turn."

Mary Jo emerged as Mirette directed her group to the stage.

When she returned, the girls passed in their next group, and this time they didn't look for her.

Audrey held up her next-to-last outfit, a sweet green-and-navy tartan dress with a full skirt held out by a ruffled slip. "I'll bring the girls in as soon as they finish."

Mary Jo rushed into the dress and zipped the back as Audrey brought her girls behind the screen to put on their smaller versions of the same dress.

"I love mother-daughter dresses." Carrie Rose turned around to be zipped.

Mary Jo grasped both girls' hands, and they walked together on the stage. The audience erupted with a chorus of "Aww" as they walked past. Both girls looked at her with sparkling eyes.

"They thought we were pretty, Mama," Penny said as Mary Jo helped her out of her dress.

"Always remember, pretty is as pretty does."

As she said the words, Audrey came to mind. She'd heard so many ugly things about Audrey, but all she'd ever *seen* was nice.

A high-pitched scream sliced through the air as she buttoned Carrie Rose's next dress.

Carrie Rose covered her ears. "Why is that lady screaming, Mama?"

Penny's bottom lip trembled.

Mary Jo gathered them close. "Stay right here."

She rushed from the changing room.

A group of models bunched together, and she couldn't see what they surrounded. She pushed through, then gasped.

Audrey stood in the middle with her hand clamped over Deanna's mouth to stifle her screams.

Deanna went limp in Audrey's arms. "Get her a chair."

No one moved.

She waited as the last group of children trooped to the staging area unaware.

Audrey locked eyes with Laurie. "A glass of water." The girl seemed rooted to the floor. Audrey snapped her fingers. "Go."

She then snagged the attention of another girl. "Get the chair from my makeup station."

The crowd parted as the demanded items appeared. She helped Deanna into the chair and pressed the cup of water into her hand. "Drink."

Deanna coughed twice before she swallowed a full sip. When her cheeks pinked, Audrey took the cup from her.

She looked at the crowd. "Those of you modeling formals, go get dressed."

Models peeled off and headed for dressings rooms.

The show had three more parts—formals, finale, then the showstopper—and she wasn't about to let this spell of Deanna's sabotage Miss Vivien. "If you're not in your finale clothes, get them on. Now."

Many bristled at her tone but complied. Miss Evelyn would have been disappointed with her again, but she couldn't help that right now.

"Deanna, what happened?"

She pointed to a dressing room set up at the far end of the backstage area. As Audrey stood, another girl's shrieking stopped the bustle in its tracks.

157

Audrey rushed to the spot.

"In there." The model held out a shaky finger.

Audrey walked around the partition, then pressed her fist against her mouth to suppress her scream.

Francis Tyler sat on the floor with her back against the wall. Blood matted her strawberry-blond hair.

She was dead.

Audrey backed out of the dressing area. She looked at the startled faces of the women around her.

Mary Jo emerged wearing a black cocktail dress. The wide taffeta skirt bowed over rows of white crinolines and rustled as she moved. "What's in there?"

The show's music twirled in Audrey's brain like a record on low speed. Fog seeped in and clouded out any assembling thoughts.

"Where are the formals?" Mirette hissed in the background.

Her mind snapped awake, and Audrey spun around. "Formals line up." As soon as they assembled, she sent them to Mirette. "The rest of you, gather for the finale."

"But what about the showstopper?" Betty Anne asked as she funneled into the line with the rest of the models.

"You worry about the dress you're wearing." Audrey rearranged other girls into the proper order.

The last group before formals filed in. Audrey addressed each one. "Get into your clothes for the finale. And stay out of that dressing room." She gestured toward the area where Francis was.

She called Laurie over. "Go get the store detective."

"If everyone's decent, I'm already here." Joshua stepped into the room from a back door.

"How—?"

"We got a call a few minutes ago that there was a—"

She rushed forward and clamped her hand over his mouth.

The music for the finale sounded, and the stragglers rushed into line.

When she'd pushed him out of earshot of the others, she removed her hand from his mouth.

"Forgive me." She gestured. "What you're looking for is in that room. Please keep this quiet until the show is over."

He scowled.

"Please, for Miss Vivien's sake."

His face softened. "Done."

"Thank you. Now I have to—"

"Miss Audrey?"

She swiveled to see Mary Jo's girls peeking from the changing room their mother had used.

Audrey's heart drummed. "What are you two doing here?"

"Mama told us to stay put." Carrie Rose patted her sister, who'd started whimpering.

"Your mama was right." She eased them back behind the screen. "Stay here. I'll send her right to you when she's off the runway."

With the girls safely tucked away from the fray, Audrey rushed to the secret dressing room that had been set up next door in Fine Dresses.

Miss Vivien had asked her to wear the showstopper, and she had exactly ten minutes to pull herself together and look amazing. She wasn't about to let Miss Vivien's original creation get nothing less than the standing ovation it deserved.

She locked herself in the room, opened the protective bag, and removed the most important garment in the show, and hopefully Wynton's Christmas season.

Ten minutes later, she stood at the makeup table securing one side of her hair back with a diamond-encrusted hair clip.

Audrey touched up her mascara.

"Wow, that's some dress." Joshua came into view in the mirror. "You're the calmest woman I've ever seen. No nerves or vapors at all when a dead body is lying a few feet from where you stand."

She sprayed her hair and grabbed a tube of lipstick. "Miss Vivien designed this dress, and I promised I'd model it in the show." She blotted her lips and adjusted the diamond choker around her neck.

Joshua looked away. "The show must go on."

The gown's long skirt wrapped around her legs as she faced him.

"That girl's name is Francis Tyler. I was there when Mr. Wynton hired her. She was a sweet, loyal employee. Everyone liked her."

"Somebody hated her. She's got a dent in the back of her skull." He shoved his hands in his coat pockets.

The music changed, and Audrey took one last look in the mirror. "That's my cue."

She met his gaze. "Please do what's best for her." She tipped her head toward the show. "They'd only be in the way, and now Francis can have the dignity and peace she deserves."

Audrey twirled around. "Grab the bottom of this dress and fluff it like you would a wet towel." She pulled on the white elbow-length gloves and fastened a diamond bracelet on her right wrist.

Ordering another man around. Miss Evelyn would have declared her completely devoid of femininity by now.

Joshua bent down, grabbed the hem with both hands, and gave a hearty shake.

The yards of snow-white chiffon and the taffeta underskirt billowed behind her. "Thank you. And please don't think poorly of me. There's more going on here than you realize." She stepped to the curtain where Mirette waited to send her out. The other models rushed in, gasping as they took one look at her and the dress.

When Audrey hit the bright lights of the runway, she chose her spot on the wall. She tipped her chin just right to show off the gown's wide neckline.

The audience jumped to their feet. Thunderous applause filled the room. She slowed her pace so every woman in the room could take in the cloudlike skirt that floated with each step. A spray of black flowers, hand-stitched by Mirette, trailed down the skirt to the end of the train. The black velvet bodice cinched her tiny waist.

She stopped at the end of the runway and flashed her 24-karat smile as the cameras from the *LTC* flashed. Miss Vivien's gown would make the front page.

When she headed off, Audrey caught Miss Vivien's gaze, saw the glimmering beads of tears resting on her well-powdered cheeks.

Thank you, she mouthed as Audrey moved past her.

Audrey nodded and winked.

The applause drowned out Miss Vivien's final remarks.

When Audrey entered the backstage area, models stared into space or talked with others. Some sat in small groups, wiping their tears. Mary Jo cuddled with her girls.

Gigi still wore the green silk cocktail dress she'd modeled as she talked with one of the store's detectives.

Levy City police officers milled around, asking their own sets of questions.

Audrey overhead Laurie talking with Betty Anne. "I was here when they wheeled the body out under that sheet."

Betty Anne clutched her throat. "How awful."

Joshua came to Audrey's side. "When you've changed?"

She nodded. "We'll talk."

Chapter 30

GIGI

Gigi snuck into the back of the kitchen during her lunch break and found Lilla removing a giant pan from the oven. "Smells like roast beef today."

Lilla set the pan on the stainless steel counter. "Hey fancy stranger." She pulled the oven mitts from her hands.

Gigi scanned the space. "Is Mary Margaret around?"

"She's down with the flu. Been nice and quiet around here." Lilla spooned the pan gravy over the meat and stirred the onions, potatoes, and carrots around in the drippings.

Gigi's bologna and cheese sandwich couldn't compete.

"Let me take these trays to the line, and we'll talk. I've got news."

When Lilla came back, she poured two glasses of iced tea from the oversize pitcher and gave one to Gigi, while she drank the other.

"With the boss out, I can enjoy my own sweet tea."

Gigi set her drink on the counter. "I think it's dumb that Mary Margaret won't let you drink the tea you make because you're pouring for yourself from the same pitchers used by the Whites in the dining room."

"Folks like me have been treated much worse." Lilla sat on a stool next to Gigi.

"You take Harry and Harriette Moore. Somebody bombed them in their bed on Christmas night. The nearest hospital refused to treat him and his wife because they were Colored. He died on the way to the one that would. His wife died a few days later, leaving two daughters without their parents. FBI never said who did it, but I think differently. I think the Klan came after them because they demanded Sheriff McCall be put in jail for his dirty, low-down deeds. He shot those young men from Groveland and killed one of them. Nobody did a thing to him."

Lilla released a deep breath, as if her anger had swelled to the point she couldn't sit still. "God didn't go to the trouble of making people for them to turn around and do such horrible things to each other."

"I'm sorry you get treated so badly." Gigi rewrapped the uneaten half of her sandwich and put it in her lunch bag. "Who you want me to yell at? I'd be happy to start with Mary Margaret."

"It's sad when the only time people pay attention"—Lilla paced the room, her fists balled—"is when someone else talks for you. I want to be heard on my own."

The oven buzzed, and Lilla donned her mitts and removed a pan of corn bread. "Sheriff McCall has been killing Colored folks for all kinds of shady reasons and using the law to make it right."

She went on. "Ruby McCollum and her husband were richer than a lot of White folks around here. But she couldn't get a fair trial because her skin color made her guilty in the White jurors' eyes no matter what she said that White doctor did to her. Lot of folks in Levy City feel the same way."

Her hand shook, and she struggled to loosen the corn bread squares from the pan. "My sister is a teacher at the Colored school, and my brother is a gardener and owns his business. My husband and I work hard, our kids go to school in clean clothes pressed just as nice as the White folks' kids. You won't find a house cleaner than mine in the whole state of Florida. But we still get treated like we're not even good enough to be second-best."

She paused her work for a moment. "I hear Florida has more registered Negro voters than any other state in the South. We've got to make things change."

Lilla was right. Things needed changing.

She used a spatula to loosen the squares from the pan. "This has to go to the line, so you'd better scoot and finish your lunch in the dining room."

When Gigi went to protest, Lilla shook her head. "We've said enough. Lots of ears around here." She lifted the pan and walked to the door, then stopped with her back against it ready to push her way into the serving line. "You're a good woman, a friend. Don't worry about me. The good Lord's got me covered. But this has got to stop."

She pushed the door open and carried out the tray.

Gigi walked out with her bag and saw Mary Jo coming up fast.

"I'm glad I caught you. Miss Vivien wants to talk about what happened in the show."

"I don't." Her mind was still brewing over what Lilla had said.

Mary Jo linked her arm through Gigi's. "Come sit with us."

When they entered, Alvid was waiting by the door and blocked their way. "Ladies, I haven't seen either of you in days. How are the new jobs going?"

"Miss Vivien is waiting. Excuse us."

Mary Jo guided Gigi by the elbow around him. "I try to avoid Mr. Ashley as much as possible now that he's not my boss. He just seems so snide lately."

"Lately? When was he not snide?"

Gigi joined Miss Vivien as Mary Jo sat across from them. "I didn't see anything backstage."

"That's not what I want to talk about," Miss Vivien said.

Gigi shot a look at Mary Jo, who shrugged.

"I'm going to help Audrey, and I want you two to join me," Miss Vivien said in a low tone.

Mary Jo shook her head. "I feel like I'd be stabbing Cissy in the back."

"Yeah, something seems off about all this."

Miss Vivien sat quietly for a moment. "It's only been a month since John T.'s accident. Knowing someone is out to ruin Mr. Wynton, maybe even threatening his life, might be too much for Cissy to bear right now."

"I hadn't thought about that." Mary Jo leaned her elbows on the table, then popped back as if she'd heard a silent reminder from her mother about manners.

"You think Audrey is protecting Cissy?" Hard to believe she would, because everyone in the store knew those two disliked each other.

"Someone is trying to ruin Wynton's."

"Why would you say that?" Mary Jo asked.

"Look at all the things that have happened."

Miss Vivien held up one finger. "Junior's accident."

Then another. "All the clothes for the show disappear, then poor Francis's death."

She held up three fingers. "The wasp attack on Mr. Wynton way back in August. That's too many odd things happening at this store."

Gigi had to admit Miss Vivien was making sense. "All those things do seem suspicious."

"If Audrey hadn't jumped in and helped with the show, I would have fallen flat on my face."

"Isn't this wonderful? All my favorite Wynton's ladies sitting together," Cissy cooed as she approached and claimed the last empty chair.

"Gigi, I hope you're liking your new job."

"I am." Gigi slid her lunch bag to her lap because the crumpled sides suddenly embarrassed her.

"I knew you'd be perfect there."

"You had me moved?"

"Of course I did. I couldn't have one of my good friends stuck in a job that's beneath her."

A sinking-rock feeling hit Gigi in the gut. She'd believed she had earned her way to the new job.

Cissy stared at her as if waiting for a response.

"Thank you."

Cissy reached across the table and grabbed Miss Vivien's hand. "I'm so sorry Audrey ruined the show."

Miss Vivien pulled free. "Whatever do you mean?"

Cissy looked around the table. "The dead body of course."

"She certainly didn't put it there."

"But Miss Vivien, she left that poor girl lying there in a heap while she pranced down the runway. And everyone knows she's the one who paid Francis to call John T. and me home from Miami."

"She did what?" Mary Jo shrieked.

"Mr. McKinnon told me just this morning that Francis confessed to him that Audrey offered her one hundred in cash to call our hotel and pretend to be her. Days later, she's dead, and Audrey barely blinked an eye over it."

Mary Jo sat back and crossed her arms. "Why would she do that?"

"I honestly think she hoped we'd be so tired driving we'd crash." Cissy's voice caught as she grabbed Mary Jo's napkin and alternated blotting her eyes and nose.

Miss Vivien looked square in Cissy's face. "That's a pretty serious accusation. Did Mr. McKinnon say he had proof?"

Cissy blew her nose, wadded up the napkin, and tossed it on Mary Jo's tray. "Not yet. But he's retired from the army and worked in intelligence in Europe and Korea, I think. He's an expert at finding the truth."

"Let's all pray he does." Miss Vivien brushed a piece of lint from her black skirt. "Fine Dresses has been calling me with requests for the showstopper, and Mirette has been reading the comment cards to me all morning. Nothing but praise for the show."

Cissy popped up like a jack-in-the-box. "Woo-hoo, Miss Vivien." She rushed off.

Mary Jo slid Cissy's chair under the table. "She got over her laryngitis fast."

"She has made a remarkable recovery. Must have gotten some kind of overnight cure from one of Mr. Wynton's nurses," Miss Vivien said.

Gigi had thought the same thing as soon as Cissy opened her mouth.

"I'm just glad she's better." Mary Jo rose from her chair. "As far as what we talked about earlier, I'm still unsure."

"How about you, Gigi?" Miss Vivien got up to leave.

How about her? Gigi sat and looked between the two of them.

Cissy had moved her into the new job, but Audrey was trying to help Mr. Wynton. He'd believed she'd move up on her own.

"I'm in."

Now to sway Mary Jo. "Remember how you said Audrey helped you on your first day and how nice she was to your girls at the fashion show?"

"Yes. But all those things Cissy just said—"

"We aren't doing this for Cissy. Or Audrey. It's for Mr. Wynton." Gigi took her bag from her lap and stood.

Mary Jo sighed. "Count me in."

Miss Vivien clasped her hands in thanks. "Meet me at the salon after work, and we'll go see Audrey."

Chapter 31

AUDREY

Audrey felt the scratchy edge of something tucked behind her steno notebook. She pulled her drawer farther open.

She choked back the bile crawling up from her stomach. A brick the size of a grapefruit lay lodged among her unsharpened pencils. Dried blood mixed with long strands of blond hair were stuck to its pointed end.

Hair the same shade as Francis Tyler's.

Joshua had said someone hit her in the head with a hard object.

She grabbed a sheet of typing paper and wrapped it around the brick, then another when the jagged edge still protruded.

Footsteps clicked in the hall. Audrey stuffed the brick back in the drawer and shoved it closed as Joshua walked into the office and removed his hat.

"Do you have a minute?"

"Sure." Audrey drawled out the word to give her heart time to stop pumping at triple speed as he pulled a chair over.

It didn't work.

"Is there something in particular you wanted to ask me?" Like did she have the murder weapon in her desk drawer?

He rested his arms on her desk and leaned forward. "During the show, you told me there was more going on here than I realized. What did you mean?"

"I think someone is trying to ruin Mr. Wynton by sabotaging the store."

Joshua seemed to be stewing on her thoughts as he looked at her.

If he'd hoped this might unnerve her, he'd wasted his time. She'd grown accustomed to being stared at by men a long time ago.

He curled his lips into a slow, lazy smile. "I think you're right."

"You do?"

"That surprises you?"

"I'm wondering how you've come to this conclusion."

"I might say the same thing to you, Miss Penault." He emphasized the French pronunciation of her name.

She matched his smile with one of her own. "Women's intuition. What's your secret?"

Joshua rested his hat on her desktop. "I don't know why people in this store don't like you. You're loaded with charm."

"Thank you ever so much. You've brought a little light into what was otherwise a dreary day."

He bounced his foot a few times. "Everything I hear from the store's gossip vine says I should be choosing you as my top suspect."

She resisted the urge to swivel her chair and press her knee against her desk drawer. "That's no surprise."

"And you're not bothered by this?"

Audrey took her time answering. "I'm here to do my job. I answer to Mr. Wynton. Not the store gossips."

"I suppose it's a waste of time asking if you stabbed Mr. Wynton's nurse in the neck and pushed her down the stairs before you left his house the other day." He uncrossed his legs and rose from his chair. "One of these days, I'd like to meet and swap notes. Maybe over a steak dinner." He slid the chair back to its original place.

"Unless you're one of those girls who only eats fancy dishes I can't pronounce or a bowl of grass clippings with a little french dressing."

Audrey fed a new sheet of paper into her typewriter. "I should get back to work."

He settled his hat on his head. "Of course."

Joshua took a few steps backward toward the door, then stopped and turned. "I saw those photographs of you in the other department next to where the fashion show was held. They're something."

Audrey collected a stack of papers from her inbox requiring her attention. "That was a long time ago."

"Why'd you retire? Those are beautiful photos, like pieces of art."

She met his gaze. "I loved modeling. But I wanted something more."

"And Mr. Wynton saw you had brains plus a good head for business."

"Yes."

"Good for him. And you."

He tipped his hat and left the office, closing the door behind him.

Audrey slumped in her chair and whistled with relief. Joshua McKinnon complimented her drive and brains. Only Mr. Wynton and her daddy had ever done so.

But was he sincere or trying to butter her up?

She pulled the brick from her desk. Her fingers shook as she unzipped the top of her satchel and crammed the weapon within. Since she was everyone's top suspect, the brick was going home with her until she figured out what to do next.

The door opened, and she half expected to see Joshua returning, but instead Miss Vivien, Mary Jo, and Gigi entered.

She struggled to yank the zipper shut around the brick. Once closed, her satchel bulged like a snake that'd eaten a whole chicken.

"Are you busy?" The three of them lined up like children waiting to be chosen for a game in a schoolyard.

"I've got a minute." Audrey put her satchel in the closet and closed the door.

Miss Vivien looked at the other two before she spoke. "We want to help you."

"You're serious?"

"As a bolt of lightning," Gigi piped in.

"What about you, Mary Jo? Will your husband mind your getting mixed up in all this?"

"Probably." She looked down at her hands. "But he and I owe Mr. Wynton."

Audrey scanned their faces. "I have to tell y'all, this will get messy.

Joshua McKinnon has been digging up who-knows-what around the store."

Gigi raised her chin. "He's talked to me twice. I don't care. I saw Francis on that gurney when they carried her out. I want to make sure no one else ends up that way. Especially not Mr. Wynton."

Audrey stood. "Can y'all come to my house, maybe one evening after work? And we can't talk about this. To anyone."

Miss Vivien held up her hand as if she were testifying in court. "I'll keep Mirette out of the employee elevator myself, sworn to secrecy on threat of bodily harm."

"Perfect. We'll meet Thursday night, say seven thirty?"

"Could we make it earlier? That's my girls' bedtime, and I need to be there."

"How about Saturday morning?"

"Sounds like our best option." Miss Vivien looked at the other two.

"I'll make the girls' breakfast and come on over," Mary Jo said.

Miss Vivien looked down the line. "How about you, Gigi?"

"Bobby's working all weekend, so I've got nothing better to do."

"Saturday then." Audrey wrote a note to herself in her steno pad.

A knock on the door caught their attention. A male employee stood in the doorway. "Is Mrs. Wynton in?"

Miss Vivien gestured to the other two. "Audrey needs to get back to work."

The phone on her desk rang, and Audrey answered on the third ring. "Mr. Wynton's office. How may I help you?" She mouthed thanks as the ladies exited into the hall.

"This is Laurel, down in Young Miss. I need to speak to Mrs. Wynton."

Audrey gestured to the gentleman to take a seat. "This is Audrey. What do you need?"

"We wanted to talk about setting up a special teen advisory board for Christmas. Have the kids talk about what they want for gifts this year, holiday parties, etc."

Audrey looked at the calendar on her desk. "What day were you thinking of doing this?" A teen board would be a great activity to add to Wynton's holiday lineup and get the kids and their mothers into the store.

"We weren't going to choose a date until we talked with Mrs. Wynton."

"I'm meeting with Mr. Wynton later today. I'll ask him and give you details tomorrow. When would be the best time to talk?"

"Afternoon?"

Audrey finished writing the details. "I'll come by after two."

"Good. See you then."

She hung up and focused on the gentleman from Sales. "You have my full attention."

He moved to the front of her desk. "I just got word from the printers that the Christmas coloring books we ordered to give out to the kids won't be here until the twentieth."

She stared at him a moment. "That won't do at all."

"No, it won't." His face bore an expression of pure frustration. "I've called three times, and they won't budge."

"I'll call them." She looked at the calendar on her desk. "We want them here tomorrow to coincide with the Christmas parade."

He blew through his lips. "I don't see how calling again is going to help."

"You go back to work, and I'll deal with getting the books to us by early tomorrow."

"Waste of time," he muttered as he walked out.

Audrey dialed Packard's Printing. It was a waste of time. For him. But she possessed a secret weapon that man from Sales did not.

Charm. And utter determination.

Packard's picked up after several rings. "Hello, this is Audrey Penault calling from Wynton's. I understand there's a problem with our order."

Once she'd hung up, she dialed Sales, who answered right away.

"Yes, this is Audrey. Please let everyone know the Christmas coloring books will be arriving here tomorrow morning at six. Can you make certain the gentleman who was just up here in Mr. Wynton's office gets this message? Thank you."

Audrey sat back in her chair and rubbed away the pinches in her shoulders.

At day's end, after she'd straightened her desk and placed the cover on her typewriter, Audrey gathered her things and hurried to the garage. The bulge in her satchel bounced against her leg as she walked to her car. On the drive home, she yawned so many times that she decided she would skip making supper and go straight to a long, hot bath.

As she got out to open her garage door, her car's headlights illuminated the edge of the wall. A strange shadow caught her eye. She walked closer to inspect and froze as her T-Bird's engine whirred behind her.

A chunk of brick, the exact size as the one hidden in her satchel, had been chiseled from the corner of her house.

Chapter 32

MARY JO

The Cottages, Audrey's neighborhood, was far too fancy for the likes of Mary Jo. The houses' windows sneered, reminding her that she didn't belong among their jade-green, cut-to-perfection lawns, gardens, gazebos, and swimming pools.

The sun spread pinkish-orange rays that hovered above the indigo water as she pulled into Audrey's driveway. Miss Vivien and Gigi were walking up the sidewalk, and Audrey waved to her from the porch. Kenny would be proud she'd found her way there without getting lost.

The smell of freshly brewed coffee and apple turnovers met her when Audrey welcomed her into the house. She was dressed in a dark green pin-tucked dress, which she protected with a green gingham and lace apron. Never in her life would she have pegged Audrey as the domestic type.

And her house didn't disappoint Mary Jo's expectations. A light blue rug dotted with white and pink roses covered the polished wood floor in her living room. A beige curving couch and two blue-and-beige chairs sat arranged around a white brick fireplace. Paintings and vases that looked like they came from *Better Homes and Gardens* magazine sat on open shelves, her mantel, and a coffee table. Everything was dust-free and in its place.

Audrey showed them to a breakfast nook with a large window over-looking a rose garden.

"Who needs coffee?" She held up a pot.

After filling their cups, she passed each of them a turnover on a matching dessert plate. She even served cubed sugar like Miss Vivien did. That must have been something the fancier folks preferred.

Mary Jo stirred her coffee as yellow bands of sunlight pierced the sky. "You must love watching sunrises and sunsets."

Audrey sat down beside her. "I do."

Mary Jo sliced off a sliver of the pastry. "Have you lived here long?"

"My parents built this house before I was born, but I moved in two years ago. I lived in a house out on County Road 44, north of Levy City, when I was young."

"You grew up in the country?" Gigi stared as if Audrey had said she'd lived on the moon.

"Until I was four."

"This tastes like Eunice's apple pie. Did you get this from the store?" Gigi asked.

Audrey shook her head. "Eunice's recipe, but I baked the turnovers this morning."

Mary Jo stopped midchew. "You had time to bake and get your house straightened this early?"

The battle to keep up with cooking, cleaning, and laundry exhausted her, and she'd give anything to have their house this neat and tidy anytime of the day.

"I only have myself to keep up with." Audrey took a bite of her turnover and managed to look glamorous as she wiped a drip of gooey apple filling from her chin with a cream-colored, lace-trimmed napkin.

Miss Vivien raised her cup to take a sip. "Rosalee retired?"

"Yes, ma'am. When I came back to Levy City, she wanted to move to Memphis to take care of her aging mother. Having a maid didn't feel right anymore, so I paid her for the rest of that year and helped her move. She makes me write her every week to make sure I'm eating and sleeping enough. If I forget, she threatens to come down here and get after me with a switch."

"Good for her." Miss Vivien tipped her cup, and the steam from the coffee within twirled about her cheeks. "What did you want to talk about that couldn't be said at the store?"

"Has Joshua McKinnon talked with y'all?"

"He asked me if I saw anybody chatting with Francis. I hadn't seen her, until. . .you know." Gigi poked at her last bite of food.

"He came up to the salon last Monday, asking about different things around the store."

"When he came to me, I told him I didn't have time to notice anything during the show because I was too busy trying to keep my girls from getting squirrely," Mary Jo added. "If I had known there was a dead girl in there, I would have grabbed my babies and run home, party dresses and all."

Miss Vivien set down her cup and looked across the table at Audrey. "Has he told you anything?"

"He's heard a lot of rumors about who might be guilty."

"Who is he saying is the prime suspect?" Miss Vivien folded her napkin and laid it next to her dishes.

Audrey released a long breath. "Me."

Surprise hit Mary Jo like a rock, while Gigi scowled and screwed her lips in a crooked line.

Miss Vivien stared straight at Audrey. "Why on earth does he think you're responsible?"

"The store's gossip chain. Who knows what he's heard there. Or believes."

Mary Jo lowered her gaze to the table. She'd believed everything she'd heard.

"Phooey," Miss Vivien said. "That's ridiculous. He needs good strong proof to make a claim like that. My bet is he's just trying to scare you."

"I don't trust him." Gigi stuck her spoon in her cup. "Always smiling, acting like he's just being friendly when he asks you something."

Audrey went to the kitchen for a serving tray.

"Who do you think is doing all these terrible things, Audrey?" As Mary Jo placed her dishes on the tray, she noticed the portrait of a woman in a flowing white gown next to a pink flower bush painted on the surface. If she used a pretty tray at home, maybe the girls would be more apt to want to help with the dishes.

"Before the accident, all clues led to Junior."

"Junior?" the other ladies chorused.

"You can't mean he'd try to kill his own father?" Mary Jo could barely get the words out. Cissy talked all the time about how much her husband loved his father. The trouble between them was caused by Audrey.

Or was it?

Audrey set down the tray. "I don't think he wanted to kill Mr. Wynton, but he did want him out of the way."

She set their dishes in her sink. "Right after Mr. Wynton was stung by the wasp, I took a phone call from George Crawford, the head of United Merchant's Federation. He claimed he had an agreement with Junior to buy the store. December first was the deadline to finish the deal."

This news sent a jolt through Mary Jo. "That's the end of this week. Do you think the deal is still on?" New owners might mean newer employees being let go. Women always went first.

"No, Mr. Wynton shut that down when he recovered from the wasp episode."

Mary Jo's fear deflated like a balloon. "Thank goodness."

Audrey grew serious. "Not yet. Someone is still trying to get rid of Mr. Wynton and ruin the store."

Miss Vivien gazed at the others. "Audrey's making perfect sense when you look at all that's happened."

She looked straight to Audrey. "Do you know who's behind all this?"

"I have an idea."

Mary Jo pounded her fists on the tabletop. "We have to tell Cissy, the police, and that Mr. McKinnon so they can be caught right away."

"Not yet." Audrey scanned their faces.

"Why not? This person could try to murder someone else. Maybe even one of us." Gigi said out loud what Mary Jo's insides had screamed.

"I need more proof, someone to ask the right questions around the store. If I do—"

"No one will give you any answers because you're doing the asking." The disgusted tone in Miss Vivien's voice cut through the room.

"Then we'll ask them." Gigi looked around the table.

The thought of asking people questions churned Mary Jo's stomach like those twirling rides at the county fair. "What do we need to know?"

"How Francis got mixed up in all of this. Mr. McKinnon said she'd been paid a hundred dollars to impersonate me. Who around the store has that kind of money to throw around? And why scare Junior and Cissy into coming back home, then blame it on me?"

"Not to mention who stole the clothes and left poor Francis there *during* the show," Miss Vivien said.

"I heard some shoppers saying they weren't going to come to Wynton's anymore. They're going to the other small dress shops and men's stores in town. My neighbor said she's thinking of driving to Tampa and doing her shopping at Maas Brothers until all this madness dies down." Repeating all these bad rumors wasn't helpful, but Mary Jo figured the group needed to know.

"Parson's Menswear put an ad in the *LTC* that they've hired extra help to ensure a safe, enjoyable holiday shopping experience. All the other stores will be watching to see if this tactic works."

Gigi wrinkled her nose. "That's so tacky."

"That's the world of retail." Audrey shrugged. "But if we figure out who's behind all this in time, we'll save the holiday season."

She met Miss Vivien's gaze. "The fashion show was a smash. Foot traffic in the store is up 5 percent over last year, and the sales for children's fashions, ladies' suits, and accessories have been strong this past week. We've had twenty requests for the showstopper in just the last three days. Wynton's hasn't had a dress make that kind of splash in years."

"That's all good, right?" Gigi leaned her elbows on the table as if she couldn't wait to hear the answer.

"Very good. But another incident in the paper and this season sinks faster than a rock." For the first time, worry flashed in Audrey's eyes.

"Then we'll get you those answers." Miss Vivien looked at her watch. "And work on squelching the rumors about the Hatchet."

She winked at Audrey.

"Yes, ma'am. I hear that Hatchet lady is a real battle-ax," Audrey said.

They laughed together as they all rose to leave, but Mary Jo caught a flicker of hurt in Audrey's eyes as she poked fun at herself.

She seemed so human. A far cry from the ogre Alvid, Cissy, and the rest of the store talked about.

As Mary Jo drove home, her mind replayed their conversations, making her head spin in confusion.

Audrey painted a different picture of the Wynton household than Cissy.

And she offered her support and encouragement when Mary Jo was ready to tuck tail and run home. And now she was rallying to save Mr. Wynton and the store—which helped all the employees, even those who talked about her behind her back.

But Cissy's account of her as a home wrecker, out for her own gain, still seemed so believable.

As Mary Jo pulled into her driveway, her brain mulled the same question over and over: *Which version was the real Audrey Penault?*

Chapter 33

GIGI

MEET ME AT THE CLOCK AFTER WORK.
—A

As Gigi waited in the cafeteria line, Lilla peeked through the kitchen door and mouthed, *Come see me.* Gigi did her best to agree without being seen, then found a seat alone where she could eat fast.

Lilla met her at the back door of the kitchen when she arrived.

"I only have a minute. I heard you're working with Audrey, and I got something to tell you."

"How did you know—"

Lilla held up her hand. "We hear too." She looked back to make sure they were alone.

"The day before the fashion show, I was hurrying home from my sister's house, and I had to go through St. Cloud."

"What were you doing in St. Cloud? That's a sundown town. They'll haul you off to jail as soon as the sun sets."

Lilla mashed her lips together in a straight line. "That's why we were in an all-fire hurry to get out of there. Now hush and let me finish."

Gigi mimed zipping her lips.

Lilla continued. "It was late afternoon, and we stopped at a fruit stand to get some orange juice. A car pulled up next to us, and I saw Francis Tyler sitting on the passenger side. The man who was driving her is out in the dining room right now."

Gigi's heart drummed like a band. "Where?"

"He's sitting at the big table at the back, talking to Mr. Ashley."

179

The door leading to the line opened, and a server peeked in. "We need more peas and carrots."

Lilla slid oven mitts over her hands and leaned back to avoid the rising cloud of steam as she pulled the lid off a tall silver pot simmering on the stove. "Tell Audrey." She headed out the door with the food.

Gigi spent the rest of the day selling candy and fruit, but her head was stuck on what Lilla's news might mean.

She met Miss Vivien and Mary Jo at the store entrance by the clock. The air puffed around them, rustling the branches of the hedges and the petunia petals, hinting colder weather might come before December arrived.

Audrey came out the revolving door. "Up for a walk?"

They grouped together, their heels striking in a quartet as they strolled along.

Once they'd ventured two blocks from the store, Gigi shared her news. "Lilla told me she saw Francis with a man from the store the day before the show. They were out near St. Cloud."

Audrey looked at Gigi. "That's two hours from here, in the middle of nowhere."

"Did Lilla say who this man was?" Miss Vivien asked as they stepped down from a curb and crossed a brick side street.

Gigi moved to avoid bumping into a man walking in the opposite direction. "She didn't know his name, but he ate lunch with Alvid today."

Audrey stopped in front of a shop. "Let's pop into the Coffee House."

As they moved to the shop's door, Gigi saw her reflection in the large windows.

She wouldn't have believed this two months ago. Here she was dressed in a suit, gloves, and the cutest matching hat, heading in for coffee with her boss's secretary, Levy City's legendary bridal consultant, and the cutest little housewife in town.

Like she was really somebody.

The host greeted Audrey like she was family and led them to a small white table surrounded by red wrought-iron chairs.

Audrey settled across from Gigi. "They have the best cherry Cokes here."

"I'll just have one of those. Then I need to scoot home and cook supper," Mary Jo said.

Gigi's stomach growled, and Audrey slid the menu to her. "Let's grab an early supper." She tapped the picture of a hamburger and fries plate. "The best in town."

"You eat hamburgers?"

"I do."

"I haven't had one in years. Sounds perfect." Miss Vivien waved at two ladies sitting nearby.

Once they'd placed their orders, Gigi churned her Coke with her red-and-white straw. "Do you have some new information?"

Audrey sipped her Coke, leaving a faint red lipstick smear on her paper straw. "No, I wanted to take time to get to know y'all a little better."

"Why? We aren't anything alike."

Audrey cocked a brow. "We both like makeup and are good at applying it."

Gigi guffawed so loudly it echoed through the room. "Mine looks nothing like yours. And costs a whole lot less."

"You've studied the fashion magazines, haven't you? Tried out all the new techniques, like Audrey Hepburn's eyeliner?"

Gigi took in her words. "But I don't look like you do."

Audrey stirred the ice in her glass. "You shouldn't. Your style looks great on you."

Mary Jo piped in. "I've been telling her that for months."

Gigi harrumphed. "Until a few weeks ago, I wore hairnets and a waitress uniform every day."

"But you still had a Marilyn Monroe way about you." Audrey sipped her Coke.

Never had a woman like Audrey complimented Gigi. Usually they picked at her like an angry mockingbird. "Are you kidding me? I'm nothing like Marilyn."

"Stop being so hard on yourself." Miss Vivien tipped her head as if she meant her words to be taken seriously.

Audrey dunked a french fry into some ketchup and pointed it at Gigi.

"If you do well in Florida Delights—and I think you will—you could be moved to Cosmetics sometime next year." Audrey stuffed the fry into her mouth.

"Is this on the level?" Gigi expected Audrey to laugh and say she was joking.

Audrey opened the burger bun and squeezed a dollop of mustard onto the lone pickle. "You'd be perfect. You know makeup, you follow the trends, and I think you'd love talking with shoppers about the products." She took a bite in the most ladylike way Gigi had ever seen.

"How do you do that?"

Audrey finished chewing her bite, then swallowed. "Do what?"

"Eat so daintily." Gigi rolled her eyes. "Everything you do is always so ladylike."

Audrey sipped her Coke. "Charm school."

"Like Miss Jenna Johnson's classes Wynton's has every summer for the kids?" Mary Jo asked.

Audrey shook her head. "I was sent away to a school for well-brought-up ladies when I was eleven."

Gigi pursed her lips in her most snobbish way. "Oh."

"Exactly." Audrey wiped her mouth.

Gigi chewed a bite. "I guess it paid off. Mr. Wynton couldn't hire just anybody to be his secretary. He needs a girl who knows how to act."

Audrey hesitated. "I've known Mr. Wynton all my life. He was my daddy's best friend. When Daddy died, Mr. Wynton stepped in and took care of me because my mother couldn't."

"What was wrong with your mother?"

Audrey's brows lowered, and Gigi worried a telling-off was about to be launched at her.

Instead, Audrey stole a look at Miss Vivien. "My mother is. . .unique." She ate the last of her burger.

"I have to know what that means." Mary Jo sipped her Coke.

Audrey took a long time to answer. "Mother married and buried three husbands, including my father. She has divorced two others and is currently in Europe shopping for number six. The last thing she needed then was a daughter hanging around. Mother took all the money Daddy left me to go husband hunting, leaving eleven-year-old me at Miss Evelyn's."

"How awful." Mary Jo stared.

Audrey went on. "Mr. Wynton paid for my schooling. I graduated at sixteen, so he talked me into modeling in one of the spring shows. He'd invited some designer friends, who asked me to model for them in New York City. He paid for my trip there, and soon after, an agency saw me in a show at Macy's, signed me, and moved me to Paris when I was barely seventeen. I modeled there until the war."

Gigi propped her chin on her fists. "This is like something from a movie."

The waiter came and removed their dirty plates and dropped off the check. Audrey opened her purse and took out her wallet. "During the war, I clerked at a department store in New York City, took business classes at night, and came home to work for Mr. Wynton."

"My life's nothing like yours." Gigi sipped the last of her Coke.

"Nonsense." Miss Vivien stirred a spoonful of sugar into her coffee. "We've all had to make choices to survive. And been judged for them."

"People judged you, Miss Vivien?" Mary Jo slurped the last of her Coke.

"When my husband, Carter, died, folks thought I should close my shop and focus on my children. I couldn't do that. Carter left me a little money, but we had a mortgage and other bills. If I wanted to keep our house and clothe and feed my children, I had to work. One elderly lady told me I was scarring them by not being home."

Mary Jo hit the tabletop. "One of the mothers at my daughters' school told me that exact same thing."

The need to share hit Gigi. "I'm twice divorced and barely finished high school."

"Which means nothing." Audrey handed the money and check to their waiter when he stopped at their table. "Mr. Wynton knew you were going to do well at the store the moment he met you. You have a don't-quit spirit."

"She's absolutely right on that." Miss Vivien touched up her lipstick. "I've got a Junior League meeting tonight, and since I'm the president, it won't do if I'm late. Is there anything else we need to talk about, Audrey?"

"What I wanted to say ties in with Lilla's news."

"You think Francis was mixed up in this?" Mary Jo leaned forward on her elbows.

"Joshua told me Francis was seen riding around with me in my car the day before her death." Audrey shook her head. "Never happened."

"Why would someone make that up?"

"I don't know, Gigi. But Cissy Wynton just walked in, and we'd better hush for now." Audrey rose from her seat. "Thanks for meeting with me."

"Well, what a surprise." Cissy spoke so loudly, other diners gawked.

Cissy took Audrey's empty chair. "Don't leave on my account." She grinned as Audrey moved out of her way.

"Have a lovely evening, ladies." Audrey's professional mask returned, and it was a marvel how quickly her entire personality changed.

"I hope I'm not intruding on a private party." Cissy's eyes narrowed as she watched Audrey leave.

Gigi jumped in quick. "We were talking about the store."

Cissy scanned her face. "Speaking of, you won't believe what I just heard." Her eyes sparkled with a hard light.

"I can't stay." Miss Vivien rose. "See y'all tomorrow."

Gigi jumped from her chair. "I've got to get back to catch the late bus." She grabbed her purse.

Mary Jo checked her watch. "I'm late." She pulled her sweater from the back of her chair.

Cissy shot up from her chair like popcorn in hot oil. "Drat. I was looking forward to some girl talk. We'll meet for lunch tomorrow."

Mary Jo slipped on her sweater. "I can't. I'm working the afternoon-to-evening shift. Kenny's not too happy about that."

"I'm off tomorrow." Gigi pushed in her chair. "I won't be back until Monday."

"But I've got loads to tell you. There's something big happening at the store."

Mary Jo flipped her hair out of her collar. "Monday, then?"

Gigi pulled on her gloves. "I can do that."

Cissy walked to the door with them.

"Did you walk here from the store, Cissy?" Mary Jo held the door open for them to exit.

"I don't walk. I drive." She pulled car keys from her purse. "See you Monday."

She left without another word.

"I think we hurt her feelings." Mary Jo fastened the chain clasp on her sweater.

Once outside, Gigi wiggled her hat onto her head. "I wasn't in the mood for gossip."

"Seems disrespectful to poor Francis, doesn't it?" Mary Jo said softly.

"Disrespectful and tacky. Bobby won't believe this day."

"How so?"

"I gabbed at the Coffee House with three of the most glamorous women in Levy City. And somehow, I belonged there."

Mary Jo stepped in front of her. "You listen to me, Gigi Woodard. You aren't dirt under anybody's shoes. Sure you made some mistakes in your life, but who cares? God forgives all of us, rich or poor." She stood taller as if to make her point stick. "So don't you ever let me hear you saying such again."

"That goes for us as well."

Gigi spun to see Miss Vivien and Audrey standing a few feet behind them.

"Where did you come from?"

"Audrey and I have been sitting on this bench, waiting for y'all. We had a few more things we wanted to talk about, without the extra ears."

Audrey and Miss Vivien sandwiched Gigi as they all walked toward the store.

"Do you know the man Lilla showed you?" Audrey asked as they waited for cars to pass so they could cross the street.

"No. But he wears really nice suits and knows Alvid."

They reached the front entrance of the store and stopped by the clock.

"Finding out his name and how he knew Francis should be our next step," Miss Vivien said.

Gigi sighed. "Maybe it's time for me to eat lunch with Alvid."

"Thank you, Gigi." Audrey entered the revolving door at the store's front entrance.

"I've got to get home." Mary Jo fished her car keys from her purse.

Miss Vivien did the same. "I'll have to rush to make my League meeting. Bye." She hurried toward the garage with Mary Jo.

Gigi walked to the bench and sat down to wait for the bus.

Chapter 34

VIVIEN

Vivien waved to Nelson as she pulled into the parking garage. Maybe someday she'd ask Mr. Wynton for her own space on the first floor, but for now the extra walk loosened her stiff muscles in the mornings.

She locked her car door, then buttoned her suit jacket against the nip in the air.

"Good morning, Miss Vivien."

She saw Mary Jo standing nearby. "You're an early bird."

"I've got big news for Audrey."

Vivien held a finger to her lips.

Mary Jo grimaced as a red hue crept up her neck. "Where is my mind?"

Vivien linked her arm through Mary Jo's. "At home with your husband and little girls."

She pulled Mary Jo along with her. "Nelson's the only one around, and he won't say anything."

"Are you sure?"

Vivien released her hold. "Sure as the day is long."

They took the sidewalk leading to the employee's entrance.

"I've got news," Gigi called as she held the door open for them.

Mary Jo and Vivien traded side glances and grins as they entered together.

"What'd I do?" Gigi asked.

"We talk too much," Mary Jo said as they made their way onto the main floor.

"I can't help it. I haven't had anyone to talk to all weekend. Bobby and

I were supposed to go out, but he stood me up."

"Again?" Mary Jo said as they reached the employee elevators.

"It's this new job calling him in at all kinds of wild hours."

They entered, and Vivien pinned Gigi with a stern look. "How many times has this young man of yours done this?"

"I've lost count."

Vivien sighed. "It's a delicate dance we girls do with our men's jobs, isn't it?"

"He loves it, so how can I fuss?"

The car dinged to a stop on their floor, and she waited as the operator moved the gate to allow them to pass.

Vivien poked Gigi when they stepped from the car. "If he doesn't straighten up, you let me know. Mirette can pop him on his noggin with her purse."

Gigi and Mary Jo giggled, then fell into step as they headed for the executive suite.

A man's angry bellows and Audrey's calm but firm responses spilled from the office.

Vivien stopped. "Let's wait."

The man's voice boomed louder. "The board is meeting tonight to vote him out, and there is nothing you can do, Audrey. It's only a temporary move until he's well enough to return."

The board was voting Mr. Wynton out? There was only one man who could run Wynton's. Vivien had half a mind to march right in there and tell this man so.

Audrey spoke up fast. "You and I both know these types of moves are never temporary, Mr. Loring. Who does the board want as his replacement—you?"

"Whether you like it or not, Cissy now holds all the Wynton family's voting shares. She's on our side. You can't stop this."

"You might be surprised, Mr. Loring."

Mr. Loring spewed words that Vivien and the others couldn't make out, which was probably best.

Vivien moved closer and saw him circling the floor with his fist pressed into his forehead. "Of course."

He swung round to Audrey and jammed his finger at her face. "You finagled him into signing something over to you, didn't you?" He threw another string of words no grandmother would have approved of.

"Isn't this a pretty picture? With the old man gone, you probably get everything." He held his hands out as if he meant to strangle Audrey, then fisted his fingers. "Joshua McKinnon will love hearing this."

"Be very careful what you share and who you threaten, Mr. Loring." Audrey's tone sent chills down Vivien's arms.

Gigi moved closer. "Who is this Mr. Loring?"

"He's head of Legal and an adviser to the board."

Mary Jo leaned against Gigi's back and peeked into the room. "That's Mr. Loring?"

"He's out to get Audrey." Gigi scowled.

"He's leaving." Vivien ushered Gigi and Mary Jo from the door.

They stood in a close huddle when Mr. Loring barreled from the office and stomped down the hallway in the opposite direction.

"Come on." Vivien led them to the office.

Audrey wasn't near her desk when they entered. "Audrey?"

The door to Mr. Wynton's office was open, so Vivien headed there with Mary Jo and Gigi close on her heels.

They found Audrey rifling through a safe in the wall. "Are you all right?"

Audrey jerked her head at them. "I'm fine."

She held two pill bottles and a gold compact, which she quickly pressed into her leg, hiding them from view.

"Are you sure?" Vivien moved closer and patted Audrey's back.

"No, really, I'm fine."

"We heard you arguing with that man." Mary Jo craned her neck, trying to get a better look at the items in Audrey's hands.

Audrey put the items back in the safe, then slammed the door and spun the dial. She pushed the portrait that hid the entire thing into place. "I'll handle Mr. Loring."

She motioned for them to follow her out. "What can I do for y'all?"

"We've got news." Vivien signaled to Gigi. "Why don't you go first."

"One of Bobby's buddies from the loading dock told me that on the day of the show, there was a strange white delivery truck parked in the loading zone. They couldn't find the driver to tell him to move, so they called store security. The truck stayed there for about an hour or so. Then a man in dark coveralls ran out the back door of the store and drove off in the truck. None of them got a good look at him because he had his collar flipped up and his hat pulled way down on his head."

"We think he's the one who killed Francis and left her in the dressing room. Nobody paid attention to him because he looked like a delivery man," Vivien said quietly.

"But how did he unlock the backstage door?" Audrey met Vivien's gaze. "Someone in the store had to be working with him."

Mary Jo joined in. "I have news too. Edie told me Francis was dating Mr. Loring."

"What?" Vivien looked at the other two. "His wife passed away less than a year ago. And he's got a good twenty years on Francis."

Mary Jo shrugged. "Edie and Francis were best friends. She said they went out several times, starting in October."

"Did you have something too, Miss Vivien?" Audrey asked.

"One of my clients was almost run down by a white truck speeding out of the parking lot the day of the show. Her description fits the truck we saw at the warehouse."

Audrey's brain clicked through these new details. "I'll add all of this to my notes. Good work."

"And if Mr. Loring threatens you again, let me know. Mirette and I will have a talk with him." Vivien gathered Gigi and Mary Jo together like a clutch of chicks and ushered them toward the door.

"Don't worry about me. I've got the Christmas parade coming this weekend. Mr. Loring is the least of my worries."

When Vivien returned to the salon, Mirette was pressing a wide swath of fabric and looked up from her work. "Get your news delivered?"

"I did."

Mirette resumed her ironing, and Vivien checked her appointment book. Her mind wandered back to the argument between Audrey and Mr. Loring as two points kept niggling at her: What power was Mr. Loring referring to, and why did Mr. Wynton sign it over to Audrey? And even more concerning, who was this murderer in the white truck?

The entrance door chimed as her first bride of the day arrived. Vivien filed her questions away and greeted the girl and her mother with an outstretched hand.

It was far more pleasant thinking about wedding gowns and veils than strange men in white trucks and murder.

Chapter 35

AUDREY

Audrey stopped on the main floor. It was December first, and the store was closed until noon when Wynton's annual Christmas parade ended at the store's main entrance. Then came the big event as Santa Claus and Mr. Wynton unlocked the front doors and welcomed all of Levy City to Wynton's Christmas season.

She covered a hefty yawn with her hand. Being up all night supervising the hanging of the lights, garlands, and giant wreaths on the main floor and on the store's front was catching up to her. But Wynton's now matched the holiday cheeriness of the giant stockings and Christmas tree decorations adorning the light poles along the street.

"Feels like I'm at the North Pole." She spun around to see Joshua McKinnon standing there.

"You like it?" She stifled another yawn.

With his hands in his pockets, he rotated on his heel. "All this red and gold mixed in with the garlands." He twirled his finger toward the ceiling. "Really snazzy."

"Our tree by the escalators came from North Carolina, a perfect twelve-footer. The employees worked all night to decorate it."

He pursed his lips as he took his hands from his pockets. "I hear the whole city turns out to see the window displays unveiled later tonight."

"This year's theme is families, and all our windows will show a family celebrating Christmas, from the nativity to now. We'll be serving hot chocolate and gingerbread cookies on the front sidewalk, and all the kids will get a little stocking filled with candy."

And after the unveiling, she was going home to hibernate for the rest of the weekend.

A young woman came running from the escalator, calling her name. "We have a big problem." She gulped in a breath. "We can't find the stockings filled with Christmas candy to pass out to the kids."

"Did you check the loading bay? They were supposed to arrive yesterday in the same shipment as the Christmas ornaments stamped with the store's logo."

"They aren't there."

Audrey resisted the urge to grab the red scarf neatly tied around her neck and mop the girl's wet forehead. "Go ask Florida Delights if they received them by mistake. If not, come find me."

"Yes, ma'am." She cantered off.

One of the other parade supervisors came in from the side hall and signaled for help.

"Mr. McKinnon, please excuse me." She moved past him, but he followed her step for step.

"Miss Penault, I need to talk with you."

She didn't even look Joshua's way. "After the parade."

There was a chance this had something to do with Mr. Loring's threat, and she didn't have time to fool with that nonsense.

"Where is Mrs. Wynton?" Joshua stayed by her side as she hurried on.

"She's coming later with Mr. Wynton."

When she met the other supervisor, his mussed hair matched the harried look in his eyes. "We have a problem."

"What?"

"Three floats are assigned to the same spot in the parade, the high school band director is mad because they're behind the horse club, and the girls holding the Wynton's banner at the front aren't here yet."

Maybe she'd hibernate for the rest of the Christmas season.

"Move the horse club to the end of the parade—"

"Won't work. That puts them in front of the Lion's Club, and their Christmas crackers scare the horses."

"Move the Lions to the front, behind the fire truck. If the girls don't show in the next ten minutes, give two of the firemen the banner, and they can lead the parade. Put the horses at the end."

"Then the elves with Santa's float will have to—"

"Move a few more elves by Santa. Give them shovels and the rolling garbage cans. If anyone complains, tell them to come find me."

The man donned a half smile. "Yes, ma'am. I'll take care of moving the floats."

Audrey followed him out the door. "I'm off to the parade's staging area, Mr. McKinnon. I'll talk with you when I get back to the store."

Joshua stayed with her. "I could use the walk."

When he and Audrey arrived at the scene, the banner girls were finally in place, the band director beamed when she revealed their new spot situated far from the horses, and the other supervisor had rearranged the floats to everyone's satisfaction.

The man in charge of starting the parade waved on the banner holders. Behind them Levy City's fire truck gleamed enough to make all the little boys watching want one of their own.

Shouting and screaming erupted where the Santa float was parked apart from the rest of the parade. Audrey took off at a speed Miss Evelyn never would have approved, happy she'd overruled wearing her usual suit in favor of a sweater, pants, and penny loafers.

The door to the miniature gingerbread house stood open, and two Wynton's employees dressed as elves yelled for onlookers to get back. Another sat on Santa's giant red throne, holding his head in his hands.

When Audrey reached the steps leading up to the trailer, she spied Santa standing by himself, his hat and fake beard crumpled in his grip.

She scurried to the open door of the gingerbread house. The two men there remained silent. One inclined his head toward something inside.

Audrey peered in, then turned away, choking back the revulsion crawling up her throat. "When did you find him?" she asked the nearest elf, whose face had gone sickly pale.

"A few minutes ago." He removed his gloves and used one to wipe his mouth. "Nobody heard or saw anything."

Joshua climbed on the float and leaned into the house for a look. He caught Audrey's eye after seeing the body. "You know him?"

"It's Mr. Loring, head of Legal at Wynton's."

"What do we do now?" one of the elves asked.

Without Santa, the entire parade and Wynton's Christmas kickoff was ruined. She looked at the group encircling the float. Many of them helped decorate the store and depended on their Christmas bonuses to finish out their year in the black.

But a man lay dead, and that couldn't be ignored. "We must get the police here. I'll call them from the store. Nothing else is open until after the parade."

Joshua nodded. "I'll take care of things here." He motioned to the crowd. "Go back to your places, folks. The police are coming, and we need you out of the way."

The man dressed as Santa approached Audrey. "I'm guessing you won't need me anymore."

She was about to agree when the next wave of the parade entered the street. Wynton's couldn't put on half a parade, and she had an idea.

Audrey grabbed Santa's hat and plopped it on his head. "Put your beard on and give it a good brushing. I'll have your sleigh here in a jiffy."

"But my reindeer ran off. They left their skins on the float." He gestured toward a pile of brown costumes left by Santa's throne.

Audrey scooped them up. "Stay here until I return. You practice your *ho ho ho*'s, being jolly, and waving."

She went back to Joshua. "Keep the employees who found Mr. Loring here so they can speak with the police. I'm sending those who weren't near the float and don't know what's happened on with the parade. And keep Santa here."

"Yes, ma'am. Good luck."

"You too." Audrey took off for the store.

Once she had phoned the police, she hurried to the fifth floor. She found Miss Vivien and Mirette hanging pink, white, and gold ornaments on a silver Christmas tree in the center of the salon.

"I have a huge favor to ask."

Mirette looked at the brown bundle in Audrey's arms. "What is that?"

"I need you and Miss Vivien to be my reindeer in the parade." She held up the costumes.

Miss Vivien stared a moment. "What happened to your first choices?"

"They ran off."

Mirette snickered. "You forget to feed them?"

"No, there was a. . .situation on the Santa float."

"Do you mean to tell me you expect us to put on those ridiculous suits and walk the entire two miles of the parade?" Miss Vivien set down the box of ornaments she'd been holding.

"No, ma'am. You're going to ride in a car. With Santa."

Miss Vivien crossed her arms. "Santa's driving a car this year?"

Audrey paused. "No, I am."

Mirette huffed. "There's no way you're going to stuff the two of us"— she swiveled her finger between herself and Miss Vivien—"some guy in a Santa suit, and you in your T-Bird."

"I'm not driving my car. Mr. Wynton is on his way in his Cadillac convertible. Plenty of room in there for all of us."

Audrey shifted her bundle to one arm, pulled out an elf's hat that she'd taken from a store display, and plopped it on her head with one hand. "We need to hurry."

"Have you lost your ever-loving mind? I'm not putting on that getup. Someone might see me." Mirette set her chin as she looked at her boss.

Miss Vivien shifted her gaze from Mirette to Audrey, then stepped forward and took the costumes. "Come along, Mirette. We'll change in the fitting rooms."

She pinned Audrey with a look. "My entire life I've worked to build my reputation of being a woman of taste, style, and fashion." She held up the costume. "And in the blink of an eye, I'm putting on something that looks like it's molting and has mange."

"This thing smells worse than my granny's house," Mirette grumbled as she headed to her dressing room. "And she had twenty cats."

After a few minutes, she came out in costume, holding the reindeer head in her arms. "I just know I'll need some sort of flea powder after this."

Miss Vivien emerged in hers. "Those fleas need to be more worried about you biting them. Get your head on straight, and let's get to the parade before it's over."

Mirette complied. "I can't see in here. Can you, Vivien?"

"Not a thing."

Audrey took each of them by the hand. "We're going to the garage. Mr. Wynton's meeting us there."

When they arrived, Cissy waited with her father-in-law. She cooed when she saw the reindeer. "Aren't you just the cutest little things?" She circled them, staring into the tiny eyeholes. "Who's in there?"

Both Mirette and Miss Vivien remained silent.

Mr. Wynton handed her the keys. "Wish you luck."

"We need a miracle." Audrey raised her eyes upward in prayer, then tucked her reindeer into the front seat. "We're off to the North Pole." She hurried into the driver's seat.

Cissy had joined Mr. Wynton. "They all look ridiculous," she mocked loudly enough for all to hear. Audrey ignored her and started the Cadillac.

She took the side streets leading to the staging area, then pulled the car into the spot first assigned to the Santa float. "You two stay here. I'll go get Santa."

Joshua met her at the car. "The police just arrived. The float's been moved off to the side, and we've managed to keep the panic to a minimum."

She touched his shoulder. "Thank you."

"Of course. What do you need now?"

She looked around. "Santa and some of the decorations from the float."

Joshua looked at the car. "Scrounged up some reindeer, I see." He waved at the occupants.

Miss Vivien and Mirette stared ahead and remained silent.

Joshua trotted off and soon returned with Santa and two other men. Their arms were filled with tinsel, garland, and some of the giant candy decorations from the float.

They hurried to get Santa settled on the back of the seat, sitting up high where the children might see him. Audrey tied ropes of golden garland into giant bows on the door handles and strung more along the car's side, tucking the ends into the back seat. She stuffed the giant candy pieces around Santa's legs and feet.

When they finished, she and Joshua stood back and took in their work.

Joshua rubbed his chin. "Looks like a sleigh full of candy and gifts. Santa looks pretty jaunty riding in a Caddy. Real modern."

Audrey walked around to the driver's seat. "Straighten your hat, Santa. We're almost ready."

She pulled on a green elf's coat she'd grabbed on her way out of the store, then fastened the outfit's wide black belt around her middle.

Miss Vivien leaned over when Audrey settled in the driver's seat. "You're the first woman who's ever driven in the parade."

Audrey adjusted her elf hat and looked into the rearview to fluff the curls around her face. "I hope they don't throw something at me."

"Me too." Miss Vivien squirmed in the seat, causing the bells on her costume to jingle.

Joshua came to the side of the car. "Looks like they're ready for Santa."

As if on cue, the man in the back seat started a round of *ho ho ho's*.

"I'll come find you at the store once the police are finished here."

He shot her two thumbs-up as she drove into her place behind the horse club and their cleanup elves.

Miss Vivien leaned in again. "What happened to the Santa float?"

"Murder." Audrey rounded the corner and pulled onto the parade route. Miss Vivien sat back and remained silent.

The crowd whooped and cheered when they saw Santa waving in the back seat, looking like the jolly elf from the old poem come to life. Children jumped and clapped.

Miss Vivien and Mirette waved too, whipping the crowd into a frenzy of holiday cheer. Audrey kept her eyes forward. She'd get Santa to Wynton's, where he could finish his job.

And God willing, help Wynton's employees keep theirs.

Chapter 36

VIVIEN

Vivien drove to the end of the street before she found a parking spot. "She must have invited the entire town." She slipped her Chrysler into PARK as a group of women chatted together on their way to Betta-John's.

"I don't know why so many people make such a fuss over Tupperware." Mirette opened her door and scooted out of the car. She peered over the top at Vivien. "Seems much more sensible to use glass jars. Snap on the lid and you're done."

Vivien tugged at the hem of her gloves to smooth them over her fingers. "We're not here just for the Tupperware."

"You know all that plastic comes from the oil companies. Nasty, nasty business." Mirette reached up and stopped her cloche hat from blowing off on the wind.

Vivien pressed her full skirt against her legs to prevent its flying up. "Don't be so dramatic. Besides, Tupperware is made from something different. 'Poly-T,' I think, is what it's called."

Mirette waited as Vivien walked around the car. "I don't care if you tell me it's made of diamonds and trimmed in gold. Burping your bowls is so uncouth."

"Then just enjoy the games and the food."

Mirette giggled. "Betta-John's such a stick-in-the-mud about keeping her carpets clean, I don't know how she's going to bear having us sit around with plates in our laps. She'll have her vacuum cleaner going the entire night."

Vivien elbowed her in the side. "You'd better behave, or Betta-John might put you out in the yard with that monstrous cat of hers."

Mirette shivered. "Every time I see that beast, the hair on the back of my neck stands up."

They stifled their laughter when Betta-John answered the door. "Y'all come on in." She swept her hand toward her cavernous living room, where card tables covered with Christmassy tablecloths had been set up in rows facing a long table filled with products. Her Christmas tree stood off to the side, filling the room with the scent of pine.

"I pity the first one who drops a crumb," Mirette teased, causing them both to bite their bottom lips to keep from breaking into laughter again.

A woman dressed in a brown wool dress and leopard-print sweater greeted them with an outstretched hand. "Hello, my name is Bennie Smith, and I'm your sales consultant tonight. I'm so glad y'all came."

Vivien and Mirette introduced themselves, then looked for a place to sit.

Mary Jo waved them over. "We saved your seats." Gigi and Audrey moved to other chairs around the table to make room.

"Never in my life would I have believed Audrey would come to a Tupperware party," Mirette said under her breath.

Vivien sat and looked around the room at all the dressed-up ladies. They all wore festive plastic Christmas corsages adorned with silver or gold bells and red velvet ribbons with fake holly tucked inside. No doubt all the husbands around town were at home wondering just what their women would be talking about all night. Excepting the Wynton's women, those attending were celebrating the chance to be out and about for a few hours.

Vivien gave her attention to her own table. Audrey looked like she'd stepped from a magazine cover in her black sweater and full black-and-white-checked skirt. The short string of pearls around her neck, matching pearl earrings, and bracelet gave the perfect touch of relaxed elegance Audrey excelled in.

Gigi wore an outfit she'd modeled in the show—a matching red cardigan set with a navy skirt and a navy-and-white polka-dotted scarf tied snugly around her neck. Mary Jo had donned a midnight-blue dress with a wide white collar. The outfit accentuated her slim figure and brought out the blue in her eyes. With her pearl choker, she was as glamorous as any other young mama there.

Vivien waved at a table of her fellow Junior League sisters eyeing her and probably wondering what she and Mirette were doing sitting with the younger women.

Betta-John came to offer her famous pink punch.

Mary Jo took a sip from her cut-glass cup. "Ooh, this punch is wonderful."

"Isn't it?" Gigi took another taste of hers. "I've never tasted anything like this."

Vivien set her cup down on the table. "Betta-John's recipe is one of Levy City's best-kept secrets. We all know there's pink lemonade, ginger ale, and pineapple juice in there. But that last ingredient has defied us all for ages."

"Who cares what's in it?" Gigi almost smacked her lips after downing the last in her cup.

Mirette leaned in. "I'll tell you one thing. Whatever that secret ingredient is, it isn't alcohol. Betta-John and her husband, Bob, are staunch Baptists."

Vivien eyed her friend and shook her head. "That could have gone without ever being said."

"Maybe so, but I had fun saying it." She grinned like a naughty schoolboy.

Vivien clicked her tongue. "I warn y'all, she's just getting warmed up. I can send her to the back corner if you'd like."

"Don't do that. I think she's fun." Gigi moved her chair closer to the table, as if to hear better.

"Ooo, I like you." Mirette raised her glass in salute to Gigi, who answered with a smile.

Since the chatter in the room was loud enough to cover their conversations, Vivien caught Audrey's eye. "You said you had something new you wanted to share?"

"It's about Mr. Loring," Audrey said in a low voice.

She was interrupted by Bennie Smith. "Good evening, ladies." She swept her arms wide before the crowd. "Welcome to a night of fun, food, and being out of the house."

The crowd clapped, and one woman whistled.

Bennie snatched a clear Tupperware bowl from the display table and flung it across the room. The item somersaulted, and the purple liquid inside rolled like stormy waves. Squeals and gasps sounded as the guests reached to prevent the bowl's tumbling onto Betta-John's spotless new mint-green carpet.

The bowl finally dropped in Gigi's lap, and she jumped from her chair to prevent any stains on her new outfit. She held up the bowl. "The lid is still on, and nothing spilled."

Bennie smiled at the titters of surprise spreading around the room. She held up her hands like a conductor before an orchestra. "Now watch this, girls." She motioned to Gigi. "Turn the bowl upside down and shake it with all your might."

Gigi shook it, and the spectators marveled to their neighbors.

Bennie took the bowl and tossed it to another group. "Come on, ladies, we'll have fun playing catch for a change."

Laughter swelled as the bowl sailed from woman to woman, tumbling top over bottom.

Audrey leaned into the group. "Since they're all entranced with the flying bowl, I'll tell you what the police said happened to Mr. Loring. He was hit on the head, then strangled."

"Oh my goodness." Vivien fought not to draw attention to their conversation.

Bennie moved near their table and raised the fervor of her sales pitch. "This seal is unbreakable." She tipped up a corner. "Once burped, this baby never spits anything out."

Vivien caught Mirette's eye and winked as her friend mouthed, *Uncouth.* Bennie flipped the bowl upside down on the floor and stood on it. "Practically unbreakable."

Bennie passed around other products, touting their usefulness, while reminding the group that Tupperware was headquartered in Kissimmee, just two hours east of Levy City. Some ladies oohed and aahed over the pastel colors and variety, while others commented on their need or love for the items.

Once her table passed around their current bowl of interest, Vivien spoke to Audrey. "Any news on what happened to Francis?"

"Only that she was hit with something solid and sharp." She passed pink and yellow tumblers to Gigi.

"I still don't see how someone lugged a dead body in without being seen." Mirette moved to avoid being handed the cups.

"There was so much chaos with girls and kids running around, an elephant could have snuck in." Vivien handed a pink pitcher on to the next group.

Mary Jo patted her heart. "Poor Francis."

"And we had a strict no-male policy backstage. How did he get in?" Gigi shrugged.

A new thought niggled at Vivien. "Come to think of it, I never designated the space where Francis was found as a dressing room. The screen was set up there when Mirette and I arrived the morning of the show."

"And it was near the door leading to the dressing rooms in Fine Dresses. The culprit could have been hiding in there the entire time. When no one was looking, he slipped out," Mirette said.

Audrey cut in. "But there's one problem. I locked the door after I hung the showstopper in my dressing room that morning. And the door was locked when I went back in to change."

"Who else had keys to that door?" Gigi looked around the table.

"Only me," Audrey said quietly. "To make sure the showstopper stayed hidden, I left the second key in Mr. Wynton's safe. He and I are the only ones who know the combination."

Vivien's heart clenched as Audrey's eyes darkened. She'd seen the look once before, when a little girl realized her daddy was gone and she was all alone.

This time she'd do what she should have done years ago. Vivien reached across the table and covered Audrey's hand with her own. "We'll get to the bottom of this."

Mirette elbowed her in the side. "Better break it up. Our sales consultant is headed over here."

Vivien sat back as Bennie approached their table with a yellow bowl containing a single carrot.

"Girls, I've had this carrot in this Wonder Bowl for over a week." She held the vegetable up for all to see. "Still fresh as a daisy and ready to eat." Bennie whisked both carrot and bowl around the room for all to see.

Mirette shook her head. "I wouldn't eat that thing if you paid me good money. It looks like it's been embalmed."

The table of Wynton's women erupted in laughter.

Bennie swiveled around and eyed them until the doorbell rang. Betta-John scowled, sprang from her hostess chair, and scurried to the door.

"As Betta-John welcomes our latecomer, let me show some of the wonderful foods you can prepare—"

The room filled with soft buzzing as Betta-John came back with Cissy at her side.

"I'm so sorry I'm late." Cissy stood before them all, dressed in a black-and-white polka-dotted silk dress and high-heeled slides decorated with black lace overlays. "Store business kept me later than I expected."

Her gaze fell on Vivien's table, and she wiggled her fingers in greeting. "Let me sneak back here."

She high-stepped like the carpet was made of hot coals. "Don't mind me," Cissy said to Bennie as she passed by.

Bennie drew in a deep breath as Cissy pulled an empty chair from another table and scooted close to Mary Jo.

"Isn't this fun?" Cissy beamed as Bennie resumed talking about all the wonderful ways to prepare food using Tupperware.

Vivien didn't miss that Cissy had greeted everyone at their table except Audrey.

As Bennie droned on, Vivien stole a glance Audrey's way. Her prized peaches-and-cream complexion had grown as sickly orange as the Tupperware-embalmed carrot.

Chapter 37

MARY JO

Mary Jo lifted her hands from the soapy dishwater and blew a cloud of bubbles at Kenny. He popped the largest one with his finger, sending their girls into fits of giggles.

"Do that again, Daddy." Penny clapped her hands.

Kenny scooped a handful of the soapy fluff and blew at both girls, bringing on more laughter.

Mary Jo rinsed the last plate and set it in the drainer. "Time to put on your pj's, girls."

The sweet giggles melted into nerve-grating whines.

Carrie Rose snuggled against her daddy's leg. "Can't we stay up a little longer? We just finished supper and our tummies are too full to sleep."

Kenny ruffled her reddish-brown crop of hair. "Mama said it's time for bed."

Mary Jo untied her apron and hung the straps over the hook by the refrigerator. "Good-night kisses are in five minutes." She swiveled her index finger at her girls. "I want to see two princesses and their dollies tucked under covers."

As the sounds of the girls brushing their teeth wafted from the bathroom, Kenny held his arm wide and beckoned Mary Jo in for a hug. "Your long workdays are hard on them. They want time to talk to their mama before they go to bed."

"Mama wishes she could stay home and play with them." Mary Jo wrapped her arms about Kenny's waist. His ribs stuck out so much she could almost use them as a washboard.

"You didn't eat much supper. Was the meat too tough?"

He rested his chin on the top of her head. "I'm just getting tired of leftovers."

Mary Jo looked him in the eyes. "I offered to get some of those TV dinners. Gigi says they aren't too bad in a pinch."

He loosened his hold on her. "Those are worse than week-old food." He pushed one of the chairs into place under the table. "The girls and I need fresh suppers."

"Kenny, I cook fresh Friday through Tuesday. Having leftovers two nights a week won't kill us."

He rubbed his jaw with his only hand. "I know."

The pipes in the bathroom clunked as the girls turned off the faucet. "We'd better get them tucked in." She squeezed his hand.

He kissed her cheek and bounded down the hall. "Here comes the dragon." Squeals erupted as he ran into the room growling and huffing.

After kisses, a story, and prayers, Mary Jo cut the light.

"Good night, loves." She loitered in their doorway.

"Night, Mama," they chorused.

She followed Kenny into their own bedroom across the hall. He lay on the bed with his head propped on the pillows.

"I may have to work late next Friday."

"Again?"

She removed her bathrobe and nightgown from the closet. "I have no choice. I'm lowest on the pecking order and assigned the worst shifts during the extended Christmas hours."

"You need to tell your manager we'd like to see you sometimes."

Why was he turning everything into a fight tonight? She put her clothes in the hamper. "You know I can't risk causing trouble at work."

"I miss spending time with my wife too." Kenny pulled off his socks and tossed them into the hamper.

"I have this Friday off plus the rest of the weekend, so I can walk the girls to school and give you my full attention. You could take some time for yourself while I'm home, maybe go fishing?"

Kenny slipped off his undershirt, and she forced her face to stay in a pleasant expression, even though the sight of his amputation scars still shattered her heart.

He changed into his pajamas and headed to the bathroom. "Fishing. Yeah, I'll tell the bass to unhook themselves and get in my bait bucket so I can bring them home for you to fry."

"You could take your dad, and he could help you."

He stopped brushing his teeth. Toothpaste foam dribbled from his lips, and he wiped the mess away with a hand towel. "Maybe."

Mary Jo raised her eyes to the ceiling. *I'm tired of maybes. Please help him see he's not worthless. Or as helpless as he thinks.*

She sat down at her vanity table and tucked her legs under the pink ruffle adorning the edge. As she pulled her brush through her hair, she stared at her husband's reflection in the oval mirror. "At the party the other night, Miss Vivien said I could think about becoming a sales representative and sell Tupperware. She's heard you can make extra money without a lot of effort."

"Just what a man wants—his wife traipsing all over town, begging other men's wives to buy stupid plastic bowls."

Mary Jo set down the brush and swiveled on her pink velvet vanity stool to face him. "Kenny, what's wrong?"

He struggled to sit upright with his legs dangling over the side of the bed. "Everything." He balled his fist and pounded the bed. "I'm sorry, honey. I'm not mad at you."

She rushed to him and wrapped her arms around his shoulders.

Kenny raked his dark hair. "I should be the one working extra hours and taking on a second job to bring home the money to pay *my* bills and protect *my* family."

She buried her face against his arm. "I know that's how you want it to be. But we have to go with how our life is. And right now, I'm the one working."

She rose from the bed. "I need to set my hair."

The doctor had warned her Kenny would slip into these moods as part of his healing process. He'd also said the responsibility for making him snap out of it fell on her. She must push him to think beyond the loss of his arm toward solutions designed to help him regain some of his lost abilities.

A pamphlet about artificial limbs and prosthetics sat tucked in the inner pocket of her purse. The doctor had slipped the information to her when she stepped out of the room to allow Kenny to get dressed.

"There are good choices these days, and your husband is a perfect candidate for one. These new prostheses help many men return to normal activities. Like working."

When he handed over the pamphlet, a glaring picture captivated her attention. A diagram on the cover depicted a metal contraption that made her heart lurch.

"You want him to use a hook? He'll never go for that. Our girls would be scared to death of that thing, of their daddy." She'd shaken her head so hard it started to throb.

The doctor closed her hand over the pamphlet. "It's your job to convince him. He needs to get over the loss of his arm and learn how to be productive again."

Her mind had searched for good excuses to keep saying no. "These must be terribly expensive."

"You work at Wynton's Department Store?" the doctor asked as the sound of Kenny's shoes tapped across the tile on the other side of the door.

"Yes."

"Order the prosthesis through the store. They do these kinds of things all the time. Set up a payment plan or use your employee discount. Make something good come of your being the breadwinner."

Her entire gut had twisted with the desire to shout in the doctor's face, "I don't want to be the breadwinner, or the strong one," but the door swooshed open.

"Having a secret chat with my missus, Doc?" Kenny slapped the doctor on the back.

Both men grinned at the joke, but there was no mirth in their eyes.

And now as she twirled her hair under and fastened it with bobby pins, a new thought dawned. "Kenny, honey, why don't we get a sitter and go Christmas shopping for the girls next Saturday night?"

He sat up. "You wouldn't be too tired?"

Her hair swayed as she answered him. "No. We could eat supper, then head over to Wynton's. The girls showed me all the things they wanted when I took them to the toy department to see Santa."

"With your 10 percent employee discount, we could get a little extra this year." He sported an excited grin she'd not seen in a long time.

But then he slumped against his pillow. "Won't work. My parents are going up to Gainesville to visit my aunt Tilda. They aren't coming back until Sunday."

She had to think fast, put that long-lost grin back on his face. "I'll find a sitter."

"You think you can find a girl you'd trust in less than a week's time?"

His doubt only spurred her on. "Yes." She'd beg every teenaged girl in Levy City if she had to.

She rose from her vanity stool and jumped in the bed beside him. "Mr. Johnson, would you go out with me next Saturday night?" Mary Jo kissed the end of his nose.

"Only if you promise to get me home by curfew, Mrs. Johnson."

He leaned in and kissed her full on the mouth.

Chapter 38

AUDREY

She'd never been this nervous in her life. Audrey paced the length of her living room, stopping at the wide picture window to check for Mary Jo's car pulling into her driveway.

What in the world possessed her to agree to babysit Mary Jo's girls? The only things she knew about children were the names of the best clothing designers and how to set up a toy display to catch their interest. How was she going to entertain them for three hours?

Car doors slammed outside. A glance out the window revealed Mary Jo coming to the door, a girl on each hand, with Kenny bringing up the rear.

Audrey smoothed the skirt of her dress and scanned the room to ensure everything was in place.

She opened the door as soon as the bell rang. "Come on in."

Mary Jo's girls each clung to her with one hand and hugged a baby doll with the opposite arm. The smaller of the two tried to hide her face in her mama's skirt, while the older stared as if she were facing a firing squad.

To avoid scaring them further, Audrey put her attention on Kenny and thrust out her hand. "I'm Audrey, so pleased to meet you."

He shook her hand. "Kenny Johnson. Nice meeting you. Heard a lot about you."

Mary Jo pulled free from her daughters' grips. "Remember all the fun you had with Miss Audrey at the fashion show?"

The tears pooling in the two pairs of baby blues looking back at her did nothing for Audrey's confidence. She looked at Mary Jo and Kenny.

Mary Jo flashed her a crooked smile as she stepped out the door. "You sure about this?"

"Nothing I can't handle." Who was she kidding?

Her heart triple flipped as she watched Mary Jo and Kenny drive away.

Audrey closed the door and faced the girls. Both stood silent, clutching their dolls to their chests, tears rolling down their cheeks and dripping onto their babies' rubber heads.

"Oh my, this won't do." She stood tall before the girls with her hands on her hips. The adults at the store cowered in fear of her, so how could she be so intimidated by two little girls?

Audrey went to a small linen chest in the corner of the room and pulled out two pink handkerchiefs. She brought them to the girls. "Let's wipe those tears."

Carrie Rose and Penny looked at one another, then took the handkerchiefs and swiped them across their faces.

They were definitely their mama's daughters.

She took them each by the hand and led them to her curving beige velvet sofa. They sat, squeezing their dolls close as Audrey stood before them.

"Your mama told me you enjoy playing tea party. I made some cookies earlier today, and I have my silver tea service set up in my dining room."

Carrie Rose raised her gaze to Audrey. "I don't want to play." She sniffed loudly.

"Me neither," Penny whined and hid her face behind her doll.

"Well, we could take a walk down to the lake and see the swans that live there. They're fun to watch."

"I hate birds." Penny stuck out her bottom lip.

"Me too." Carrie Rose wrapped both arms around her doll.

"We could take a walk around the neighborhood. We have some lovely houses up the block, with beautiful flowers in their yards."

"Flowers make me sneeze." Carrie Rose crumpled Audrey's handkerchief in her palm.

"I'm afraid of bees." Penny's lip stuck out far enough for a chicken to roost on it.

This was no easy crowd. "I see." Audrey stole a glance at the clock on her mantel. Twelve minutes and all her best plans had been rejected.

Penny looked at her big sister, and the next thing Audrey knew, both girls sat caterwauling worse than two cats crammed together in a croker sack.

Miss Evelyn said a lady must never give up on trying to please guests. She keeps searching until she finds that special thing that makes everything right.

Audrey rubbed her temples as the girls' boo-hoos grew louder. If this kept up much longer, she was going to go hide in one of her closets and plug her ears.

Then the idea hit.

She cleared her throat, because Miss Evelyn said ladies never raised their voices to their guests, no matter how boisterous they may have become.

Both girls looked up from their sorrows.

"Who would like to play princess dress-up?"

The girls passed a look, and Carrie Rose spoke up. "How do you play that?"

Penny pulled her lip back into place and set her attention on Audrey.

Thank You, God, for Miss Evelyn.

"You're sure you'd like to play?"

They nodded in sync.

"One moment then." Audrey went to a cedar chest she kept in her hallway and removed two woolen shawls.

She took them back to the living room. "First, we need to put these babies to bed." She handed each girl a shawl and one of the couch's throw pillows.

Carrie Rose and Penny laid their dolls on a pillow, tucked them under a shawl, and planted kisses on their cheeks. As soon as they finished, they looked to Audrey for the next instruction.

"Follow me." Audrey led them into another room and stopped before the double doors of the closet.

"Ready?"

"Yes, ma'am."

"Here are the rules. You may try on any dress you'd like, but you must let me help you get into it. Understand?"

Their heads bobbed so fast Audrey didn't doubt they got dizzy.

"Rule number two. We will take turns, so no fussing for your sister's dress when she's wearing it."

Carrie Rose clapped her hands, and Penny bounced like a bunny.

"Close your eyes." Audrey didn't know why they should, but it added to the excitement.

She opened the door to the closet. "Ladies, you may enter." She swept her hand to welcome them in.

The girls squealed and ran into the huge walk-in closet she'd had specially made to store the gowns she'd kept from her modeling days.

"This really is a princess closet." Carrie Rose twirled in circles, as if trying to see every gown at once.

"I want that one." Penny pointed to an aquamarine silk-and-chiffon cocktail dress Audrey had modeled in a Paris show.

She removed it from the hanger and slipped the soft folds over Penny's head.

Penny pulled the wide skirt out and did her best curtsy to Audrey and her sister. She then pirouetted, giggling as the chiffon lifted and twirled around her.

"I like this one." Carrie Rose pointed to a purple, tea-length Balenciaga gown.

Audrey pulled the dress down for her. "This is one of my favorites. And look what it comes with." She held up the matching cape.

Carrie Rose's mouth fell open. "A queen's cape."

She shivered with glee as Audrey slid the dress on and zipped up the back. "The cape too. Please?"

Audrey couldn't help smiling as she bowed low. "As you wish, mademoiselle."

She draped the cape over Carrie Rose's shoulders.

"Look, Penny, I'm a queen." Carrie Rose stuck her nose in the air.

Penny twirled in her dress again. "Can't be a queen until you have a crown."

Audrey reached for a wooden box on the shelf.

Both girls moved in as she opened the dusty lid.

"You have a real crown?" Penny shrieked as Audrey lifted a small rhinestone tiara from the black velvet interior. The light sparkled around the flower-petal design, casting rainbows in the rhinestones.

"I have more than one." She placed the tiara on Carrie Rose's head.

"I want one," Penny whined.

"Mama told you not to beg for stuff, Penny," Carrie Rose corrected in a big-sister voice.

"Your mama is right." Audrey brought a second wooden box down from the shelf. Penny squealed when the lid was raised.

"It's so pretty. The little leaves are made of diamonds."

Audrey removed the second tiara and placed it on Penny's head. "Rhinestones, not diamonds."

She did own a couple of diamond tiaras, but those were locked away in her safe upstairs. She couldn't imagine what Mary Jo might say if she allowed the girls to play in those.

Penny looked up at Audrey. "Are you a princess?"

"No."

Carrie Rose's brows puckered with confusion. "Then why do you have crowns?"

"Because my mother liked to pretend that she was a princess." Audrey set the second box back on the shelf. "Who wants to see how pretty they look?"

"I do, I do," the girls sang together.

"Then let's go look in the big mirror in the other bedroom."

"How many bedrooms do you have?" Carrie Rose asked as Audrey led them from the room.

"Enough."

As they paraded together, movement outside the picture window caught Audrey's eye. A dark figure stood among her front hedges, pointing something at her and the girls.

Gunshots rang out, shattering the window. Audrey pushed the girls to the floor.

She dropped to her knees when more shots sailed into the room.

"Crawl back into the room and shut yourselves in my closet."

They clung to each other, too scared to move.

Audrey scooted on her knees to them as another round of shots exploded into her living room. She scurried ahead of them, scraping her bare knees raw on the nap of her carpet. "Hurry, girls!"

Both girls struggled against the long skirts but kept going until they were back in the dress-up room.

Audrey herded them into the closet. "Stay here until I come and get you."

As she shut them in, her mind flashed back to the show when she'd had to keep the girls from seeing Francis. "Mary Jo's never going to let me near them again."

The firing had stopped, so she peered around the doorframe into the living room. The black figure hurled a ball glowing orange into the living room.

The fiery object landed inside the window and ignited Audrey's sheers. Flames licked their way to the ceiling as lines of sparks ignited her carpet. The branches of her Christmas tree lit up, and the smell of sizzling pine sap and melting glass ornaments permeated the room.

Audrey ran to the closet. "We have to get outside."

She grabbed each girl by the hand and dragged them out to the fence at the far perimeter of her backyard. "I'll get some chairs."

Audrey settled the sobbing girls into her metal patio chairs.

"I'm going around to the front to see what's happening inside my house."

Carrie Rose grabbed her hand. "Please don't leave us. It's dark." She dug her nails into the skin on the back of Audrey's hand.

Audrey wrapped her hand around the little girl's. "I'll stay."

Which was a better idea, seeing as she didn't know if the attacker was hanging around out front. She sat in one of the chairs, and both girls crawled into her lap. They snuggled against her, and their tears wet the front of her dress.

At long last, the wails of a fire engine broke into the night. "See, girls? That means help is coming. Everything's going to be fine."

"I want my mama," Penny cried.

"Our babies are still on the couch," Carrie Rose screamed.

If she could have gotten away with it, Audrey would have cried herself. "I'm so sorry, girls. I can't go back in there."

"Hello?" a man's voice yelled above the sounds of the other men pulling hoses free and shouting orders.

Audrey took the girls by the hand. "We're going out front." Surely their attacker would have run off by now, not wishing to be seen by the fire crew.

She led them through the gate and around the corner of her house. One of the firemen noticed and trotted up to them.

"Are you ladies hurt?"

"Our babies are in there on the couch," Carrie Rose said in between sobs.

The man looked at Audrey. "Babies?"

Audrey shook her head. "Dolls."

"I see. Excuse me." He walked back to the fire truck.

Audrey looked at the girls, but words wouldn't come.

Yards of hose were unfurled and dragged into her house. Men barked more orders as they rushed around her and the girls. Water gushed from the hose and flooded the flames engulfing her couch, chairs, bookshelves, and art pieces she'd bought from street vendors in Paris. The scorching heat had turned her white fireplace black.

Tires screeched in the street. Mary Jo and Kenny leaped out of their car, leaving the doors open as they came running.

Mary Jo bounded to the girls first and gathered them into her arms. "Oh, my darlings, are you all right?" She smothered them with more hugs as the girls burst into another round of tears. Kenny stooped down and circled his family with his arm.

Audrey saw he was fighting back emotions, so she moved to a spot in the yard where she could survey the progress against the flames.

The largest of the plumes of fire had been vanquished, and firemen doused and beat the last of the flames down to smoldering sparks. With the absence of firelight, night once again enfolded her yard.

She fought back tears of her own. The scents of charred fabric and wood burned her nose. Her sweet cottage had been marred. A stranger had come to her sanctuary and attacked. Burned away her life, including the box storing Daddy's gold cuff links. Monogrammed with his initials, same as hers.

She rubbed her forehead. Her beautiful window to the lake was shattered. She'd spent more than she cared to say on remodeling her living room, adding that window so she could sit on her couch and watch dawn arrive and dusk close the day.

The fire chief came to speak with her. "Are you Audrey Penault?"

Her dry throat wouldn't allow her to speak.

"Good news. We were able to contain the blaze to your living room. Your hallway is partly scorched, as well as your kitchen door."

He paused while another of his crew came and spoke to him in low tones.

The chief turned back to her. "I'm afraid all the furniture and knick-knacks in there are gone."

He watched as his crew dragged the hoses from her house. "Were you smoking?"

Burning rage crept up from her gut and flamed her cheeks. "I don't smoke. A man was outside. He shot through my window with a gun, then lit something and threw it inside. My curtains and Christmas tree caught on fire, and the flames spread from there."

A muscle in his jaw twitched. "A strange man shot at you and tried to burn your house down? That's what you're saying happened?"

Audrey stood to her full height and met him eye to eye. "That *is* what happened."

He removed his helmet and scratched his head. "The police are on their way. You can explain it all to them." He dipped his head. "Ma'am."

Audrey laid her hand on his arm to stop him from walking away. "Thank you for saving the rest of my house."

"Yes, ma'am." He looked at the smoldering wreckage of her living room. "You did good to get your girls out."

"They aren't mine." She pointed to Mary Jo, who was charging their way. "They're hers."

"Excuse me." The chief walked away as Mary Jo reached Audrey.

She shoved the gowns into Audrey's arms and held out the tiaras until Audrey was able to hook them with one of her fingers.

"I have no words." Mary Jo's voice shook. She stalked to her car, where Kenny was helping the girls into the back seat.

Mary Jo started the car and turned around in the street. The final remnants of the smoke parted like filmy curtains as the Johnson family drove away without a second look at Audrey.

A tap on her shoulder almost stopped her heart. Audrey swirled around to find Miss Vivien standing behind her, wrapped in a coat covering her robe.

She gathered Audrey into a hug. "My goodness, honey, are you all right?"

"No, ma'am."

Miss Vivien enfolded her. "I saw the flames clear across the lake at my house. I raced over here as fast as I could, but the police blocked the street. I came through when they let Mary Jo in."

Audrey lifted her head. "A man came—"

Miss Vivien held her at arm's length. "You can tell me later. They've got the fire out, so you go inside and pack your bags. You're going to stay with me until we can get this sorted."

Audrey tried to pull her thoughts together to decline, but Miss Vivien held up her hand before she could speak. "Don't even try to argue."

"You there." Miss Vivien waved a young fireman over to where they stood. "Audrey needs to get in there and pack some of her things."

He shook his head. "No, ma'am, it's not safe for her—"

"Then hose it down again, stay in there while she packs, and then walk her back out. What's she supposed to do, live in these clothes until y'all get this cleaned up?"

Audrey drew in a deep breath. "I could go in my back door and straight to my room."

The fireman bowed his head. "Come on. We'll ask the chief."

Once she'd talked to the chief and relayed the night's events to the police, Audrey sat tucked into Miss Vivien's car with a few belongings and her work satchel, plus a box of store items locked in the trunk.

Vivien had just put the coffee on when Audrey padded softly down the kitchen stairs. Her stomach twitched as she gave the space a third look around to make certain all was in place. She then rolled her eyes at her own behavior.

Many years had passed since she'd entertained a Penault woman in her little breakfast room. The last time became one of the worst days of her life.

But that wasn't now, and she needed to be a good hostess since she'd practically forced Audrey to come.

"Oh my goodness, those cinnamon rolls smell delicious," Audrey said as she came into the room.

Vivien took two cups from the cabinet and set them on the table. "Have a seat. Coffee will be ready in a second." She removed the rolls from the oven to cool.

Dark circles hung beneath Audrey's puffy eyes.

"Were you able to get any sleep at all?" Vivien set out sugar and cream as the coffee percolated.

"Watched the sun rise."

"Good thing I made the coffee strong this morning."

Audrey slipped on a drooping, tired smile. "Every bit helps." She looked around the room. "You've changed things since I was last here."

Vivien set the coffeepot on a trivet on the table, then looked around the room. "I put the terrazzo floors in soon after Carter died." She motioned to the wallpaper. "Found this cherry pattern when Mirette and I were in Charleston for a bridal show. She and I put it up ourselves. Took us three weekends to finish and about ruined our friendship."

Audrey held out her coffee cup. "I love the little cherry pattern." Steam twirled like a mini tornado as she blew on her coffee. "The yellow appliances dress things up nicely. Very modern." She took a sip.

"All from Wynton's." Vivien cut a cinnamon roll from the pan and placed it on a plate for Audrey.

"Did you make the curtains?"

Vivien fixed herself a roll and sat across from Audrey. "I did—found that yellow gingham at the store. Whipped those up on a Saturday afternoon." She gulped down a large sip of coffee before jumping into a long-overdue conversation.

"I'm sorry, Audrey."

She met Vivien's gaze and shrugged. "The damage to my house was limited to the living room and a few walls. I'll get everything fixed soon enough."

"I'm not talking about your house."

Understanding filled Audrey's eyes. "I never blamed you for what happened, Miss Vivien."

She crossed her arms on the tabletop. "Mother was your best friend and business partner and tried to steal the salon from you after Daddy died. Then lied to get money from Mr. Carter behind your back."

Vivien ran her finger around the rim of her cup. "She went from your grandparents' house to your father's. All she knew was how to be a socialite."

"And snag rich husbands." Audrey poured cream into her coffee.

Vivien went on. "Fiona did me a great favor. After she took the buy-out, I promoted Mirette, and we built Miss Vivien's into a premier salon. And Carter never gave me cause to believe he and Fiona. . . Listening to gossip and blaming the Penault women for that falls squarely on me."

Audrey cut a small bite of cinnamon roll. "I was so glad when Mr. Wynton shipped Mother off to Europe. You and Mr. Carter reconciled, and everyone's life improved." She popped the piece in her mouth and closed her eyes while she chewed. "These are wonderful."

"They were Carter's favorite. I like to make them when my grandchildren come to stay. Or other special guests." She smiled at Audrey.

As soon as Audrey swallowed her last bite, Vivien refilled her cup.

"Do you feel like telling me what happened last night? I noticed Mary Jo gave you no chance to speak to her."

Audrey set down her cup. "The girls and I were playing dress-up, and I saw a man outside my picture window. He had a gun and shot into the house several times. We hid until he started the fire. I rushed the girls to the backyard and stayed there until we heard the fire department arrive."

"You didn't see who it was?" Vivien cut another piece of cinnamon roll and placed it on Audrey's plate.

"He was dressed all in black, and it was dark. I couldn't see his face." Audrey cradled her head in her hands. "I can't imagine how frightened Mary Jo's girls must be. They probably didn't sleep a wink."

Vivien poured herself a second cup of coffee. "I'll call her later."

Audrey groaned. "This is all so ugly." She pounded the table with her fist.

"You think this has something to do with what's happening at the store?" Vivien stirred a spoonful of sugar into her coffee.

"Don't you?"

Vivien hesitated. "I just wish I knew who and why."

"The why is easy. Money."

Vivien poured Audrey another cup. "And the who?"

Audrey didn't answer.

Though she wasn't certain she wanted the information, Vivien asked anyway. "Someone we know?"

"Folks at the store think I'm the guilty party." Audrey finished her coffee. "I need to show you something." She left the room.

She returned with her work satchel stacked on top of the box she'd brought from home. "If you'll clear a space, I'll show you what I've found so far."

"What's all this?"

Audrey pulled a store ledger from the box. "Junior's unintended breadcrumbs."

Vivien glanced over the ledger. "I'm going to need my glasses for this. And we'd better move to my dining room table so you can spread all this out. It seats eight, twelve if I put the leaves in."

The clock read far past noon when Vivien sat back in her chair, head spinning with the information Audrey presented for over two hours.

"I never dreamed Junior had this much low-down in him."

"I put him on notice shortly before he died." Audrey rubbed her eyes. "He threatened I'd be gone by the end of the month."

Vivien drummed her fingers on the tabletop. "What did you put in my safe the day Mr. Wynton was stung by the wasps?"

Audrey organized a pile of ledgers into a neat stack, gathered her paperwork, and slid the sheets back into a folder. "A copy of Mr. Wynton's will, a declaration of voting shares, and his succession wishes for chairman of the board."

"Who knows the combination to my safe?"

"Mr. Wynton, you, and me. He keeps those numbers in his wallet for protection."

"Who do you think is behind all this, Audrey?"

Audrey gave Vivien a long stare before answering. "Cissy."

"You can't be serious. I'm sure she helped Junior when he was alive, but. . .murdering four people, poisoning Mr. Wynton, and trying to sell the store behind his back? No one would believe she'd do any of this."

Audrey picked up the box. "Exactly."

Vivien pulled the bundle from Audrey. "We'll spread all your evidence on my table again. I'm calling Gigi and Mary Jo. They need to see this."

"But they're friends with Cissy."

"We'll figure all that out once they get here."

Audrey sighed. "Maybe if we told them Cissy's full story, they might believe us?"

"Maybe so. For now, you need a nap."

"Yes, ma'am. But first I need to call the store and order a pair of baby dolls. May I use your phone."

"Of course, it's—"

Audrey held up her hand. "I remember. Thank you."

A few hours later, Vivien stood at her stove, stirring a pot of Brunswick stew to perfection, when soft thumps sounded on the kitchen stairs.

"You look a bit more bright eyed." Vivien went to the cabinet and removed two bowls and glasses.

"It's a wonder what a nap and a bath can do for a person. Did you talk to Gigi and Mary Jo?"

Vivien switched off the stove and set the pot aside to cool. She bent down and pulled a tray of biscuits from the oven. "Mary Jo flat-out refused. Gigi's got a head full of curlers and her mind on a date with Bobby Bridges. I didn't say more because she's on a party line."

Audrey propped her elbow on the table and cradled her chin in her hand. "We could go to Gigi's house."

Vivien plopped a lid on the pot and looked straight into Audrey's eyes. "We are. As soon as we finish eating."

Chapter 40

GIGI

The rollers yanked at her scalp, but Gigi decided to leave them in a little longer to make tighter curls. She propped her feet on a kitchen chair and leaned over to blow on her freshly polished toenails.

And Edie had said Fire and Ice wasn't her color. She huffed and puffed at her toes like the Big Bad Wolf until soft knocking sounded on the door.

Better not be Bobby coming to surprise her. "Come in."

"What are y'all doing here?" She blew on her still wet nails. "I'm sorry I couldn't let you in." Sorrier they'd now see how she lived.

Miss Vivien and Audrey sat on the couch. "I'm perfectly capable of opening a door." Miss Vivien set her jaw as if she meant business. "We came to talk."

"About the fire? Mary Jo said the police were there looking around when they arrived. Do they think someone started the fire on purpose?"

Audrey exchanged a look with Miss Vivien. "The police haven't shared what they think with me."

"Was your house badly damaged?"

"Nothing that can't be fixed. How are Carrie Rose and Penny?" Audrey asked softly.

"They ended up sleeping in Mary Jo's bed last night. They've been clinging to her all day, and she can't get her housework done."

Audrey groaned and covered her face with her hands.

"We'll all pray the police grab whoever did this soon." Miss Vivien shifted in her spot.

"Mary Jo's really steamed." Gigi whistled. "When I called her this morning, I had to hold the phone out from my ear because of her hollering."

Audrey clamped her eyes shut. "Lovely."

Miss Vivien patted her on the hand. "She'll come around."

She met Gigi's gaze. "Audrey has some news."

"Another clue into who's been doing all the"—she dropped her voice low—"murders?"

Gigi's legs cramped, so she moved her feet, careful to avoid bumping them on the chair's padded back. She wanted to wear her open-toed heels tonight, and having smeared polish would look tacky. "Tell me what's new."

Miss Vivien spoke first. "Gigi, we need you to listen with an open mind."

"How else would I listen?"

Miss Vivien grew serious. "You're going to hear things you won't want to believe."

"Well, now you've got me worried."

Audrey drew in a deep breath. "I think Cissy Wynton is the guilty party."

Even though Audrey spoke each word clearly, her message didn't stick. "Are you joking?"

"No."

"You think Cissy killed her own husband, a nurse, Francis, and Mr. Loring? And made Mr. Wynton sick all those times?"

"She may also be behind the fire at my house."

"Cissy never hurt anyone. She helped Mary Jo and I get promoted. She's taken care of Mr. Wynton and the store. And no one cried harder at Junior's funeral than her. She wouldn't kill him."

Miss Vivien took a long time before she spoke. "Audrey's evidence says otherwise."

Gigi slammed her hands on her head, then jerked them back when the curlers pulled her hair. "Why would she do this?"

"Money," Audrey quickly added.

"But Cissy has plenty."

"As long as he's alive, it's Mr. Wynton's money."

She should have jumped to her feet and started arguing for Cissy, but then she'd ruin her nail polish. "Junior was the hair parent to the whole fortune."

"Do you mean heir apparent?" Miss Vivien asked.

"I don't know. Alvid told me he was whatever-that-word-is at lunch one day. Right around the time Mr. Wynton was stung."

Audrey scowled. "How would Alvid know about the Wynton family finances?"

"He said everybody in town knew Junior got everything."

"Alvid's wrong. Mr. Wynton changed his will when he discovered Junior's dirty deals. Neither one would get the entire fortune. They'll only get what's set up in a trust," Audrey said.

Miss Vivien jumped into the conversation. "Audrey believes Cissy wants Mr. Wynton out of the way so she can sell the store and keep all the money."

Gigi threw up her hands. "I don't believe any of this. Mr. Wynton wouldn't leave his son and Cissy out in the cold."

"You promised to listen to all Audrey has to say," Miss Vivien said softly.

"Cissy's shared plenty of stuff to make you look guilty too, Audrey. How you snuggled up to Mr. Wynton to get special favors, pushed your way between him and his son. And the whole store knows he bought that car for you."

Audrey's cheeks burned red as she stood. "I'm sorry I upset you." She stepped over Miss Vivien's feet on her way to the door.

"Cissy and Bobby warned me about you," Gigi yelled after her.

Audrey left without another word, which suited Gigi fine.

Miss Vivien rose from the couch, tucked her purse under her arm, and followed Audrey out the door.

++

Gigi looked for signs of Mary Margaret before she bolted through the kitchen's back door. She needed to find Lilla.

After taking a seat at the steel food-prep counter in the back of the kitchen, she laid her head on her arms.

"Long night?"

Lilla entered with a small bucket of soapy water in one hand and a wet dishrag in the other.

Gigi yawned. "Never-ending."

Lilla gestured for her to sit up so the counter could be wiped clean. "Trouble with Bobby again?" She moved the rag in quick circles across the surface, then dropped it in the bucket.

"How'd you know?"

"Whenever you come to work with them big black bags under your eyes, he's responsible." Lilla poured out the water and put the bucket under the sink.

"He stood me up last night. I'm worried he's gator bait or dead in a ditch somewhere."

Lilla leaned against the counter. "Go eat lunch with your friend. She'll cheer you up."

"She's not here. Her little girls are. . .sick."

Lilla washed her hands with a bar of Lava soap. "They're still scared from the fire the other night?"

"How'd you know about that?"

"Nelson. He talks with Miss Penault every morning. She brings him breakfast."

Gigi wrinkled her nose in disbelief. "She does what?"

"She's been bringing him breakfast ever since his wife died. About the same time she started working here."

"I can't believe she'd be that nice."

"She's always been nice to you, hasn't she?" Lilla should have been a judge. She could shoot a person "the eye" and make the truth flow out of them faster than water through a sieve.

"I guess."

"Then why are you dancing with the green-eyed monster?"

"I'm not jealous of her."

Lilla pulled up the chair she used when she sat and shelled peas into her giant stainless steel bowl. "Most folks around here are. She's pretty and smart but closed up too. Earned Mr. Wynton's respect and made lots of people mad because she's good at working hard. You know, I heard her own mama took money that was supposed to be hers. She went off to model so she could have something to live on."

"I've heard."

"She got Eunice and me a bonus for the holidays for all the extra baking."

"I thought Cissy did that." At least she claimed that at lunch one day.

Lilla shook her head. "Miss Audrey got Nelson's nephew a job at the warehouse when nobody else would hire him because he went to jail for stealing. Miss Audrey didn't believe he did it, so when he got out, she talked Mr. Wynton into hiring him, and he's been a perfect employee since."

She held out a cookie bar to Gigi. "Good people don't brag about their good deeds."

Gigi nibbled on her cookie bar. "I heard rumors from her last night that would curl a cow's tail."

"Straight from Miss Audrey?"

"They were about Cissy Wynton. Terrible things."

"She doesn't gossip. Maybe you heard wrong."

"I didn't." Gigi shook her head. "Cissy's been nothing but nice to me."

"Unlike that man of yours." Lilla sat down in her chair again. "Been on my feet since five this morning. Feels nice to sit."

Heels tapped on the tile in the hallway. Lilla rose from her chair.

Mary Margaret limped into the room but adjusted her gait as soon as she noticed Lilla and Gigi watching. Her feet had swelled over the sides of her low-heeled pumps.

Gordon Holbrook in Ladies' Shoes told Gigi once that Mary Margaret refused to wear her true size 8 shoes, declaring herself to be a size 6. He claimed lots of women did the same to seem more delicate and ladylike.

She stared down her nose at Gigi. "Miss Woodard, there is a young man loitering in the hallway—says he's looking for you. And why are you here?"

Bobby. But why did he come looking for her in the cafeteria? She told him about her new job a week ago. "I came by to say hey to Lilla."

"Don't waste her time." Mary Margaret toddled off to the serving line.

Gigi rolled her eyes. "Why do they keep her?"

"She got this job during the war when all the men went off to fight. When they came back, none of them wanted it, so they kept her on." Lilla opened the oven door, and the aroma of a roast filled the room.

"But she's awful to everybody, especially you."

Lilla closed the oven door. "Lots of folks fare worse."

"You shouldn't have to take that from her."

"Maybe someday soon I won't have to." Lilla pulled a large knife from the rack on the wall and sliced a pan of cookie bars.

"Are you planning on calling people out on things like the Moores did?"

"Too much going on not to think about it. I want my family to have it better."

Gigi jumped from her chair. "Be careful, Lilla."

"You need to do the same. People aren't always what they seem when you're standing too close."

"What is that supposed to mean?"

"Open your eyes, Gigi."

Lilla tilted her head toward the door. "You'd better go."

As Gigi slipped out, her head reeled with Lilla's advice. Who did she need to watch?

Cissy? She wouldn't hurt a flea.

And Bobby always apologized after being a lunkhead.

She must have meant Audrey.

Gigi hurried around the corner and caught sight of Bobby pacing the floor, that old, beat-up hat of his bunched in his hand.

Poor Bobby. The last time they went out, she'd argued with him over Audrey, and he'd gone home early in a huff because she said he was being childish.

She'd apologize because he was right about Audrey.

Then smack him for standing her up and scaring her half to death.

Chapter 41

AUDREY

Reality slapped Audrey in the face when she opened the door to her house. Asking Miss Vivien to take her there may have been a mistake.

"Well?" Miss Vivien peeked around her. "Oh. My. Stars."

Audrey's couch was now a pile of char. Her scorched hi-fi system had been dumped over, and her record collection lay in melted heaps across the floor, including her newest Sinatra album.

The cherry bookcases lay face down in the back of the room. The books they once held were now hills of pages mixed with ashes.

Audrey fought back tears. "Why?"

Miss Vivien grabbed her arm. "Let's go." She tugged, but Audrey slipped free.

She headed to the den, where she kept her desk and filing cabinet. As Audrey hurried down her hallway, she glanced into the kitchen. The drawers and cabinet doors stood wide open; her dishes, glassware, and silverware lay scattered all over the floor.

In the den, her easy chairs and desk chair had suffered the same fate. Pushed over and sliced open. Broken frames and portraits slashed to colorful ribbons covered the rug.

Miss Vivien stood in the doorway. "Oh, Audrey."

Audrey stepped over the chair pieces and hurried to the closet. Her belongings lay spread out as if they'd been swept away in a flood. She dug through the mass of boxes and her old modeling portfolios twice, slinging items left and right. At last she covered her mouth with shaky fingers. She'd hidden the dead wasp, the brick used to kill Francis, her broken compact, and the medicine bottles from Mr. Wynton's safe in a Wynton's hatbox.

The box was gone.

She almost jumped a country mile when Miss Vivien tapped her on the shoulder. She held out a piece of paper stained with a dirty footprint from a man's work boot. "I know this isn't yours."

Audrey snatched the sheet from Miss Vivien. "There's a brand name stamped on the sole. We sell this kind at the store."

"What now?"

Audrey waffled between being angry enough to kick whoever did this in both shins and fear for those close to her. "I can't stay with you anymore, Miss Vivien."

"You're certainly not staying here."

Audrey swept her hand around the room. "This person came after me when children were present. He shot at me and them." She picked up a fragment of a painting. "I can't put anyone else in danger."

"Where are you going to go?"

Audrey folded the piece of paper with the boot print and stuck it in the pocket of her suit jacket. "That's going to remain a secret." She walked past Miss Vivien. "I've got to pack."

Miss Vivien followed her into her bedroom, which had also been ransacked. "How will we know if you're dead or alive?"

Audrey pulled her large suitcase from her closet and laid it open on her bed. She gathered what she needed from the garments tossed about the room. "You'll see me at the store. I'll be the one wearing all the wrinkles." She held up her favorite Chanel suit jacket for Miss Vivien to see.

Miss Vivien tsk-tsked the damage. "Will you at least ask Joshua McKinnon about having some sort of extra protection while you're at the store?"

Audrey folded a skirt and laid it in the suitcase. "Why? He thinks I'm the guilty party."

"Have you thought about sharing your Cissy suspicions with him?"

"She hired him to. . .to investigate me."

Miss Vivien looked away. "I see."

Audrey gathered shoes and gloves from the floor and brought them to her suitcase. "I have a feeling whoever left that boot print is our mysterious truck driver."

She pulled pairs of silk stockings hanging from her dresser's open drawers. "He's connected to Cissy somehow."

When it came time to close her suitcase, she had to sit on the lid before the latch would catch.

Miss Vivien pushed Audrey's cedar chest lid closed and sat. "You've packed enough to go on a world tour."

Audrey retrieved a second suitcase from her closet and began the packing process again. "I'm not coming back here until my living room is repaired."

She stuffed undergarments, shoes, jeans, and sweaters in a smaller bag. All her best evidence had been stolen. In the wrong hands, they spun a story coloring her guilty. But she wasn't about to tell that to anyone.

She'd protected herself her entire life, and she'd do so now.

A new thought bolted through her, and Audrey rushed from the room.

"Audrey?" Miss Vivien trailed after her.

Audrey pushed through the swinging door in her kitchen. Her heart cartwheeled as she checked the knob on the door leading into her garage. She'd kept that entrance locked since discovering the missing brick from the side of her house.

The knob turned easily.

Miss Vivien came up behind her and caught her by the arm. "Do you think he might be hiding in the garage?"

"If he is, I'll scream, and you run to your car."

Audrey opened the door and flipped on the light.

Her entire body sagged as she leaned against the doorframe for support.

Her T-Bird sat untouched.

After peering under her car to ensure no one was hiding there, she turned to Miss Vivien, who waited in the doorway. "Empty."

She went back in the house with Miss Vivien. "I always leave the kitchen door locked."

Miss Vivien leaned down, picked the toaster off the floor, and set it on the counter. "Do you think something scared the man off?"

Audrey walked through a maze of shattered glass. "Maybe. Or he found what he was looking for."

Miss Vivien looked around the room. "Shouldn't we call the police?"

Audrey walked to the phone hanging on the wall. She put the receiver to her ear, then laid it back in the cradle. "Phone's dead."

"Load your stuff into your car, and we'll go back to my house. You can call the police from there." Miss Vivien looked around the room. "I guess it's best we leave all this for them to look through."

She checked her watch. "We'd best hurry back so you can have time to dress. I'll call ahead and let Cissy know you'll be late."

"Don't bother. You're already dressed for the salon, and I don't want you to get mussed. I'll be perfectly fine to finish here. Besides, I only need fifteen minutes to get dressed." Audrey walked out of the kitchen.

Miss Vivien directed Audrey to retrieve her things. "You'll follow me back to the house. And no more arguments."

✛✛

Miss Vivien surveyed Audrey from head to toe when she came down the front stairs. "I've never seen a woman so put together in that short a time."

"I had a lot of practice during my modeling days. I'll need to grab my satchel from your car; then I'm off to the store."

"I love that suit." Miss Vivien circled Audrey. "That dark green color is stunning. The black-velvet trim on the lapels and buttons finishes it off so well. Is that a Lilli Ann?"

"No, Marionne Leslie."

"I love her clothes. I wish I didn't have to drive all the way to Atlanta or Charleston to find them."

Audrey picked up her purse from a side table. "You won't have to now. I inked a deal with her a few weeks ago. She's designing a line for us."

"Her label or exclusive for Wynton's?"

Audrey smiled. Miss Vivien thought like a businesswoman. "Exclusive. The line will debut next fall. Collegian and Ladies."

"She's so reclusive. How did you get a meeting with her?" Miss Vivien followed Audrey out the door.

"I've modeled for her many times. I called on behalf of the store and asked to speak with her. She waited over a month to return my call. She's a tough negotiator, but after several conversations she accepted my proposal. She's coming to see the store after Christmas."

"You did all this without Mr. Wynton?"

Audrey paused. Miss Evelyn always said ladies didn't do business, that things having to do with money were better left to the men.

But Miss Vivien would understand. "Yes."

"No wonder Cissy wants to get rid of you." Miss Vivien patted her on the arm. "I'll see you at the store."

Chapter 42

MARY JO

Mary Jo craned her neck, searching the noon lunch rush for Gigi. They hadn't spoken since the fire at Audrey's three days ago, and she was bursting with news.

When she spotted Gigi in the serving line, Mary Jo flailed her arms, trying to get her attention, and was sure she looked like a bird trying to take off in a tornado.

"You're wound up today," Gigi said when she joined Mary Jo at the table.

"I've done something."

"Unlawful?" Gigi sipped her tea.

"No, but it'll probably stir up just as much trouble."

Gigi raised her brows. "What did you do?"

Mary Jo couldn't believe what she'd done. The thought popped into her head while she drove to work and kept tapping her on the shoulder until she could stand it no longer. "I ordered that prosthesis for Kenny."

"The one in the pamphlet the doctor gave you?"

Disbelief pushed Gigi's eyes wide. "You didn't."

"I did."

"I thought Kenny told you to absolutely not do that."

"He did."

"And you went and ordered it anyway?"

"I did." Regret ripples hit Mary Jo, like when she was seven and her parents punished her for wearing her Sunday shoes to school when she had been strictly told not to.

"What's he going to say?"

Mary Jo chewed her thumbnail a moment before she pulled it away to avoid chipping the polish. "I don't think there'll be much he won't say."

Gigi stirred the mound of peas and carrots on her plate. "What's gotten into you?"

"Kenny and I had a fight last Friday night after we finally got the girls settled."

Gigi swallowed her vegetables fast. "But y'all never fight. What happened?"

"We were both overtired because it was after midnight, and the girls had been screaming and weeping because of what happened at Audrey's. They cried themselves to sleep, but Kenny and I were still worked up, so we decided to sit down and try to calm our nerves."

What had happened next brought a swell of sadness. "I know he was tired, and we were both upset, but Kenny blamed me for what happened."

Gigi sat poised to take a sip from her tea glass but instead held the dripping cup aloft. "He did not."

"He said if I wasn't working at Wynton's and neglecting my motherly duties, the girls wouldn't have been put in danger. Then he yelled at me for letting Audrey babysit." She buried her face in her hands. "Gigi, it was awful. We said things to each other I'm still ashamed of."

"Oh, Mary Jo, I'm so sorry."

Mary Jo used her napkin to wipe away a tear stream dripping down her cheek. "He's still not speaking to me. Carrie Rose noticed this morning while she was eating her breakfast. She thought her daddy was mad at her and Penny for being scared of the fire." She sniffed. "The doctor is right. I've got to find a way to get Kenny back to work and me back home. The sooner the better." Mary Jo paused before going on. "When I was driving to the store today, I passed by Mercer's hardware store. That's when the idea for the prosthesis came to me."

Gigi wiped her mouth. "Why?"

Mary Jo couldn't help but smile, because the more she got used to the idea, the more perfect the thought became. "No one knows more about tools, building things, or painting than my Kenny. He could work in a hardware store."

"But do you think he would?"

"The prosthesis won't be in for at least eight weeks. Gives me plenty of time to figure out how to sweeten him on the idea."

Gigi laid her silverware on her now empty tray. "I can't believe you did this."

"I had to. After what happened, my heart aches every time I leave the girls."

"Mama cat wants to protect her kittens." Gigi's face darkened as she reached for her tea.

"What's the matter, Gigi?"

"Bobby and I had our makeup date last night. And we fought."

Mary Jo couldn't recall a time when they hadn't fought lately. "Again?"

"I don't understand him. He comes to the store all sweet with his hat in his hand, begging me for forgiveness. Two days later, he corrects everything I say and insults my new job."

Now it was Mary Jo's turn to offer comfort. "I'm so sorry, Gigi."

She grunted. "You should have heard the way he was talking to our waiter. I kept thinking about how nasty Mary Margaret is to Lilla. Bobby was being worse. I got so embarrassed, I wanted to crawl under the table. He carried on like he lived in Audrey's neighborhood."

The sound of her name clenched Mary Jo's heart again.

"Sorry. I shouldn't have said that."

Mary Jo set her tea glass on her tray. "We're quite a pair, aren't we?"

Gigi rolled her eyes. "One good thing happened. He finally told me where he's working. It's Mahon's fruit-packing house."

"Well, at least you got that. You've been asking for months."

"He didn't mean to tell me. It slipped out when we were yelling at each other in his truck on the way home."

"Gigi, why do you stay with him?"

"Because he used to be fun." Gigi narrowed her eyes as she looked at something behind Mary Jo.

"What's the matter?" Mary Jo twisted around and saw Cissy talking to Alvid near the cafeteria's entrance. "She looks mad."

Gigi grimaced at Mary Jo. "She's blessing him up one side and down the other."

"I wonder what he did."

Gigi stole another glance at them. "I wouldn't want to be him right now."

Her eyes widened. "Uh-oh."

Mary Jo twisted around again and saw Joshua McKinnon take a wide track to avoid Cissy and Alvid. He caught her looking at him and waved as he headed toward their table.

She swung round to Gigi. "He makes me so nervous. All those questions. I'm always afraid I'll say the wrong thing and end up convicted of something."

"Me too," Mary Jo whispered as footsteps announced his approach.

He stopped at the end of the table. "Hello, ladies." He motioned to the empty chair next to Mary Jo. "May I?"

"We only have ten minutes left on our lunch break." Mary Jo moved her tray.

"I only need five."

"What do you want?" Gigi stared, as if daring him to take longer than he promised.

"I know you're friends with Audrey—"

"We're not close at all." Gigi gathered her silverware together.

"I barely know her," Mary Jo added.

He smiled in the friendliest way that for some reason sent chills running down Mary Jo's arms. "Have you ever seen her act in a way you'd call. . .suspicious?"

"No." Gigi put her glass on her tray.

Joshua gave his full attention to Mary Jo. "And how about you, Mrs. Johnson?"

The memory of Audrey standing in Mr. Wynton's office by the safe came to mind. "I saw her take some things out of Mr. Wynton's wall safe. She tried to hide them against her leg, then put them back in."

He switched his gaze to Gigi. "I saw that too," she admitted.

Joshua looked back and forth between them. "What did she take?"

Gigi spoke first. "Small stuff, like a gold compact—"

"And some medicine bottles," Mary Jo said.

Joshua pursed his lips and rocked his head twice. "And you saw her put these things back in the safe?"

"Yes," Mary Jo answered, and Gigi agreed with a quick chin dip.

"Did you see her put anything else in the safe?"

"No." Mary Jo grabbed her tray. "But she seemed surprised those things were in there. She put them back pretty fast."

She looked at Gigi. "I need to go."

Gigi rose quickly. "Me too."

Joshua pulled Mary Jo's chair out for her. "Thank you, ladies. You've been gracious and helpful."

After he'd gone, Mary Jo sidled up to Gigi as they headed to drop off their trays. "Do you think Audrey's in trouble?"

"Sounds like she might be." Gigi put her tray on the belt. "I need to tell you something."

"Make it fast. I have to get back."

Gigi lowered her voice. "In the hall."

When they were alone, she continued. "Audrey and Miss Vivien think Cissy is behind all the bad things happening around here, even the murders."

"What?" Mary Jo's voice blasted through the hallway, and Gigi shushed her.

Mama always told her she bellowed like a cow when she got worked up. Mary Jo made sure to use a ladylike whisper. "Why do they think that?"

"They came to my apartment and tried to tell me all about this evidence Audrey had. I couldn't believe what she was telling me."

"What don't you believe?" Alvid's voice booming behind them gave them both a jolt.

Mary Jo swiveled on her heel to walk away. "I'm going to be late."

"Me too." Gigi hurried with her from the employee hallway to the main floor, leaving Alvid behind.

Before they parted ways in the main aisle, Gigi grabbed Mary Jo by the wrist. "I don't know why, but something tells me we'd better stay away from Alvid."

"I was thinking the same thing." Mary Jo scurried back to Ladies' Accessories.

Chapter 43

AUDREY

Audrey waited for Gordon to finish ringing up a mother corralling her toddler son before she approached him with the boot imprint. He once claimed he knew the shoe size of every citizen of Levy City.

As with most Wynton's employees, his face grew serious when he saw her heading his way. Miss Evelyn taught that pleasant faces and demeanors won favor better than a hard-set jaw or scowling brow.

She relaxed her face into her most pleasant expression. He'd need a dose of sweetening before he'd help her. "Good morning, Gordon."

He squared his shoulders. "Morning."

Audrey spread the imprinted paper on the counter. "I need your help identifying this boot size, and I know you're the only man for the task."

He half smiled as he slipped on his eyeglasses, which hung on a chain around his neck. "Utility boots, a brand we sell." He removed the glasses. "Large feet, size 13½ or 14. Wide width."

"Is there anything else you can tell me?"

Gordon put on his glasses again. "This is our bestselling brand, but this size must be special ordered." He bent over and inspected the print more closely. "And these are new. The sole hasn't been scuffed much."

New and special order meant she could search the store receipts from the last few months and see who bought a size 14 boot.

Audrey refolded the paper. "Gordon, you're amazing. You've made my morning."

His cheeks reddened as his mouth slid into a lopsided grin. "Doing my job."

"And no one does this better than you."

His face blushed bright red, and he opened his mouth as if to say something, then pressed his lips together and cleared his throat. "Thank you, Miss Penault."

"No, thank you, Gordon." Audrey left him to do his work.

Audrey found Joshua waiting for her in the executive suite. Dressed in a blue-flannel suit obviously custom made, he rose as soon as she entered, smoothing his blue-and-white-dotted tie. "Not even fire compels you to take a day off."

She tucked the boot print into the pocket of her suit jacket. Miss Evelyn always taught that a lady never dwells on her hardships. "Is there something you needed?"

His face fell into more serious lines. "Sit with me a moment?" He motioned to a chair beside him.

Was the spider this charming when asking the fly to join him in his parlor? She paused, trying to read the expression in his eyes, but couldn't. Audrey took the chair next to the one he offered, leaving a wider space between them.

She clasped her hands in her lap. "You have five minutes."

Joshua sat facing her. "I've learned something."

"Go ahead."

"I've been looking into the phone call made to the hotel where Mrs. Wynton and her husband were staying in Miami."

He shifted in his chair. "You didn't make that call."

And she'd thought talking with Gordon was the best news she'd hear. "I'm glad you believe me. What makes you so certain?"

"I'll only say that whoever is trying to pin this on you makes mistakes."

She met his eyes. "You think someone is trying to frame me?"

The line along his jaw flexed as his expression darkened. "Possibly." He glanced at his gold watch. "My five minutes are up."

Audrey rose when he did. "Do you have any idea who?"

His response was interrupted by Cissy entering the office.

She stood in the doorway, staring bullets at Audrey.

"Mrs. Wynton, are you all right?" Joshua asked.

Cissy's brows lowered. "No, I am not all right."

Joshua put his hand on the small of Cissy's back and guided her to the empty chairs. When he'd settled her into one, he pulled another around to face her. "Tell me what's going on." His deep voice remained steady and calm.

"Daddy's had another spell. We've called the doctor."

Joshua motioned to Audrey. "Get her some water."

Not again. How much more could his poor body take? She splashed water everywhere as she tried to pour Cissy a glass.

Her shaking hands caused more to spill onto Joshua's suit pants when she handed the glass to Cissy. She tried to apologize, but he waved her off with an understanding look.

Cissy took a sip. "Thank you, Joshua." She spoke in a high-pitched, girlish tone.

After a second sip, she sat straighter in her chair. "Oh dear, Audrey, you've spilled water on your Cassini suit."

Audrey glanced down at the small damp circle on the peplum of her suit jacket. "It'll dry."

Her brain latched onto the fact that Cissy's concern for Mr. Wynton seemed to have evaporated. And as a former buyer for Wynton's, she'd misidentified the designer of Audrey's suit.

She shook away the thought, as now was not the time to be thinking of so petty a thing when Mr. Wynton was poorly again.

Cissy laid a hand on Joshua's arm. "I'm so worried about Daddy."

She set a hard gaze on Audrey. "Which is why I'm glad you're finally here. I wished you'd called to tell me you'd be in late. I need to give you an assignment before I can go home and care for Daddy."

"I'm happy to help." Miss Evelyn would have been proud of Audrey's efforts to resist telling Cissy to go jump in a swamp and chat with a water moccasin.

Cissy lifted her chin in the air. "You'll be taking over the New Year's Eve Ball this season." She cocked a brow at Audrey, as if waiting to see her explode.

Audrey went stock-still, not even allowing herself to blink. She feared she might break one of Miss Evelyn's most stringent rules. Ladies never ever showed anger in public.

Cissy had always handled the event and began her planning in June, with millions of final details to be worked out in the days leading up to the event.

But it was mid-December. The ball was in two weeks.

And Audrey still needed to catch a murderer, prove Cissy was an accessory to the murders and Mr. Wynton's health crises, and fix her house.

She relaxed her face. "It will be my pleasure."

Cissy popped from her chair, and Joshua rose with her. She wrapped him in a hug. "You are the nicest man."

She slid her arms slowly from around his neck. "And Audrey, I want the budget by the end of the day."

"I've got to get home." Cissy pivoted on the pointed heels of her strapped sandals and exited without another word.

Audrey sat at her desk as her brain spun like a pinwheel. She needed to hire a caterer, but none would agree to take the job this late. Then there were the decorations and a thousand other things she'd have to figure out.

She pulled out her steno pad and jotted down a quick list.

"Guess you're starting that budget?" Joshua stood before her desk.

Audrey cast him a side-eyed glance. "Boss's orders."

"I won't keep you then."

He stepped to the door.

Audrey swiveled in her chair and found him paused at the entryway, still looking her way. "I'm sorry, Joshua. I didn't mean to be rude."

"Your mind is on more important things. Hope that spot on your Lilli Ann dries soon." He walked out whistling "Jingle Bells."

Unlike Cissy, he knew his designers. Miss Evelyn would have liked Joshua McKinnon. She always said attention to small details was what set a lady apart from the others.

Apparently this held true for store detectives.

A bit unnerving. . .but also intriguing.

Chapter 44

GIGI

Gigi clamped her teeth together to keep from screaming as Alvid launched into another story. How he managed to get any work done when it seemed he lived to spread the juiciest stories from the gossip vine stumped her.

"I heard today that the Hatchet checked into the Floridian Hotel this morning. Guess her humble abode is still smoldering." He snickered at his joke.

She jabbed her elbow against his ribs, causing him to jump and spill tea from his glass. He glared as he mopped the brown puddle on the table. "Must you do that?"

No, but she also wasn't going to let him go on about what happened to Audrey with Mary Jo sitting right across from them. Mary Jo's face paled to a sick chartreuse the moment he mentioned the fire.

"We'd like to go one meal without hearing about you-know-who." Gigi handed him her napkin to clean up the last of the spilled tea.

"Ditto," Mary Jo said.

Alvid crumpled the used napkins and dropped them onto his tray. "But you haven't heard the best part yet."

Gigi rolled her eyes. "Don't care."

Alvid glanced at them both. "You're a pair of spoilsports."

"Two innocent little girls were scared out of their wits." Mary Jo looked down at the table.

"Precisely. How could Audrey put your daughters in such a horrible setup?" His eyes didn't show much sympathy as he kept staring at Mary Jo.

"I don't want to talk about that anymore." Mary Jo shot Gigi a look, begging her to steer the conversation to another topic.

"How have the Christmas sales been on your floor, Alvid?" The only thing he loved more than gossip was bragging about his sales numbers.

He tilted his head back as if the question had slapped him in the face. "Terrible. I've had the worst year. Ever."

"But there were so many kids here for the teen Christmas advisory board event, I could hardly get through the aisles last week," Gigi said.

Mary Jo joined in. "Pamela up in the toy department said they've had so many children come to see Santa that the poor man's lap had gone flat. And Christmas is still a week away."

"I don't care. Mr. McKinnon may have increased the number of floor walkers for the holidays, and word has gotten around town that Wynton's is extra safe, but I've heard the numbers. And they're terrible."

"How do you know the numbers for the entire store when you're a floor manager?"

His eye twitched a moment before he answered. "Gigi, my dear, the bookkeeping folks talk, and I'm a good listener."

"What does Cissy think about all this?"

Alvid glared at Mary Jo's question. "How would I know what Cissy thinks? She's not talking store business with me."

Mary Jo didn't wilt from his sneer like she usually did. "I see you two talking all the time."

Alvid grunted. "Cissy is head of personnel and loves her employees. She stops and asks me how things are going. Just like she does with the two of you." He pulled at his collar and readjusted his purple tie decorated with a green, blue, and yellow peacock.

"That's good because she's headed our way." Gigi sipped her tea.

"Merry Christmas, my sweet friends." Cissy bent down and pressed her cheek against Mary Jo's, then came around the table and did the same to Gigi, leaving her in a cloud of Chanel No. 5.

"Do we all have plans for the big day next week?" The heavy gold charms on her pearl bracelets clinked together as she clasped her hands and waited for them to answer.

Alvid went first. "The ball and chain and I are having dinner at her mother's."

He went on about his in-laws, but Gigi tuned him out.

She had her own troubles. On their last date, Bobby said she shouldn't get too fond of her new job because she'd be back in the cafeteria line after the holiday rush ended. She wasn't the clerk type.

What did he know? He couldn't keep his job at Wynton's.

Because of Audrey. The thought of her urged Gigi to give Cissy a warning.

She tuned into the conversation going round the table and found that Alvid and Cissy had brought up Audrey on their own.

"Audrey won't have so much time on her hands. I've put her in charge of the New Year's Eve Ball."

"You didn't." Alvid bore a smile worthy of the cat that snacked on the canary.

Cissy wrinkled her nose and grinned so wide it seemed every tooth in her mouth showed. "I did."

"She'll never be able to pull off such a huge event in two weeks." Alvid shook his head as he and Cissy laughed together.

Cissy went on. "I have more surprises waiting for her after she finishes."

As Alvid leaned forward, waiting for Cissy's next words like a dog for a table scrap, his eyes gleamed. "What have you done?"

He and Cissy kept their attention on each other, and Gigi and Mary Jo shared a shrug and a confused look.

Cissy tossed her head, making her dangly earrings sway. "I discovered that she went missing right after Daddy was stung by those wasps. No one could find her. The store detectives and the police wanted to question her since she was the last to speak to him. She was seen coming out of the executive suite with a box."

Cissy paused and looked around the table. "A box that no one, not even Joshua McKinnon, can account for."

"What do they think is in the missing box?" The pink drained from Mary Jo's cheeks.

"Wasps may not have been the only reason for Daddy's troubles that day. Joshua discovered that the sugar used in the coffee was tainted with rat poison. Audrey is the only one who stocks the coffee cart in Daddy's office."

Gigi's head spun. Audrey said she had evidence against Cissy. Cissy now claimed she had evidence against Audrey.

She looked to make sure Mary Jo hadn't fainted dead away at the news. But Mary Jo stared at the table, her face screwed into a deep scowl.

Cissy sprang from her chair as if she possessed springs in her seat. "I've got to run. Audrey owes me a budget for the ball, and I want it now." She blew a kiss to the table, pulled her tight black cashmere sweater over the top of her fitted black skirt, and walked to the door.

Several employees greeted her as she passed the tables, but Cissy acknowledged none of them.

Alvid blew out a loud breath. "Can you believe it? Audrey tried to poison Mr. Wynton. She's like a black widow spider."

"What do you mean?" Gigi asked.

"Kills her latest paramour and moves on."

Gigi didn't know what paramour meant, but she elbowed him in the ribs anyway. "That's awful."

He looked at her with wide eyes. "Did you not hear what Cissy just said? Audrey Penault is a killer." He looked at Mary Jo. "Just ask her little girls."

Alvid motioned to their trays. "I'll take them up."

Gigi slid hers his way as he reached across the table for Mary Jo's.

She couldn't wait for him to stack them and leave. There was much she wanted to talk about with Mary Jo.

With the stacked trays in hand, he bowed low. "Ladies, lunch was a pleasure as always."

When he'd moved far enough away, Gigi moved to the other side of the table and sat next to Mary Jo. "Can you believe what Cissy just told us?"

"Something's wrong," Mary Jo said in a low voice.

"What do you mean?"

"I know where Audrey was when the police and the detectives

were in Mr. Wynton's office. And I know what's in the missing box and where it is."

Gigi's jaw dropped. "You do?"

"Remember I told you how I ran out of the bathroom at my orientation."

Mary Jo continued. "I was in the sixth-floor ladies' lounge. Audrey was there with me, helping me fix my face. That missing box was a make-up kit. She gave it to me because she believed I was going to be moved to Cosmetics, and she wanted me to practice at home. I told her I didn't want to be in Cosmetics; I liked Ladies' Accessories better."

Gigi's swirling mind came to a screeching halt. "And you got moved to Accessories."

"Right. That missing box is at my house."

Gigi sat back. "Audrey found out Mary Margaret was making me fill out the orders for the cafeteria. I got promoted to Florida Delights, where I do orders and shipping all day long."

They looked each other square in the eyes.

Mary Jo paled. "I was so mad at her. . . And those things I told Joshua McKinnon."

She closed her eyes and pressed fingers to her forehead as if she had a blistering headache. "I don't believe Audrey would hurt Mr. Wynton, Gigi."

Gigi pressed her hand against her flip-flopping stomach to calm things before her bologna and cheese came back up. "Cissy flat-out lied to us." She got up to leave. "Meet me after work."

Mary Jo followed her. "I can't. I've got to get home and fix supper."

"I have to know what's going on, Mary Jo," Gigi said as they parted ways when they entered the main floor.

Chapter 45

VIVIEN

I f she hadn't looked up from her notebook, Vivien would have been knocked to the floor when Gigi plowed out of the elevator like a tractor.

She put her hands up to stop Gigi's mad dash. "My heavens, girl, what's got you in such a rush?"

"I need to talk to you." Gigi's cheeks flushed bright red.

"You're huffing like you've been chased by lightning. What's going on?"

"I'm about to bust, Miss Vivien."

Mirette joined them. "What's going on out here?"

"I don't know. Gigi came barreling out of the elevator and nearly put me on the floor." She looked at Gigi. "Care to tell me what this is all about?"

Gigi huffed. "What's going on between Audrey and Cissy? They're both tossing accusations at each other, and my head is spinning so fast, I feel like I'm in a hurricane."

Vivien slipped her notebook into her work bag. "Come on back to the salon, and I'll tell you everything you need to know."

She turned the lights back on and led Gigi to the back room. She offered her the mother-of-the-bride bucket chair, then pulled two others up for her and Mirette.

Vivien laid her belongings on the fabric cutting table. "First, let me tell you about Cissy. Her maiden name is Mahon, and she comes from one of Levy City's oldest and proudest families. They are southern blue bloods who can trace their lineage all the way back to the first settlers who came to Georgia with Oglethorpe."

"Mahon? Like the packing house?"

"Yes. Cissy's people came here with nothing and in a few years managed to become one of the wealthiest names around. They moved to Florida and were some of the first to make it big in the citrus industry."

Vivien continued. "Her grandfather saved the family fortune during the Depression, but he passed away soon after, and Cissy's father took over the family business."

"Ran the company and the family into the ground." Mirette gestured at the floor.

Gigi's brows crinkled above her eyes. "How?"

"Cissy's daddy was a better playboy than businessman. In ten years, he'd lost all his cash through bad investments and living like money fell from trees."

"You mean Cissy's family went broke?"

"Not the whole family, just her daddy's branch of the Mahon tree. He died shortly after," Vivien said softly.

"Under questionable circumstances," Mirette added.

"Her daddy's sister, Dorella Mahon, took over, invested the money smartly, and amassed quite a fortune. She never married, so all that money just went into her own bank account. She took Cissy and her mother in." Vivien paused to let Gigi soak up all the information.

"I feel bad for her," Gigi said softly.

"Don't. Dorella Mahon petted and spoiled Cissy as much as possible. But at a cost. She never let Cissy or her mother forget they were sympathy cases she had to save."

"She's the meanest kind of old biddy you'll ever find," Mirette said and jumped when Vivien smacked her on the arm. She glared at her boss. "We both know that's true."

"Be that as it may, Cissy and Audrey grew up together, ran in the same circles. Being a part of the social set was very important to Cissy's mother and aunt. They worked hard to be front and center every week in the *LTC* society page."

Gigi sat forward in her chair. "What does that have to do with Audrey?"

Vivien traded another look with Mirette. "Because of her daddy's history, Cissy's family had to work hard to fit in with the country club set. But with Audrey and her mother, Fiona, the country club set chased after them.

"Audrey's father was famed architect Arthur Penault. He designed city hall, the Floridian Hotel, and Wynton's Department Store. He and Mr. Wynton were best friends. In fact, if you were to visit all the large cities in Florida, you'd find an Arthur Penault design. Her mother came from Charleston wealth."

"So there was jealousy between the families?" Gigi asked.

"Only on the Mahon side. Dorella had to sell off a portion of her real estate holdings to pay off her brother's debts. She sold to Audrey's father." Vivien waited as Gigi put the pieces together.

A light flashed in Gigi's eyes. "Who owns Mahon's packing plant?"

"Dorella, as well as the acres of Mahon orange groves outside of Levy City."

"Bobby works at the packing house. He loves it, and they treat him really nice. His boss gave him a new watch a few months ago for doing a great job."

Mirette scowled with disbelief. "My brother has been a manager there for thirty years, and nobody ever gave him anything but a pay-check. Dorella is such a penny-pincher, I can't see her approving a watch for a new employee."

Gigi swelled like a toad. "I saw the watch. Bobby got it for working extra jobs and overtime."

"Everybody at the packing house works on shifts. Dorella is a stickler about not paying overtime to anybody." Mirette shook her head.

Gigi reared to argue in support of Bobby, so Vivien stepped in. "There is no loss of love between Cissy and Audrey. They competed against each other in everything.

"When Audrey went away to Miss Evelyn's school, Cissy demanded to go there as well. But Dorella refused and sent Cissy to the Carlson School for Ladies instead. Still a nice school but not Miss Evelyn's. Audrey finished early and went on to modeling, then college. Cissy finished later, came back, and landed Junior Wynton."

Mirette looked over the rim of her glasses at Vivien. "Don't forget to tell her how all that came about."

"How what came about?"

Vivien hesitated, but since they'd come this far, Gigi ought to know all the details. "Since you ran in different circles, I'll tell you the short version. There was a time when Junior Wynton chased both Cissy and Audrey. Audrey didn't want to be caught, and Cissy reeled Junior in with no trouble at all."

Gigi whistled. "Drama, drama."

"Cissy thrives on drama," Mirette said.

"But another thing has me puzzled," Gigi said.

"What's that?" Vivien asked.

"Why does everyone around here hate Audrey so much?"

"Rumors. Hard to fight those when everyone is willing to believe the worst of what they hear."

Gigi dropped her gaze to the floor. "Yes, it is. But I still don't understand why Audrey would accuse Cissy of trying to kill four people. She's just not the type."

Miss Vivien locked eyes with Gigi. "Are you sure about that?"

Gigi fingered a button on her cardigan. "Mary Jo and I realized Cissy lied to us. She took credit for our job promotions when we're pretty sure Audrey made the changes. I came up here to find out the truth."

Vivien rose from her chair. "I'm sure Audrey's still here." She pushed her chair back to its original spot while Mirette gathered her things.

"Let's go ask." Vivien ushered them out as she cut off the lights and followed them out of the salon. "Let's take the stairs. I need to ask Gigi a question and don't want extra listeners."

Their steps echoed off the walls in the stairwell as they made their way to the seventh floor.

"I think we're alone. What did you want to ask?"

"You said Bobby works at the packing house. Does he wear work boots? The kind with a thick sole and heavy heel?"

"Yes. He has huge feet and sounds like an elephant clomping around when he has them on. Why?"

"And you said Audrey got him fired from Wynton's?"

Gigi blocked Vivien's way. "What's going on, Miss Vivien?"

"Audrey has something I want to show you."

"What's this about?" Gigi's eyes filled with suspicion.

"Keep going and you'll see." Vivien ushered Gigi forward.

As Gigi went on ahead, Mirette leaned close to Vivien's ear. "Do you think her big-footed boyfriend is the one who dumped Francis at the fashion show?"

"For Gigi's sake, I sincerely hope I'm wrong."

Chapter 46

AUDREY

A udrey was sitting at her desk, going over the New Year's Eve Ball to-do list, when the phone rang. "Wynton's Department Store, Mr. Wynton's office. How may I help you?"

"This is Cissy. I need to know what designer and what type of gown you're wearing to the ball."

Audrey covered the mouthpiece. Mr. Wynton was still ailing, and all Cissy could worry about was standing out at the ball. "I'm wearing a custom gown."

"By who?"

"Trust me, Cissy, you and I will not look anything alike at the ball."

Cissy huffed on the other end of the line. "What color?"

"Emerald green, taffeta and chiffon."

"Oh good, I hate that color and those fabrics. By the way, your budget was small and that worries me. You know this is the social event of the holidays. If the ball isn't picture perfect, it's all on you." Cissy hung up.

And when it went swimmingly, she'd make sure to smile pretty when her picture landed on the front page of the *LTC* and brag that it was all Mr. Wynton. Audrey set the receiver in the cradle.

She was rechecking her notes for the ball when Miss Vivien, Mirette, and Gigi entered. "What are y'all doing here this late?" She rose to greet them.

"Girl talk." Miss Vivien set down her things, then sat in a chair and draped her coat across her lap. Gigi and Mirette took the chairs next to hers.

Miss Vivien tilted her head to the side. "I think Gigi needs to go first."

Gigi's eyes widened with surprise. "Me?"

"Didn't you want to ask about the job promotions?"

Audrey had been waiting for this opportunity for so long she couldn't wait to spill the truth. "I'm responsible."

Gigi's surprise filled her face. "Why?"

"You and Mary Jo are great assets to the store. Mr. Wynton agreed."

Gigi's surprise flared into anger. "Then why'd you get Bobby fired? He worked hard down in the loading bay."

The truth was going to hurt, but Gigi needed to be told. "Bobby was stealing from the store. He snuck merchandise and sold the items on the side, then pocketed the profits."

Gigi sprang from her chair. "He'd never steal."

Miss Vivien tugged on the hem of her sweater until Gigi sat down again. "There's something you need to see, honey." She switched her focus to Audrey. "Do you still have the paper with the boot print?"

Audrey walked to her desk drawer, removed the folded paper, and gave it to Gigi.

Gigi peered at the imprint. "What is that?"

"Miss Vivien and I found this in my house the day after the fire. She took me there to get clothes. When we arrived, we discovered my house had been ransacked." Audrey held up the imprint. "Whoever broke in left this behind."

Gigi shuddered. "Do you think this is the same man who shot at you and Mary Jo's girls?"

"I do."

"Do you know who he is?"

Sharing all she suspected would break Gigi's heart. Small doses were probably best until she had ironclad proof. "I know where he works because I found the invoice for the boots."

"I know Wynton's has supplied work boots for Mahon's employees ever since Cissy and Junior married," Miss Vivien explained.

She laid her arm across her lap. "If Cissy is behind all this, I'm certain she'd be happy to take a disgruntled employee ready to grind his axe against Wynton's and Audrey and have him perform the dirty work for her. When Cissy pours on the charm, I've never known a man who'd say no."

"Even Mr. Wynton gives in," Audrey said softly.

"Y'all still think Cissy would commit murder?" Gigi asked.

Mirette clasped Gigi's hand. "Sweetie, haven't you been listening? She's sweet-talked some poor man into getting blood on his hands and keeping hers clean."

As she released Gigi, Mirette locked eyes with Audrey. "If she's after the store and the Wynton money, she's probably leading him by a ring in his nose, and he's got dollar signs in his eyes."

Audrey rubbed her arms. "I can't follow this trail now. I've got to finish planning for the ball. It may be the only thing left to save the store. And Mr. Wynton."

Gigi slunk in her chair. "Bobby wants me to go, but I don't have anything to wear."

"I can help you with that," Audrey said. "I've got closets full of gowns."

Gigi harrumphed. "It would take a miracle for something of yours to fit me."

Miss Vivien and Mirette squeezed Gigi between them. "Meet your fairy godmothers."

"I'll take you to my house tonight, and you can pick something out. We'll bring it to the store tomorrow, and Miss Vivien and Miss Mirette will fix you right up. It will need airing out from the smoke."

"May I join the fairy godmother league too?"

Mary Jo stood in the doorway of the suite.

"I thought you had to go home and fix supper," Gigi said as Mary Jo came to them.

She gave Audrey a long look before speaking. "I owe you an apology."

"Nonsense. You had every right to be angry with me—"

Mary Jo held up her hands to stop Audrey from going on. "No, I didn't. I acted as if you'd invited that man over to shoot at you and try to burn your house down."

She dropped her gaze a moment, then looked around the group.

"I'm sure Gigi told you what happened with Cissy. I didn't know what to think."

Mary Jo shrugged. "I went to the garage, and I've been sitting in my car, trying to get up the nerve to come say I'm sorry."

Audrey stared at her for a moment. She'd not received many apologies in her life, and as Miss Evelyn taught, a lady always accepted one with grace.

She hadn't hugged anyone in ages, but she put her arm around Mary Jo's shoulders and squeezed. "Thank you." She released her as soon as the words left her mouth.

Miss Vivien, Mirette, and Gigi surrounded them, and hugs were spread among the group. Audrey stepped back, but Gigi pulled her into the fray. "If I'm stuck in all this, you are too."

Audrey allowed Mary Jo to hug her around the neck, while Miss Vivien patted her on the back.

Funny how such simple gestures could make a body feel they belonged.

Chapter 47

GIGI

Gigi held her mirror out as far as her arm could reach but couldn't see her full reflection. She propped the mirror's handle between two soup cans, as she did when applying her makeup and doing her hair. Then she tried twirling before the glass. No luck.

"I guess I'll just have to hope and pray I've got this big old skirt smoothed over all those crinolines." She flounced the wide, floor-length skirt again and held her mirror behind her. As far as she could tell, all was in order.

She patted her middle to settle the flutter of nerves that started the moment she stepped into the strapless black velvet gown Audrey had given her. Miss Vivien, Mirette, and Mary Jo did nothing short of magic in their shortening of the hemline, letting out the waist, and restyling the neckline to fit her shape.

Now dotted with rhinestones Mirette found in the salon, the dress sparkled like the night sky. Gigi still couldn't believe this gown belonged to her.

Complete with a name on a label that she couldn't pronounce no matter how many times Audrey tried to help her say it.

"Ba-len-ci-a-ga," Gigi said aloud. She wanted to tell Bobby the name so he wouldn't think she didn't belong in such a gown.

Oh, if only Mama and Daddy could see her. They'd be tickled pink and blue. Maybe she'd take the dress with her for a surprise visit and model it for them while she was there.

Gigi checked her makeup. As soon as Bobby invited her to go, she ran to the drugstore to buy the latest fan magazine with Grace Kelly on the front to use as a guide. She'd practiced every night for a week to get the mascara, rouge, and lipstick just right. Her final attempt wasn't too shabby if she said so herself.

She adjusted the pearl choker Miss Vivien insisted she borrow. As she moved her head to give her hair a final look, the overhead light sparkled in the rhinestone-and-pearl earrings Audrey had supplied.

Car brakes squeaked outside, announcing Bobby's arrival. Gigi pulled on the long white gloves she'd bought at Wynton's, grabbed her gown's matching black velvet cape, and draped it around her shoulders. At the sound of Bobby's feet pounding up the steps, she moved to close the blinds behind the couch but caught sight of her image in the window.

Her head looked twice the size of her body, even with the billowing skirt of her gown. She pulled the cord to hide the image. She was Cinderella for a night, and no one was going to take this away from her.

Bobby knocked on the door, and she smooshed the sides of her skirt so she'd fit past the couch. She paused a moment. "Gigi Woodard, just who do you think you are going out with in this getup?"

Bobby pounded a second time, and after drawing in a shaky breath, she swung the door open slowly, her eyes set to catch his reaction.

He stood in the doorway, his eyes bugging. "Say. . ."

"Say what?" She swallowed hard as his gaze scanned her from head to toe and back.

His new black suit, pleated shirt, and bow tie made him look like a short Cary Grant.

"I think I'm at the wrong apartment. No girl I know ever looked this beautiful." He took her hands in his. "Spin around."

He whistled as she twirled. "Baby, you look good from every angle."

She dipped her head as she moved out to the stoop and locked her apartment door. Bobby offered his arm and held on tight as he guided her down the steps.

The night air chilled her bare neck as she stopped and stared at the ivory-colored Chevy Bel Air parked in the driveway. "Whose car is this?"

Bobby opened the door and bowed low. "Your coach."

Her gown swished as she settled into the car. She took care to tuck her skirt around her legs in the way Audrey and Miss Vivien made her practice over and over.

Bobby closed the door, and she watched him in the rearview mirror as he scurried around the car with an enormous smile on his face.

Gigi leaned back in her seat and clasped her gloved hands in her lap. Miss Vivien and Audrey had filled her head with so many pointers for ladylike behaviors to remember, she feared she'd forget one and make a. . .what was it Audrey called it?

A *fo pa*?

Then Miss Vivien's voice rang in her head with a final word of advice. "Gigi, if all else fails, smile, let out a deep breath, and just be yourself."

That one she could do.

Bobby popped open his door and slid into the seat beside her. He leaned over and kissed her cheek. "All the men at the ball are gonna be jealous of my date."

Her stomach shivered at his compliment. "You look like a movie star."

He straightened his bow tie and pretended to brush lint from his shoulder. "Don't I?"

Bobby started the car and pulled from the driveway.

"You didn't say who you borrowed this car from," she reminded him as he drove down the street.

"I didn't borrow it." He cocked a crocodile-sized grin at her. "I own it."

"What? Where did you get money to buy a new car?"

"Earned it. And this car is a year old. Got it for a steal from a guy over in Ocala."

"What happened to your old truck?"

His smile faded. "I had to junk it."

"Why"

Bobby squirmed in his seat. "The engine quit running." He turned into the street. "I'd rather talk about how beautiful you look tonight. You get that dress from the fashion show?"

"No. Audrey gave it to me."

"Funny joke."

Gigi shook her head. "I'm not joking. She has this closet full of gowns she saved from her modeling days and told me to come pick one. Miss Vivien, Miss Mirette, and Mary Jo fixed the gown to fit me."

"My aren't we fancy? *Miss* Vivien, *Miss* Mirette, and Audrey herself all jumping and fetching to help you out." His tone cut through the car and Gigi's happy mood.

"What's the matter with you? You say these women don't know how to be nice all the time. Well, they've been plenty nice to me."

Nicer than he was at the moment. And lately, if she were being honest with herself.

"They must want something."

"What's that supposed to mean?"

"Women like them take on girls like you as a charity case. Makes 'em feel good about themselves."

Heat traveled up from her innards and flamed across her entire body. "You don't believe they could like me as a friend?"

"Not hardly," he mumbled.

He clammed up as he drove past the orange juice factory and other warehouses on Gigi's side of town. The only sound breaking up the silence the entire trip was the clicking of his turn signal when he maneuvered onto Main Street.

When Bobby rounded the corner and pulled into the line of cars waiting to enter Wynton's parking garage, Nelson stood at the entrance, checking invitations and directing folks into the spaces.

Bobby rolled down his window, then wiggled his fingers at Gigi. "Give me those invites so I can flash them at this—"

Gigi's stomach curled at the word he called Nelson. She thought of Lilla and Eunice and the other Colored employees at the store who'd always worked hard—and treated her with more respect than Bobby did.

She pulled the linen invitations from the evening bag Mary Jo had given her and handed them over.

She'd never been to the ballroom, and she gasped as they entered. The red-and-gold planters filled with poinsettias and ferns, and shiny bunting in the same colors draped around the ceiling and wall made the room look like a palace.

The food table stood off to the right of the entrance, and the aroma made her stomach growl. She'd know Lilla's cooking anywhere, even if Audrey hadn't told her she'd paid Lilla and Eunice to cook for the ball.

No caterers could have done better, Audrey said, and Gigi couldn't agree more. "Bobby, let's get some food. I'm starving."

But he wasn't listening. Instead, he unwound her arm from his as he looked around the room. "Later. I need to take care of something."

He went back through the entrance, leaving her standing alone.

"Bobby?" Gigi called after him, but he hurried through the doors and never looked back.

"Gigi."

Mary Jo came her way, dragging Kenny by the hand toward her.

Mary Jo wore the blue cocktail dress from the fashion show. The updo Gigi had shown her in a magazine highlighted her high cheekbones and tiny nose, bringing the image of homecoming queen to life.

Even the antique mother-of-pearl brooch she'd pinned to the front of her neckline and the matching earrings Mary Jo said came from her great-aunt Somebody-or-other looked perfect.

Her friend's eyes sparkled when she took Gigi in. "You look absolutely amazing." She leaned close. "Did Bobby flip when he saw you?"

"He fawned for a minute, but as soon as we got here, he hotfooted out of here and left me standing."

"What a bubblehead." Mary Jo pulled Kenny closer.

"Honey, this is Gigi, from work."

Kenny offered his hand. "Nice to put such a pretty face with the name I hear so often." His warm fingers closed around hers when he shook her hand.

No wonder Mary Jo mooned over him. He was quite the dish with his black, slicked-back hair and big hazel eyes. And Gigi couldn't remember seeing a man with more perfect, white teeth.

She gave his hand a firm shake before releasing it. "Nice to meet you too. She talks about you and the girls all the time."

He leaned over and kissed the top of Mary Jo's head. "That's my girl." Kenny draped his arm about her shoulders and pulled her close.

Kenny was the kind of guy Gigi had dreamed of her whole life but could never seem to find or catch.

The band switched to a new song, and Kenny gazed at Mary Jo. "This is one of our favorite songs, so if you don't mind, I'm going to steal my wife away for a dance."

He did the pulling this time as he maneuvered her to the circle of light on the floor filled with all the other dancing couples.

Gigi watched the dancers. There were so many red, blue, and black gowns, some strapless like hers, others with tiny sleeves. Some with big skirts, others tight-fitting. And all the women, except Mary Jo, were decked in diamonds or pearls. It was like a scene out of a Cary Grant or Grace Kelly movie. And here she was dolled and perfumed up, living it instead of just watching in a dark movie house.

But Bobby had been gone too long, and she didn't come to the ball to be left standing alone. Gigi went back to the hallway to search for him.

After looking both ways, she chose to head to the right. The music from the ballroom faded as she moved farther down the hallway. Voices sounded ahead—a woman's high-pitched coos and a man's responding low laugh.

She rounded a corner and saw Cissy and Bobby at the end of another hallway. Cissy had her hand on Bobby's chest and seemed to be whispering something in his ear.

He rubbed the bare skin between her shoulders and the hem of her long black gloves.

Cissy stuck her face so close to his, their noses almost touched. "Bobby Bridges, you're too much."

Gigi took a step toward them. "Bobby? Cissy?"

They both jerked their heads in her direction. Cissy stepped back so fast, one would think Bobby had changed into a giant rattlesnake.

She held out her arms as she scurried forward. "Gigi."

Cissy grabbed her by the hands. "Let me get a look at you." She spun Gigi in a circle.

"Oh, honey, you look like a million." Cissy let go and clapped her hands. "No, two million, maybe even three."

Gigi took in Cissy's bright red satin dress. The bodice and skirt clung to her slim figure, then flared at the ruffled bottom like a fish tail. Her necklace was made of diamonds the size of malted milk balls, and her dangling diamond earrings almost brushed her shoulders.

"You look like a queen." The words tumbled out before she checked them, and Gigi hoped she hadn't made one of those fo pas Audrey warned her about.

But Cissy smiled. "John T. loved me in red, so I picked this dress in his honor. It's a Charles James."

Gigi nodded like she understood, even though she had no idea what Cissy was talking about.

"Where did you get yours?" Cissy asked as she straightened the cape about Gigi's shoulders.

"A friend."

Cissy's eyes darkened as she checked the tag sewn into the cape's neckline. "Balenciaga. What a nice friend." She didn't pronounce the name the same as Audrey did, and her voice had lost its friendly tone.

Bobby came beside Cissy. "Audrey gave her the dress."

Cissy curled her nose as if she'd sniffed something dead. "How kind."

They snickered together like a couple of school chums, leaving Gigi as a very unhappy third wheel.

"I'm going back to the ballroom." Gigi picked up her skirt like Miss Vivien had taught her, swung around, and left Bobby and Cissy behind.

She heard their loud whispers, then Bobby's trotting footsteps coming up behind her. "You leaving me?"

Gigi hurried her pace back to the ballroom.

Bobby came round and blocked her progress. He stood before her with outstretched arms and the crooked smile he used to butter her up when she was steamed at him.

"Honey, she's my boss. I went looking for the men's room and ran into her. She asked me about a problem at the packing house, and I couldn't tell her to take a leap in the lake, could I?"

He clasped both her arms and looked straight into her eyes. "This is the best job I've ever had, and I've got a chance to finally make enough money to be somebody. Don't ruin it for me."

Gigi wriggled from his grip. Money didn't make you a somebody.

Her parents had taught her that, but until this moment she'd not really understood what they meant.

"I'm going to the ball." She stepped past Bobby and headed for the ballroom.

He walked by her side until she found an empty table along the wall. When she'd slipped out of her cape, Bobby whistled softly. "You're so pretty." He held out his arm and escorted her to the dance floor.

After swaying through two songs, he took her by the hand. "Let's sit. I'm starving and thirsty."

He pulled out her chair and helped her settle, then took off for the food and drink tables. Bobby returned with two plates filled with Lilla's and Eunice's best goodies, and they ate in silence.

Bobby downed a glass of something sparkly, then two more. Gigi kept her eyes on the array of women in beautiful gowns, playing a game with herself, guessing which dresses came from Wynton's.

When they danced again, Bobby swayed and stepped on her toes. "You keep watching all the rich stiffs."

"I like looking at the dresses. They're pretty." She looked around the room. "Audrey did a nice job with the decorating. You know she only had two weeks to pull this together?"

"Audrey this, Audrey that. I'm going back to the table."

Bobby grabbed another drink from a waiter weaving through the crowd and downed it while they moved to their table. A cloud of his alcohol-laced breath hit Gigi's nose when he leaned in close. He tried to prop his elbow on the table for support, but it slipped and he almost fell from his chair. His cackling laughter echoed above the music. People stared.

Gigi searched the room for Mary Jo and Kenny to see if their table had an empty chair for her to claim.

They were on the dance floor again, but a vacant chair was available. She went to rise, but Bobby caught her arm and pulled her down. "Where you going?" He seemed to be fighting to keep his eyes open, and she wouldn't have been a bit surprised if he slid under the table and fell asleep.

"Leave me alone, Bobby." She snatched her arm from his grip.

He wobbled toward her. "You got on one of Audrey's ritzy rags, and now you're too good to sit with me?"

He hiccuped. "I got me some rich friends too." Bobby's eyes narrowed and his mouth curled into a crocodile grin. "They already paid me to do a big job."

Gigi's heart clenched as she sat forward. "Bobby, what have you done?"

He hiccuped. "I lit up the sky, baby. And now I'm gonna make it fall, like in that story about the chicken."

Fear stabbed through her as she mulled his words. "Are you talking about Audrey's house?" Gigi fought back tears.

"Took away my job when I didn't do nothing wrong."

She stared at him a moment as ugly thoughts came to her mind. "What are you mixed up in?"

The fog in his glassy eyes seemed to lift a moment. "Don't ask me that. You'll get me killed."

"You tell me right now, Bobby Bridges."

Bobby squirmed in his chair. He grabbed Gigi's evening bag and shoved it in her lap. "We're going."

He grabbed her wrist, but she yanked free. "I'm not going anywhere with you. You're so drunk, you can't see straight."

Bobby hovered by her ear. "We have to go. Before something bad happens."

Gigi jerked away from him. "You have something planned tonight. Here?"

He clamped his jaws together so tightly she could see the muscles rippling in his cheek. "Either you come with me now, or I'm leaving you here. What's it gonna be, Gigi?"

She tipped her chin. "I'm staying."

"I'm gone." Bobby slammed his chair under the table and staggered from the ballroom, leaving Gigi at the table.

Alone.

Gigi practically burst from anger, fear, and nerves as she searched the room for Audrey and Miss Vivien.

She had to tell somebody that trouble was coming.

Chapter 48

AUDREY

Audrey stepped to the side as Bobby Bridges stumbled out of the ballroom. Tradition held that the hostess of the New Year's Eve Ball arrived late, then made her welcome speech to the attendees. She'd taken her time getting ready and rode in with Miss Vivien and Mirette. Bobby's quick retreat wasn't a good sign.

"You two owe me a steak dinner," Mirette said as she and Miss Vivien joined Audrey in the hallway outside the ballroom. She checked her watch. "He lasted forty-five minutes or less, by my count."

Miss Vivien peeked into the room. "Looks like Gigi found Mary Jo and Kenny." She turned back to Audrey. "She's sitting with them, looking mad as fire."

"Good. Maybe she threw the no-good—"

"Mirette, you're in ladylike clothes tonight." Miss Vivien gave her assistant a warning glance.

"Speaking of which, how in the world did you manage to get changed and dolled up so fast, Audrey? You were the last to get started, beat me and Vivien by twenty minutes, and yet you look like you stepped out of a magazine." Mirette waved her hand over Audrey as if she were an appliance for sale in a TV commercial.

"Practice." Audrey fluffed the emerald-green chiffon flounces at the back of her skirt. They billowed like butterfly wings from the back of her form-fitting, draped taffeta gown.

"Y'all go on in and see how Gigi's doing." Audrey adjusted the pearl bracelet she wore over the wrist of her long white glove.

"The sooner I'm off these heels, the better." Mirette followed Miss Vivien to the ballroom as squeals from friends greeting her and happy-new-year wishes broke out around them.

Audrey held back, listening as the band played a jazzy version of "Winter Wonderland." Thankfully, their leader honored her request to mix plenty of holiday tunes into the dance selection. Mr. Wynton was a firm believer that the Christmas spirit shouldn't end until the day after New Year's.

Other than Bobby's hasty exit, everything seemed to be going well. The waiters milled through the crowd, offering goodies from their trays, while other guests visited the food and drink tables. The dance floor was full, the air filled with happy voices, and as far as she could tell, all the attendees, minus Gigi, were smiling and having fun.

Cissy came up beside her. "Don't you think it's time you went in?" She cast a side-eye at a waiter who stared a second longer than he should have when he passed her by.

"Almost. I thought Mr. Wynton was coming tonight. He was so happy to be feeling better. Already in his tux when I stopped by to give him his medicine earlier."

Cissy released a long sigh. "He was, but shortly before I left he looked pale and complained of a headache, so I made him stay home. I promised to bring him some cake and a plateful of Eunice and Lilla's goodies."

"Nurse Ethel won't like that very much."

Cissy waved off her comment. "She'll be asleep by the time I get home. And Daddy won't tell on me."

"Thank you for the extra handyman you sent in last night." Audrey looked around the room once more. "He did a great job hanging the glass ball. I think the guests will enjoy having our own version, like they do in Times Square."

"Anything to help." Cissy nudged Audrey. "I can walk in with you if you'd like."

"I'll be fine." Where did this kinder Cissy come from?

"Your dress is lovely, Cissy. Very bold statement with the black gloves against the red gown."

"John T. loved me in red. Daddy wanted me to look festive as well. I wore the gloves because I'm still in mourning."

She stared at Audrey. "You'll be the first hostess ever to walk in alone. Aren't you a little worried that might stir up the crowd?" She reached down and adjusted the ruffles in her skirt.

"We were always greeted with such love when we walked in together to lead the hostess dance." Cissy pressed her hand against her middle. "I'll never have the fun of dancing with him again. Thanks to you."

Audrey squared her shoulders.

She'd walked into worse situations, and if she had to grab the first man she saw to dance with her for the hostess dance, she'd make it a memorable choice.

"I'm so sorry I'm late, Audrey. There was a mix-up with my invitation," a male voice called behind her.

She and Cissy gawked as Joshua threw his overcoat to the attendant manning the cloak room. He hurried to Audrey's side and tucked her arm within his.

Joshua inclined his head toward Cissy. "Mrs. Wynton. You're looking lovely." He flashed Audrey a bright smile. "Time to walk you in?"

Cissy locked eyes with Audrey. She smirked. "Have fun, you two."

Cissy entered to a loud round of applause. She blew kisses to the crowd, bent low at the waist as if she were addressing a royal court, and made her way to the VIP table in the front of the room.

Joshua patted Audrey's hand. "I hope you didn't mind my saving you."

"I would have been fine walking in alone."

"I know."

The crowd parted as they walked in together, and the band leader raised his baton. She'd asked them to play a version of "Mood Indigo," Mr. Wynton's favorite song.

Joshua placed his arm around her waist and waltzed her to the middle of the dance floor. After the first round of the song was completed, the band leader welcomed everyone to the floor. Other couples joined them.

"Green is a good color for you." He twirled her in a circle and continued. "And the scent you're wearing. Evening in Paris. I'd have thought you'd go for something a little fancier."

"I'm really just a simple girl." Take every compliment with a grain of salt to keep from feeding vanity, Miss Evelyn always said. Besides, she'd received so many gushes from men her entire life, she barely listened to them anymore.

"You don't like compliments, do you?" Joshua maneuvered her to a less crowded side of the dance floor.

"Depends on the source."

"Leftovers from your modeling days?"

"Partly."

"I have to confess, I don't believe your answer about why you quit. From what I see tonight, your heart is still very much in the fashion world."

"Whatever do you mean?"

"This is a custom dress, Miss Penault. If I remember, this very frock debuted in Paris in 1952, Givenchy's collection."

She wanted to ask how he knew this, but he continued. "For someone who didn't want to be treated like a product, you still dress like one."

She shrugged away his words. "I love how well-made clothes feel when you wear them."

"Still doesn't answer my question."

He watched as he awaited her answer.

"Perhaps I developed a crush on a well-known photographer who discovered me and whisked me off to Paris. After a whirlwind romance all over Europe, he broke my heart by marrying another, more famous model."

She paused as a couple swayed past them. "Or maybe I got tired of fighting off the advances of a wealthy octopus who only wanted me as an accessory."

Audrey tapped her fingers on his shoulder. "Then there's always the chance I saw other girls forced out because the clock never stopped chasing them, and decided to leave by my own choice."

Joshua shook his head. "You don't care much for straight answers, do you?"

The band finished their song, and he removed his hand from her waist but stayed close as the leader prepared for the next tune.

"Not so. I gave you three very plausible answers."

"None of them were the right answer."

She had to give him credit—he was interesting. "Then maybe the truth lies somewhere in the midst of them."

"It usually does." He grinned, and she couldn't help responding in kind.

As their conversation lulled, Audrey was certain she heard a cracking noise.

Then another.

They grew so loud the band leader halted his musicians. All the dancers stopped, looking around with questioning eyes.

Audrey looked at the huge glass ball hanging above them and saw that the plaster around it was cracking. The ornament jerked.

"Get off the dance floor!" she yelled.

Voices rose as bodies rushed to the sides of the room.

A final cracking sounded. The glass ball fell from the ceiling and crashed to the floor, sending jagged shards in all directions. Screams filled the ballroom.

Chapter 49

AUDREY

Audrey tried to hand Nelson his breakfast, but he waved her offering away. "There's trouble today."

The concern in his eyes drilled straight to her gut. "What's wrong, Nelson?"

He tilted his head toward Junior's Corvette. "She got here at six. Scrambled in like a scalded cat, slammed the door, and stomped to the store. A few minutes later, the other gentlemen on the board of directors came. I heard two of them saying Mr. Wynton's bad off."

"I knew something was wrong. When I stopped by to give him the medicine, Nurse Ethel met me at the door and said the doctor strictly forbade any visitors today." Audrey choked out the words.

She buttoned her coat to ward off the cold and her own shivering. Audrey held up the thermos and bag. "You're sure you don't want these?"

Nelson shook his head.

Audrey locked her car, then shoved both thermos and twists into her satchel. As she hurried from the garage, Joshua pulled up in his car. He stopped and rolled down the window. "Were you called in early too?"

"What's going on?"

He put the car in PARK but left it running. "I got a call from Cissy around five. She said her father-in-law had a spell with his heart at midnight, and things look bad."

"She never called me."

Another car pulled into the garage. The driver honked at Joshua to move along. "I'll see you in the suite." He drove into the garage.

Once she arrived in the office, Audrey put her things away. The red button on her phone was lit, and she could hear Cissy chattering fast on Mr. Wynton's side of the office walls.

But who would she be talking to this early in the morning? The temptation to quietly lift the receiver and listen in was hard to ignore.

But she wouldn't.

Instead, she hung her coat in the closet, sat in her chair, and stared at Mr. Wynton's closed door.

"Audrey."

She swiveled in her chair to see Joshua rushing in. Audrey held a finger to her lips. "Cissy's on the phone." She gestured toward the closed door.

Joshua didn't grab a chair like he usually did, but squatted before her desk and met her eye to eye. "Good. I'll tell you this fast. Cissy has apparently been on the phone with the board members since she got here. She's called an emergency meeting."

Audrey's stomach twisted, untwisted, and curled again. "She doesn't have that authority."

Joshua leaned in. "She seems to now."

"How? The only way she could is if Mr. Wynton—" Her voice broke off as another thought screamed into her head.

"Oh no."

"What's the matter?"

Before she could answer him, the door opened and Cissy walked out.

Her face paled above the high-necked, full-skirted black dress she wore. Her usual stilettos were gone, and she wore simple black pumps.

Joshua rose to his feet. "Mrs. Wynton, are you all right?"

Cissy stared past him with a glassy-eyed gaze. "Daddy is dying. His doctors say he won't last much longer."

Her words sliced through Audrey. "This can't be true." Her voice shook as she fisted both hands and pressed them hard against her chest to keep from crying.

Mr. Wynton couldn't be dying.

Audrey snapped to her feet, but her head spun and she plopped back in her chair.

Cissy's eyes snapped to attention and flashed with dark anger. "Don't you dare sit there all innocent and caring." She rushed to the desk and jabbed her finger in Audrey's face. "You did this." Cissy melted into the same loud wails she'd had at Junior's funeral.

She drew up straight and dabbed the tears away with her fingertip. She locked eyes with Audrey. "That ends today."

Cissy laid her hand on Joshua's arm. "I want you at the meeting. Eight o'clock sharp."

She switched her gaze to Audrey. "You too."

Cissy stalked into Mr. Wynton's office and slammed the door.

Audrey grabbed her coat and satchel from the closet.

"Where are you going?" Joshua tried to follow her out the door.

"I'll see you at eight."

Audrey ran down the stairs. Locked inside her car was her only hope of fixing things.

✝✝

Audrey made her way to the conference room with two minutes to spare. A store security guard standing by the entrance held his hand out when she tried to enter. "This meeting is closed."

He was one of Cissy's newest hires and probably wasn't told she always attended board meetings to take the minutes. She held up her steno pad and pencil. "I'm Mr. Wynton's secretary. I'm supposed to be here."

The guard moved to block the doorway. "Mrs. Wynton said board members only." He crossed his arms behind his back and stood with his feet a little farther apart.

"She can't do that."

The door cracked open, and Cissy poked her head through. "Actually, I can. I'm now the acting chairman of the board. When we need you, Audrey, I'll send Gill here to come and get you. Until then, you go wait in the office."

Cissy patted Gill on the shoulder, then shut the door.

"Do you need me to walk you back?" Gill smirked as he spoke.

Audrey left on her own.

When she walked in, Joshua was waiting for her. "What's going on?"

Audrey laid her pad and pencil on her desk. "Cissy has declared herself the acting chairman." She sat on the edge of her desk.

Joshua sat beside her. "Can she do that?"

"No. But somehow she is anyway."

"What happens next?"

The night she snuck over to Mr. Wynton's house came to mind. He'd said he'd fight back, but now it seemed whatever he'd planned was not going to happen.

"Nothing good."

Gill appeared in the doorway. "They're ready for you." He switched his gaze to Joshua. "Are you McKinnon?"

"I am."

"You come too."

As they followed Gill down the hallway, Joshua brushed his shoulder against Audrey's. She glanced at him, and he mouthed, *Good luck.*

She prayed for more than luck as they reached the door to the conference room.

When they entered, Audrey's gaze went to Mr. Wynton's chair at the end of the long table. In his place sat a man who stared at her as if she were a slice of chocolate cake he'd ordered for dessert.

He looked to Cissy. "This her?"

"All day long."

He looked Audrey over from head to toe. "You look as good as you sound."

Shock stabbed through her. "You're George Crawford."

He cocked one brow. "You have a good memory."

"Cissy, why is he here?"

"He's buying the store."

"What? How?" Audrey scanned the faces of the board members.

The president of First Bank of Levy City, Ronald Blackmoore, met her gaze. "The store's in trouble, and she's got controlling interests." He motioned to the other members. "They want to go with her plan. The rest of us aren't convinced yet."

"Cissy, how could you do this to Mr. Wynton? You know what this store means to him. How he started the company because his father—"

Cissy tipped her chin. "Daddy is dying. This store is dying. I'm trying to save what's left of his legacy since I'm the only Wynton you haven't killed yet."

Audrey met the stares of the men in the room. "She doesn't have the power to do this. Mr. Wynton appointed—"

Cissy rose from her chair. "I know what you thought you'd forced Daddy to set up. But I figured everything out before you could kill him and make that happen."

Audrey fought to remain calm. "You can't be serious. I didn't try to kill—"

"If you gentlemen will follow me, I'll prove it." Cissy walked to the door and waited for the board members.

The men on the board rose, as did George Crawford. He kept his eyes on Audrey as he made his way to the door.

He held out his arm. "I'll walk you there."

Audrey was about to tell him she'd rather walk through a pile of fire ants barefoot when Joshua took her by the arm. "I'm to escort you. Mrs. Wynton's orders."

George Crawford held up his hands as Joshua tightened his grip and held her back while the others went into the hall.

They walked a few steps in silence before Joshua spoke. "I'm sorry about all this."

"You know what she's up to, don't you?"

The line of his jaw hardened. "Not completely."

He slowed his pace. "Tell me about Mr. Wynton and his father."

She'd heard Mr. Wynton share his history many times and loved the story more with each retelling.

"He grew up desperately poor, just him and his father. His father couldn't read or write and knew nothing but farming or grove work, so they moved around. When Mr. Wynton was old enough to go to school, his father settled near Jacksonville and took a job as a janitor. He was paid a little more than nothing but wanted his son to have new shoes and pants when he started school so the city kids wouldn't tease him."

She stopped and faced Joshua. "They went to a store, and the clerks humiliated his father when he asked to see clothes for himself and his son. Mr. Wynton said he saw tears in his father's eyes as the clerks forced them off the premises. He vowed he'd build a store where everyone, from the richest to the poorest, would feel welcome and be able to buy what they wanted."

Joshua steered her toward the office again. "We'd better get in there."

When they entered the suite, Miss Vivien, Mary Jo, and Gigi waited by her desk.

Joshua released her arm. "I'll go see what Mrs. Wynton wants you to do now."

The women surrounded Audrey.

"What is going on? Cissy ignored us when she came in," Mary Jo said.

"She's trying to get the board to vote to sell the store."

"What?" the women said in unison.

"It's true. Somehow, she's got controlling shares, and I think she's made a deal with George Crawford."

Gigi looked toward Mr. Wynton's office, then back. "I found out this morning that Francis wasn't dating Mr. Loring. She was sneaking around with the man who owns the big sawmill outside of town."

Audrey rubbed her forehead. "He's on the board. Cissy must have blackmailed him, so he sold her his shares."

Miss Vivien motioned for them to huddle closer. "Mirette heard Raymond Spurling was behind on the mortgages on his house and business, so Cissy paid them off in trade for his shares."

Audrey exhaled. "Add those shares to what she inherited from Junior, and she owns more of the store now than Mr. Wynton."

"Joshua, I'm ready. Bring Audrey in," Cissy called from the inner office.

"Excuse me." Joshua cut into the ladies' circle and motioned for Audrey.

"We're right behind you." Miss Vivien patted Audrey as she followed Joshua into the office.

The door to the wall safe was open, and Cissy stood nearby, the center of attention. "I've said all along"—she pointed at Audrey—"that she's been out to get Daddy. Today I've got proof."

She reached into the safe and brought out an object.

Audrey's heart pounded so hard she was sure everyone in the room heard it.

"This brick was used to kill Francis Tyler. Her hair and blood were found on it when I showed it to the police. It came from the corner of Audrey's house."

Cissy laid the brick on a table and reached into the safe again. She held up Audrey's gold compact, then opened the lid, exposing the broken mirror. "A piece of this mirror was used to kill Daddy's nurse, Nancy. This compact belongs to Audrey."

Audrey's knees melted and she swayed. Joshua grabbed her around the waist and held her up.

Cissy took out the empty cold cream jar with the wasp. "Daddy's doctors have confirmed that this was the kind of wasp that stung him. This jar came from Audrey's house." She added the jar to the array.

She then removed the medicine bottles. "These are the bottles Audrey has been using when she gives Daddy his medicine."

Cissy motioned to Joshua. "He found rat poison in Daddy's sugar bowl weeks ago. Audrey is the only one who fills that bowl and fixed Daddy's coffee. The police found the same kind of poison in these pill bottles."

Audrey's stomach threatened to erupt. All the items she'd hidden in her hatbox at home now sat before the world, stolen from her for just this moment.

"And there's one more thing."

Audrey jerked her attention back to the safe. What else was there?

Cissy removed a large file folder and opened it. She held a single sheet of paper up for all to see. "This is a will drafted by the late Mr. Loring, for Daddy."

She touched the date at the top. "This was written in late July of this year, one month before Daddy's wasp attack."

Cissy handed the will to Mr. Blackmoore. "Please read what it says."

He pulled his glasses from his pocket and slid them on his nose, then focused his attention to the will. Creases in his forehead deepened the longer he read.

He looked up. "Audrey Penault gets everything when Mr. Wynton dies."

"That's not true." She looked at her friends, and they stared back with unbelief and shocked expressions. "He made me temporary chairman of the board until his chosen successor could fill the spot. But nothing else."

Audrey pulled away from Joshua. She stepped toward Cissy, but George Crawford blocked her way.

"I think we've heard enough."

"That will is a fake."

Cissy shoved the document at Audrey's face as she ran her finger over the signatures at the bottom. "Daddy, Mr. Loring, and you signed this. You talked him into this, then plotted to kill him and my sweet John T. You pulled poor Francis and Mr. Loring into your scheme, then killed them when they threatened to expose you. Nancy figured out you were poisoning Daddy, so you killed her too."

"I never signed any such document." Audrey tried to take the document and look at her supposed signature, but Cissy pulled it from her reach.

"But she doesn't need the money." Joshua moved to stand before the crowd. "The entire town has told me Audrey's loaded. So why kill for more?"

Cissy looked at him as if he were a silly little boy. "She's greedy."

"What's next, Mrs. Wynton?" George Crawford plopped his over-sized body into one of the chairs sitting in front of Mr. Wynton's desk.

Cissy looked right at Audrey. "The police are on their way here. Mr. McKinnon, they want you to take her to the store's security offices."

"Yes, ma'am." Joshua clicked a pair of handcuffs around her wrists, then took her by the arm and led her from the room.

As she passed by her friends, Audrey caught their eyes. "Please make sure Nelson gets his thermos back. I rinsed it out and put it on my desk. "

They stood stone-still and said nothing.

The expressions on their faces told all she needed to know.

They believed everything Cissy had told them.

I t wasn't until she'd tasted the chicken and dumplings that Mary Jo realized she'd forgotten to add salt and pepper. Cooking supper proved hard when her mind kept jumping back to the events at the store.

She couldn't shake Audrey's downcast eyes when Cissy accused her of all those awful things. Or how Cissy's mouth curled up at the corners when the police marched Audrey in front of all the employees and customers through the main floor and out the front doors.

Kenny came in and sniffed the air. "Smells like supper's almost ready. You want me to fix the girls' milk?"

The phone on the wall in the hall rang.

"Go get that, will you, please? I'll fix the girls' plates."

Kenny came back looking annoyed. "It's Miss Vivien. I told her we're sitting down to supper, but she said this couldn't wait."

"She wouldn't call if it weren't serious." Mary Jo wiped her hands on a towel.

Kenny had left the receiver hanging when he'd come to get her, so Mary Jo grabbed it up. "Miss Vivien, I'll be right with you. I've got to call the girls to supper."

"I'll be here," she answered.

Mary Jo herded Penny and Carrie Rose to the table, making sure they bowed their heads when Kenny started to pray. She tiptoed away after the amens and went back to the phone.

"I'm here, Miss Vivien. What's the matter?"

"I can't stop thinking about what happened to Audrey today."

A burst of giggles sounded in the kitchen, making it hard to hear, so Mary Jo moved down the hallway until the curls in the phone cord straightened.

"I can't believe she did all those things Cissy said."

"She didn't. You remember that boot print we found at Audrey's? It belongs to Bobby Bridges. Mahon's packing house ordered him a size 14 right around the time of the show."

Mary Jo coiled a section of the cord around her finger. "Does Gigi know?"

"She told me."

"Oh, she must be devastated or mad as a nest of hornets."

"Bit of both."

"I'll be asking for forgiveness for this later, but I hope he gets what's coming to him."

"I understand. It's hard to be Christian in circumstances like these, isn't it?"

He shot at her babies. "I want Bobby to go to jail, Miss Vivien." She'd never wished ill on anyone in her life.

"We all do."

"Is that what you wanted to tell me?"

"There's more. Joshua McKinnon caught up with me and Mirette as we were leaving the salon. He said Audrey's in jail. She's been booked for murder, attempted murder, fraud, conspiracy to commit murder, and theft."

Mary Jo's heart ached. "Poor Audrey."

"I think there's evidence in my safe that will save her. Mirette, Gigi, and I are going over to the store now. You're welcome to come too."

Mary Jo's stomach knotted. She'd promised the girls she'd read the next chapter of *Peter Pan* to them before bed. And Kenny would never approve of her leaving the house at night without him.

"I don't know. . ."

Kenny peeked his head into the hallway. "What's the matter?"

"Hang on, Miss Vivien." Mary Jo covered the mouthpiece with her hand. "They put Audrey in jail today."

Kenny's brows shot up. "Jail?"

"For a whole list of terrible things."

"You think she's guilty?"

Mary Jo shook her head. "Miss Vivien says she's got proof in her salon that Audrey's innocent, and wants to go there tonight to get it. She's asked me to come along."

The girls peeked around the corner. "Mama, what are you doing?" Carrie Rose asked.

Kenny herded them back into the kitchen. "Mama's talking to her friend. You two need to put your dirty dishes in the sink."

He returned and inclined his head toward the phone. "How many are going?"

"Miss Vivien, Miss Mirette, and Gigi."

"Where are you going again?"

"Miss Vivien's salon."

He kissed her forehead. "Go help your friend."

"I love you." Mary Jo removed her hand from the mouthpiece. "I'll be waiting on my front steps."

Mary Jo pulled her coat around her as the January cold crept up her legs, happy that Wynton's had the thicker stockings for sale during the Christmas season.

What would Mama say about her gallivanting after dark when she should be home putting her girls to bed?

For once in her life, she didn't care what Mama might say.

✝✝

As Miss Vivien opened the door for her to climb into the back seat, Mary Jo felt a pang of excitement flutter in her stomach. The moment she landed in the car, Miss Mirette hit the gas, leaving Miss Vivien to pull the front passenger-side door closed.

Mirette took a sharp right at the end of the street, sending Gigi sliding across the seat into Mary Jo. "Miss Mirette drives like she's been shot out of a cannon."

"I heard that," Mirette called from the front seat as she took another sharp turn, sending Mary Jo bumping into Gigi.

"This is like those twirly rides at the county fair." Gigi linked her arm through Mary Jo's.

"I didn't know you owned a car, Miss Mirette." Mary Jo tightened her grip on Gigi's arm as the car's engine roared to a higher speed.

Miss Vivien faced the back seat. "She's kept this locked up in an old shed behind her house. We weren't even sure it would start."

As if to prove its vigor in the face of their doubts, the car backfired, sending Mary Jo's heart into frantic beats.

Miss Vivien braced against the door as Mirette took another turn. "Everyone would recognize my car, so we decided to use Mirette's and be less conspicuous."

They screeched to a stop at the traffic signal. Beams from a streetlight illuminated strands of cobwebs stretching from the ceiling above Miss Vivien's perfectly coiffed hair to the back window.

"How long has this car been in your shed?" Mary Jo shivered, hoping no spiders or rats lived in the car.

"Since the war."

"Which one?" Gigi sneezed.

"Does it matter?" The car's tires spun as Mirette took off again.

When they parked in the garage, Nelson limped over to them. "No parking after seven."

Miss Vivien exited. "Nelson, it's Vivien Sheffield."

He halted when Mirette, Gigi, and Mary Jo got out and joined Miss Vivien.

Nelson looked along the line. "What are you ladies doing?"

"Nelson, Audrey's in jail. We're here to find a way to get her out."

His face softened. "How is she, Miss Vivien?"

"We don't know. They wouldn't let us talk to her."

Mary Jo and Gigi spun to face Miss Vivien and Mirette.

"Y'all went down to the jailhouse? Alone?" Women of their age visiting a jailhouse was unthinkable.

"We went to ask Audrey where she'd put her notes detailing everything she found about Junior and Cissy's dirty dealings. I've scoured the things she brought to my house, but they weren't there. Those notes and whatever papers she put in my safe are her only hope, I'm afraid. She must have hidden them in her office somewhere."

Nelson unfastened the flashlight hanging on his belt. "Use this when you take the sidewalk into the store." He walked away from them.

Miss Vivien clicked on the light and shined the beam on the grease-stained floor. "Who's ready?"

As she walked ahead of them, Mary Jo leaned into Gigi. "I've never seen Miss Vivien or Miss Mirette wearing pants before."

"I guess they mean business."

The employee side door was locked, so they went around to the front.

Mirette knocked several times, but the hums of the floor-polishing machines must have drowned out the noise. The night maids dusted off the wooden counters and around the bases of the many mannequins dressed in winter wear. They concentrated on their work and never looked up.

"Now what?" Mary Jo huddled close to Gigi. What if another night guard came by and caught them? She might find herself sitting in jail next to Audrey.

How would she explain all this to the girls?

"I've got an idea." Gigi grabbed Mary Jo. "Come with me."

She led them to the back of the store where the night stockers were unloading a delivery truck. "Bobby said they keep one of the doors back here unlocked so the guys can sneak out for a smoke."

Mary Jo almost cheered when the knob turned easily and Gigi opened the door.

They filed into the stairwell and headed for the fifth floor. At the landing, Mirette opened the door and peeked inside. "Empty." She waved the others through.

Once in Miss Vivien's salon, they gathered around the safe in the storeroom.

Miss Vivien used Nelson's flashlight as she entered the combination and opened the safe. She pulled out an envelope.

"Audrey left this with us the day Mr. Wynton had the reaction to the wasps."

"My first day here," Mary Jo whispered.

Miss Vivien lifted the flap and pulled out a sheet of paper. She walked to the desk and retrieved her glasses, then began to read.

Mary Jo leaned in close. "What does it say?"

"Junior got everything. With him gone, Cissy gets to be the winner who takes it all."

She folded the document. "This is no help at all."

Vivien looked at the others. "We all knew Junior didn't have the sense God gave a goose, especially in business. Why would Mr. Wynton leave the entire thing to a son he knows would run it into the ground?"

"But what about the one Cissy pulled out of Mr. Wynton's safe that said Audrey got everything?" Mary Jo asked.

"Probably a fake." Miss Vivien shut the safe door. "The only people who knew the combination to this safe are me, Audrey, and Mr. Wynton. She said he kept the combinations for both his and mine in his wallet." Miss Vivien slid the boxes in front of the safe.

"I think Audrey put the original in our safe that day, and Cissy stole the combinations, tracked down all the originals, and replaced them with the fakes."

Gigi looked at the group. "I think Cissy did something else. She got Bobby to kill Francis."

Mary Jo couldn't believe what she was hearing. "Gigi, are you sure?"

She nodded. "Right after Cissy started the rumor Francis was seen riding around with Audrey, Francis was killed. Then, when the nurse and Mr. Loring were seen talking to Audrey, they ended up dead too. And Bobby disappeared for a few days after each of their deaths."

Mary Jo looked around the group. "Cissy fooled us all."

Miss Vivien herded them from the storeroom. "We've got another stop to make."

A male voice greeted them as they walked out. "You ladies going fishing?" Joshua stood in the middle of the sales floor with his hands clasped behind his back.

Mary Jo shuddered.

Miss Vivien joined the group. "We're trying to help Audrey."

Joshua motioned for the paper Miss Vivien held in her hand. "Please?"

She handed it over.

He read, then held the paper to his nose. "Ladies, you just landed a prize catch."

Gigi clapped her hands on her cheeks. "I know where Audrey's notes are."

She took off for the elevator. Miss Vivien, Mirette, and Mary Jo followed.

"Mr. McKinnon, you want to help Audrey, don't you?" Mary Jo called over her shoulder.

"Yes, ma'am, I do."

"Then come on. We've got more fish to catch."

Chapter 51

AUDREY

Audrey stared at the black smudges on her icy-cold fingertips. Miss Evelyn had no advice for ladies who ended up in jail. True ladies tended homes, husbands, and children, never getting themselves soiled in the grime of the world.

She huddled deeper into her cashmere coat and rose from the cell's cement bench, shuddering against the cold seeping into her bones. The radio weatherman had warned a storm was bringing crop-killing frost from up north.

She couldn't focus on the cold. Not when she'd failed Mr. Wynton.

The wall clock ticktocked away the moments. Were they his last? What if she never got to say a proper goodbye or thank-you. . . ?

She muffled her sobs with the back of her hand.

Cissy had fixed her but good.

The wind shrieked outside. Inside, an officer sat reading, feet propped on his desk. He dog-eared a page corner, rose, and stretched.

The drunk in the next cell snorted in his sleep. The officer chuckled, then crossed to a table and poured coffee from the percolator.

The door burst open, shattering the silence, as Miss Vivien, Mirette, Gigi, and Mary Jo rushed in.

Startled, the officer sloshed coffee on his uniform shirt, then angrily blotted it. "Y'all can't be here."

"Ferrell Hatcher"—Miss Vivien brushed raindrops from her clothing—"after the night we've had, we aren't about to leave." She motioned to Mary Jo. "Show him."

Mary Jo held up Nelson's thermos.

"What is that?" the officer bellowed.

"A thermos full of truth." Miss Vivien winked at Audrey. "And more is on the way."

Gigi approached the cell, beckoning for Audrey.

"What are y'all doing here?" Audrey asked.

"Digging you out of a trouble hole." Gigi gripped the bars. "And hopefully burying Bobby and Cissy in it."

"How?"

Mary Jo joined them. "You'll see when Joshua gets here."

"Joshua?" Audrey gaped. "What have y'all been up to?"

Gigi and Mary Jo exchanged a look as Miss Vivien pulled a chair up to Audrey's cell.

Miss Vivien rubbed her arms. "It's like an icebox in here. Don't you have heat, Ferrell?"

The officer ceased his dabbing. "The chief doesn't want us to waste kerosene."

"I can barely feel my feet." Miss Vivien jerked her finger at the heater. "The rain and cold are burrowing into my bones. Fire that thing up."

"Not without the chief's approval. He'll take the extra cost out of my paycheck."

Crossing the room, Mirette reached for the phone. "I play Hearts with his wife every week. I'll just call her and ask."

Ferrell lifted his hands in surrender. "I'll turn it on."

"Thank you." Miss Vivien wrapped the heavy woolen shawl she'd brought around her shoulders.

The heater clicked on, filling the room with the smell of burnt dust. Mary Jo and Mirette brought three more chairs and formed a semicircle in front of Audrey's cell like a bulwark of protection.

"How did you get Nelson's thermos?" Audrey eyed the item.

"We told him you were in trouble." Mirette settled by Mary Jo.

The door opened again, and the Levy City police chief, Bill Young-blood, whooshed in, smoothing his rumpled salt-and-pepper hair, which stood on end.

He looked around the room. "For Pete's sake, Vivien, why'd you have to drag me out of a warm, dry bed?"

"You'll know soon enough, Bill." Miss Vivien rubbed her chilled fingers.

Another storm gust carried Bobby in. His old hat lay soaked against his head.

Cissy followed in a bedraggled vision of red—wide-legged pants, a cherry-red coat, and a candy-striped silk blouse that matched her coat's lining. Even her sodden pumps were red. Pulling off her soggy wool hat, she gave her drenched locks an I'm-too-far-above-this-to-care flip.

Joshua entered on a gust of rain-soaked wind, with leaves clinging to his shoes and pants legs. He shoved the door closed.

Chief Youngblood motioned at Ferrell. "A chair. And coffee."

Once he'd settled in, he studied the room. "Who's going first?"

Mary Jo held the thermos out to the chief. "Audrey kept notes of all the illegal things John. . .John T. cooked up at the store."

"Show me." He sipped his coffee.

Mary Jo held up the notes, but he scowled. "I don't read shorthand."

"Audrey can read those to you, Chief," Joshua said.

Cissy jumped to her feet. "Don't you believe a word she says. She's been after Daddy's money since she was a teenager. She killed dear, sweet Francis, Mr. Loring, and Daddy's poor nurse."

"And my husband," She hissed at Audrey.

Audrey gripped the bars. "I did not kill your husband. Or anyone else."

"You caused the crash." Cissy moaned into her hands.

"She couldn't have."

As Joshua spoke, Cissy snatched her hands from her face, chest heaving. "How would you know?"

He met her gaze. "A mispronounced name."

The chief yawned. "Go on."

"The clerk in Miami told me the caller spelled out Miss Penault's name—twice. I asked him to demonstrate the caller's pronunciation."

Joshua winked at Audrey, as if this were a game. Half of her relished his confidence, the other wanted to wring his neck.

"Audrey is quite particular about how her name is pronounced." He gestured to Cissy. "Say it for me, please, Mrs. Wynton."

Cissy hoisted her nose into the air. "Pen-ult."

Joshua held his hand out to Miss Vivien. "You know her preference. Would you, please?"

"Pee-null. As the French would say." Miss Vivien shivered.

"And to your knowledge, she's been correcting Levy City folks ever since she moved back?"

"Yes."

"Would we find folks who'd confirm this if the chief and I asked them?"

"Yes." Miss Vivien's firm nod punctuated her assurance.

Joshua continued. "The clerk repeated the caller's pronunciation." He motioned to Cissy. "It was hers. Audrey never made that call."

Angry fire lit Cissy's eyes. "Pray tell, how did I phone my husband when I was at the hotel *with my husband*?" Her voice pitched higher with each word.

"You paid Francis to make the call," Mary Jo cut in. "She told Edie all about it."

Cissy spun around and looked like she could spit nails in Mary Jo's face. "I did not."

"A two-hundred-dollar fraudulent refund for a nonexistent client and a deposit in Francis Tyler's bank account for the same amount says you did." Joshua signaled at Audrey's notes. "I'd bet the proof is in there." His bright blue eyes sparkled her way.

Miss Evelyn always said that ladies never wasted time defending themselves but rather allowed their friends to do so.

Audrey's heart pounded.

Chapter 52

AUDREY

The chief gave Joshua a squinty-eyed look. "And who are you?"

Joshua produced his credentials and handed them to Chief Youngblood. "Mrs. Wynton hired me to investigate the strange happenings at the store."

Cissy pointed to Bobby. "He can't say her name either. And he hates Audrey." She cast pleading puppy-dog eyes at Gigi. "Doesn't he?"

Gigi turned away, stone-faced.

"You didn't find my footprint in Audrey's house, did you?" Cissy demanded.

Miss Vivien scowled. "How did you know about the boot print?"

"Gordon told Alvid. Alvid told me." Cissy pounded her fist in her palm. "Besides, Audrey was seen driving Francis around, not me."

"That wasn't Audrey's car." Miss Vivien tucked her hands into her shawl as she spoke. "It was Junior's Corvette, driven by you."

Cissy's jaw dropped. "That's an outright lie."

The chief leaned in. "Who reported this?"

"The one man who'd know best." Miss Vivien smiled. "Nelson, Wynton's parking garage attendant."

The chief bolted upright. "I can't go on the word of one Colored guard."

"Thank goodness a better head is in charge." Cissy looked like she might kick Miss Vivien.

The chief motioned to Ferrell. "Let her out."

When she was freed, the chief handed Audrey her notes. "Read these to me."

Audrey riffled through pages, then passed a few to the chief.

"What's this?"

"Receipts, invoices, and evidence where Junior and Cissy worked together to defraud the store. They wanted to get Mr. Wynton out of the way so they could sell Wynton's."

She held up two airline tickets. "They planned to run away to France and live off Mr. Wynton's fortune and the proceeds from the sale."

Audrey pulled another paper out. "This is Bobby's boot print. Miss Vivien and I found it in my house after the fire. He works for Mahon's packing house, and they special ordered a size 14 boot from Wynton's a few weeks ago." She shuffled her notes. "Here's the sales slip."

The chief looked, then handed it back to Audrey. "Not worth a hill of beans without more proof."

She wasn't going to be deterred. "Bobby wears this same size. Cissy bought the boots for him so he could sneak into my house after the fire and not get his feet burned as he ransacked it."

"Why was he in your house?" The chief placed the papers on his desk.

Audrey pointed to the evidence box. "May I?"

The chief held up his hands. "If it gets me back to bed faster, by all means."

Audrey removed the cold cream jar, the brick, and her compact. After unscrewing the cap, she showed the dead wasp to the chief. "I found this in Mr. Wynton's desk drawer. It's the very wasp he's allergic to. John T., Cissy, and I were the only ones who knew about his allergy."

She put the jar back and held out the brick. "This was chiseled from the corner of my garage. I found it in my desk after Francis was killed. It bore evidence of being used in her murder."

Audrey exchanged the brick for her compact. "This was in my purse, which was locked in my desk drawer. It went missing, then returned with the broken mirror after Mr. Wynton's nurse Nancy was murdered." She dropped the compact in the box.

"I realized these made me look guilty, so I hid them in my house until I could figure out what was going on. They were the only items Bobby took from my house. Cissy removed them from Mr. Wynton's safe yesterday and used them as evidence against me."

Chief Youngblood rubbed his chin. "That's interesting."

Cissy charged at him. "What about the fake will she forced Daddy to sign?"

"About that will." Joshua presented a rolled-up paper from his inside pocket, and Cissy's questions ceased.

"This paper was also in Mr. Wynton's safe. It states Audrey gets the store, the chairman's position on the board, and the Wynton fortune."

He pulled a second document out. "This one says John T. Wynton inherited everything, and upon his death, Mrs. Clarissa Mahon Wynton gets it all. Audrey's friends found it in Miss Vivien's safe tonight."

He went on. "Our biggest problem here is trying to figure out which of these is legal and binding." He handed both to the chief. "Would you smell them, please?"

Joshua might as well have asked him to kiss a pig.

"Please, just sniff."

The chief complied. "They smell like perfume."

"They do indeed. Do you have the other items you took from Mr. Wynton's office earlier?"

The chief motioned for the box, and Audrey carried it to him.

He removed one of the pill bottles and sniffed. "Same scent."

Mary Jo perked up. "A perfume's scent lasts at most a couple of weeks unless it's been locked in an air-tight environment. Like Mr. Wynton's safe." She grinned. "I read that in a perfume ad that came to the store."

She reached for the copies of the wills and smelled each one. "I was a perfume spritzer, and that is Chanel No. 5, Cissy's favorite."

Joshua sat in the last empty chair. "Audrey favors Evening in Paris."

Audrey's cheeks warmed when all swiveled their attention to her.

Miss Vivien cleared her throat. "Since all the evidence smells like Cissy, we believe both wills are fake and planted in the safes by her. She was going to produce the one giving everything to her once Audrey was convicted."

"And"—Gigi joined Mary Jo—"we think Bobby killed Francis. And Cissy helped him do it."

Cissy tossed her head. "That's impossible. I was home sick in bed."

Gigi shook her head. "We're pretty sure you stole the safe combinations from Mr. Wynton's wallet. Miss Vivien called his nurse Ethel, and she said his wallet went missing months ago. You gave Bobby the combination to Mr. Wynton's safe so he could get the key and sneak backstage to dump poor Francis. And you put the fake wills in both safes."

Mirette piped up. "My brother works at Mahon's, and he's never seen Bobby there. Right around the time those work boots were ordered, he said one of their new white delivery trucks disappeared. So new, it didn't have Mahon's logo painted on it yet."

"The same truck that tried to steal my crates from the warehouse." Miss Vivien looked straight at Bobby. "Frederick described you as the man in the driver's seat, right down to your dirty hat."

"Wynton's entire loading bay saw a white truck speeding away around the time Francis was found." Mary Jo turned to Audrey. "Blanche, down in Gift Wrapping, saw Bobby sneak into the basement with a large crate on a dolly before the fashion show started."

Cissy cast a hard look at Bobby. "You cannot believe I'd carry on with the help at the packing house."

Bobby's shoulders drooped, and for an instant pain registered in his eyes before his jaw firmed and his spine stiffened.

Audrey almost felt sympathy for him. She'd seen that same expression in her own mirror once when her heart was broken.

"Didn't you once drive an old Ford, Mr. Bridges?" Joshua pinned Bobby with a narrowed glance. "Because one of the employees at the parade said an old, beat-up truck was parked near the Santa float shortly before Mr. Loring's body was found."

The chief held up his hand. "Enough." He motioned to Bobby. "Ferrell, lock him up."

Bobby wrenched free from Ferrell. "For what?"

"Because I'm suspicious." The chief gestured toward the cells.

Gigi stood over Bobby and gestured at his watch. "It's time to come clean."

"Aw, Gigi, honey, you can't believe I'd—"

Mary Jo turned on him. "Don't you 'honey' her after you've treated her like dirt."

A red hue crept up Bobby's neck and settled on his cheeks. "You'd better put Cissy in there with me because she killed her husband."

Cissy gasped and slapped him. The crack echoed through the room. "I loved my husband."

Bobby sneered. "Until he lost his nerve. Then you just loved his money."

He stared at the chief. "The night of the wreck, she bashed him in the head with a bottle of champagne she paid me to buy at Latham Liquors. She jumped out of the car before it crashed, figuring the police would think his wounds came from the crash."

Bobby flashed his watch at the chief. "She gave me this for helping her."

Cissy rushed at the chief. "I'm a Mahon. I married a Wynton. Why would I get mixed up with a dirty, low-down—"

"She stuffed the wasps in Mr. Wynton's desk." Bobby wiped his mouth with the back of his hand. "That morning, Alvid Ashley was to hold Audrey up so Cissy could get them bugs in without being seen. He kept an eye on Audrey and was always reporting stuff back to Cissy."

He snickered. "She got Loring to write up new wills. Told him that after Junior was gone, they'd run off together and keep the money."

Bobby shook his head. "She sweet-talked him into driving Francis to Daytona for a date with her secret boyfriend. He was supposed to kill her on the way there, but he lost his nerve and tried to blackmail Cissy. She paid me to kill them both."

Truth now stampeded from Bobby. "She sprinkled drain cleaner on the old man's pills and in his elixir to poison him. Nurse Nancy caught her, so I killed her too. The fire and the glass ornament at the ball—she gave me a new car for doing those."

"Ferrell, put him in with the drunk, and put Cissy in the cell Audrey vacated. Then call the hospital. Tell them they'd better pump Wynton's stomach, if they haven't already. And haul Alvid in here too," Chief Youngblood ordered.

Cissy screamed in his face, "How dare you? I'm a Mahon."

The chief blinked his eyes once. "I don't care if you're the queen of Sheba. You cook up a plot to murder people, you're going to sit in my jail until your trial."

"Call my aunt. Now."

"We'll call tomorrow." He held up Audrey's notes. "Can you translate all this into English?"

"Yes, sir."

"Tomorrow, after three, and we'll go over this piece by piece."

He motioned to Ferrell. "You think this department has a kerosene reserve somewhere? Who told you to turn on the heat?"

Ferrell's Adam's apple bobbed, and he swept his hand at the ladies. "They threatened to call your wife if I didn't."

The chief shuddered. "We wouldn't want that."

He bowed his head to Audrey. "My deepest apologies. And ladies, please promise me that none of you will ever show up in my jail again."

Once Chief Youngblood ushered them outside, Miss Vivien grabbed Audrey in a tight embrace, and the others joined in. "We weren't leaving that horrid place without you."

A tear slipped from the corner of Audrey's eye. This time she was certain Miss Evelyn would have approved.

✝✝

A new sign met Audrey as she motored her T-Bird into her spot:

WELCOME BACK!

She gathered her belongings and Nelson's breakfast items, then slid from her seat.

"Good morning." Nelson smiled when she walked his way.

"One of the best in years." She handed him the thermos and his cinnamon twists.

He pointed to the new sign. "That's from Lilla, Eunice, Frederick, and me." Nelson chuckled. "You are something else."

Audrey buttoned her coat around her. "You're not the first man who's told me that, but you're the first who meant it as a compliment."

Nelson chuckled again, sat in his resting chair, and set the thermos down beside him.

Audrey motioned to Mr. Wynton's Cadillac. "Good to see that back in the garage."

"He's moving slow but glad to be back." Nelson munched a bit of cinnamon twist.

Audrey adjusted her hat and pulled on her gloves.

Nelson swallowed a bit of cinnamon twist. "Keep them dancing today, Miss Audrey."

"Do you want a jive or a jitterbug?"

"A waltz. Folks are still tired."

"Better days are coming, Nelson. For all of us."

Sooner rather than later, she hoped as she hurried from the garage. Mr. Wynton waited at the employee's entrance and waved when he saw her approaching.

"We're all glad you're back."

He patted her arm. "I've been away far too long."

"I'm so sorry for—"

He held up his hand. "It's a new year and a blank slate."

Mr. Wynton guided her to the main entrance. "Let's enter in style today."

When they walked through the revolving door, the main floor exploded with cheers. Wynton's employees filled the aisles, with others waving from the upper floors' balconies.

Audrey stood back from the fray. This was all for Mr. Wynton, and he should enjoy it alone.

He walked to the center of the room, rotated slowly, and waved, then gestured for her to join him. The cheers increased. Faces melded together until she spied Miss Vivien, Mary Jo, Gigi, and Mirette standing together in the main aisle, grinning and blowing kisses at her.

In the back corridor, Nelson, Eunice, Lilla, and Frederick clapped and whistled.

A faint chant started, then swelled until the space filled with the sound.

Audrey, Audrey, Audrey!

Miss Evelyn would have been proud at how well she hid her emotions, even though the effort ached in her chest by the time Mr. Wynton quieted the room.

As he stood under the lights, surrounded by the store he'd created to honor his father, Mr. Wynton's eyes danced with the old spark.

"Thank you all." He held out his hands to her. "And thank you, Audrey."

He looked around the room. "You're all my most valuable assets. Thank you."

The old vitality crackled around him. "It's almost nine o'clock. Let's get to work."

Another round of cheers followed Audrey and Mr. Wynton to the elevators.

When they reached the suite, Joshua waited in one of the chairs. He leapt to his feet and grabbed Mr. Wynton's hand. "Nice to see you again, sir."

Mr. Wynton gave his hand a vigorous shake. "It's fantastic to be seen."

He turned to Audrey. "Get George Crawford on the phone. It's time he talked to the Wynton in charge." He went into his office and closed the door.

"And how is the greatest crime-solving mind around today?" Joshua grinned.

Audrey sat in her chair. "Don't you play coy with me. How did you know those wills were fake?"

Joshua's eyes danced with mischief as he sat on the corner of her desk. "I have the real one in my office back home. Chief Youngblood will be receiving a copy by courier today. You had a copy too."

Her brain fumbled with his revelation; then she snapped her fingers. "The envelope I was to open if he. . . You knew about that?"

"When he discovered Junior and Cissy were plotting to take over, he chose me as his successor. I'm an exec for Loveman's in Birmingham. My dad is his personal lawyer and drew up the papers."

"Of course. Any executive worth his grits would know his designers and perfumes. And Mr. Wynton said he was going to fight. You were his weapon."

She smiled and shook her head. "He outsmarted every single one of us."

Joshua ran his finger along the wood grain of her desktop. "You do realize this makes me your future boss." A slow, easy grin spread across his face and flickered in his eyes.

Audrey flashed her 24-karat smile. "Mr. McKinnon, I wouldn't be so sure about that. I just might be saying the same to you someday."

Author's Note

The 1950s is an era in American history that continues to capture the interest of generations. The movies, music, and fashion of that time never seem to fall out of style or favor.

During this era in the South, and especially Florida, a delicate dance took place between wanting to join in the determined push to the future while also clinging to the traditions of the past. New people from up north streamed into the state, causing a population and building explosion that brought changes to the landscape that continues today.

These new people introduced different ideas and challenged many of the old ways. Roles for men, women, and African Americans seemed to be set in stone. But there were also whispers of change that would eventually lead to the civil rights movement and new opportunities for women. Those whispers became the seeds for this story.

In writing this book, I wanted to be true to what was happening and show the good and the bad. To gain a better understanding of the time period and what was happening to the African American community, I studied the works of Zora Neale Hurston, as well as other early civil rights advocates. A very dear friend of mine also pointed me to the tragic murders of Harry and Harriette Moore. The impact of that injustice was still felt years later, and it spurred others to fight for their rights. Florida's culture at the time presented the same struggles felt across the South. Many Whites disagreed with how things were but also feared the trouble that pushing against the old ways might bring upon them. Others were fine with the old system and fought against change. I hope I've treated these experiences as accurately as possible.

Choosing the department store for the setting turned out to be one of the most enjoyable aspects of writing this story, especially the research. Growing up in rural Florida, I didn't have any large department stores near my home. We had a local Sears and J. C. Penney, but to go to a more upscale store meant driving south for two hours to Maas Brothers in Tampa or east to shop at Jacobson's, Burdines, or Robinson's near Orlando. Those trips were saved for special occasions like Christmas shopping or searching for formal wear. To me, visiting these large stores was the height of glamour, and I wanted to capture that feeling again when creating Wynton's Department Store.

I never realized the impact department stores had on American culture. I wanted to include as much of this as I could in this story but had to leave out a lot of interesting facts. Many started out as small, local dry goods establishments and grew to become huge retail palaces offering everything from clothing, furniture, and housewares to doctor offices, post offices, places to pay bills, and dentists. The stores provided nurseries where mothers could leave their children in the care of uniformed nursemaids and go on to do their shopping. These stores were the centers of commerce in cities and reflected the area's growing economies. People dressed up to go shopping, and most had upscale tearooms or cafés that became *the* place to meet for a special meal in town. These department stores became the center of activities around their communities, with annual events such as parades and the unveiling of Christmas display windows. On an upper floor of their buildings, many stores had huge banquet rooms that were used for weddings, receptions, balls, high school proms and dances, or other formal events.

Like everything else, time marched on, and shopping preferences changed as American cities spread out to the suburbs. Many of the old downtown stores struggled to keep up, were bought out by large conglomerates, and were absorbed into the last remaining big-name stores. Others closed their doors, and the downtown shopping experience was forever changed.

During World War II, women filled jobs in the stores vacated by the men who went off to war. When the men returned, female employees were pushed to return to their homes. The glamorous 1950s housewife became the ideal, and the stores promoted products to encourage them to embrace their homemaker roles by offering cooking demonstrations, makeup workshops, fashion shows, sewing classes, and charm schools for children and teens.

But something else was quietly happening during this time. Single women and older women continued to work, and the department stores held many opportunities for them. Clerking in a store became a prestigious position, and many women worked their way into positions as clothing buyers, heads of bookkeeping departments, and secretaries for top executives. Some women became executives themselves.

A perfect example of this was Dorothy Shaver, who started out selling her sister's homemade dolls to the toy departments at various stores. She possessed a knack for marketing that was noticed by an executive in one of the stores she sold to. He hired her, and eventually she rose to become the first woman in the United States to head a multimillion-dollar firm, Lord and Taylor.

Tupperware had also entered the market, giving women the chance to become entrepreneurs and earn their own money separate from their husbands.

There is so much to this period, and I've barely scraped the surface. I wanted to share many more facts, but stories aren't meant to be textbooks, especially this one. I had a mystery that needed solving, and my characters had to focus on finding out who dunnit.

I believe in a story's ability to transport, teach, and transform. My goal in writing this book was to do all three while also giving my readers a place to amuse their imaginations. Because, as Audrey says, we all need a little fun in our lives.

Acknowledgments

The inspiration for this book came from my love of the movies and fashions of the 1950s. I would look at fashion photographs and wonder what the women who wore those clothes were like, how they lived, and what they held close in their hearts.

I had a small picture of this time in Florida from my parents. They came of age and married in the '50s. Remembering the stories of what they encountered when they settled in rural Florida and how they fell in love with the people and their ways was always in the back of my mind while writing *The Women of Wynton's*. I'm thankful I had the opportunity to grow up hearing them and could draw from them, the good and the bad, to bring the world of Wynton's Department Store to life.

Thank you, Linda, my fabulous agent. When I first presented the idea to you, your enthusiastic "Yes, write that one!" made my day. You helped me find this little story a publishing home and offered loads of support when I needed it most.

Huge thanks to Becky and the Barbour family. You took a chance on me and my story and helped me share it with the world. Your kindness and support made working with you a wonderful experience.

To Eva, thank you for everything. It meant the world to me to know you were there in the good and the bad.

My ever-faithful Word Weavers of Tampa chapter, thank you for your support during this year. You've helped me fix bad sentences and pare down my long-winded tendencies. You cheered me on and told me to finish this book so y'all could find out what happened. Now you'll know!

To Sharron and a long, long ride home. We brainstormed so much for these ladies on that trip, and I will forever be grateful for your input and excitement over this story idea. The women of Wynton's thank you for helping bring them to life. You shared a little piece of personal history then, and I hope you find it when you read the book.

Jan, your uncanny ability to know just when I needed a pick-me-up text or phone call amazes me still. Having you in my cheering section is a blessing for sure.

Jen, you are the world's greatest accountability partner. The daily check-ins and late-night texting to iron out story issues, and your unwavering support mean more than I can ever express.

I couldn't go on without thanking my local librarians for their help and assistance in researching this book. They sent me in the right direction to find all I needed to know and more.

To Denise, Sue, Sharon, Genice, Stacie, and Michelle: You've proven that you can't make old friends. They are something to be nurtured and cherished over time. Buckman rules!

To Jessica: Big thanks for the early edits and steering me in the right direction when I first started writing this story. Your excitement made me think I might possibly pull this off.

Marianne, thank you for forcing me away from my desk for lunch and great talks. You're a special friend, and I look forward to the next time we meet. I have more to tell you.

To my three guys: Love y'all with all my heart and then some.

And lastly, I thank God for leading me down this path and helping me put all my daydreaming and love of old movies to good use.

Donna Mumma perfected storytelling in her first-grade classroom, spinning tales exciting enough to settle a roomful of antsy six-year-olds. She is an award-winning author who loves to blend history, mystery, and a dash of hope in stories that explore ordinary people who learn extraordinary life lessons. Donna is an active member of Word Weavers International, serving as president for the Tampa chapter as well as a mentor for chapters around the country. She was recognized as the Word Weavers traditional groups president and mentor of the year in 2022. She also serves as a line editor and contributor for Inskpirationsonline.com, a site featuring devotions written for writers by writers. An avid believer in education, Donna earned her master of education degree in elementary education and writes educational blogs and articles to assist teachers overseas for the International School Project. A native Floridian, she loves sharing life with family and her energetic collie, Duke.